KNIGHT ON THE CHILDREN'S WARD

BY
CAROL MARINELLI

CHILDREN'S DOCTOR, SHY NURSE

BY
MOLLY EVANS

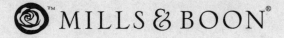
MILLS & BOON

FALLING FOR THE CHILDREN'S DOCTOR

Meet two men who go above and beyond
to save the lives of their tiny patients!

These dedicated doctors are incredible with their
little charges, but their talents don't stop there…

Gorgeous, charismatic and charming,
these men have nurses falling at their feet!

But what—or who!—will it take for them
to fall in love themselves?

Find out in…

**KNIGHT ON THE CHILDREN'S WARD
by Carol Marinelli**

and

**CHILDREN'S DOCTOR, SHY NURSE
by Molly Evans**

KNIGHT ON THE CHILDREN'S WARD

BY
CAROL MARINELLI

™ MILLS & BOON®

For Helen Browne, thank you for your friendship, Carol x

DID YOU PURCHASE THIS BOOK WITHOUT A COVER?

If you did, you should be aware it is **stolen property** as it was reported *unsold and destroyed* by a retailer. Neither the author nor the publisher has received any payment for this book.

All the characters in this book have no existence outside the imagination of the author, and have no relation whatsoever to anyone bearing the same name or names. They are not even distantly inspired by any individual known or unknown to the author, and all the incidents are pure invention.

All Rights Reserved including the right of reproduction in whole or in part in any form. This edition is published by arrangement with Harlequin Enterprises II BV/S.à.r.l. The text of this publication or any part thereof may not be reproduced or transmitted in any form or by any means, electronic or mechanical, including photocopying, recording, storage in an information retrieval system, or otherwise, without the written permission of the publisher.

This book is sold subject to the condition that it shall not, by way of trade or otherwise, be lent, resold, hired out or otherwise circulated without the prior consent of the publisher in any form of binding or cover other than that in which it is published and without a similar condition including this condition being imposed on the subsequent purchaser.

® and TM are trademarks owned and used by the trademark owner and/or its licensee. Trademarks marked with ® are registered with the United Kingdom Patent Office and/or the Office for Harmonisation in the Internal Market and in other countries.

First published in Great Britain 2010
Harlequin Mills & Boon Limited,
Eton House, 18-24 Paradise Road, Richmond, Surrey TW9 1SR

© Carol Marinelli 2010

ISBN: 978 0 263 87897 4

Harlequin Mills & Boon policy is to use papers that are natural, renewable and recyclable products and made from wood grown in sustainable forests. The logging and manufacturing process conform to the legal environmental regulations of the country of origin.

Printed and bound in Spain
by Litografia Rosés, S.A., Barcelona

Dear Reader

A couple of years ago I wrote about two brothers from the Kolovsky family. But you don't need to have read about them to enjoy their sister Annika's story. They are a rich, fascinating family, with lots of scandal and secrets, and after two years away from them I was looking forward to visiting the Kolovsky family again—especially as I had worked out Annika's story.

I forgot that in two years people can change a lot!

Naively, I had expected to pick up where I had left off—but while I had been busy getting on with life, so too had Annika. She had grown up and made a lot of changes in the time since I last met her, and all the neat plans I had for her soon fell by the wayside!

It was fun getting to know her all over again—and working out a hero who would suit such a complex woman. I have to say—I do like her taste.

Happy reading!

Carol x

Carol Marinelli recently filled in a form where she was asked for her job title and was thrilled, after all these years, to be able to put down her answer as 'writer'. Then it asked what Carol did for relaxation. After chewing her pen for a moment Carol put down the truth—'writing'. The third question asked—'What are your hobbies?' Well, not wanting to look obsessed or, worse still, boring, she crossed the fingers on her free hand and answered 'swimming and tennis'. But, given that the chlorine in the pool does terrible things to her highlights, and the closest she's got to a tennis racket in the last couple of years is watching the Australian Open, I'm sure you can guess the real answer!

**Carol also writes for
Mills & Boon® Modern™, where you can find out
what the Kolovskys do next in:**

THE LAST KOLOVSKY PLAYBOY

**Available in August 2010 from
Mills & Boon® Modern™**

PROLOGUE

'CAN I ask what happened, Reyes?'

Ross didn't answer his mother for a moment—instead he carried on sorting out clothes, stray earrings, books, make-up, and a shoe that didn't have a partner. He loaded them into a suitcase.

He'd been putting the job off, and when he'd finally accepted his mother's offer to sort Imelda's things, he had accepted also that with her help might come questions.

Questions that he couldn't properly answer.

'I don't know.'

'Were you arguing?' Estella asked, and then tried to hold back a sigh when Ross shook his head. 'I loved Imelda,' Estella said.

'I know,' Ross said, and that just made it harder—Imelda had loved his family and they had loved her too. 'She was funny and kind and I really, really thought I could make it work. I can't honestly think of one thing that was wrong... It was just...'

'Just what, Reyes?' His mother was the only person who called him that. When he had arrived in Australia aged seven, somehow his real name had slipped away. The other children, fascinated by the little dark-haired, olive-skinned Spanish boy who spoke no English, had translated Reyes to Ross—and that was who he had become.

Ross Wyatt.

Son of Dr George and Mrs Estella Wyatt. Older brother to Maria and Sophia Wyatt.

Only it was more complicated than that, and all too often far easier *not* to explain.

Sometimes he *had* to explain—after all, when he was growing up people had noticed the differences. George's hair, when he had had some, had been blond, like his daughters'. George was sensible, stern, perfectly nice and a wonderful father—but it wasn't his blood that ran in Ross's veins.

And he could tell from his mother's worried eyes that she was worried *that* was the problem.

Estella's brief love affair at sixteen with a forbidden Gitano, or Romany, had resulted in Reyes. The family had rallied around. His grandmother had looked after the dark baby while his mother had worked in a local bar, where, a few years later, she'd met a young Australian man, just out of medical school. George had surprised his rather staid family by falling in love and bringing home from his travels in Europe two unexpected souvenirs.

George had raised Reyes as his own, loved him as his own, and treated him no differently from his sisters.

Except Reyes, or rather Ross, *was* different.

'It wasn't…' His voice trailed off. He knew his mother was hoping for a rather more eloquent answer.

He knew that she was worried just from the fact she was asking, for his mother never usually interfered. 'There wasn't that…' He couldn't find the word but he tried. He raked his mind but couldn't find it in English and so, rarely for Ross, he reverted to his native tongue. *'Buena onda.'* His mother tensed when he said it, and he knew she understood—for that was the phrase she used when she talked about his father.

His real father.

Buena onda—an attraction, a connection, a vibe from another person, from *that* person.

'Then you're looking for a fairytale, Reyes! And real-life fairytales don't have happy endings.' Estella's voice was unusually sharp. 'It's time you grew up. Look where *buena onda* left me—sixteen and pregnant.'

Only then, for the first time in his thirty-two years did Ross glimpse the anger that simmered beneath the surface of his mother.

'Passion flares and then dims. Your father—the father who held you and fed you and put you through school— stands for more than some stupid dream. Some gypsy dream that you—' She stopped abruptly, remembering perhaps that they were actually discussing him. 'Imelda was a good woman, a loyal and loving partner. She would have been a wonderful wife and you threw it away—for what?'

He didn't know.

It had been the same argument all his life as his mother and George had tried to rein in his restless energy. He struggled with conformity, though it could hardly be called rebellion.

Grade-wise he had done well at school. He had a mortgage, was a paediatrician—a consultant, in fact—he loved his family, was a good friend.

On paper all was fine.

In his soul all was not.

The mortgage wasn't for a bachelor's city dwelling—though he had a small one of those for nights on call, or when he was particularly concerned about a patient—no, his handsome wage was poured into an acreage, with stables and horses, olive and fruit trees and rows of vines, and not another residence in sight.

Just as there had been arguments about his attitude at school, even as a consultant he found it was more of the same. Budgets, policies, more budgets—all he wanted to do was his job, and at home all he wanted to do was *be*.

There was nothing wrong that he could pin down.

And there was no one who could pin him down.

Many had tried.

'Should I take this round to her?' Ross asked.

'Put it in the cupboard for now,' Estella said. 'If she comes for her things, then at least it is all together. If she doesn't…' She gave a little shrug. 'It's just some clothes. Maybe she would prefer no contact.'

He felt like a louse as he closed the zipper. Packed up two years and placed it in the cupboard.

'Imelda wanted to decorate the bedroom.' Task over, he could be a bit more honest. 'She'd done the bathroom, the spare room…' It was almost impossible to explain, but he felt as if he were being slowly invaded. 'She said she wanted more of a commitment.'

'She cared a lot about you, Reyes…'

'I know,' he admitted. 'And I cared a lot about her.'

'It would have hurt her deeply, you ending it.'

It had. She had cried, sobbed, and then she had hit him and he'd taken it—because he deserved it, because she had almost been the one. He had hoped she was the one and then, when he could deny no longer that she wasn't... What was wrong with him?

'She loved you, Reyes!'

'So I should have just let it carry on? Married her...?'

'Of course not,' Estella said. 'But it's not just Imelda...'

It wasn't.

Imelda was one of a long line of women who had got too close—and, despite his reputation, Ross hated the pain he caused.

'I don't like it that my son hurts women.'

'I'm not getting involved with anyone for a while,' Ross said.

'You say that now...'

'I've never said it before,' Ross said. 'I mean it; I've got to sort myself out. I think I need to go back.' It took a lot of courage to look at his mum, to watch her dark eyes widen and her lips tighten. He saw the slight flinch as he said the words she had braced herself to hear for many years. 'To Spain.'

'What about your work in Russia?' Estella asked. 'All your annual leave is taken up with that. You said that it's the most important thing to you.'

It had been. As a medical student he had taken up the offer to work in a Russian orphanage on his extended summer break, with his fellow student Iosef Kolovsky. It had changed him—and now, all these years on, much of his spare time was devoted to going back. Even though Iosef was married now, and had a new baby, Ross had been determined to return to Russia later in the year. But now things had changed.

'I want to go to Spain, see my *abuelos*…' And that was a good reason to go—his grandparents were old now—but it didn't quite appease his mother. 'I'm going back next month, just for a few weeks….'

'You want to find him, don't you?'

He saw the flash of tears in her eyes and hated the pain he was causing, but his mother, whether she believed it or not, simply didn't understand.

'I want to find myself.'

CHAPTER ONE

'THERE is room for improvement, Annika.' Heather Jameson was finding this assessment particularly difficult. In most areas the student nurse was doing well. In exams, her pass-rates had been initially high, but in her second year of study they were now merely *acceptable*. In her placements it was always noted how hard she worked, and that she was well turned out, on time, but there were still a couple of issues that needed to be addressed.

'It's been noted that you're tired.' Heather cleared her throat. 'Now, I know a lot of students have to work to support themselves during their studies, but…'

Annika closed her eyes, it wouldn't enter Heather's head that she was amongst them—no, she was a Kolovsky, why on earth would *she* have to work?

Except she did—and that she couldn't reveal.

'We understand that with all your family's charity work and functions…well, that you have other balls to juggle. But, Annika, your grades are slipping—you have to find a better balance.'

'I am trying,' Annika said, but her assessment wasn't over yet.

'Annika, are you enjoying nursing?'

No.

The answer was right there, on the tip of her tongue, but she swallowed it down. For the first six months or so she had loved it—had, after so much searching, thought that she had found her vocation, a purpose to her rich and luxurious life. Despite the arguments from her mother, despite her brother Iosef's stern warning that she had no idea what she was taking on, Annika had dug in her heels and, for six months at least, she had proved everyone wrong.

The coursework had been interesting, her placements on the geriatric and palliative care wards, though scary at first, had been enjoyable, and Annika had thought she had found her passion. But then gradually, just as Iosef had predicted it would, the joy had waned. Her surgical rotation had been a nightmare. A twenty-one-year-old had died on her shift and, sitting with the parents, Annika had felt as if she were merely playing dress-up.

It had been downhill since then.

'Have you made any friends?'

'A few,' Annika said. She tried to be friendly, tried to join in with her fellow students' chatter, tried to fit in, but the simple truth was that from the day she had started, from the day her peers had found out who she was, the family she came from, there had been an expectation, a pressure, to dazzle on the social scene. When Annika hadn't fulfilled it, they had treated her differently, and Annika had neither the confidence nor the skills to blend in.

'I know it's difficult for you, Annika…' Heather really didn't know what else to say. There was an aloofness to Annika that was hard to explain. With her thick blonde hair and striking blue eyes, and with her family's connections, one would expect her to be in constant demand, to be outgoing and social, yet there was a coldness in her that had to be addressed—because it was apparent not just to staff but to the patients. "A large part of nursing is about putting patients at ease—'

'I am always nice to the patients,' Annika interrupted, because she was. 'I am always polite; I introduce myself; I…' Annika's voice faded. She knew exactly what Heather was trying to say, she knew she was wooden, and she didn't know how to change it. 'I am scared of saying the wrong thing,' Annika admitted. 'I'm not good at making small talk, and I also feel very uncomfortable when people recognize my name—when they ask questions about my family.'

'Most of the time people *are* just making small talk, not necessarily because of who you are,' Heather said, and then, when Annika's eyes drifted to the newspaper on the table, she gave a sympathetic smile, because, in Annika's case people would pry!

The Kolovsky name was famous in Melbourne. Russian fashion designers, they created scandal and mystery and were regularly in the tabloids. Since the founder, Ivan, had died his son Aleksi had taken over the running of the business, and was causing social mayhem. There was a picture of him that very morning on page one, coming out of a casino, clearly the worse for wear, with the requisite blonde on his arm.

'Maybe nursing is not such a good idea.' Annika could feel the sting of tears behind her eyes but she would not cry. 'At the start I loved it, but lately…'

'You're a good nurse, Annika, and you could be a *very* good nurse. I'm more concerned that you're not happy. I know you're only twenty-five, but that does mean you're older than most of your group, and it's a bit harder as a mature student to fit in. Look…' She changed tack. This wasn't going the way Heather had wanted it—she was trying to bolster Annika, not have her consider quitting. 'You're starting on the children's ward today. Most of them won't have a clue about the Kolovsky name, and children are wonderful at…'

'Embarrassing you?' Annika volunteered, and managed a rare smile. 'I am dreading it.'

'I thought you might be. But children are a great leveller. I think this might be just the ward for you. Try and enjoy it, treat it as a fresh start—walk in and smile, say hello to your colleagues, open up a little, perhaps.'

'I will try.'

'And,' Heather added in a more serious tone, because she had given Annika several warnings, 'think about managing your social engagements more carefully around your roster. Request the weekends off that you need, plan more in advance.'

'I will.' Annika stood up and, unlike most other students, she shook Heather's hand.

It was little things like that, Heather thought as Annika left the room, which made her stand apart. The formal handshake, her slight Russian accent, even though she had been born in Australia. Heather skimmed through Annika's personal file, reading again that she had been home tutored, which explained a lot but not all.

There was guardedness to her, a warning that came from those blue eyes that told you to keep out.

And then occasionally, like she had just now, Annika would smile and her whole face lifted.

She was right about one thing, though, Heather thought, picking up the paper and reading about the latest antics of Annika's brother Aleksi. People did want to know more. People were fascinated by the Kolovsky family—even Heather. Feeling just a touch guilty, she read the article and wondered, not for the first time, what someone as rich and indulged as Annika was trying to prove by nursing.

There was just something about the Kolovskys.

There was still half an hour till Annika's late shift started and, rather than walk into an unfamiliar staffroom and kill time, unusually for Annika she decided to go to the canteen. She had made a sandwich at home, but bought a cup of coffee. She glanced at the tables on offer, and for perhaps the thousandth time rued her decision to work at Melbourne Bayside.

Her brother Iosef was an emergency doctor at Melbourne Central. His wife, Annie, was a nurse there too, but Iosef had been so discouraging, scathing almost, about Annika's ability that she had applied to study and work here instead. How nice it would be now to have Annie wave and ask to join her. Perhaps too it would have been easier to work in a hospital where there were already two Kolovskys—to feel normal.

'Annika!'

She felt a wash of relief as one of her fellow students waved at her. Cassie was down for the children's ward rotation too and, remembering to smile, Annika made her way over.

'Are you on a late shift?' asked Cassie.

'I am,' Annika said. 'It's my first, though. You've already done a couple of shifts there—how have you found it?'

'Awful,' Cassie admitted. 'I feel like an absolute beginner. Everything's completely different—the drug doses, the way they do obs, and then there are the parents watching your every move.'

It sounded awful, and they sat in glum silence for a moment till Cassie spoke again. 'How was your assessment?'

'Fine,' Annika responded, and then remembered she was going to make more of an effort to be open and friendly 'Well, to tell the truth it wasn't great.'

'Oh?' Cassie blinked at the rare insight.

'My grades and things are okay; it is more to do with the way I am with my peers...' She could feel her cheeks burning at the admission. 'And with the patients too. I can be a bit stand-offish!'

'Oh!' Cassie blinked again. 'Well, if it makes you feel any better, I had my assessment on Monday. I'm to stop talking and listen more, apparently. Oh, and I'm to stop burning the candle at both ends!'

And it did make her feel better—not that Cassie hadn't fared well, more that she wasn't the only one who was struggling. Annika smiled again, but it faded when she looked up, because there, handing over some money to the cashier, *he* was.

Dr Ross Wyatt.

He was impossible not to notice.

Tall, with thick black slightly wavy hair, worn just a touch too long, he didn't look like a paediatric consultant—well, whatever paediatric consultants were supposed to look like.

Some days he would be wearing jeans and a T-shirt, finished off with dark leather cowboy boots, as if he'd just got off a horse. Other days—normally Mondays, Annika had noticed—it was a smart suit, but still with a hint of rebellion: his tie more than a little loosened, and with that silver earring he wore so well. There was just something that seemed to say his muscled, toned body wanted out of the tailored confines of his suit. And then again, but only rarely, given he wasn't a surgeon, if he'd been on call he might be wearing scrubs. Well, it almost made her dizzy: the thin cotton that accentuated the outline of his body, the extra glimpse of olive skin and the clip of Cuban-heeled boots as she'd walked behind him in the corridor one morning....

Ross Wyatt was her favourite diversion, and he was certainly diverting her now. Annika blushed as he pocketed his change, picked up his tray and caught her looking. She looked away, tried to listen to Cassie, but the slow, lazy smile he had treated her with danced before her eyes.

Always he looked good—well, not in the conventional way: her mother, Nina, would faint at his choices. Fashion was one of the rules in her family, and Ross Wyatt broke them all.

And today, on her first day on the paediatric ward, as if to welcome her, he was dressed in Annika's personal favourite and he looked divine!

Black jeans, with a thick leather belt, a black crew-neck jumper that showed off to perfection his lean figure, black boots, and that silver earring. The colour was in his lips: wide, blood-red lips that curved into an easy smile. Annika hadn't got close enough yet to see his eyes, but he looked like a Spanish gypsy—just the sort of man her mother would absolutely forbid. He looked wild and untamed and thrilling—as if at any minute he would kick his heels and throw up his arms, stamp a flamenco on his way over to her. She could almost smell the smoke from the bonfire—he did that to her with a single smile...

And it was madness, Annika told herself, utter madness to be sitting in the canteen having such flights of fancy. Madness to be having such thoughts, full stop.

But just the sight of him did this.

And that smile *had been* aimed at her.

Again.

Maybe he smiled at everyone, Annika reasoned—only it didn't feel like it. Sometimes they would pass in the corridor, or she'd see him walking out of ICU, or in the canteen like this, and for a second he would stop...stop and smile.

It was as if he was waiting to know her.

And that was the other reason she was dreading her paediatric rotation. She had once let a lift go simply because he was in it. She wanted this whole eight weeks to be over with, to be finished.

She didn't need any more distractions in an already complicated life—and Ross Wyatt would be just that: a huge distraction.

They had never spoken, never even exchanged pleasantries. He had looked as if he was going to try a couple of times, but she had scuttled back into her burrow like a frightened rabbit. Oh, she knew a little about him— he was a friend of her brother's, had been a medical student at the same time as Iosef. He still went to the orphanages in Russia, doing voluntary work during his annual leave—that was why he had been unable to attend Iosef and Annie's wedding. She had paid little attention when his name had been mentioned at the time, but since last year, when she had put his face to his name, she had yearned for snippets from her brother.

Annika swallowed as she felt the weight of his eyes still on her. She had the craziest notion that he was going to walk over and finally speak to her, so she concentrated on stirring her coffee.

'There are compensations, of course!' Cassie dragged her back to the conversation, only to voice what was already on Annika's mind. 'He's stunning, isn't he?'

'Who?' Annika flushed, stirring her coffee, but Cassie just laughed.

'Dr Drop-Dead Gorgeous Wyatt.'

'I don't know him.' Annika shrugged.

'Well, he's looking right over at you!' Cassie sighed. 'He's amazing, and the kids just love him—he really is great with them.'

'How?'

'I don't know…' Cassie admitted. 'He just…' She

gave a frustrated shrug. 'He *gets* them, I guess. He just seems to understand kids, puts them at ease.'

Annika did not, would not, look over to where he sat, but sometimes she was sure he looked over to her— because every now and then she felt her skin warm. Every now and then it seemed too complicated to move the sandwich from her hand up to her mouth.

Ross Wyatt certainly didn't put Annika at ease.

He made her awkward.

He made her aware.

Even walking over to empty out her tray and head to work she felt as if her movements were being noted, but, though it was acutely awkward, somehow she liked the feeling he evoked. Liked the thrill in the pit of her stomach, the rush that came whenever their paths briefly crossed.

As she sat in handover, listening to the list of patients and their ages and diagnoses, he popped his head around the door to check something with Caroline, the charge nurse, and Annika felt a dull blush on her neck as she heard his voice properly for the first time.

Oh, she'd heard him laugh on occasion, and heard his low tones briefly as they'd passed in the corridor when he was talking with a colleague, but she'd never fully heard him speak.

And as he spoke now, about an order for pethidine, Annika found out that toes did curl—quite literally!

His voice was rich and low and without arrogance. He'd made Caroline laugh with something he said— only Annika couldn't properly process it, because instead she was feeling her toes bunch up inside her sensible navy shoes.

'Back to Luke Winters…'

As the door closed so too did her mind on Ross, and she began concentrating carefully on the handover, because this rotation she *had* to do well.

'He's fifteen years old, Type 1 Diabetes, non-compliant…'

Luke Winters, Annika learnt, was causing not just his family but the staff of the children's ward a lot of problems.

It was his third admission in twelve months. He was refusing to take his insulin at times, ignoring his diet, and he had again gone into DKA—a dangerous, toxic state that could kill. He had an ulcer on his leg that had been discovered on admission, though had probably been there for some time. It would take a long time to heal and might require a skin graft. His mother was frantic—Luke had come to the ward from ICU two days ago and was causing chaos. His room was a mess, and he had told the domestic this morning, none too politely, to get out.

He was now demanding that his catheter be removed, and basically both the other patients and the staff wanted him taken to an adult ward, though Ross Wyatt was resisting.

'"Teenagers, even teenagers who think they are adults, are still children."' Caroline rolled her eyes. 'His words, not mine. Anyway, Luke's mum is at work and not due in till this evening. Hopefully we can have some order by then. Okay…' She stared at the patient sheet and allocated the staff, pausing when she came

to Annika. 'I might put you in cots with Amanda…'
She hesitated. 'But you haven't been in cots yet, have
you, Cassie?'

When Cassie shook her head and Caroline changed
her allocation Annika felt a flood of relief—she had
never so much as held a baby, and the thought of looking
after a sick one petrified her.

'Annika, perhaps you could have beds eight to
sixteen instead—though given it's your first day don't
worry about room fifteen.'

'Luke?' Annika checked, and Caroline nodded.

'I don't want to scare you off on your first day.'

'He won't scare me,' Annika said. Moody teenagers
she could deal with; it was babies and toddlers that
scared her.

'His room needs to be sorted.'

'It will be.'

'Okay!' Caroline smiled. 'If you're sure? Good luck.'

Lisa, who was in charge of Annika's patients, showed
her around the ward. It was, as Cassie had said, completely different. Brightly painted, with a detailed mural
running the length of the corridor, and divided pretty
much into three.

There were cots for the littlest patients—two large
rooms, each containing four cots. Then there were eight
side rooms that would house a cot or a bed, depending
on the patient's age. Finally there were three large four-
bedded rooms, filled with children of various ages.

'Though we do try to keep ages similar,' Lisa said,
'sometimes it's just not possible.' She pointed out the
crash trolley, the drug room, and two treatment rooms.

'We try to bring the children down here for dressings and IV's and things like that.'

'So they don't upset the other children?' Annika checked.

'That, and also, even if they are in a side room, it's better they have anything unpleasant done away from their bed. Obviously if they're infectious we can't bring them down, but generally we try to do things away from the bedside.'

Annika was offered a tabard to replace her navy one. She had a choice of aprons, all brightly coloured and emblazoned with cartoon characters, and though her first instinct was to politely decline, she remembered she was making an effort, so chose a red one, with fish and mermaids on it. She felt, as she slipped it over her head, utterly stupid.

Annika started with the obs. Lunches were being cleared away, and the ward was being readied for afternoon rest-time.

The children eyed her suspiciously—she was new and they knew it.

'What's that for?' A mother demanded angrily as her first patient burst into tears when Annika went to wrap a blood pressure cuff around her arm.

Lisa moved quickly to stop her.

'We don't routinely do blood pressure,' Lisa said, showing her the obs form. 'Unless it's stated on the chart.'

'Okay.'

'Just pulse, temp and respirations.'

'Thank you.'

The little girl wouldn't stop crying. In fact she

shrieked every time Annika tried to venture near, so
Lisa quickly took her temperature as Annika did the rest
of the obs. In the room, eight sets of eyes watched her
every awkward move: four from the patients, four from
their mothers.

'Can I have a drink?' a little boy asked.

'Of course,' Annika said, because that was easy. She
checked his chart and saw that he was to be encouraged
to take fluids. 'Would you like juice or milk…?'

'He's lactose intolerant!' his mother jumped in. 'It
says so above his bed.'

'Always look at the whiteboard above the bed,' Lisa
said. 'And it will say in his admission slip too, which is
clipped to his folder.'

'Of course.' Annika fled to the kitchen, where Cassie
was warming a bottle.

'Told you!' Cassie grinned when Annika told her all
that had happened. 'It's like landing on Mars!'

But she wasn't remotely nervous about a sullen Luke.
She knew he had no relatives with him, and was glad to
escape the suspicious eyes of parents. It was only when
she went into the side ward and realised that Ross was
in there, talking, that she felt flustered.

'I can come back.'

'No.' He smiled. 'We're just having a chat, and Luke
needs his obs done.'

'I don't want them done,' Luke snarled as she approached the bed.

That didn't ruffle her either—her extra shifts at the
nursing home had taught her well, because belligerence
was an everyday occurrence there!

'I will come back in five minutes, then,' Annika said, just as she would say to Cecil, or Elsie, or any of the oldies who refused to have their morning shower.

'I won't want them done then either.'

'Then I will come back five minutes later, and five minutes after that again. My name is Annika; it would seem that you'll be seeing a lot of me this afternoon.' She gave him a smile. 'Every five minutes, in fact.'

'Just take them now, then.'

So she did.

Annika made no attempt at small talk. Luke clearly didn't want it, and anyway Ross was talking to him, telling him that there was no question of him going home, that he was still extremely ill and would be here for a few weeks—at least until the ulcer on his leg was healed and he was compliant with his medication. Yes, he would take the catheter out, so long as Luke agreed to wee into a bottle so that they could monitor his output.

Luke begrudgingly agreed to that.

And then Ross told him that the way he had spoken to the cleaner that morning was completely unacceptable.

'You can be as angry as you like, Luke, but it's not okay to be mean.'

'So send me home, then.'

'That's not going to happen.'

Annika wrote down his obs, which were all fine, and then, as Ross leant against the wall and Luke lay on the bed with his eyes closed, she spoke.

'When the doctor has finished talking to you I will come back and sort out your room.'

'And I'll tell *you* the same thing I said to the cleaner.'

She saw Ross open his mouth to intervene as Luke snarled at her, but in this Annika didn't need his help.

'Would you rather I waited till children's nap-time is over?' Annika asked. 'When you feel a little less grumpy.'

'Ha-ha…' he sneered, and then he opened his eyes and gave a nasty sarcastic grin. 'Nice apron!'

'I hate it,' she said. 'Wearing it is a bit demoralising and…' She thought for a moment as Luke just stared. 'Well, I find it a bit patronising really. If I were in cots it would maybe be appropriate. Still…' Annika shrugged. 'Sometimes we have to do things we don't want to.' She replaced his chart. 'I'll be back to clean your room shortly.'

Ross was at the nurses' station writing notes when she came over after completing the rest of the obs. He grinned when he saw her.

'Nice apron.'

'It's growing on me!' Annika said. 'Tomorrow I want to wear the one with robots!'

'I can't wait!' he replied, and, oh, for a witty retort—but there wasn't one forthcoming, so instead she asked Lisa where the cleaning cupboard was and found a bin liner. She escaped to the rather more soothing, at least for Annika, confines of Luke's room.

It was disgusting.

In the short time he had been in the room he had accumulated cups and plates and spilt drinks. There were used tissues on the floor. His bed was a disgrace because he refused to let anyone tidy it, and there were loads of cards from friends, along with all the gadgets fifteen-year-olds seemed to amass.

Luke didn't tell her to leave—probably because he sensed she wouldn't care if he did.

Annika was used to moods.

She had grown up surrounded by them and had chosen to completely ignore them.

Her father's temper had been appalling, though it had never been aimed towards her—she had been the apple of his eye. Her brothers were dark and brooding, and her mother could sulk for Russia.

A fifteen-year-old was nothing, *nothing*, compared to that lot.

Luke ignored her.

Which was fine by Annika.

'Everything okay?' Lisa checked as she finally headed to the kitchen with a trolley full of used plates and cups.

'All's fine.' The ward was quiet, the lights all dimmed, and Ross was still at the desk. 'Do you need me to do anything else, or is it okay if I carry on with Luke's room?'

'Please do,' Lisa said.

Luke wasn't ignoring her now—instead he watched as she sorted out his stuff into neat piles and put some of it into a bag.

'Your mum can take these home to wash.'

Other stuff she put into drawers.

Then she tacked some cards to the wall. All that was messy now, Annika decided as she wiped down the surfaces in his room, was the patient and his bed.

'Now your catheter is out it will be easier to have a shower. I can run it for you.'

He said neither yes nor no, so Annika headed down the ward and found the linen trolley, selected some towels and then found the showers. She worked out the taps and headed back to her patient, who was a bit wobbly but refused a wheelchair.

'Take my arm, then.'

'I can manage,' Luke said, and he said it again when she tried to help him undress.

'You have a drip…'

'I'm not stupid; I've had a drip before.'

Okay!

So she left him to it, and she didn't hover outside, asking if he was okay every two minutes, because that would have driven Luke insane. Instead she moved to the other end of the bathroom, so she could hear him if he called, and checked her reflection, noting the huge smudges under her eyes, which her mother would point out to her when she went there for dinner at the weekend.

She was exhausted. Annika rested her head against the mirror for a moment and just wanted to close her eyes and sleep. She was beyond exhausted, in fact, and from this morning's assessment it seemed it had been noticed.

Heather would never believe that she was working shifts in a nursing home, and the hardest slots too—five a.m. till eight a.m. if she was on a late shift at the hospital, and seven p.m. till ten p.m. if she was on an early. Oh, and a couple of nights shifts on her days off.

She was so tired. Not just bone-tired, but tired of arguing, tired of being told to pack in nursing, to come home, to be sensible, tired of being told that she didn't need to nurse—she was a Kolovsky.

'Iosef is a doctor,' Annika had pointed out.

'Iosef is a fool,' her mother had said, 'and as for that slut of a wife of his…'

'Finished.'

She was too glum thinking about her mother to smile and cheer as Luke came out, in fresh track pants and with his hair dripping wet.

'You smell much better,' Annika settled for instead, and the shower must have drained Luke because he let Annika thread his T-shirt through his IV.

'What are you looking so miserable about?' Luke asked.

'Stuff,' Annika said.

'Yeah,' Luke said, and she was rewarded with a smile from him.

'Oh, that's *much* better!' Lisa said, popping her head into the bathroom. 'You're looking very handsome.' Annika caught Luke's eyes and had to stop herself from rolling her own. She sort of understood him—she didn't know how, she just did. 'Your mum's here, by the way!' Lisa added.

'Great,' Luke muttered as Annika walked him back. 'That's all I need. You haven't met her yet…'

'You haven't met mine!' Annika said, and they both smiled this time—a real smile.

Annika surprised herself, because rarely, if ever, did she speak about her family, and especially not to a patient. But they had a little giggle as they walked, and she was too busy concentrating on Luke and pushing his IV to notice Ross look up from the desk and watch the unlikely new friends go by.

* * *

'Are you still here?' Caroline frowned, quite a long time later, because, as pedantic as Ross was, consultants didn't usually hang around all day.

'I just thought I'd catch up on some paperwork.'

'Haven't you got an office to go to?' she teased.

He did, but for once he didn't have that much paperwork to do.

'Annika!' Caroline called her over from where Annika was stacking the linen trolley after returning from her supper break. 'Come and get started on your notes. I'll show you how we do them. It's different to the main wards.'

He didn't look up, but he smelt her as she came around the desk.

A heavy, musky fragrance perfumed the air, and though he wrote it maybe twenty times a day, he had misspelled *diarrhoea*, and Ross frowned at his spiky black handwriting, because the familiar word looked completely wrong.

'Are you wearing perfume, Annika?' He didn't look up at Caroline's stern tone.

'A little,' Annika said, because she'd freshened up after her break.

'You can't wear perfume on the children's ward!' Caroline's voice had a familiar ring to it—one Ross had heard all his life.

'What do you mean—you just didn't want to go to school? You can't wear an earring. You just have to, that's all. You just don't. You just can't.'

'Go and wash it off,' Caroline said, and now Ross did look up. He saw her standing there, wary, tight-lipped, in that ridiculous apron. 'There are children with allergies, asthma. You just *can't* wear perfume, Annika—didn't you think?'

Caroline was right, Ross conceded, there were children with allergies and, as much as he liked it, Kolovsky musk post-op might be a little bit too much, but he wanted to step in, wanted to grin at Annika and tell her she smelt divine, tell her *not* to wash it off, for her to tell Caroline that she wouldn't.

And he knew that she was thinking it too!

It was a second, a mere split second, but he saw her waver—and Ross had a bizarre feeling that she was going to dive into her bag for the bottle and run around the ward, ripping off her apron and spraying perfume. The thought made him smile—at the wrong moment, though, because Annika saw him and, although Ross snapped his face to bland, she must have thought he was enjoying her discomfort.

Oh, but he wanted to correct her.

He wanted to follow her and tell her that wasn't what he'd meant as she duly turned around and headed for the washroom.

He wanted to apologise when she came back unscented and sat at her stool while Caroline nit-picked her way through the nursing notes.

Instead he returned to his own notes.

DIAOR… He scrawled a line through it again.

Still her fragrance lingered.

He got up without a word and, unusually for Ross, closed his office door. Then he picked up his pen and forced himself to concentrate.

DIARREA.

He hurled his pen down. Who cared anyway? They knew what he meant!

He was not going to fancy her, nor, if he could help it, even talk much to her.

He was off women.

He had sworn off women.

And a student nurse on his ward—well, it couldn't be without complications.

She was his friend's little sister too.

No way!

Absolutely not.

He picked up his pen and resumed his notes.

'*The baby has,*' he wrote instead, '*severe gastro-enteritis.*'

CHAPTER TWO

HE DID a very good job of ignoring her.

He did an excellent job at pulling rank and completely speaking over her head, or looking at a child or a chart or the wall when he had no choice but to address her. And at his student lecture on Monday he paid her no more attention than any of the others. He delivered a talk on gastroenteritis, and, though he hesitated as he went to spell *diarrhoea*, he wrote it up correctly on the whiteboard.

She, Ross noted, was ignoring him too. She asked no questions at the end of the lecture, but an annoying student called Cassie made up for that.

Once their eyes met, but she quickly flicked hers away, and he, though he tried to discount it, saw the flush of red on her neck and wished that he hadn't.

Yes, he did a very good job at ignoring her and not talking to her till, chatting to the pathologist in the bowels of the hospital a few days later, he glanced up at the big mirror that gave a view around the corridor and there was Annika. She was yawning, holding some blood samples, completely unaware she was being watched.

'I've been waiting for these…' Ross said when she turned the corner, and she jumped slightly at the sight of him. He took the bloodwork and stared at the forms rather than at her.

'The chute isn't working,' Annika explained. 'I said I'd drop them in on my way home.'

'I forgot to sign the form.'

'Oh.'

He would rather have taken ages to sign the form, but the pathologist decided they had been talking for too long and hurried him along. Annika had stopped for a moment to put on her jacket, and as his legs were much longer than hers somehow, despite trying not to, he had almost caught her up as they approached the flapping black plastic doors. It would have been really rude had she not held it open—and just plain wrong for him not to thank her and fall into step beside her.

'You look tired,' Ross commented.

'It's been a long shift.'

This had got them halfway along the corridor, and now they should just walk along in silence, Ross reasoned. He was a consultant, and he could be as rude and as aloof as he liked—except he could hear his boots, her shoes, and an endless, awful silence. It was Ross who filled it.

'I've actually been meaning to talk to you…' He had—long before he had liked her.

'Oh?' She felt the adrenaline kick in, the effect of him close up far more devastating than his smile, and yet she liked it. She liked it so much that she slowed down her pace and looked over to him. 'About what?'

She could almost smell the bonfire—all those smiles, all that guessing, all that waiting was to be put to rest now they were finally talking.

'I know your brother Iosef,' Ross said. 'He asked me to keep an eye out for you when you started.'

'Did he?' Her cheeks were burning, the back of her nose was stinging, and she wanted to run, to kick up her heels and run from him—because all the time she'd thought it was her, not her family, that he saw.

'I've always meant to introduce myself. Iosef is a good friend.' It was her jacket's fault, Ross decided. Her jacket smelt of the forbidden perfume. It smelt so much of her that he forgot, for a second, his newly laid-down rules. 'We should catch up some time…'

'Why?' She turned very blue eyes to him. 'So that you can report back to Iosef?'

'Of course not.'

'Tell him I'm doing fine,' Annika snapped, and, no, she didn't kick up her heels, and she didn't run, but she did walk swiftly away from him.

A year.

For more than a year she'd carried a torch, had secretly hoped that his smile, those looks they had shared, had meant something. All that time she had thought it had been about her, and yet again it wasn't.

Again, all she was was a Kolovsky.

It rankled. On the drive home it gnawed and burnt, but when she got there her mother had left a long message on the answer machine which rankled rather more.

They needed to go over details, she reminded her daughter.

It was the charity ball in just three weeks—as if Annika could ever forget.

When Annika had been a child it had been discovered that her father had an illegitimate son—one who was being raised in an orphanage in Russia.

Levander had been brought over to Australia. Her father had done everything to make up for the wretched years his son had suffered, and Levander's appalling early life had been kept a closely guarded family secret.

Now, though, the truth was starting to seep out. And Nina, anticipating a public backlash, had moved into pre-emptive damage control.

Huge donations had been sent to several orphanages, and to a couple of street-kid programmes too.

And then there was *The Ball*.

It was to be a dazzling, glitzy affair they would all attend. Levander was to be excused because he was in England, but the rest of the family would be there. Iosef and his wife, her brother Aleksi, and of course Annika. They would all look glossy and beautiful and be photographed to the max, so that when the truth inevitably came out the spin doctors would be ready.

Already were ready.

Annika had read the draft of the waiting press release.

The revelation of his son Levander's suffering sent Ivan Kolovsky to an early grave. He was thrilled when his second-born, Iosef, on qualifying as a doctor, chose to work amongst the poor in Russia, and Ivan would be proud to know that his daughter, Annika, is now studying nursing. On

Ivan's deathbed he begged his wife to set up the Kolovsky Foundation, which has gone on to raise huge amounts (insert current figure).

Lies.

Lies based on twisted truths. And only since her father's death had Annika started to question them.

And now she had, everything had fallen apart.

Her mother had never hit her before—oh, maybe a slap on the leg when she was little and had refused to converse in Russian, and once as a teenager, when her mother had found out she was eating burgers on her morning jog, Annika had nursed a red cheek and a swollen eye…but hardly anything major…

Until she had asked about Levander.

They had been sorting out her father's things, a painful task at the best of times, and Annika had come across some letters. She hadn't read them—she hadn't had a chance to. Nina had snatched them out of her hands, but Annika had asked her mother a question that had been nagging. It was a question her brothers had refused to answer when she had approached them with it. She asked whether Ivan and Nina had known that Levander was in an orphanage all those years.

Her mother had slapped her with a viciousness that had left Annika reeling—not at the pain but with shock.

She had then discovered that when she started to think, to suggest, to question, to find her own path in life, the love and support Annika had thought was unconditional had been pulled up like a drawbridge.

And the money had been taken away too.

Annika deleted her mother's message and prepared a light supper. She showered, and then, because she hadn't had time to this morning, ironed her white agency nurse's uniform and dressed. Tying her hair back, she clipped on her name badge.

Annika Kolovsky.

No matter how she resisted, it was who she was—and *all* she was to others.

She should surely be used to it by now.

Except she'd thought Ross had seen something else—thought for a foolish moment that Ross Wyatt had seen her for herself. Yet again it came back to one thing.

She was a Kolovsky.

CHAPTER THREE

'SLEEP well, Elsie.' Elsie didn't answer as Annika tucked the blankets round the bony shoulders of the elderly lady.

Elsie had spat out her tablets and thrown her dinner on the floor. She had resisted at every step of Annika undressing her and getting her into bed. But now that she was in bed she relaxed, especially when Annika positioned the photo of her late husband, Bertie, where the old lady could see him.

'I'll see you in the morning. I have another shift then.'

Still Elsie didn't answer, and Annika wished she would. She loved the stories Elsie told, during the times when she was lucid. But Elsie's confusion had worsened because of an infection, and she had been distressed tonight, resenting any intrusion. Nursing patients with dementia was often a thankless task, and Annika's shifts exhausted her, but at least, unlike on the children's ward, where she had been for a week now, here Annika knew what she was doing.

Oh, it was back-breaking, and mainly just sheer hard work, but she had been here for over a year now, and knew the residents. The staff of the private nursing home had been wary at first, but they were used to Annika now. She had proved herself a hard worker and, frankly, with a skeleton staff, so long as the patients were clean and dry, and bedded at night or dressed in the morning, nobody really cared who she was or why someone as rich as Annika always put her hand up for extra shifts.

It was ridiculous, though.

Annika knew that.

In fact she was ashamed that she stood in the forecourt of a garage next to a filthy old ute and had to prepay twenty dollars, because that was all she had until her pay from the nursing home went in tomorrow, to fill up the tank of a six-figure powder-blue sports car.

It had been her twenty-first birthday present.

Her mother had been about to upgrade it when Annika had declared she wanted to study nursing, and when she had refused to give in the financial plug had been pulled.

Her car now needed a service, which she couldn't afford. The sensible thing, of course, would be to sell it—except, despite its being a present, technically, it didn't belong to her: it was a company car.

So deep in thought was Annika, so bone-weary from a day on the children's ward and a twilight shift at the nursing home, that she didn't notice the man crossing the forecourt towards her.

'Annika?' He was putting money in his wallet. He had obviously just paid, and she glanced around rather than look at him. She was one burning blush, and not just because it was Ross, but rather because someone from work had seen her. She had done a full shift on the children's ward, and was due back there at midday tomorrow, so there was no way on earth she should be cramming in an extra shift, but she clearly was—two, actually, not that he could know! The white agency nurse dress seemed to glow under the fluorescent lights.

He could have nodded and left it there.

He damn well *should* nod and leave it there—and maybe even have a quiet word with Caroline tomorrow, or Iosef, perhaps.

Or say nothing at all—just simply forget.

He chose none of the above.

'How about a coffee?'

'It's late.'

'I know it's late,' Ross said, 'but I'm sure you could use a coffee. There's an all-night cafe a kilometre up the road—I'll see you there.'

She nearly didn't go.

She was *extremely* tempted not to go. But she had no choice.

Normally she was careful about being seen in her agency uniform, but she didn't have her jacket in the car, and she'd been so low on petrol… Anyway, Annika told herself, it was hardly a crime—all her friends did agency shifts. How the hell would a student survive otherwise?

His grim face told her her argument would be wasted.

'I know students have to work…' he had bought her a coffee and she added two sugars '…and I know it's probably none of my business…'

'It *is* none of your business,' Annika said.

'But I've heard Caroline commenting, and I've seen you yawning…' Ross said. 'You look like you've got two black eyes.'

'So tell Caroline—or report back to my brother.' Annika shrugged. 'Then your duty is done.'

'Annika!' Ross was direct. 'Do you go out of your way to be rude?'

'Rude?'

'I'm trying *not* to talk to Caroline; I'm trying to talk to *you*.'

'Check up on me, you mean, so that Iosef—'

He whistled in indignation. 'This has nothing to do with your brother. It's my ward, Annika. You were on an early today; you're on again tomorrow…'

'How do you know?'

'Sorry?'

'My shift tomorrow. How do you know?'

And that he couldn't answer—but the beat of silence did.

He'd checked.

Not deliberately—he hadn't swiped keys and found the nursing roster—but as he'd left the ward he had glanced up at the whiteboard and seen that she was on tomorrow.

He had noted to himself that she was on tomorrow.

'I saw the whiteboard.'

And she could have sworn that he blushed. Oh, his cheeks didn't flare like a match to a gas ring, as Annika's did—he was far too laid-back for that, and his skin was so much darker—but there was something that told her he was embarrassed. He blinked, and then his lips twitched in a very short smile, and then he blinked again. There was no colour as such to his eyes—in fact they were blacker than black, so much so that she couldn't even make out his pupils. He was staring, and so was she. They were sitting in an all-night coffee shop. She was in her uniform and he was telling her off for working, and yet she was sure there was more.

Almost sure.

'So, Iosef told you to keep an eye out for me?' she said, though more for her own benefit—that smile wouldn't fool her again.

'He said that he was worried about you, that you'd pretty much cut yourself off from your family.'

'I haven't,' Annika said, and normally that would have been it. Everything that was said stayed in the family, but Ross was Iosef's friend and she was quite sure he knew more. 'I see my mother each week; I am attending a family charity ball soon. Iosef and I argued, but only because he thinks I'm just playing at nursing.'

This wasn't news to Ross. Iosef had told him many things—how Annika was spoilt, how she stuck at nothing, how nursing was her latest flight of fancy. Of course Ross could not say this, so he just sat as she continued.

'I have not cut myself off from my family. Aleksi and I are close…' She saw his jaw tighten, as everyone's did these days when her brother's name was mentioned. Aleksi was trouble. Aleksi, now head of the Kolovsky fortune, was a loose cannon about to explode at any moment. Annika was the only one he was close to; even his twin Iosef was being pushed aside as Aleksi careered out of control. She looked down at her coffee then, but it blurred, so she pressed her fingers into her eyes.

'You *can* talk to me,' Ross said.

'Why would I?'

'Because that's what people do,' Ross said. 'Some people you know you can talk to, and some people...' He stopped then. He could see she didn't understand, and neither really did Ross. He swallowed down the words he had been about to utter and changed tack. 'I am going to Spain in three, nearly four weeks.' He smiled at her frown. 'Caroline doesn't know; Admin doesn't know. In truth, they are going to be furious when they find out. I am putting off telling them till I have spoken with a friend who I am hoping can cover for me...'

'Why are you telling me this?'

'Because I'm asking you to tell *me* things you'd rather no one else knew.'

She took her fingers out of her eyes and looked up to find *that* smile.

'It would be rude not to share,' he said.

He *was* dangerous.

She could almost hear her mother's rule that you discussed family with no one breaking.

'My mother does not want me to nurse,' Annika tentatively explained. And the skies didn't open with a roar, missiles didn't engage. There was just the smell of coffee and the warmth of his eyes. 'She has cut me off financially until I come back home. I still see her, I still go over and I still attend functions. I haven't cut myself off. It is my mother who has cut me off—financially, anyway. That's why I'm working these shifts.'

He didn't understand—actually, he didn't fully believe it.

He could guess at what her car was worth, and he knew from his friend that Annika was doted upon. Then there was Aleksi and his billions, and Iosef, even if they argued, would surely help her out.

'Does Iosef know you're doing extra shifts?'

'We don't talk much,' Annika admitted. 'We don't get on; we just never have. I was always a daddy's girl, the little princess…Levander, my older brother, thinks the same…' She gave a helpless shrug. 'I was always pleading with them to toe the line, to stop making waves in the family. Iosef is just waiting for me to quit.'

'Iosef cares about you.'

'He offers me money,' Annika scoffed. 'But really he is just waiting for this phase to be over. If I want money I will ask Aleksi, but, really, how can I be independent if all I do is cash cheques?'

'And how can you study and do placements and be a Kolovsky if you're cramming in extra shifts everywhere?'

She didn't know how, because she was failing at every turn.

'I get by,' she settled for. 'I have learnt that I can blowdry my own hair, that foils every month are not essential, that a massage each week and a pedicure and manicure…' Her voice sounded strangled for a moment. 'I am spoilt, as my brothers have always pointed out, and I am trying to learn not to be, but I keep messing up.'

'Tell me?'

She was surprised when she opened her screwed up eyes, to see that he was smiling.

'Tell me how you mess up?'

'I used to eat a lot of takeaway,' she admitted, and he was still smiling, so she was more honest, and Ross found out that Annika's idea of takeaway wasn't the same as his! 'I had the restaurants deliver.'

'Can't you cook?'

'I'm a fantastic cook,' Annika answered.

'That's right.' Ross grinned. 'I remember Iosef saying you were training as a pastry chef…in Paris?' he checked.

'I was only there six months.' Annika wrinkled her nose. 'I had given up on modelling and I so badly wanted to go. It took me two days to realise I had made a mistake, and then six months to pluck up the courage to admit defeat. I had made such a fuss, begged to go… Like I did for nursing.'

He didn't understand.

He thought of his own parents—if he'd said that he wanted to study life on Mars they'd have supported him. But then he'd always known what he wanted to do. Maybe if one year it had been Mars, the next Venus and then Pluto, they'd have decided otherwise. Maybe this was tough love that her mother thought she needed to prove that nursing was what she truly wanted to do.

'So you can cook?' It was easier to change the subject.

'Gourmet meals, the most amazing desserts, but a simple dinner for one beats me every time…' She gave a tight shrug. 'But I'm slowly learning.'

'How else have you messed up?'

She couldn't tell him, but he was still smiling, so maybe she could.

'I had a credit card,' she said. 'I have always had one, but I just sent the bill to our accountants each month…'

'Not now?'

'No.'

Her voice was low and throaty, and Ross found himself leaning forward to catch it.

'It took me three months to work out that they weren't settling it, and I am still paying off that mistake.'

'But you love nursing?' Ross said, and then frowned when she shook her head.

'I don't know,' Annika admitted. 'Sometimes I don't even know why I am doing this. It's the same as when I wanted to be a pastry chef, and then I did jewellery design—that was a mistake too.'

'Do you think you've made a mistake with nursing?' Ross asked.

Annika gave a tight shrug and then shook her head— he was hardly the person to voice her fears to.

'You can talk to me, Annika. You can trust that it won't—'

'Trust?' She gave him a wide-eyed look. 'Why would I trust you?'

It was the strangest answer, and one he wasn't expecting. Yet why should she trust him? Ross pondered. All he knew was that she could.

'You need to get home and get some rest,' Ross settled for—except he couldn't quite leave it there. 'How about dinner…?'

And this was where every woman jumped, this was where Ross always kicked himself and told himself to slow down, because normally they never made it to dinner. Normally, about an hour from now, they were pinning the breakfast menu on the nearest hotel door or hot-footing it back to his city abode—only this was Annika, who instead drained her coffee and stood up.

'No, thank you. It would make things difficult at work.'

'It would,' Ross agreed, glad that one of them at least was being sensible.

'Can I ask that you don't tell Caroline or anyone about this?'

'Can I ask that you save these shifts for your days off, or during your holidays?'

'No.'

They walked out to the car park, to his dusty ute and her powder-blue car. Ross was relaxed and at ease, Annika a ball of tension, so much so that she jumped at the bleep of her keys as she unlocked the car.

'I'm not going to say anything to Caroline.'

'Thank you.'

'Just be careful, okay?'

'I will.'

'You can't mess up on any ward, but especially not on children's.'

'I won't,' Annika said. 'I don't. I am always so, so careful…' And she was. Her brain hurt because she was so careful, pedantic, and always, *always* checked. Sometimes it would be easier not to care so.

'Go home and go to bed,' Ross said. 'Will you be okay to drive?'

'Of course.'

He didn't want her to drive; he wanted to bundle her into his ute and take her back to the farm, or head back into the coffee shop and talk till three a.m., or, maybe just kiss her?

Except he was being sensible now.

'Night, then,' he said.

'Goodnight.'

Except neither of them moved.

'Why are you going to Spain?' Unusually, it was Annika who broke the silence.

'To sort out a few things.'

'I'm staying here for a few weeks,' Annika said, with just a hint of a smile. 'To sort out a few things.'

'It will be nice,' Ross said, 'when things are a bit more sorted.'

'Very nice,' Annika agreed, and wished him goodnight again.

'If you change your mind…' He snapped his mouth closed; he really mustn't go there.

Annika was struggling. She didn't want to get into her car. She wanted to climb into the ute with him, to forget about sorting things out for a little while. She wanted him to drive her somewhere secluded. She wanted the passion those black eyes promised, wanted out of being staid, and wanted to dive into recklessness.

'Drive carefully.'

'You too.'

They were talking normally—extremely politely, actually—yet their minds were wandering off to dangerous places: lovely, lovely places that there could be no coming back from.

'Go,' Ross said, and she felt as if he were kissing her. His eyes certainly were, and her body felt as if he were.

She was shaking as she got in the car, and the key was too slim for the slot. She had to make herself think, had to slow her mind down and turn on the lights and then the ignition.

He was beside her at the traffic lights. Ross was indicating right for the turn to the country; Annika aimed straight for the city.

It took all her strength to go straight on.

CHAPTER FOUR

ELSIE frowned from her pillow when Annika awoke her a week later at six a.m. with a smile.

'What are you so cheerful about?' Elsie asked dubiously. She often lived in the past, but sometimes in the morning she clicked to the present, and those were the mornings Annika loved best.

She recognised Annika—oh, not all of the time, sometimes she spat and swore at the intrusion, but some mornings she was Elsie, with beady eyes and a generous glimpse of a once sharp mind.

'I just am.'

'How's the children's ward?' Elsie asked. Clearly even in that fog-like existence she mainly inhabited somehow she heard the words Annika said, even if she didn't appear to at the time.

Annika was especially nice to Elsie. Well, she was nice to all the oldies, but Elsie melted her heart. The old lady had shrunk to four feet tall and there was more fat on a chip. She swore, she spat, she growled, and every now and then she smiled. Annika couldn't help but spoil her, and sometimes it annoyed the other staff, because many showers had to be done before the day shift appeared, and there really wasn't time to make drinks, but Elsie loved to have a cup of milky tea before she even thought about moving and Annika always made her one. The old lady sipped on it noisily as Annika sorted out her clothes for the day.

'It's different on the children's ward,' Annika said. 'I'm not sure if I like it.'

'Well, if it isn't work that's making you cheerful then I want to know what is. It has to be a man.'

'I'm just in a good mood.'

'It's a man,' Elsie said. 'What's his name?'

'I'm not saying.'

'Why not? I tell you about Bertie.'

This was certainly true!

'Ross.' Annika helped her onto the shower chair. 'And that's all I'm saying.'

'Are you courting?'

Annika grinned at the old-fashioned word.

'No,' Annika said.

'Has he asked you out?'

'Sort of,' Annika said as she wheeled her down to the showers. 'Just for dinner, but I said no.'

'So you're just flirting, then!' Elsie beamed. 'Oh, you lucky, lucky girl. I loved flirting.'

'We're not flirting, Elsie,' Annika said. 'In fact we're now ignoring each other.'

'Why would you do that?'

'Just leave it, Elsie.'

'Flirt!' Elsie insisted as Annika pulled her nightgown over her head. 'Ask him out.'

'Enough, Elsie,' Annika attempted, but it was like pulling down a book and having the whole shelf toppling down on you. Elsie was on a roll, telling her exactly what she'd have done, how the worst thing she should do was play it cool.

On and on she went as Annika showered her, though thankfully, once Annika had popped in her teeth, Elsie's train of thought drifted back to her beloved Bertie, to the sixty wonderful years they had shared, to shy kisses at the dance halls he had taken her to and the agony of him going to war. She talked about how you must never let the sun go down on a row, and she chatted away about Bertie, their wedding night and babies as Annika dressed her, combed her hair, and then wheeled her back to her room.

'You must miss him,' Annika said, arranging Elsie's table, just as she did every morning she worked there, putting her glasses within reach, her little alarm clock, and then Elsie and Bertie's wedding photo in pride of place.

'Sometimes,' Elsie said, and then her eyes were crystal-clear, 'but only when I'm sane.'

'Sorry?'

'I get to relive our moments, over and over…' Elsie smiled, and then she was gone, back to her own world, the moment of clarity over. She did not talk as Annika wrapped a shawl around her shoulders and put on her slippers.

'Enjoy it,' Annika said to her favourite resident.

* * *

He had his ticket booked, and four weeks' unpaid leave reluctantly granted. They had wanted him to take paid leave but, as Ross had pointed out, that was all saved up for his trips to Russia. This hadn't gone down too well, and Ross had sat through a thinly veiled warning from the Head of Paediatrics—there was no such thing as a part-time consultant and, while his work overseas was admirable, there were plenty of charities here in Australia he could support.

As he walked through the canteen that evening, the conversation played over in his mind. He could feel the tentacles of bureaucracy tightening around him. He wanted this day over, to be back at his farm, where there were no rules other than to make sure the animals were fed.

His intention had been to get some chocolate from the vending machine, but he saw Annika, and thought it would be far more sensible to keep on walking. Instead, he bought a questionable cup of coffee from another machine and, uninvited, went over.

'Hi!'

He didn't ask if he could join her; he simply sat down.

She was eating a Greek salad and had pushed all the olives to one side.

'Hello.'

'Nice apron.' She was emblazoned with fairies and wands, and he could only laugh that she hated it so.

'It was the only one left,' Annika said. 'Ross, if I do write my notice—if I do give up nursing—in my letter there will be a long paragraph devoted to being made to wear aprons.'

'So you're thinking of it?'

'I don't know,' she admitted. 'I asked for a weekend off. There is a family function—there is no question that I don't go. I requested it ages ago, when I found out that I would be on the children's ward. I sent a memo, but it got lost, apparently.'

'What are you going to do?'

'Caroline has changed my late shift on Saturday to an early, and she has changed the early shift on Sunday to a late. She wasn't pleased, though, and neither am I.' She looked over to him. 'I have to get ready….' And then her voice trailed off, because it sounded ridiculous, and how could he possibly know just what getting ready for a family function entailed?

And he didn't understand her, but he wanted to.

And, yes, he was sworn off women, and she had said no to dinner, and, yes, it could get very messy, but right now he didn't care.

He should get up and go.

Yet he couldn't.

Quiet simply, he couldn't.

'I told them I'm going to Spain.'

She looked at his grim face and guessed it hadn't gone well. 'It will be worth it when you're there, I'm sure.'

'Do you ever want to go to Russia?' Ross asked. 'To see where you are from.'

'I was born here.'

'But your roots…'

'I might not like what I dig up.'

He glanced down at her plate, at the lovely ripe olives she had pushed aside. 'May I?'

'That's bad manners.'

'Not between friends.'

He would not have taken one unless she'd done what she did next and pushed the plate towards him. She watched as he took the ripe fruit and popped it in his mouth, and Annika had no idea how, but he even looked sexy as he retrieved the stone.

'They're too good to leave.'

'I don't like them,' she said. 'I tried them once…' She pulled a face.

'You were either too young to appreciate them or you got a poor effort.'

'A poor effort?'

'Olives,' Ross said, 'need to be prepared carefully. They take ages—rush them and they're bitter. I grow them at my farm, and my grandmother knows how to make the best… She's Spanish.'

'I didn't think you were Spanish, more like a pirate or a gypsy.'

It was the first real time she had opened the conversation, the first hint at an open door. It was a glimpse that she did think about him. 'I am Spanish…' Ross said '…and I prefer Romany. I am Romany—well, my father was. My real father.'

His eyes were black—not navy, and not jade; they were as black as the leather on his belt.

'He had a brief affair with my mother when they were passing through. She was sixteen…'

'It must have caused a stir.'

'Apparently not,' Ross said. 'She was a wild thing

back then—she's a bit eccentric even now. But wise…' Ross said reluctantly. 'Extremely wise.'

She wanted to know more. She didn't drain her cup or stand. She was five minutes over her coffee break, and never, ever late, yet she sat there, and then he smiled, his slow lazy smile, and she blushed. She burnt because it was bizarre, wild and crazy. She was blue-eyed and blonde and rigid, and he was so very dark and laid-back and dangerous, and they were both thinking about black-haired, blue-eyed babies, or black-eyed blonde babies, of so many fabulous combinations and the wonderful time they'd have making them.

'I have to get back.'

Annika had never flirted in her life. She had had just one boring, family-sanctioned relationship, which had ended with her rebellion in moving towards nursing, but she knew she was flirting now. She knew she was doing something dangerous and bold when she picked up a thick black olive, popped it in her mouth and then removed the pip.

'Nice?' Ross asked

'Way better than I remember.' And they weren't talking about olives, of that she was certain. She might have to check with Elsie, but she was sure she was flirting. She blushed—not from embarrassment, but because of what he said next.

'Oh, it will be.'

And as she sped back to the ward late, she was burning. She could hardly breathe as she accepted Caroline's scolding and then went to warm up a bottle for a screaming baby. Only when he was fed, changed and settled did she pull up the cot-side and let herself think.

Oh, she didn't need to run it by Elsie.

Ross had certainly been flirting.

And Annika had loved it.

CHAPTER FIVE

'I DON'T want a needle.'

Hannah was ten and scared.

She had flushed cheeks from crying, and from the virus that her body was struggling to fight, and Annika's heart went out to her, because the little girl had had enough.

Oh, she wasn't desperately ill, but she was sick and tired and wanted to be left alone. However, her IV site was due for a change, and even though cream had been applied an hour ago, so that she wouldn't feel it, she was scared and yet, Annika realised, just wanted it to be over and done with.

So too did Annika.

Ross was putting the IV in.

'I'll be in in a moment,' he had said, popping his head around the treatment room door—and Annika had nodded and carried on chatting with Hannah, but she was exhausted from the hyper-vigilant state he put her in. She knew he was in a difficult position; he was a consultant, she a student nurse—albeit a mature one. She also knew a relationship was absolutely the last thing she needed. Chaos abounded in her life; there was just so much to sort out.

Yet she wanted him.

Elsie, when Annika had discussed it with her, had huffed and puffed that it should be Ross who asked *her* out, Ross who should take her out dancing. But things were different now, Annika had pointed out, and she'd already said no to him once.

'Ask him,' Cecil had said when she had taken him in his evening drink. He had a nip of brandy each night, and always asked for another one. 'You lot say you want equal rights, but only when it suits you. Why should he risk his job?'

'Risk his job?'

'For harassing you?' Cecil said stoutly. 'He's already asked you and you said no—if you've changed your mind, then bloody well ask him. Stop playing games.'

'How do you know all this?' Annika had demanded, and then gone straight to Elsie's room. 'That was a secret.'

'I've got dementia.' Elsie huffed. 'You can't expect me to keep a secret.'

'You cunning witch!' Annika said, and Elsie laughed.

She hadn't just told Cecil either!

Half of the residents were asking for updates, and then sulking when Annika reported that there were none.

So, when Ross had asked her to bring Hannah up to the treatment room to have her IV bung replaced, even though Cassie had offered to do it for her, Annika had bitten the bullet. Now she was trying to talk to her patient.

'The cream we have put on your arm means that you won't feel it.'

'I just don't like it.'

'I know,' Annika said, 'but once it is done you can go back to bed and have a nice rest and you won't be worrying about it any more. Dr Ross is very gentle.'

'I am.'

She hadn't heard him come in, and she gave him a small smile as she turned around to greet him.

'Hannah's nervous.'

'I bet you are,' Ross said to his patient. 'You had a tough time of it in Emergency, didn't you? Hannah was too sick to wait for the anaesthetic cream to work,' he explained to Annika, but really for the little girl's benefit, 'and she was also so ill that her veins were hard to find, so the doctor had to have a few goes.'

'It hurt,' Hannah gulped.

'I know it did.' Ross was checking the trolley and making sure everything was set up before he commenced. Hannah was lying down, but she looked as if at any moment she might jump off the treatment bed. 'But the doctor in Emergency wasn't a children's doctor…' Ross winked to Hannah, 'I'm used to little veins, and you're not as sick now, so they're going to be a lot easier to find and because of the cream you won't be able to feel it…'

'No!'

She was starting to really cry now, pulling her arm away as Ross slipped on a tourniquet. The panic that had been building was coming to the fore. He did his best to calm her, but she wasn't having it. She needed this IV; she had already missed her six a.m. medication, and she was vomiting and not able to hold down any fluids.

'Hannah, you need this,' Ross said, and as she had done for several patients now, Annika leant over her, keeping her little body as still as she could as Ross tried to reassure her.

'Don't look,' Annika said, holding the little girl's frightened gaze. 'You won't feel anything.'

'Just because I can't see it, I still know that you're hurting me!' came the pained little voice, and something inside Annika twisted. She felt so hopeless; she truly didn't know what to say, or how to comfort the girl.

'Watch, then,' Ross said. 'Let her go.'

He smiled to Annika and she did so, sure that the little girl would jump down from the treatment bed and run, but instead she lay there, staring suspiciously up at Ross.

'I know you've been hurt,' he said, 'and I know that in Emergency it would have been painful because the doctor had to have a few goes to get the needle in, but I'm not going to hurt you.'

'What if you can't get the needle in, like last time?'

'I'm quite sure I can,' Ross said, pressing on a rather nice vein with his olive-skinned finger. 'But if, for whatever reason, I can't, then we'll put some cream elsewhere—you're not as sick now, and we can wait…'

His voice was completely serious; he wasn't doing the smiling, reassuring thing that Annika rather poorly attempted.

'I am going to do everything I can not to hurt you. If for some reason there's ever a procedure that will hurt,

I will tell you, and we'll work it out, but this one,' Ross said, 'isn't going to hurt.'

He tightened the tourniquet and Hannah watched. He swabbed the vein a couple of times and then got out the needle, and she didn't cry or move away, she just watched.

'Even I'm nervous now.' Ross grinned, and so too did Annika, that tiny pause lifting the mood in the room. Even Hannah managed a little smile. She stared as the needle went in, and flinched, but only because she was expecting pain. When it didn't come, when the needle was in and Ross was taping it securely in place, her grin grew much wider when Ross told her she had been very brave.

'Very brave!' Annika said, like a parrot, because she could never be as at ease with children as he was. She was attaching the IV and Ross was looking through his drug book, working out the new medication regime that he wanted Hannah on.

Brighter now it was all over, Hannah looked up at Annika.

'You're pretty.'

'Thank you.' She hated this. It was okay when Elsie said it, or one of the oldies, but children were so probing. Annika was still trying to attach the bung, but the little hard bit of plastic proved fiddly, and the last thing she wanted was to mess up the IV access. She almost did when Hannah spoke next.

'Have you got a boyfriend?'

'No.' Her cheeks were on fire, and she could feel Ross looking at her, though she was *so* not going to look at him.

'I thought you did, Annika.' He spoke then to Hannah. 'He's a very nice guy, apparently.'

'It's very early days.' The drip was attached, and now she had to strap it in place.

'I like a boy in my class,' Hannah said, with a confidence Annika would never possess. 'He sent me a card, and he wrote that he's coming to visit me once I'm allowed visitors that aren't my mum.'

'That's nice.'

'So, where does your boyfriend take you?' Hannah probed.

'I'm more a stay-at-home person…' Annika blew at her fringe and pressed in the numbers. Ross was beside her, checking that the dosage was correct and signing off on the sheet. She could feel that he was laughing, knew he was enjoying her discomfort—and there and then she decided to be brave.

Exceptionally brave—and if it didn't work she'd blame Cecil and Elsie.

'I was thinking of asking him over for dinner on Saturday.' Annika swallowed. She knew her face was on fire, she was cringing and burning, and yet she was also excited.

'That sounds nice. I'm sure he'd love it,' was all Ross said.

She got Hannah back to bed, and then, as she went back into the treatment room to prepare Luke's dressing, Ross came in.

'I don't want to talk at work.'

'Fine.'

'So can we just keep things separate?'

'No problem, Annika.'

'I mean it, Ross.'

'Of course,' he said patiently. 'Annika, do you know where the ten gauge needles are kept? They've run out on the IV trolley…'

And he was so matter-of-fact, so absolutely normal in his behaviour towards her, that Annika wondered if she actually had asked him out at all. At six a.m. on a Saturday, when he hadn't asked for a time, or even an address, she wasn't sure that she had.

CHAPTER SIX

'How's the children's ward?' Elsie was wide awake before Annika had even flicked the lights on.

'It's okay,' Annika said, and then she admitted the truth. 'I'll be glad when it's over.'

'What have you got next?'

'Maternity,' Annika said, as Elsie slurped her tea.

She seemed to have caught her second wind these past few days: more and more she was lucid, and the lucid times were lasting longer too. She was getting over that nasty UTI, Dianne, the Div 1 nurse had explained. They often caused confusion in the elderly, or, as in Elsie's case, exacerbated dementia. It was good to have her back.

'I'm not looking forward to it.'

'What *are* you looking forward to?'

'I don't know,' Annika admitted.

'How's your boyfriend?' Elsie asked when they were in the shower, Annika in her gumboots, Elsie in her little shower chair. 'How's Ross?'

'I don't know that either,' Annika said, cringing a little when Elsie said his name. 'It's complicated.'

'Love isn't complicated,' Elsie said. 'You are.'

And they had a laugh, a real laugh, as she dried and dressed Elsie and put her in her chair. Then Annika did something she had never done before.

'I've got something for you.' Nervous, she went to the fridge and brought out her creation.

It was a white chocolate box, filled with chocolate mousse and stuffed with raspberries.

'Where's my toast?' Elsie asked, and that made Annika laugh. Then the old lady peered at the creation and dipped her bony finger into the mousse, licked it, and had a raspberry. 'You bought this for me?'

'I made it,' Annika said. 'This was my practice one…' She immediately apologised. 'Sorry, that sounds rude…'

'It doesn't sound rude at all.'

'You have to spread the white chocolate on parchment paper and then slice it; you only fill the boxes at the end. I did a course a few years ago,' Annika admitted. 'Well, I didn't finish it…'

'You didn't need to,' Elsie said. 'You could serve this up every night and he'd be happy. This is all you need…it's delicious…' Elsie was cramming raspberries in her mouth. 'This is for your man?'

'I'm worried he'll think I've gone to too much effort.'

'Is he worth the effort?' Elsie asked.

'Yes.'

'Then don't worry.'

'I think I've asked him to dinner tonight.'

'You think?' Elsie frowned. 'What did he say?'

'That it sounded very nice.' Annika gulped. 'Only we

haven't confirmed times. I'm not even sure he knows where I live…'

'He can find out,' Elsie said.

'How?'

'If he wants to, he will.'

'So I shouldn't ring him and check…?'

'Oh, no!' Elsie said. 'Absolutely not.'

'What if he doesn't come?'

'You have to trust that he will.'

'But what if he doesn't?'

'Then you bring in the food for us lot tomorrow,' Elsie said. 'Of course he's coming.' She put her hands on Annika's cheeks. 'Of *course* he'll come.'

CHAPTER SEVEN

IT KILLED her not to ring or page him, but Elsie had been adamant.

She had to trust that he would come, and if he didn't… Well, he had never been going to.

So, when she finished at the nursing home at nine a.m., she went home and had a little sleep, and then went to the Victoria Market. She bought some veal, some cream, the most gorgeous mushrooms, some fresh fettuccini and, of course, some more raspberries.

It was nice to be in the kitchen and stretching herself again.

Melting chocolate, whisking in eggs—she really had loved cooking and learning, but cooking at a high level had to be a passion. It was an absolute passion that Annika had realised she didn't have.

But still, she could love it.

She didn't know what to wear. She'd gone to so much trouble with the dessert that she didn't want to make too massive an effort with her clothes, in case she terrified him.

She opened her wardrobe and stared at a couple of Kolovsky creations. She had a little giggle to herself, wondering about his reaction if she opened the door to him in red velvet, but settled for a white skirt and a lilac top. She put on some lilac sandals, but she never wore shoes at home—well, not at this home—and ten minutes in she had kicked them off. She was dusting the chocolate boxes and trying not to care that it was ten past eight. She checked her hair, which was for once out of its ponytail, and put on some lip-gloss. Then she went to the kitchen, opened the fridge. The chocolate boxes hadn't collapsed, and the veal was all sliced and floured and waiting—and then she heard the knock at her door.

'Hi.' His voice made her stomach shrink.

'Hi.'

He was holding flowers, and she was so glad that she had taken Elsie's advice and not rung.

He kissed her on the cheek and handed her the flowers—glorious flowers, all different, wild and fragrant, and tied together with a bow. 'Hand-picked,' he said, 'which is why I'm so late.'

And she smiled, because of course they weren't. He'd been to some trendy place, no doubt, but she was grateful for them, because they got her through those first awkward moments as he followed her into the kitchen and she located a vase and filled it with water.

Ross was more than a little perplexed.

He hadn't known quite what to expect from tonight, but he hadn't expected this.

Okay, he'd known from her address that she wasn't

in the smartest suburb. He hadn't given it that much thought till he'd entered her street. A trendy converted townhouse, perhaps, he'd thought as he'd pulled up— a Kolovsky attempt at pretending to be poor.

Except her car stuck out like a sore thumb in the street, and as he climbed the steps he saw there was nothing trendy or converted about her flat.

There was an ugly floral carpet, cheap blinds dressed the windows, and not a single thing matched.

The kitchen was a mixture of beige and brown and a little bit of taupe too!

There was a party going on upstairs, and an argument to the left and right. Here in the centre was Annika.

She didn't belong—so much so he wanted to grab her by the hand and take her back to the farm right now, right this minute.

'I'll start dinner.'

She poured some oil in a large wok, turned the gas up on some simmering water, and then glanced over and gave him a nervous smile, which he returned. Then she slipped on an apron.

And it transformed her.

He stood and watched as somehow the tiny kitchen changed.

She pulled open the fridge and put a little meat in the wok. It was rather slow to sizzle, so she pulled out of the fridge some prepared plates, and he watched as she tipped coils of fresh pasta into the water and then threw the rest of the meat into the wok. Her hair was in the way, so she tied it back in a knot. He just carried on watching as this awkward, difficult woman relaxed and transformed garlic, pepper, cream and wine. He had never thought watching someone cook could be so sexy, yet before the water had even returned to the boil Ross was standing on the other side of the bench!

'Okay?' Annika checked.

'Great,' Ross said.

In seven minutes they were at the table—all those dishes, in a matter of moments, blended into a veal scaloppini that was to die for.

'When you said dinner…'

'I love to cook…'

And she loved to eat too.

With food between them, and with wine, somehow, gradually, it got easier.

He told her about his farm—that his sisters didn't get it, but it must be the gypsy blood in him because there he felt he belonged.

'I've never been to a farm.'

'Never?'

'No.'

'You're a city girl?'

'I guess,' Annika said.

She intrigued him.

'You used to model?'

'For a couple of years,' Annika said. 'Only in-house.'

'Sorry?'

'Just for Kolovsky,' she explained. 'I always thought that was what I wanted to do—well, it was expected of me, really—but when I got there it was just hours and hours in make-up, hours and hours hanging around, and…' she rolled her eyes '…no dinners like this.' She registered his frown. 'Thin wasn't thin enough, and I like my food too much.'

'So you went to Paris…?'

'I did.'

'What made you decide to do nursing?'

'I'm not sure,' Annika admitted. 'When my father was ill I watched the nurses caring for him…' It was hard to explain, so she didn't. 'What about you? Are you the same as Iosef? Is medicine your vocation?'

'Being a doctor was the only thing I ever wanted to be.'

'Lucky you.'

'Though when I go to Russia with your brother, sometimes I wonder if there is more than being a doctor in a well-equipped city hospital.'

'You're not happy at work?'

'I'm very happy at work,' Ross corrected. 'Sometimes, though, I feel hemmed in—often I feel hemmed in. I just broke up with someone because of it.' He gave her a wry smile. 'I'm supposed to be sworn off women.'

'I'm not good at hemming.'

Ross laughed. 'I can't picture you with a needle.' And then he was serious. 'Romanys have this image of being cads—that is certainly my mother's take. I understand that, but really they are loyal to commitment, and virginity is important to them, which is why they often marry young…' He gave an embarrassed half-laugh. 'There is more to them than I understand…'

'And you need to find out?'

'I think so,' Ross answered. 'Maybe that is why I get on with the orphans in Russia. I am much luckier, of course, but I can relate to them—to that not knowing, never fully knowing where you came from. I don't know my father's history.'

'You could have a touch of Russian in you!' Annika smiled.

'Who knows?' Ross smiled. 'Do you go back to Russia?'

She shook her head. 'Levander does, Iosef as you know does work there...'

'Aleksi?' Ross asked.

'He goes, but not for work...' She gave a shrug. 'I don't really know why. I've just never felt the need to.'

'You speak Russian, though?'

'No.' She shook her head. 'Only a little—a very little compared to my family.'

'You have an accent.'

'Because I refused to speak Russian...' She smiled at his bemusement. 'I was a very wilful child. I spoke Russian and a little English till I was five, and then I realised that we lived in Australia. I started to say I didn't understand Russian—that I only understood English, wanted to speak English.' He smiled at the image of her as a stubborn five-year-old. 'It infuriated my mother, and my teacher...I learnt English from Russians, which is why I have an accent. Do you speak Spanish?'

'Not as much as I'd like to.'

'You're going in a couple of weeks?'

'Yeah.' And he told her—well, bits... 'Mum's upset about it. I think she's worried I'm going to find my real father and set up camp with him. Run away and leave it all behind...'

'Are you?'

'No.' Ross shook his head. 'I'd like to meet him, get to know him if I can find him. I only have his first name.'

'Which is?'

'Reyes,' Ross said, and then he gave her a little part of him that he didn't usually share. 'That's actually my real name.'

'I lived with my father. Every day I saw him,' Annika said, giving back a little part of herself, 'but I don't think I knew him at all.'

'I know about Levander.' He watched her swallow. 'I know that Levander was raised in the Detsky Dom.'

'Iosef shouldn't talk.'

'Iosef and I have spent weeks—no, months, working in Russian orphanages. It's tough going there—sometimes you need to talk. He hates that Levander was raised there.'

'My parents were devastated when they found out…' She was glad she'd read that press release now. 'On his deathbed my father begged that we set up the foundation…' Her voice cracked. She was caught between the truth and a lie, and she didn't know what was real any more. 'We are holding a big fundraiser soon. If nursing doesn't work out then I am thinking of working full-time on the board…'

'Organising fundraisers?'

'Perhaps.' She shrugged. 'I'll get dessert…'

'You made these?' He couldn't believe it. He took a bite and couldn't believe it again—and then he said the completely wrong thing. 'You're wasted as a nurse.'

And he saw her eyes shutter.

'I'm sorry, Annika; I didn't mean it like that.'

'Don't worry.' She smiled. 'You're probably right.'

'Not wasted…'

'Just leave it.'

'I can't leave it,' Ross said, and her eyes jerked up to his. 'But I ought to.'

'At least till I have finished on the ward,' Annika said, and her throat was so tight she didn't know how to swallow, and her chocolate box sat unopened.

'I'll be in Spain,' Ross said.

'Slow is good.' Annika nodded. 'I don't want to rush.'

'So we just put it on hold?' Ross checked, and she nodded. 'Just have dinner?' He winced. 'When I say *just*…'

'Maybe one kiss goodnight,' Annika relented, because Elsie would be so disappointed otherwise.

'Sounds good,' Ross said. 'Now or later?'

'You choose.'

Four hours of preparation: tempering the chocolate, slicing the boxes, choosing the best raspberries. And the mousse recipe was a complicated one. All that work, all those hours, slipped deliciously away as he pulled her across the table and her breast sank into her own creation.

His tongue tasted better than anything she could conjure. They both had to stretch, but it was worth it. He tasted of chocolate, and then of him. His hair was in her fingers and she was pressing her face into him, the scratch of his jaw, the press of his lips. She wanted more, so badly she almost climbed onto the table just to be closer, but it was easier to stand. Lips locked, they kissed over the table, and then did a sort of crab walk till they could properly touch—and touch they did.

The most touching it was possible to do with clothes on and standing. She felt his lovely bum, and his jeans, and she pressed him into her. It was still just a kiss, one kiss, but it went on for ever.

'Oh, Annika,' he said, when she pulled back for a gulp of air, and then he saw the mess on her top and set to work.

'That's not kissing…' He was kissing her breast through the fabric, sucking off the mousse and the cream, and her fingers were back in his hair.

'It is,' he said.

And the raspberries had made the most terrible stain, so he concentrated on getting it out, and then she had to stop him. She stepped back and did something she never did.

She started to laugh.

And then she did something really stupid—something she'd cringe at when she told Elsie—well, the edited version—but knew Elsie would clap her approval.

She told him to dance—ordered him, in fact!

She lay on the sofa and watched, and there was rather more noise than usual from Annika's flat—not that the neighbours noticed.

She lay there and watched as his great big black boots stamped across the floor, and it was mad, really, but fantastic. She could smell the gypsy bonfire, and she knew he could too—it was their own fantasy, crazy and sort of private, but she would tell Elsie just a little.

And she did only kiss him—maybe once or twice, or three times more.

But who knew the places you could go to with a kiss?

Who knew you could be standing pressed against the door fully dressed, but naked in your mind?

'Bad girl,' Ross said as, still standing, she landed back on earth.

'Oh, I will be!' Annika said.

'Come back to the farm…'

'We said slowly.'

So they had—and there was Spain, and according to form he knew he'd hurt her, but he was suddenly sure that he wouldn't. She could take a sledgehammer to his bedroom wall if she chose, and he'd just lie on the bed and let her.

'Come to the farm.' God, what was he doing?

'I've got stuff too, Ross.'

'I know, I know.'

'Don't rush me.'

'I know.' He was coming back to earth as well. He'd never been accused of rushing things before. It was always Ross pulling back, always Ross reluctant to share—it felt strange to be on the other side.

'And I've never been bad.'

He started to laugh, and then he realised she wasn't joking.

'The rules are different if you're a Kolovsky girl, and till recently I've never been game enough to break them.'

Oh!

Looking into her troubled eyes, knowing what he knew about her family, suddenly he was scared of his own reputation and knew it was time to back off.

Annika Kolovsky he couldn't risk hurting.

CHAPTER EIGHT

AT HER request, things slowed down.

Stopped, really.

The occasional text, a lot of smiles, and a couple of coffees in the canteen.

It was just as well, really. There was no time for a relationship as her world rapidly unravelled.

Aleksi had hit a journalist and was on the front pages again.

Her mother was in full charity ball mode, and nothing Annika could say or do at work was right.

'He's *that* sick from chicken pox?' Annika couldn't help but speak up during handover. Normally she kept her head down and just wrote, but it was so appalling she couldn't help it. An eight-year-old had been admitted from Emergency with encephalitis and was semi-conscious—all from a simple virus. 'You can get *that* ill from chicken pox?'

'It's unusual,' Caroline said, 'but, yes. If he doesn't improve then he'll be transferred to the children's hospital. For now he's on antiviral medication and hourly obs. His mother is, of course, beside herself. She's got two others at home who have the virus too. Ross is just checking with Infectious Diseases and then he'll be contacting their GP to prescribe antivirals for them too.' Caroline was so matter-of-fact, and Annika knew she had to be too, but she found it so hard!

Gowning up, wearing a mask, dealing with the mum.

She checked the IV solutions with a nurse and punched in the numbers on the IVAC that would deliver the correct dosage of the vital medication. She tried to wash the child as gently as she could when the Div 1 nurse left. The room was impossibly hot, especially when she was all gowned up, but any further infection for him would be disastrous.

'Thank you so much.' The poor, petrified mum took time to thank Annika as she gently rolled the boy and changed the sheets. 'How do you think he's doing?'

Annika felt like a fraud.

She stood caught in the headlamps of the mother's anxious gaze. How could she tell her that she had no idea, that till an hour ago she hadn't realised chicken pox could make anyone so ill and that she was petrified for the child too?

'His observations are stable,' Annika said carefully.

'But how do *you* think he's doing?' the mother pushed, and Annika didn't know what to say. 'Is there something that you're not telling me?'

The mother was getting more and more upset, and so Annika said what she had been told to in situations such as this.

'I'll ask the nurse in charge to speak with you.'

* * *

It was her first proper telling-off on the children's Ward.

Well, it wasn't a telling-off but a pep talk—and rather a long one—because it wasn't an isolated incident, apparently.

Heather Jameson came down, and she sat as Caroline tried to explain the error of Annika's ways.

'Ross is in there now.' Caroline let out a breath. 'The mother thought from Annika's reaction that there was bad news on the way.'

'She asked me how I thought he was doing,' Annika said. 'I hadn't seen him before. I had nothing to compare it with. So I said I would get the nurse in charge to speak with her.'

She hadn't done anything wrong—but it was just another example of how she couldn't get it right.

It was the small talk, the chats, the comfort she was so bad at.

'Mum's fine.' Ross knocked and walked in. 'She's exhausted. Her son's ill. She's just searching for clues, Annika.' He looked over to her. 'You didn't do anything wrong. In fact he is improving—but you couldn't have known that.'

So it was good news—only for Annika it didn't feel like it.

'It's not a big deal,' Ross said later, catching her in the milk room, where she was trying to sort out bottles for the late shift.

'It is to me,' Annika said, hating her own awkwardness. She should be pleased that her shift was over, and tonight she didn't have to work at the nursing home, but tonight she was going to her mother's for dinner.

'Why don't we—?'

'You're not helping, Ross,' Annika said. 'Can you just be a doctor at work, please?'

'Sure.'

And she wanted to call him back—to say sorry for biting his head off—but it was dinner at her mother's, and no one could ever understand what a nightmare that was.

'How's the children's ward?'

Iosef and Annie were there too, which would normally have made things easier—but not tonight. They had avoided the subject of Aleksi's latest scandal. They had spoken a little about the ball, and then they'd begun to eat in silence.

'It's okay,' Annika said, pushing her food around her plate.

'But not great?' Iosef checked.

'No.'

They'd been having the same conversation for months now.

She'd started off in nursing so enthusiastically, raving about her placements, about the different patients, but gradually, just as Iosef had predicted, the gloss had worn off.

As it had in modelling.

And cooking

And in jewellery design.

'How's Ross?' Iosef asked, and luckily he missed her blush because Nina made a snorting sound.

'Filthy gypsy.'

'You've always been *so* welcoming to my friends!' Iosef retorted. 'He does a lot of good work for your chosen charity.' There was a muscle pounding in Iosef's cheek and they still hadn't got through the main course.

'Romany!' Annika said, gesturing to one of the staff to fill up her wine. 'He prefers the word Romany to gypsy.'

'And I prefer not to speak of it while I eat my dinner,' Nina said, then fixed Annika with a stare. 'No more wine.'

'It's my second glass.'

'And you have the ball soon—you'll be lucky to get into your dress as it is.'

There was that feeling again. For months now out of nowhere it would bubble up, and she would suddenly feel like crying—but she never, ever did.

What she did do instead, and her hand was shaking as she did it, was take another sip of wine, and for the first time in memory in front of her mother she finished everything on her plate.

'How are you finding the work?' Iosef attempted again as Nina glared at her daughter.

'It's a lot harder than I thought it would be.'

'I was the same in my training,' Annie said happily, sitting back a touch as seconds were ladled onto her plate.

Annika wanted seconds too, but she knew better than to push it. The air was so toxic she felt as if she were choking on it, and then she stared at her brother, and for the first time ever she thought she saw a glimmer of sympathy there.

Annie chatted on. 'I thought about leaving—nursing

wasn't at all what I'd imagined—then I did my Emergency placement and I realised I'd found my niche.'

'I just don't know if it's for me,' Annika said.

'Of course it isn't for you,' Nina said. 'You're a Kolovsky.'

'Is there anything you want help with?' Iosef offered, ignoring his mother's unhelpful comment. 'Annie or I can go over things with you. We can go through your assignments…'

He was trying, Annika knew that, and because he was her brother she loved him—it was just that they had never got on.

They were chalk and cheese. Iosef, like his twin Aleksi, was as dark as she was blonde. They were both driven, both relentless in their different pursuits, whereas all her life Annika had drifted.

They had teased her, of course, as brothers always did. She'd been the apple of her parents' eyes, had just had to shed a tear or pout and whatever she wanted was hers. She had adored her parents, and simply hadn't been able to understand the arguments after Levander, her stepbrother, had arrived.

Till then her life had seemed perfect.

Levander had come from Russia, an angry, displaced teenager. His past was shocking, but her father had done his best to make amends for the son he hadn't known about all those years. Ivan had brought him into the family and given him everything.

Annika truly hadn't understood the rows, the hate, the anger that had simmered beneath the surface of her family. She had ached for peace, for the world to go back to how it was before.

But, worse than that, she had started to wonder why the charmed life she led made her so miserable.

She had been sucked so deep into the centre of the perfect world that had been created for her it had been almost impossible to climb out and search for answers. She couldn't even fathom the questions.

Yet she *was* trying.

'You could do much better for the poor orphans if you worked on the foundation's board,' Nina said. 'Have you thought about it?'

'A bit,' Annika admitted.

'You could be an ambassador for the Kolovskys. It is good for the company to show we take our charity work seriously.'

'And very good for you if it ever gets out that Ivan's firstborn was a Detsky Dom boy.' Iosef had had enough; he stood from his seat.

'Iosef!' Nina reprimanded him—but Iosef was still, after all these years, furious at what had happened to his brother. He had worked in the orphanages himself and was struggling to forgive the fact that Levander had been raised there.

'I'm going home.'

'You haven't had dessert.'

'Annie is on an early shift in the morning.'

Annie gathered up the baby, and Annika kissed her little niece and tried to make small talk with Annie as Iosef said goodbye to her mother, who remained seated.

'Can I hold her?' Annika asked, and she did. It felt

so different from holding one of the babies at work. She stared into grey trusting eyes that were like the baby's father's, and smiled at the knot of dark curls that came from her mother. She smelt as sweet as a baby should. Annika buried her face in her niece's and blew a kiss on her cheek till she giggled.

'Annika?' Iosef gestured her out to the hall. 'Would some money help?'

'I don't want your money.'

'You're having to support yourself,' Iosef pointed out. 'Hell, I know what she can be like—I had to put myself through medical school.'

'But you did it.'

'And it was hard,' Iosef said. 'And...' He let out a breath. 'I was never their favourite.' He didn't mean it as an insult; he was speaking the truth. Iosef had always been strong, had always done his own thing. Annika was only now finding out that she could. 'How *are* you supporting yourself?'

'I'm doing some shifts in a nursing home.'

'Oh, Annika!' It was Annie who stepped in. 'You must be exhausted.'

'It's not bad. I actually like it.'

'Look...' Iosef wrote out a cheque, but Annika shook her head. 'Just concentrate on the nursing. Then—*then*,' he reiterated, 'you can find out if you actually like it.'

She could...

'Give your studies a proper chance,' Iosef said.

She stared at the cheque, which covered a year's wage in the nursing home. Maybe this way she *could* concentrate just on nursing. But it hurt to swallow her pride.

'We've got to go.'

And they did. They opened the front door and Annika stood there. She stroked Rebecca's cheek and it dawned on her that not once had Nina held or even looked at the baby.

Her own grandchild, her own blood, was leaving, and because she loathed the mother Nina hadn't even bothered to stand. She could so easily turn her back.

So what would she be like to a child that wasn't her own?

'Iosef…' She followed him out to the car. Annie was putting Rebecca in the baby seat and even though it was warm Annika was shivering. 'Did they know?'

'What are you talking about, Annika?'

'Levander?' Annika gulped. 'Did they know he was in the orphanage?'

'Just leave it.'

'I can't leave it!' Annika begged. 'You're so full of hate, Levander too…but in everything else you're reasonable. Levander would have forgiven them for not knowing. You would too.'

He didn't answer.

She wanted to hit him for not answering, for not denying it, for not slapping her and telling her she was wrong.

'You should have told me.'

'Why?' Iosef asked. 'So you can have the pleasure of hating them too?'

'Come home with us,' Annie said, putting her arm around Annika. 'Come back with us and we can talk…'

'I don't want to.'

'Come on, Annika,' Iosef said. 'I'll tell Mum you're not feeling well.'

'I can't,' Annika said. 'I can't just leave…'

'Yes, Annika,' Iosef said, 'you can—you can walk away this minute if you want to!'

'You still come here!' Annika pointed out. 'Mum ignores every word Annie ever says but you still come for dinner, still sit there…'

'For you,' Iosef said, and that halted her. 'The way she is with Annie, with my daughter, about my friends… Do you really think I want to be here? Annie and I are here for you.'

Annika didn't fully believe it, and she couldn't walk away either. She didn't want to hate her mother, didn't want the memory of her father to change, so instead she ate a diet jelly and fruit dessert with Nina, who started crying when it was time for Annika to go home.

'Always Iosef blames me. I hardly see Aleksi unless I go into the office, and now you have left home.'

'I'm twenty-five.'

'And you would rather have no money and do a job you hate than work in the family business, where you belong,' Nina said, and Annika closed her eyes in exhaustion. 'I understand that maybe you want your own home, but at least if you worked for the family… Annika, think about it—think of the good you could do! You are not even *liking* nursing. The charity ball next week will raise hundreds of thousands of dollars— surely you are better overseeing that, and making it bigger each year, than working in a job you don't like?'

'You knew about Levander, didn't you?' Had Annika

thought about it, she'd never have had the courage to ask, but she didn't think, she just said it—and then she added something else. 'If you hit me again you'll never see me again, so I suggest that you talk to me instead.'

'I was pregnant with twins,' Nina hissed. 'It was hard enough to flee Russia just us two—we would never have got out with him.'

'So you left him?'

'To save my sons!' Nina said. 'Yes.'

'How could Pa?' Still she couldn't cry, but it was there at the back of her throat. 'How could he leave him behind?'

'He didn't know…' Annika had seen her mother cry, had heard her wail, but she had never seen her crumple. 'For years I did not tell him. He thought his son was safe with his mother. Only I knew…'

'Knew what?'

'We were ready to leave, and that *blyat* comes to the door with her bastard son…' Annika winced at her mother's foul tongue, and yet unlike her brothers she listened, heard that Levander's mother had turned up one night with a small toddler and pleaded that Nina take him, that she was dying, that her family were too poor to keep the little boy…

'I was pregnant, Annika…' Nina sobbed. 'I was big, the doctor said there were two, I wanted my babies to have a chance. We would never have got out with Levander.'

'You could have tried.'

'And if we'd failed?' Nina pleaded. 'Then what?' she demanded. 'So I sent Levander and his mother away, and for years your father never found out.'

'And when he did Levander came here?'

'No.' Nina was finally honest. 'We tried for a few more years to pretend all was perfect.' She looked over to her daughter. 'So now you can hate me too.'

CHAPTER NINE

But Annika didn't want to hate her mother.

She just didn't know how to love her right now.

She wanted Ross.

She wanted to hide in his arms and fall asleep.

She wanted to go over and over it with him.

The truth was so much worse than the lies, and yet she could sort of understand her mother's side.

The family secret had darkened many shades, and her mother had begged her not to tell anyone.

Oh, Annie knew, and no doubt so did Millie, Levander's wife, but they were real partners. Ross and Annika…they were brand spanking new!

How could she land it on him?

And anyway, he would soon be heading off for Spain!

For the first time in her life she had a tangible reason to sever ties with her mother. Instead she found herself there more and more, listening to Nina's stories, understanding a little more what had driven her parents, what had fuelled their need for the castle they had built for their children.

* * *

'I haven't seen you so much,' Elsie commented.

'I've cut down my shifts,' Annika said, with none of her old sparkle. 'I need to concentrate on my studies.'

Cashing the cheque had hurt, but then so too did everything right now. When push had come to shove, she'd realised that she actually *liked* her shifts at the nursing home, so instead of cutting ties completely, she'd drastically reduced her hours.

Ross was around, and though they smiled and said hello she kept him at a distance.

She had spent the past week in cots, which didn't help matters.

The babies were so tiny and precious, and sometimes so ill it terrified Annika.

She was constantly checking that she had put the cot-sides up, and double- and triple-checking medicine doses.

She longed to be like the other nurses, who bounced a babe on their knee and fed with one hand while juggling the phone with the other.

She just couldn't.

'How's that man of yours?' Elsie asked, because Annika was unusually quiet.

'He goes to Spain soon—when he gets back we will maybe see each other some more.'

'Why wait?'

'You know he's a doctor—a senior doctor on my ward?'

'Oh.' Elsie pondered. 'I'm sure others have managed—you can be discreet.'

'There's stuff going on.' Annika combed through her

hair. 'With my family. I think it's a bit soon to land it all on him.'

'If he's the right one for you, he'll be able to take it,' Elsie said.

'Ah, but if he's not…' Annika could almost see the news headlines. 'How do you know if you can trust someone?'

'You don't know,' Elsie said. 'You never know. You just hope.'

CHAPTER TEN

Ross always liked to get to work early.

He liked a quick chat with the night staff, if possible, to hear from them how things were going on the ward, rather than hear the second-hand version a few hours later from the day nurses.

It was a routine that worked for him well.

A niggle from a night nurse could become a full-blown incident by ten a.m. For Ross it was easier to buy a coffee and the paper, have a quick check with the night staff and then have ten minutes to himself before the day began in earnest. This morning there was no such luxury. He'd been at work all night, and at six-thirty had just made his way from ICU when he stopped by the nurses' station.

'Luke's refused to have his blood sugar taken,' Amy, the night nurse, explained. 'I was just talking him round to it and his mum arrived.'

'Great!' Ross rolled his eyes. 'Don't tell me she took it herself?'

'Yep.'

It had been said so many times, but sometimes working on a children's ward would be so much easier without the parents!

'Okay—I'll have another word. What else?'

There wasn't much—it was busy but under control—and so Ross escaped to his office, took a sip of the best coffee in Australia and opened the paper. He stared and he read and he stared, and if *his* morning wasn't going too well, then someone else's wasn't, either.

His pager went off, and he saw that it was a call from Iosef Kolovsky. He took it.

'Hi.'

'Sorry to call you for private business.' Iosef was, as always, straight to the point. 'Have you seen the paper?'

'Just.'

'Okay—now, I think Annika is on your ward at the moment…' Iosef had never asked for a favour in his life. 'Could you just keep an eye out for her—and if the staff are talking tell them that what has been written is nonsense? You have my permission to say you know me well and that this is all rubbish.'

'Will do,' Ross said, and, because he knew he would get no more from Iosef, 'How's Annie?'

'Swearing at the newspaper.'

'I bet. I'll do what I can.'

He rang off and read it again. It was a scathing piece—mainly about Iosef's twin Aleksi.

On his father's death two years ago he had taken over as chief of the House of Kolovsky, and now, the reporter surmised, Ivan Kolovsky the founder must be turning in his grave.

There had been numerous staff cuts, but Aleksi, it was said, was frittering away the family fortune in casinos, on long exotic trips, and on indiscretions with women. A bitter ex, who was allegedly nine weeks pregnant by him, was savage in her observations. Not only had staff been cut, but his own sister, a talented jewellery designer, had been cut off from the family trust and was now living in a small one-bedroom flat, studying nursing. Along with a few pictures of Aleksi looking rather the worse for wear were two of Annika— one of her in a glamorous ballgown, looking sleek and groomed, and the other... Well, it must have been a bad day, because she was in her uniform and looking completely exhausted, teary even, as she stepped out into the ambulance bay.

There was even a quote from an anonymous source that stated how miserable she was in her job, how she hated every moment, and how she thought she was better than that.

How, Ross had fathomed, was she supposed to walk into work after that?

She did, though.

He was sitting in the staffroom when she entered, just as the morning TV news show chatted about the piece. An orthopaedic surgeon was reading the paper, and a couple of colleagues were discussing it as she walked in. Ross felt his heart squeeze in mortification for her.

But she didn't look particularly tense, and she didn't look flushed or teary—for a moment he was worried that she didn't even know what was being said.

Until she sat down, eating her raisin toast from the canteen, and a colleague jumped up to turn the television over.

'It's fine,' she said. 'I've already seen it.'

The only person, Ross surmised as the gathering staff sat there, who didn't seem uncomfortable was Annika.

Ross called her back as the day staff left for handover. 'How are you doing?'

'Fine.'

'If you want to talk…?'

'Then I'll speak with my family.'

Ross's lips tightened. She didn't make things easy, but he didn't have the luxury of thinking up a smart retort as his pager had summoned him to a meeting.

'I'm here if you need me, okay?'

The thing with children, Annika was fast realising, was that they weren't dissimilar from the residents in the nursing home. There, the residents' tact buttons had long since been switched off—on the children's ward they hadn't yet been switched on.

'My mum said you were in the paper this morning!' A bright little five-year-old sang out as Annika did her obs.

'What's "allegedly" mean?' asked another.

'Why don't you change your name?' asked Luke as she took down his dressing just before she was due to finish. Ross wanted to check his leg ulcer before it was re-dressed, and Annika was pleased to see the improvement. 'Then no one would know who you are.'

'I've thought about it,' Annika admitted. 'But the

papers would make a story out of that too. Anyway, whether I like the attention or not, it is who I am.'

His dressing down, she covered his leg with a sterile sheet and then checked off on his paperwork before the end of her shift.

'What's your blood sugar?'

'Dunno.'

It had been a long day for Annika, and maybe her own tact button was on mute for now, but she was tired of reasoning with him, tired of the hourly battles when it was really simple. 'You know what, Luke? You can argue and you can kick and scream and make it as hard as you like, but why not just surprise everyone and do it for yourself? You say you want your mum to leave you alone, to stop babying you—maybe it's time to stop acting like one.'

It was perhaps unfortunate that Ross came in at that moment.

'His dressing's all down,' Annika gulped.

'Thanks. I'll just have a look, and then you can re-dress.'

'Actually, my shift just ended. I'll pass it on to one of the late staff.'

She turned to go, but Ross was too quick for her.

'If you could wait in my office when you've finished, Annika,' Ross said over his shoulder. 'I'd like a quick word.'

Oh, she was really in trouble now.

She hadn't been being mean—or had she?

Maybe she should have been more tactful with Luke…

She couldn't read Ross's expression when he came in.

He was dressed in a suit, even though he hadn't been in one this morning, and he looked stern and formidable. Unusually for Ross, he also looked tired, and he gave a grim smile when she jumped up from the chair at his desk.

'Is Luke okay?'

'He's fine. I asked Cassie to do his dressing.'

'Was he upset?'

'Upset?'

'Because I told him he should be taking his own blood sugars?'

'He just took it.'

'Oh.'

Ross frowned, and then he shook his head in bewilderment. 'Do you think you're here to be told off?'

'I told him he was acting like a baby.'

'I've told him the same,' Ross said. 'Many times. You were fine in there—would you please stop doubting yourself all the time?'

'I'll try.'

'How come you're finishing early?'

'I worked through lunch; I'm going home at three.' She let out a breath. 'It's been a long day.'

'That offer's still there.' He saw her slight frown. 'To talk.'

'Thank you.'

And when she didn't walk off, neither did Ross.

'Do you want to come riding?' There was an argument raging in his head—he was going away soon, they had promised to keep things on ice till he returned, and yet he couldn't just leave her like this.

'Riding?'

'At the farm.'

'I've never ridden.'

'It's the best thing in the world after a tough day,' Ross said. 'You'll love it.'

'How do you know?' Annika said.

'I just know.' He watched her cheeks darken further. 'Annika, I will not lay a finger on you. It's just a chance to get away…'

'I don't like talking like this when I'm on duty.'

'Then give me half an hour to call in a favour and I'll meet you in the canteen.'

She *wasn't* going back to the farm with him. Her hand was shaking as she opened her locker, and then she picked up her phone and turned it on. She saw missed calls from her mother, her family's agent, her brother Iosef, a couple from Annie and four from Aleksi. She turned it off. Right now she was finding it very hard to breathe.

She didn't want to go home.

Didn't want to give a comment.

Didn't want a spin doctor or a night out at some posh restaurant with her family just to prove they were united.

Which was why she turned left for the canteen.

He drove; she followed in her own car. He had a small flat near the hospital, Ross had explained, for nights on call, but home was further away, and by the time they got there it was coming up for five. As they slid into his long driveway, she saw the tumbled old house and sprawling grounds. For the first time since she had been awoken by a journalist at five a.m., asking her to offer a comment, Annika didn't have to remember to breathe.

It just happened.

And when she stepped out of the car she saw all the flowers waving in the breeze—the same kind of flowers he had brought for her.

Ross *had* picked them.

The inside was scruffy, but nice: boots in the hallway, massive couches, and a very tidy kitchen, thanks to the cleaner who was just leaving.

'Hungry?' Ross asked, and she gave a small shrug.

'A bit.'

'I'll pack a picnic.'

'Am I to learn to ride in my uniform?'

He laughed and found her some jodhpurs that he said belonged to one of his sisters, some boots that belonged to someone else, though he wasn't sure who, and an old T-shirt of his.

Annika didn't know what she was doing here.

But it was like a retreat and she was grateful for it.

She was grateful too for familiarity in the strangest of places. There were pictures of Iosef there with Ross, from twenty years old to the present day. They grew up before her eyes as she walked along the hallway—and, though she had never really discussed the Detsky Dom with her brother, somehow with Ross she could.

'I expected them to be more miserable,' Annika said, staring at a photo of some grinning, pimply-faced teenagers, with Ross and Iosef beaming in the middle. It was a Iosef she had never seen.

'Our soccer team had just won!' Ross grinned at the memory. 'It's not all doom and gloom.'

'I know,' Annika said, glad that now she did, because

there were so many questions she felt she couldn't ask her brothers.

'There's an awful lot of love there,' Ross said, 'there's just not enough to go around. The staff are wonderful…'

And she was glad to hear that.

She was glad too when she walked back into the kitchen. They had had very little conversation—she was too tired and confused and brain-weary to talk—but he got one essential thing out of the way.

He held her.

It was as if he had been waiting for her, and she stepped so easily into his arms. She never cried, and she certainly wouldn't now, but it had been a horrible day, a rotten day, and although Iosef, Annie, Aleksi, her friends, would all do their best to offer comfort—she was sure of that—Ross was far nicer. He didn't ask, or make her explain, he just held her, and the attraction that had always been there needed no explanation or discussion. It just was. It just *is*, Annika thought.

His chest smelt as she remembered. He was, she decided as she rested in his arms, an absolute contradiction, because he both relaxed and excited her. She could feel herself unwind. She felt the hammer of his heart in her ear and looked up.

'One kiss,' she said.

'Look where that got us last time.'

'Just one,' Annika said, 'to chase away the day.'

So he kissed her. His lovely mouth kissed hers and her wretched day disappeared. He tasted as unique as he had the first time he'd kissed her, as if blended just for her. His mouth made hers an expert. They moved as if they were reuniting, tongues blending and chasing. His body was taut, and made hers do bold things like press a little into him. Her fingers wanted to hook into the loop of his belt and pull him in harder, and so she did. Their breathing was ragged and close and vital, and when he pulled back he gave her that delicious smile.

'Come on.'

He gave her his oldest, slowest, most trustworthy horse to ride, and helped her climb on, but even as the horse moved a couple of steps she felt as if the ground was giving way and let out a nervous call.

'Sit back in the saddle.' Ross grinned. 'Just relax back into it.'

She felt as if she would fall backwards, or slide off, every muscle in her body tense as they clopped at a snail's pace out of the stables.

'Keep your heels down,' Ross said, as if it were that easy. Every few steps she lost a stirrup, but the horse, along with Ross, was so endlessly patient that soon they were walking. Annika concentrated on not leaning forward and keeping her heels down, and there was freedom, the freedom of thinking about nothing other than somehow staying on. After a little while Ross goaded her into kicking into a trot.

'Count out loud if it helps.' He was beside her, holding his own reins in one hand as she bumped along. It was *exciting* for maybe thirty seconds, as she found her rhythm and then lost it. She pulled on the reins to stop, and then the only thing Annika could do was laugh. She laughed with a strange freedom, exhilaration ripping through her, and Ross was laughing too.

'Better?'

'Much.' She was breathless—from laughing, from riding, from dragging in the delicious scent of dusk, and then, when she slid off the horse and he spread out a picnic, she was breathless from just looking at him.

'It helped,' Annika said. 'You were right.'

'After a bad day at work,' Ross said, 'or a difficult night, this is what I do and it works every time.' He gave her a smile. 'It worked for me today.'

'Was today a bad day?' Annika asked, and he looked at her.

'Today was an exceptionally bad day.'

'Really?' She cast her mind back. Was there something she had missed on the ward? An emergency in ICU, perhaps?

But Ross smiled. 'I had a meeting with the CEO!'

'I wondered what was with the suit.'

'On my return they want me to commit to a three-year contract. So far I have managed to avoid it…'

'Does a three-year contract worry you?'

'More the conditions.' He gave a tight smile. 'I'm a good doctor, Annika, but apparently wearing a suit every day will make me a better one.'

'At least it's not an apron,' she joked, but then she was serious. 'You *are* a good doctor—but why would you commit if you are not sure it is what you want?'

And never, not once, had he had that response.

Always, for ever and always, it had been, 'It's just a suit. What about the mortgage? What if…?'

'I love my job,' Ross said.

'Do you love the kids or the job?' Annika checked,

and Ross smiled again. 'There will always be work for you, Ross.'

'I've also been worrying about you.'

'You don't have to worry about me.'

'Oh, but I do.'

They ate cold roast beef and hot mustard sandwiches and drank water. The evening was so still and delicious, so very relaxing compared to the drama waiting for her at home.

'I should get back…' She was lying on her back, staring up at an orange sky, inhaling the scent of grass, listening to the sounds of the horses behind them. Ross was so at ease beside her—and she'd never felt more at home with another person.

She looked over to him, to the face that had taken her breath away for so long now, and he was there, staring back and smiling.

A person, Annika reminded herself, who barely knew her—and if he did…

If she closed her eyes, even for a moment, she knew she would remember his kiss, knew where another kiss might lead, right here, where the air was so clear she could breathe, the sky so orange and the grass so cool.

'I should get back,' she said again. She didn't want to, but staying would be far too dangerous.

'You don't have to go,' Ross said.

'I think I do,' was her reluctant reply. 'Ross, it's too soon.'

'Annika, you are welcome to stay. I'm not suggesting a weekend of torrid sex.' Low in her stomach, something curled in on itself. 'Though of course…' he grinned '…that can be an optional extra…' And then he laughed, and so too did she. 'There's a spare room, and you're more than welcome to use it. If you want a break, a bit of an escape, here's the perfect place for it. I can go and stay at the flat if you prefer…'

'You'd offer me your home?'

'Actually, yes!' Ross said, surprised at himself, watching as she turned on her phone again and winced at the latest flood of incoming messages. 'Hell, I can't imagine what you have to go home to.'

'A lot,' Annika admitted. 'I have kept my phone off all day.'

'You can keep it off all weekend if you like.'

Oh, she could breathe—not quite easily, but far more easily than she had all day.

'I don't want to stay here alone.'

'Then be my guest,' he said.

'I have a shift at the nursing home tomorrow night.'

'I'm not kidnapping you—you're free to come and go,' Ross replied, and after a moment she nodded.

'I'd love to stay, but I should let Aleksi know.'

She rang her brother, and Ross listened as she checked if he was okay and reassured him that she was fine.

'I'm going to have my phone off,' Annika said. 'Tell Mum not to worry.'

He busied himself packing up the picnic, but he saw her run a worried hand through her hair.

'No, don't—because I'm not there,' she said. 'I'm staying with a friend.' She caught his eye. 'No, I'd rather not say. Just don't worry.'

She clicked off her phone and stood. Ross called the horses, and they walked them slowly back.

'It's nice,' Annika said. 'This…' She looked over to him. 'Do your grandparents have horses?'

'They do.'

And he'd so longed for Spain, longed for his native land, yearned to discover all that had seemed so important, so vital, but right now he had it all here, and the thought of Spain just made him homesick.

Homesick for here.

It was relaxing, settling the horses for the night, then heading back to his house.

'Have a bath,' Ross suggested.

'I have nothing to change into. Maybe I should drive back and pack. I haven't got anything.'

'You don't need anything,' Ross said. 'My sisters always leave loads of stuff—they come and stay with the kids some weekends when I'm on call.' He went upstairs and returned a few moments later with some items of clothing and a large white towelling robe. 'Here.' He handed her a toothbrush. 'Still in its wrapper—you're lucky I did a shop last week.'

'Very lucky.'

'So now you have no excuse but to relax and enjoy.'

He poured her a large glass of wine and told her to take it up to the bath, and then he showed her the spare room, which had a lovely iron bed with white linen.

'You have good taste.'

'Spanish linen,' Ross said, 'from my grandmother… She's the one who has good taste.' On the way to the bathroom he kicked open another door. 'I, on the other hand, have no taste at all.'

His bedroom was far more untidy than his office, with not a trace of crisp linen in sight. It was brown on black, with boots and jeans and belts, a testosterone-laden den, with an unmade bed and a massive music system.

'This reminds me of Luke's room.'

'You can come in with your bin liner any time,' Ross said. 'My door is always open…' Then he laughed. 'Unless family's staying.'

The bathroom was lovely. It had a large freestanding bath that took for ever to fill, a big mirror, and bottles of oils, scents and candles.

His home confused her—parts looked like a rustic country home, other parts, like his bedroom, were modern and full of gadgets. It was like Ross, she thought. He was doctor, farmer, gypsy—an eclectic assortment that added up to one incredibly beautiful man.

Settling into the warm oily water, she could, as she lay, think of no one, not one single other person, whose company could have soothed her tonight.

His home was like none she had ever been in.

His presence was like no other.

She washed out her panties and bra, but stressed for a moment about hanging them over the taps to dry. They were divine: Kolovsky silk in stunning turquoise. In fact all her underwear was divine—it was one of the genuine perks of being a Kolovsky. It was seductive, suggestive, and, Annika realised, she could *not* leave it in the bathroom!

So she hung it on the door handle in her bedroom and

then headed downstairs, where he sat, boots on the table, strumming at a guitar, a dog looking up at him. She thought about using her fingers as castanets and dancing her way right over to his lap, but they'd both promised to be good.

'Why would you do this for me?' She stood at the living room door, wrapped in his sister's dressing gown, and wondered why she wasn't nervous.

'Because my life's not quite complicated enough,' Ross said, with more than a dash of sarcasm. 'Just relax, Annika, I'm not going to pounce.'

So she did—or she tried to.

They watched a movie, but she was so acutely aware of the man on the sofa beside her that frankly her mother would have been more relaxing company. When she gave in at eleven and went to bed, it was almost frustrating when he turned and gave her a very lovely kiss, full on the lips, that was way more than friendly but absolutely going nowhere. It was, Annika realised as she climbed the steps, a kiss goodnight.

She could taste him on her lips.

So much so that she didn't want to remove the toothbrush from its wrapper. But she did, and she brushed her teeth, and then when she heard him coming up the stairs she raced to her bedroom. She slipped off her dressing gown and slid naked into bed, then cursed that she hadn't been to the loo.

He was filling the bath.

She could hear it, so she decided to make a quick dash for it, but she came out to find him walking down the landing wearing only a black towel round his loins.

His body was delicious, way better than her many imaginings, and his hair looked long, and his early-morning shadow was a late-night one now. She just gave a nod.

'Feel free…' He grinned at her awkwardness.

'Sorry?'

'To wash your hands…'

'Oh.'

So she had to go into the bathroom, where his bath was running, as he politely waited outside. She washed her hands and tried not to look at the water and imagine him naked in it.

'Night, Annika.'

'Night.'

How was she to sleep? He was in the bath for ever, and then she heard the pull of the plug and the lights ping off. She lay in the dark silence and knew he was just metres away. And then, just as she thought she might win, as a glimpse of sleep beckoned, she heard music.

There was no question of sleeping here in a strange house, with Ross so close. She couldn't sleep, so instead she did a stupid thing—she checked her phone.

Even as she turned it on it rang, and foolishly she answered. She listened as her mother demanded that she end this stupidity and come home immediately—not to the flat, but home, where she belonged. She was wreaking shame on her family, and her father would be turning in his grave. Annika clicked off the phone, her heart pounding in her chest, and headed out for a glass of water.

The low throb of music from his room somehow beckoned, and his door was, as promised, open. She glanced inside as she walked past.

'Sorry.'

'For what?'

'I'm just restless.'

'Get a drink if you want…' He was lying in the bed reading, hardly even looking up.

'I'll just go back to bed.'

'Night, then.'

She just stood there.

And Ross concentrated on his book.

His air ticket was his bookmark. He'd done that very deliberately—ten days and he was out of here; ten days and he would be in Spain. And then, when he returned—well, then maybe things could be different.

'Night, Annika.'

She ignored him and came and sat on the bed. They kept talking. And it was hard to talk at two a.m. without lying down, so she did, and even with her dressing gown on it was cold. So she went under the covers, and they talked till her eyes were really heavy and she was almost asleep, and then he turned out the light.

'The music…'

'It will turn itself off soon.'

She turned away from him; there were no curtains on the window, just the moon drifting past, and he spooned right into her. She could feel his stomach in her back, and the wrap of his arms, and it was sublime—so much so that she bit on her lip. Then he kissed the back of her head, pulled her in a little bit more, and she could feel every breath he took. She could feel the lovely tumid length of him, and just as she braced herself for delicious attack, just as she wondered how long it would be polite to resist, she felt him relax, his breathing even, as she struggled to inhale.

'Ross, how can you just lie there…?' He wasn't even pretending; he really was going to sleep!

'Relax,' he said to her shoulder. 'I told you, nothing's going to happen—I had a *very* long bath.'

And she laughed, on a day she had never thought she would, on a day she had done so many different things. She lay in bed and counted her firsts: she had been cuddled, and she had hung up the phone on her mum.

The most amazing part of it all, though, was that for the first time in ages she slept properly.

CHAPTER ELEVEN

IT WAS midday when she woke up.

Annika never overslept, and midday was unthinkable, but his bed was so comfortable, and it held the male scent of him even though he had long since gone. Instead of jumping guiltily out of bed she lay there, half dozing, a touch too warm in her dressing gown, smiling at the thought that there was really no point getting up as she had nothing to wear—and there was no way she was getting on a horse today!

She hurt in a place she surely shouldn't!

'Afternoon!' He pushed the bedroom door open, and the door to her heart opened a little wider too. He hadn't shaved, and looked more gypsy-like, dark and forbidden, than she had ever seen him, but he was holding a tray and wearing a smile that she was becoming sure was reserved solely for her. She smiled back at him.

'What did I do to deserve breakfast in bed?'

'You didn't snore, which is very encouraging,' he said, waiting till she sat up before placing a tray on her lap, 'and it's actually *lunch* in bed.'

It was *the* nicest lunch in the world: omelette made from eggs he had collected that morning, with wild mushrooms and cheese. The coffee was so strong and sweet that if she had given orders to the chef at her mother's home he could not have come up with better.

'You're yesterday's news, by the way,' Ross said. 'In case you were wondering.'

She had been.

'Lucky for you some bank overseas has gone into liquidation and the papers have devoted four pages to it—you don't even get a mention.'

'Thank you.'

She had finished her lunch, and he took the tray from her, but instead of heading off he put it on the floor and lay on top of the bed beside her.

'I like having you here.'

'I like being here.'

She could feel his thigh through the sheet. She felt so safe and warm and relaxed, in a way she never would have at the movies with him, or across the table in some fancy restaurant—so much so that she could even get up and go to the loo, brush her teeth and then come to the warm waiting bed.

'I am being lazy,' Annika said as she crossed the room.

'Why not?' Ross said. 'You have to work tonight.'

And he might never know how nice that sentence was—for surely he could never understand the battle of wills, the drama it entailed, merely for her to work.

Ross accepted it.

It was warm. The sun was streaming through the window, falling on the crumpled bed. After hot coffee and the omelette, wearing a thick dressing gown under the covers was suddenly making her feel way too hot. She stared at him, wanting to peel her dressing gown off, to stand naked before him and climb in bed beside him. He stared back for the longest time. The air was thick with lust and want, but with patience too.

'Sleep.' He answered the heavy unvoiced question by standing up. He stood in front of her, and she thought he would go, but she didn't want him to.

There was a mire of confusion in her mind, because it was too soon and sometimes she wondered if she was misreading him. What if he was just a very nice guy who perhaps fancied her a little?

And then he answered her fleeting doubt.

His hands untied the knot of her dressing gown, and she stood as he slid it over her shoulders. She saw his calm features tighten a fraction, felt the caress of his gaze over her body and the arousal in the air.

She was naked in front of him, and he was dressed, and yet it felt appropriate. She could not fathom how, but if felt right that he should see her, that they glimpsed the future even if it was too soon to reach for it. She felt safe as he pulled the bedcovers over her.

Only then did he kiss her. He kissed the hollows of her throat, sitting on the bed, leaning over where she lay. He kissed her till she wanted him to lie down beside her again, but he didn't. He kissed her until her hands were in his thick black hair, her body stretched to drag him down, but he didn't lie down. He just kissed her some more, till her breath was as hard and as ragged as his. It was just a kiss, but it brought with it indecent thoughts, because they both explored what they knew was to come. Their faces and lips met, but their minds were meshed too. It was a dangerous kiss, that went on and on as her body flared for him, and then he lifted his head and smiled down.

'Go back to sleep.'

'You are cruel.'

'Very.' He smiled again, and then he left her, a twitching mass of desire, but relaxed too. She had never slept more, never felt more cherished or looked after. The horrors were receding with every hour she spent in his presence.

She slept till seven, and then showered and pulled on her uniform. She made his bed before heading downstairs. He offered her some dinner but she wasn't hungry.

'I need to go home and get my agency uniform, and perhaps…' she blushed a little at her own presumption '…perhaps I should pack a change of clothes for tomorrow.'

'Here.' He handed her a key. 'I lie in on Sunday. Let yourself in.' And he handed her something else—a brown paper bag. 'For your break.'

He had made her lunch—well, a lunch that would be eaten at one a.m., after she had helped to get twenty-eight residents into bed and answered numerous call bells.

She deliberately didn't look inside until then. She sat down in the staffroom and took the bag out of the fridge and opened it as excited as a kid on Christmas morning.

He had made her lunch!

A bottle of grapefruit juice, a chicken, cheese and salad sandwich on sourdough bread, a small bar of chocolate and, best of all, a note.

> *Hope you are having a good shift.*
> *R x*
> *PS I am no doubt thinking about you. R xx*

He *was* thinking of her.

Even though she had slept for most of the day, it had been nice knowing Annika was there, and without her now the house seemed empty and quiet.

He had never felt like this about anyone, of that he was sure.

Gypsy blood did flow in his veins, and it wasn't just his looks that carried the gene. There was a restlessness to him that so many had tried and failed to channel into conventional behaviour.

He didn't feel like that with Annika.

Yet.

Her vulnerability unnerved him, his own actions sideswiped him—it had taken Imelda months to get a key; he had handed it to Annika without thought.

He was going away in little more than a week, digging deep into his past, thinking of throwing in his job… He could really hurt her, and that was the last thing he wanted to do.

Ross headed upstairs and stepped into his room. He smiled at the bed she had made. The tangled sheets were tucked into hospital corners, his pillows neatly arranged. If it been Imelda it would have incensed him, but it was Annika, and it warmed him instead.

And that worried him rather a lot.

CHAPTER TWELVE

SHE flew through the rest of her shift.

There would be no words of wisdom from Elsie, though.

As Annika flooded the room with light at six the following morning, Elsie stared fixedly ahead, lost in her own little world. And though, as Elsie had revealed, she enjoyed being there, this morning Annika missed her. She would have loved some wise words from her favourite resident.

Instead she propped Elsie up in bed and chatted away to her as she sorted out clothes from Elsie's wardrobe, her stockings, slippers, soap and teeth. Then Annika frowned.

'Drink your tea, Elsie.'

No matter Elsie's mood, no matter how lucid she was, every morning that Annika had worked there the old lady had gulped at her milky tea as Annika prepared her for her shower.

'Do you want me to help you?'

She held the cup to her lips, but Elsie didn't drink. The tea was running down her chin.

'Come on, Elsie.'

Worried, Annika went and found Dianne, the Registered Nurse.

'Perhaps just leave her shower this morning,' Dianne said when she came at Annika's request and had a look at Elsie. Instead they changed her bed, combed her hair, and Annika chatted about Bertie and all the things that made Elsie smile—only they didn't this morning.

Annika checked her observations, which were okay. The routine here was different from a hospital: there was no doctor on hand. There was nothing to report, no emergency as such.

Elsie just didn't want her cup of tea.

It was such a small thing, but Annika knew that it was vital.

It felt strange, driving home to *someone*.

Strange, but nice.

Since her mother had refused to talk to her about her work since she had supposedly turned her back on her family to pursue a 'senseless' career, Annika had felt like a ball-bearing, rattling around with no resting place, careering off corners and edges with no one to guide her, no one to ask where she was.

It felt different, driving to someone who knew where you had been.

Different letting herself in and knowing that, though he was asleep, if the key didn't go in the lock she would be missed.

She felt responsible, almost, but in the nicest way.

She dropped the bag she had packed on the bathroom

floor, and then slipped out of her uniform and showered, using her own shampoo that she had brought from home. It felt nice to see it standing by his shampoo, to wrap herself in his towel and brush her hair and teeth, then put her toothbrush beside his.

The house was still and silent, and she had never felt peace like it.

Nothing like it.

She had never felt so sure that the choice she made now would be right, no matter what it was. The decision was hers.

She could step out of the bathroom and turn right for the spare room and that would be okay.

She could go downstairs and make breakfast and that would be fine too.

Or she could slip into bed beside him and ask for nothing more than his warmth, and that would be the right choice too.

It was her choice, and she was so grateful he was letting her make it.

His door *was* always open, and she stepped inside and stood a moment.

He needed to shave—his jaw was black and he looked like a bandit. His eyes were two slits and she knew he was deeply asleep. He was beautiful, dark and, no doubt—according to her mother—completely forbidden, but he was hers for the taking—and she wanted to take.

Annika slipped in bed beside him, her body cool and damp from the shower, and he stirred for a moment and pulled her in, spooned in beside her, awoke just enough to ask how her shift had been.

'Good.'

And then she felt him fall back to sleep.

His body was warm and relaxed, and hers was cold, tired and weary, drawing warmth from him. She felt him unfurl, felt him harden against her, and then he turned onto his back. She lay there for a moment, till his breathing evened out again, and then she rested her wet hair on his chest and wrapped her cold foot between his warm calves. She slid her hand down to his hardening place, heard his breath held beneath her ear, and turned her head and kissed his flat nipple. Her hand stroked him boldly—because this was no sleepy mistake.

'Annika…'

'I know.' She did—she knew they were supposed to be taking it slow, knew he was going away, knew it was absolutely bad timing—but… 'I want it to be you.'

'What if…?'

'Then I still want it to be you.'

Her virginity, in that moment, was more important to Ross than it was to her. To him it denoted a commitment that he thought he wasn't capable of making, yet he had never felt more sure in his life.

She traced his lovely length to the moist tip, and then he lifted her head, gently pulled at her hair so that he could kiss her. His hand was on her breast, warming it, holding its weight. Then he was stroking her inside, her warm centre was moist, and she was glad his mouth had left hers because she wanted to bite on her lip.

He kissed her low in the neck, a deep, slow kiss, and

he was restraining himself in case he bruised her, but she wanted his bruise, so she pushed at his head, rocking a little against him as his lips softly branded her.

'Put something on,' she begged, because she wanted to part her legs so badly.

'Are you sure?' It was the right thing to say, but it seemed stupid, and Annika clearly thought the same.

'Yes!' she begged. 'Just put something on.'

He was nuzzling at her breasts now, as his fingers still slid inside her, and his erection was there too, heavy on her inner thigh, teasing her as his other hand frantically patted at the bedside drawer.

She was desperate.

Little flicks of electricity showered her body. She was wanton as he suckled at her breast and searched un-seeing in the drawer. Then she held him again, because she wanted to. She took his tip and slid it over her, and he moaned in hungry regret because he wanted to dive in. Side by side they explored each other's bodies as still he searched for a condom.

'Here…' He waved it as if he had found the golden ticket, his hand shaking as he wrestled with the foil.

Still she held him, slid him over and over the place he wanted to be till it was almost cruel. He was so hard, so close, and she didn't want him sheathed. She wanted to see and feel—but he had a shred of logic and he used it. He sheathed himself more quickly than he ever had, but he didn't dive in, because he didn't want to hurt her. He claimed her breast again with his mouth, and she cupped him and stroked him again. She teased him, but she could only tease for so long—and then she got her reaction: he was gently in. She was breaking every in-grained rule and it felt divine.

'Did I hurt you?' he checked.

'Not yet.'

And he swore to himself that he wouldn't.

Yes, he'd made that promise more than a few times before, but this time he hoped he meant it.

She wanted more, and he pushed so hard into her that she had to lie back. She wanted to accommodate him, to orientate herself to the new position. Those little flicks of electricity had merged into a surge—she couldn't breathe. He was bucking inside her and she was frantic. She thought she might swear, or cry out his name, but she held back from that. She could feel his rip of release and she wanted to scream, but she wouldn't allow herself. She bit on his shoulder instead, sucked his lovely salty flesh and joined him—*almost*.

Not with total abandon, because she didn't yet know what that was, but she joined him with a rare freedom she had never envisaged.

Then, after, he waited.

As she fell asleep, still he waited.

For the thump of regret, the sting of shame, for him to convince himself that he was just a bastard—but it never came.

CHAPTER THIRTEEN

HE WAS a very patient teacher—and not just in the bedroom. Round and round the field she bobbed, trot, trot, and she even, to her glee, got to gallop. Then Ross showed her the sitting trot, in which her bottom wasn't to lift out of the seat. He did it with no hands, made it look so easy, but it was actually hard work.

Around Ross she was always starving.

'It's all the exercise!'

She laughed at her own little joke and he kissed her. Then, when she wanted so much more than a kiss, very slowly he took off her boots and she lay back. She could feel the sun on her cheeks and the breeze in the trees, and life was, in that moment, perfect. He sorted out her zip and she let him. In everything she was inhibited—at work, with friends, with family—but not with Ross.

In this, with him, there was no fear or shame, just desire.

'There,' she told him, because where he was kissing her now was perfect.

'Again,' she said, when she wanted it there again.

'More,' she said, when she wanted some more.

She pulled his T-shirt over his head, berating him the second his mouth stopped working so it resumed duty again.

She wanted more—and not just for herself, so she pulled at her own T-shirt till all she wore was a bra. Then she didn't care what she was wearing. She could feel his ragged breathing on her tender skin and sensed her pleasure was his.

He was unshaved, and she was tender, so she had to push him back, just once, and yet she so much wanted him to go on.

And he dived in again, but she was still too tender.

So she pulled at his jodhpurs and freed him instead.

He was divine, his black curls neat and manicured, the erection glorious and dark, so that she had to touch. Her fingers stroked, guided, and he was there at her entrance, moistening it a little. It was so fierce to look at, yet on contact more gentle than his lips.

'Please...' She was so close to coming she lifted her hips.

'They're in there...' He was gesturing to the backpack, a lifetime away, or more like ten metres, but it was a distance that was too far to fathom. He might just as well have left the condoms in the bathroom.

It was the most delicious tease of sex to come. He was stroking against her and she was purring, her hips rising, begging that he fill her and for it not to stop.

'Just a little way...' Her voice was throaty, and he stared down at her, so pink and swollen. How could he not? He entered her just a little.

He was kneeling up, holding her buttocks, and his

eyes roamed her body. He thought he would come. She was all blonde and tumbled, and in underwear that would make working beside her now close to impossible, because if he even pictured her in that... He pushed it in just a little bit more as Annika—shy, guarded Annika—gave him a bold, wanton smile that had his heart hammering. He pulled down the straps on her bra and freed her breasts, and she boldly took his head and led him there. She kissed his temple as he suckled her. He moved within her till he wanted more than just a little way, and so too did she.

He leant back and guided her, up and down his length. She had never felt more pliant, moving as his hands guided her. She could see his dark skin against her paleness, and she felt as if she were climbing out of her mind and watching them, released from inhibition. She cried out, could see her thighs trembling, her back arching. Then she climbed back into her body and felt the deep throb of an orgasm that didn't abate. It swelled and rolled like an ocean, took away her breath and dragged her under, and she said his name, thought she swore. Still he was pounding within her, so fast and hard that even as her orgasm faded she thought it would happen again.

And it did—because he was mindful. Just as he satisfied her he gave in, pulled out of her warmth and shivered outside her. She watched. It was startling and beautiful and intimate.

Their intimacy shocked her.

It shocked her that this was okay, that *they* were okay, that they could do all that and afterwards he could just pull her to him.

They lay for a long time in delicious silence, and all Ross knew was that they had completely crossed a line—it wasn't about condoms, or trips to Spain, or families, or all things confusing.

It was, in that moment, incredibly simple.

They were both home.

CHAPTER FOURTEEN

'You might want to get dressed…' They were both half dozing when Ross heard the crunch of tyres. 'I think we've got visitors.'

And, though they were miles from being seen, Annika was horrified. As she dressed quickly Ross took his time and laughed. She tripped over herself pulling on her jodhpurs.

'No one can see,' he assured her.

'Who is it?'

'My family, probably…' Ross said, and then there were four blasts of a horn, which must have confirmed his assumption because he nodded. 'There's no rush; they'll wait.'

'I'll go home.' Annika was dressed now. The horses were close by, and she would put up with *any* pain just to make it to the safety of her car. 'I'll just say a quick hello and then go.'

'Don't rush off.' For the first time ever he looked uncomfortable.

'What will they think, though?' Annika asked,

because if *her* mother had turned up suddenly on a Sunday evening to find a man at her home she would think plenty—and no doubt say it too.

'That I've got a friend over for the afternoon,' Ross said, but she knew he was uncomfortable.

As they rode back her heart was hammering in her chest—especially when another car pulled up and several more Wyatt family members piled out. His father was very formal, his sisters both much paler in colouring than Ross, and his mother, Estella, was raven-haired and glamorous. Grandchildren were unloaded from the car. His sisters said hi and bye, and relieved them of their horses before heading out for a ride in what was left of the sun.

'Hi, Imelda!'

The sun must have gone behind a cloud, because it was decidedly chilly.

'This is Annika,' Ross said evenly. 'She's a friend from the hospital. Iosef's sister…'

'Oh, my mistake.' His mother gave a grim smile. 'It's just with the blonde hair, and given that she's wearing Imelda's things, you'll forgive me for being confused.'

Ross's brain lurched, because never before had his mother shown her claws.

She had never been anything other than a friend to him, but now she was stomping inside. A row that had never before happened between them was about to start—and it was terrible timing, because he had to deal with Annika as well.

'Imelda?'

'My ex,' Ross said.

'How ex?'

'A few weeks.'

And she wasn't happy with that, so she demanded dates and he told her.

'Was there time to change the sheets?'

'Annika, I never said I didn't have a past.'

'And I'm standing here dressed in her things!'

'It's not as bad as it sounds…'

'It's worse,' Annika said. 'Can you get my keys?'

'Don't go.'

'What—do you expect me to go in and make small talk with your family? Can you please go and get my things?'

It was like two patients collapsing simultaneously at work. Two blistering things he had to deal with.

Annika refused to bend—she wanted her keys and no more.

Ross stomped into the house.

'What the hell?' His voice was a roar. 'How *dare* you do that to her?'

'She'll thank me!' Estella shouted. 'And don't, Reyes—don't even try to justify it to me. "I've got to sort myself out." "I want to find myself." "I'm not getting involved with anyone…"' She hurled back everything he had said, and then she called him a *cabrón* too! He vaguely remembered it meant a bastard. 'I had Imelda on the phone last night, and again this morning. You shred these girls' hearts and we're supposed to say *nothing*?'

'Annika's different!'

'Oh, it's *different* this time, is it?' Estella shouted, and the windows were open, so Ross knew Annika could hear. 'Because apparently you said that to Imelda too!'

And then she really let him have it.

Really!

She called him every name she could think of. Later, Ross would realise that she had probably been talking to Reyes senior. Every bit of hurt his biological father had caused his mother, all the shame, anger and fury that had never come out, had chosen that afternoon to do so.

And his time was up. Annika was storming through the house, finding her keys for herself as his mother continued unabated.

Ross raced out behind her to the car.

'It's not that bad…'

'Really?' Annika gave him a wide-eyed look as she turned the key in the ignition. 'From the sounds inside your home, you're the only who thinks that way.'

'You're just going to drive off…?' He couldn't believe it. He didn't like rows, but he didn't walk away from them either. 'All that's happened between us and you'll just let it go…?'

'Watch me!' Annika said, and she did just that. She gunned the car down his drive, still dressed in Imelda's things. His mother's words about her own son still ringing in her ears.

It was only when she went into her flat, kicked off her boots and ripped off those clothes that she calmed down.

Well, she didn't calm down, exactly, but she realised it wasn't that she had been wearing Imelda's things, or what his mother had said, or anything straightforward that had made her so angry. It was that, just like her family, he had fed her a half-truth.

And, as she had with her family, she had been foolish enough to trust him.

CHAPTER FIFTEEN

ELSIE was right—you should never let the sun go down on a row, because as the days moved on life got more complicated. It was cold and lonely up there on her high horse, and next Tuesday Ross flew out to Spain. More importantly, her midway report on her time with the children's ward was less than impressive, and she was considering the very real good she could do working on the family foundation board.

She wanted his wisdom.

She attempted a smile, even tried to strike up a conversation. She finally resorted to wearing the awful wizard apron that always garnered comment. But Ross didn't bat an eye.

Because Ross was sulking too.

Yes, he'd messed up, but the fact that she hadn't let him explain incensed him. His mother, two minutes after Annika had left, had burst into tears, and George had had to give her a brandy.

Then George, who had always been a touch lacking in the emotion department, had started to cry and revealed he was dreading losing his son!

Ross had problems too!

So he ignored her—wished he could stop thinking about her, but ignored her.

Even on Saturday.

Even as she left the ward, still he didn't look up.

'Enjoy the ball!' Caroline called. 'You can tell us all about it tomorrow.'

'I will,' Annika said. 'See you then.'

He could feel her eyes on the top of his head as he carried on writing his notes.

'See you, Ross.'

Consultants didn't need to look up; he just gave her a very clipped response as he continued to write.

'Yep.'

Annika consoled herself that this was progress.

'You're not working this afternoon, are you?' Dianne frowned as Annika came into the office.

'No,' Annika said. 'I just popped in to check my roster.'

It was a lie and everyone knew it. She wasn't due for a shift for another week, and anyway she could have rung to check. She had, to her mother's disgust, worked on the children's ward this morning, but they had let her go home early. Instead of taking advantage of those extra two hours, and racing to her mother's to have her hair put up and her make-up applied for the ball, she'd *popped in to check her roster*.

'How's Elsie?' Annika asked. 'I rang yesterday and the GP was coming in…'

'She's not doing so well, Annika,' Dianne said.

'She's got another UTI, and he thinks she might have had an infarct.'

'Is she in hospital?'

'She's here,' Dianne said, 'and we're making her as comfortable as we can. Why don't you go in and see her?'

Annika did. Elsie wasn't particularly confused, but she didn't recognize Annika out of uniform.

'Is any family coming?' Annika asked Dianne.

'Her daughter's in Western Australia, and she's seventy,' Dianne said. 'She's asked that we keep her informed.'

Annika sat with Elsie for a little while longer, but her phone kept going off, which disturbed the old lady, so in the end Annika kissed Elsie goodbye and asked Dianne if she could ring later.

'Of course,' Dianne said. 'She's your friend.'

CHAPTER SIXTEEN

STARING out of her old bedroom window, Annika felt the knot in her stomach tighten at the sight of the luxury cars waiting lined up in the driveway.

She could hear chatter and laughter downstairs and was loath to go down—but then someone knocked at the door.

'Only me!' Annie, her sister-in-law, popped her head round and then came in. 'You look stunning, Annika.'

'I don't feel it.' She stared in the mirror at the curled blonde ringlets, at the rouge, lipstick, nails and the thousands of dollars worth of velvet that hugged her body and felt like ripping it off.

'But you look gorgeous,' Annie protested.

How did Annie balance it? Annika wondered. She had probably spent half an hour getting ready. Her dark curls were damp at the ends, and she was pulling on a pair of stockings as she chatted. Her breasts, huge from feeding little Rebecca, were spilling out her simple black dress. And her cheeks had a glow that no amount of blusher could produce—no doubt there was a very good reason why she and Iosef were so late arriving for pre-dinner drinks!

'It's going to be fun!' Annie insisted. 'Iosef was dreading it too, but I've had a fiddle and we're on the poor table.'

'Pardon?'

'Away from the bigwigs!' Annie said gleefully. 'Well, we're not sitting with the major sponsors of the night.'

And then Annie was serious.

'Iosef meant it when he said if you needed a hand.'

'I cashed the cheque.'

'We meant with your studies.' Annie blew her fringe out of her eyes. Iosef's family were all impossible—this little sister too. There was a wall that Annie had tried to chip away at, but she'd never even made a dint. 'I know it must be hell for you now—finding out what your mother did…'

'Had she not…' Annika's blue eyes glittered dangerously '…your beloved Iosef wouldn't be here. Do you ever think of *that* when you're so busy hating her?'

'Annika, please, let us help you.'

'No!' Annika was sick of Annie—sick of the lot of them telling her how she felt. 'I don't need your help. I'm handing in my notice, and you'll get your money back. All my mother did was try and look after her family—well, now it's my turn to look after her!'

She stepped out of the car and smiled for the cameras. She stood with her mother and smiled ever brighter, and then she walked through the hotel foyer and they were guided to the glittering pre-dinner drinks reception.

Diamonds and rare gems glittered from throats and ears, and people sipped on the finest champagne.

Annika dazzled, because that was what was expected of her, but it made no sense.

Hundreds of thousands would have been spent on tonight.

Aside from the luxury hotel and the fine catering, money would have been poured into dresses, suits, jewels, hairdressers, beauticians, prizes and promotion. All to support a cluster of orphanages the Kolovskys had recently started raising funds for.

All this money spent, all this gluttony, to support the impoverished.

Sometimes, to Annika, it seemed obscene.

'You have to spend it to make it,' her mother had said.

'Annika…' Her mother was at her most socially vigilant. Everything about tonight had to be perfect. The Kolovskys had to be seen at their very best—and that included the daughter. 'This is Zakahr Belenki, our guest speaker…'

'*Zdravstvujte*,' he greeted her formally, in Russian, and Annika responded likewise, but she was relieved when he reverted to English.

He was a Detsky Dom boy made good—a self-made billionaire and the jewel in the crown that was tonight. He poured numerous funds into this charity, but he was, Zakahr said, keen to raise awareness, which was why he had flown to the other side of the world for this ball.

This, Nina explained, was what tonight could achieve, proof of the good they could do. But though Zakahr nodded and answered politely to her, his grey eyes were cold, his responses slightly scathing.

'I've heard marvellous things about your outreach programme!' Annika attempted.

'What things?' Zakahr asked with a slight smirk, but Annika had done her homework and spoke with him about the soup kitchen and the drop-in centre, and the regular health checks available for the street children. She had heard that Zakahr was also implementing a casual education programme, with access to computers…

'We would love to support that,' Nina gushed, and then dashed off.

'Tell me, Annika?' Zakahr said when they were alone. 'How much do you think it costs to clear a conscience?'

She looked into the cool grey eyes that seemed to see right into her soul and felt as if a hand was squeezing her throat, but Zakahr just smiled.

'I think our support for the education programme is assured,' she said.

He knew, and he knew, and it made her feel sick.

Soon everyone would know, and she could hardly stand it. She wanted to hide, to step off the world till it all blew over, but somehow she had to live through it and be there for her mother too.

'Excuse me…' She turned to go, to escape to the loo, to get away from the throng—except there was no escape tonight, because she collided into a chest and, though she didn't see his face for a second, the scent of him told her that a difficult night had just become impossible.

'Ross.' Annika swallowed hard, looked up, and almost wished she hadn't.

Always she had considered him beautiful; tonight he was devastatingly handsome.

He was in a dinner suit, his long black hair slicked back, his tie knotted perfectly, his shirt gleaming against his dark skin, his earring glittering. His face was, for the first time, completely cleanshaven. She looked for the trademark mockery, except there was none.

'How come…?' She shook her head. She had never for a second factored him into tonight, had never considered that their worlds might collide here.

'I work in the orphanages with your brother.' Ross shrugged. 'It's a very good cause.'

'Of course.' Annika swallowed. 'But…' She didn't continue. How could she? This was her world, and she had never envisaged him entering it.

'I'm also here for the chance to talk to you.'

'There's really not much to say.'

'You'd let it all go for a stupid misunderstanding? Let everything go over one single row?'

'Yes,' Annika said—because her family's shame was more than she could reveal, because it was easier to go back to the fold alone than to even try to blend him in.

'Hello!' Nina was all smiles. Seeing her daughter speaking to a stranger, she wormed her way in for a rapid introduction, lest it be someone famous she hadn't met, or a contact she hadn't pursued.

'This is my mother, Nina.' Annika's lips were so rigid she could hardly get the words out. 'Mother, this is Ross Wyatt—Dr Ross Wyatt.'

'I work at the hospital with Annika; I'm also a friend of Iosef's.' Ross smiled.

Only in her family was friendship frowned upon; only for the Kolovskys was a doctor, a *working* doctor, considered common.

Oh, Nina didn't say as much, and Ross probably only noticed her smile and heard her twenty seconds of idle chatter, but Annika could see the veins in her mother's neck, see the unbreakable glass that was her mother's eyes frost as she came face to face with the 'filthy gypsy' Iosef had spoken so often about.

She glanced over to Annika.

'You need to work the room, darling.'

So she did—as she had done many times. She made polite conversation, laughing at the right moment and serious when required. But she could feel Ross's eyes on her, could sometimes see him chatting with Iosef, and a job that had always been hard was even harder tonight.

She was the centre of attention, the jewel in the Kolovsky crown, and she had to sparkle on demand.

Just as she had been paraded for the grown-ups on her birthdays as a child, or later at dinner parties, so she was paraded tonight.

Iosef, Aleksi, and later Levander had all teased her, mocked her, because in her parents' eyes Annika had been able to do no wrong. Annika had been the favourite, Annika the one who behaved, who toed the line. Yes, she had, but they just didn't understand how hard that had been.

And how much harder it would be to suddenly stop.

She stood at the edge of the crowd, heard the laughter and the tinkle of glass, felt the buoyant mood, and how she wanted to head over to Ross, to Iosef and Annie, to relax. She almost did.

'Aleksi isn't here...' Her mother's face was livid behind her bright smile, her words spat behind rigid teeth. 'You need to speak to the Minister, and then you need to—'

'I'm just going to have a drink with my friends, with Iosef...'

'Have you *any* idea what people are paying to be here tonight?' Nina said. 'Any idea of the good we can do? And you want to stop and *have a drink*?'

'Annie and Iosef are.'

'You know what I think of *them*. You are better than that, Annika. Your father wanted more for you. Iosef thinks his four weeks away a year helping the orphans excludes him from other duties. Tonight *you* can make a real difference.'

So she did.

She spoke to the Minister. She laughed as his revolting son flirted with her. She spoke fluent French with some other guests, forgetting that she was a student nurse and that she wiped bums in a nursing home. She shone and made up for the absent Aleksi and she impressed everyone—except the ones that mattered to her the most.

'It's going well!' Annika said, slipping into her seat at their table, putting her hand over her glass when the waiter came with wine. 'Just water, thanks.'

'Ross was just saying,' Iosef started, 'that you're...' His voice trailed off as his mother appeared and spoke in Annika's ear.

'I have to go and sit with them...' Annika said.

'No, Annika, you don't,' Iosef said.

'I want to.' She gave Ross a smile, but he didn't return it.

'It's hard for her,' Annie said, once Annika had gone, but Iosef didn't buy it. He had done everything he could to keep Annika in nursing, and his mother had told him earlier today that Annika was quitting.

'No, she loves this,' he said. 'She always has.' He looked over to his wife. 'Has she told you that she's handing in her notice at the end of her rotation?'

'Sort of.'

'I told you she wouldn't stick at it.' He glanced at Ross. 'Model, pastry chef, jewellery designer, student nurse…' He looked to where his sister was laughing at something the Minister's son had said. 'I think she's found her vocation.'

Aleksi did arrive. Dinner had already been cleared away, and the speeches were well underway, but because it was Aleksi, everyone pretended not to notice his condition.

A stunning raven-haired beauty hung on his arm and he was clearly a little the worse for wear—and so was she. Their chatter carried through the room, once at the most inappropriate of times, when Zakahr Belenki was speaking of his time in the Detsky Dom.

Abandoned at birth, he had been raised there, but at twelve years of age he had chosen the comparative luxury of the streets. The details were shocking, and unfortunately, as he paused for effect, Aleksi's date, clearly not listening to the speaker, called to the waiter for more wine.

And Ross watched.

Watched as the speaker stared in distaste at Aleksi.

Watched as a rather bored Annika played with her napkin and fiddled with the flower display, or occasionally spoke with her brother's revolting date.

He saw Aleksi Kolovsky yawn as Zakahr spoke of the outreach programme that had saved him.

Clothed him.

Fed him.

Supported him.

Spoke of how he had climbed from the gutters of the streets to become one of Europe's most successful businessmen.

He asked that tonight people supported this worthy cause.

And then Ross watched as for the rest of the night Annika ignored him.

He'd clearly misread her. Here she was, being how he had always wanted her to be—smiling, talking, dancing, laughing—she just chose not to do it with him.

'Why don't I give you a lift home?'

'There's an after-party event.'

'How about we stay for an hour and then…?'

'It's exclusive,' Annika said.

And he got the point.

Tonight he had seen her enjoying herself in a way that she never had with him.

For once instinct had failed him.

He had been sure there was more, and was struggling to accept that there wasn't.

'It was a good speech from Zakahr…' Ross said, carefully watching her reaction.

'It was a little over the top,' Annika said, 'but it did the job.'

'Is that what this is to you?'

'Ross.' Annika's cheeks were burning. 'You and Iosef are so scathing, but you don't mind spending the funds.'

'Okay.' She had a point, but there was so much more in the middle.

Iosef and Annie were leaving, and they came over and said their goodnights.

'You've got work tomorrow,' Iosef pointed out, when Annika declined a lift from them and said where she was heading.

And then it was just the two of them again, and, though he had no real right to voice an opinion, though she had promised him nothing, he felt as if he had been robbed.

'Are you giving up nursing?'

'Probably,' Annika answered, but she couldn't look at him. Why wouldn't he just leave her? Why, every time she saw him, did she want to fall into his arms and weep? 'Ross, I need to be here for my mother, and there's a good work opportunity for me. Let's face it— I'm hardly nurse of the year. But I haven't properly made up my mind yet. I'm going to finish my paediatric rotation—'

'Come back with me,' Ross interrupted.

How badly she wanted to—to go back to the farm, where she could breathe, where she could think. Except Ross would be gone on Tuesday, and all this would still be here.

Her mother was summoning her over and Annika took her cue. 'I have to go.'

'I'll see you at work on Monday,' Ross said, and suddenly he was angry. 'If you can tear yourself away from the Minister's son!'

CHAPTER SEVENTEEN

ROSS'S words rang in her ears as she raced home and pulled on her uniform. After this afternoon, she knew it would confuse Elsie to see Annika in anything else.

Yes, she was supposed to be at the after-party event, and, yes, her mother was furious, but even though she wouldn't get paid for tonight, even though she wasn't on duty, she *had* to be here.

'How is she?' Annika asked, as Shelby, one of the night nurses, let her in.

'Close to the end,' Shelby said. 'But she's lucid at times.'

'Hi, Elsie.'

They were giving her some morphine when Annika walked in, and the smile on the old lady's face was worth all the effort of coming. Now she was in her uniform Elsie recognised her. Yes, Annika would be tired tomorrow, and, no, she didn't have to be here, but she had known and cared for the old lady for over a year now, and it was a very small price to pay for the friendship and wisdom Elsie had imparted.

'My favourite nurse,' Elsie mumbled. 'I thought you weren't on for a while…'

'I'm doing an extra shift,' Annika said, so as not to confuse her.

'That's good.' Elsie said. 'Can you stay with me?'

She couldn't.

She really couldn't.

She'd only popped in to check on her, to say good-night or goodbye. She had to be at work at twelve tomorrow. The charity do would be all over the papers—it was unthinkable that she call in sick.

But that was exactly what she did.

She spoke to a rather sour voice on the other end of the phone and said she was getting a migraine and that she was terribly sorry but she wouldn't be in.

There was going to be trouble. Annika knew that.

But she'd deal with it tomorrow. Tonight she had other things to do.

Elsie's big reclining seat was by her bed, and Annika put a sheet over it and sat down beside her. She took the old bony hand in hers and held it, felt the skinny fingers hold hers back, and it was nice and not daunting at all.

She remembered when her father had been so ill. Annie had been his nurse on his final night. How jealous Annika had been that Annie had seemed to know what to do, how to look after him, how to take care of him on his final journey.

Two years on, Annika knew what to do now.

Knew this was right.

It was right to doze off in the chair, to hold Elsie's hand and wake a couple of hours later, when the morphine wore off a little and Elsie started to stir. She walked out to find Shelby.

'I think her medication's wearing off.'

And Shelby checked her chart, and then Elsie's, and agreed with Annika's findings.

Gently they both turned Elsie, and Annika combed her hair and swabbed her mouth so it tasted fresh, put some balm on her lips. Elsie was lucid before the medicine started to kick in again.

'How's Ross?' Elsie asked.

'Wonderful,' Annika said, because she knew it would make Elsie happy.

'He's good to you?' the old lady checked.

'Always.'

'You can be yourself?'

And she should just say yes again, to keep Elsie happy, but she faltered.

'Be yourself,' Elsie said, and Annika nodded. 'That's the only way he can really love you.'

The hours before dawn were the most precious.

Elsie slept, and sometimes Annika did too, but it was nice just to be there with her.

'I'm very grateful to you,' Elsie said, her tired eyes meeting Annika's as the nursing home started to wake up. The hall light flicked on and the drug trolley clattered. 'You're a wonderful nurse.'

Annika was about to correct her, to say she wasn't here as a nurse but as a friend, and then it dawned on her that she could be both. Here, she knew what she was doing, and again Elsie was right.

She *was*, at least to the oldies, a wonderful nurse.

'I'm very grateful to you too,' Annika said.

'For what?'

'You've worked it out for me, Elsie.' And she took Bertie's photo and gave it to Elsie, who held it instead of Annika's hand.

The next dose of morphine was her last.

Annika stepped out into the morning without crying. Death didn't daunt her, it was living that did, but thanks to Elsie she knew at least something of what she was doing.

Her old friend had helped her to map out the beginnings of her future.

CHAPTER EIGHTEEN

'ANNIKA.' Caroline had called her into the office immediately after handover. 'I appreciate that you have commitments outside of nursing, and I know that your
off-duty request got lost, but I went out of my way to
accommodate you. I changed your shift to a late and you
accepted it!'

'I thought I would be able to come in.'

'Your photo is in the paper—dining with celebrities,
drinking champagne…' Caroline was having great
trouble keeping her voice even. 'And then you call at
four a.m. to say you're unable to come in. Even this
morning you're…' Her eyes flicked over Annika's puffy
face and the bags under her eyes. 'Do you even want to
be here, Annika?'

Just over twenty-four hours ago her answer would
have been very different. Had it not been for Elsie, Annika
might well have had her notice typed up in her bag.

But a lot had changed.

'Very much so.' Annika saw the dart of surprise in her
senior's eyes. 'I have been struggling with things for a

while, but I really do want to be here.' Annika was trying to be honest. It wasn't a Kolovsky trait, in fact her life was a mire of lies, but Annika took a deep breath. All she could do was hope for the best. 'I wasn't sick yesterday.'

'Annika, I should warn you—'

'I am tired on duty at times but that is because I have been doing shifts at a private nursing home. Recently I have tried to arrange it so that it doesn't impinge on my nursing time, but on Saturday I found out that my favourite resident was dying. She has no visitors, and I went in to see her on my way home from the party. I ended up staying. Not working,' she added, when Caroline was silent. 'Elsie had become a good friend, and it didn't seem right to leave her. I'm sorry for letting everyone down.'

'Keep us informed in the future,' Caroline said. 'You've got a lecture this morning in the staffroom— why don't you get a coffee?'

She had expected a reprimand, even a written warning. She was surprised when neither came, and surprised, too, when Ross caught up with her in the kitchen.

'Caroline said you were at the nursing home on Saturday night?'

'I'm surprised she discusses student nurses with you.'

'I heard her on the phone to Heather Jameson.'

'Oh.'

'Is that the truth?' He didn't know. 'Or did it take you twenty-four hours to come up with a good excuse?'

'It's the truth.' She filled her mug with hot water.

'So why couldn't you tell me that?' Ross demanded. 'Why did you make up some story about an after-party event?'

'I thought I was just going to drop in on Elsie; I didn't realise that I'd stay the night.'

'You could have told me.'

'And have you tell Caroline?' Annika said. 'Or Iosef? He's given me some money so that I don't have to work there any more.' She swallowed hard. 'I wasn't actually working. I don't expect you to understand, but Elsie has been more than a patient to me, and it didn't seem right to leave her—'

'Hey.' He interrupted her explanations with a smile. 'Careful—you're starting to sound like a nurse.'

'I thought I would be in trouble,' Annika admitted. 'I didn't expect Caroline to understand.'

'You could have told me,' Ross said. 'You could have trusted me…'

'I don't, though,' Annika said.

Her tongue could be as sharp as a razor at times, but this time it didn't slice. He stared at her for a long moment.

'Why do you push everything good away?'

He didn't expect an answer. He was, in fact, surprised when she gave one.

'I don't know.'

Each Monday, patients permitting, one of the senior staff did an informal lecture for the nursing staff, and particularly the students. As they sat in the staffroom and waited for a few stragglers to arrive, Ross struggled to make small talk with the team. His mind was too full of her.

He watched as she came in and took a seat beside Cassie. She smiled to her fellow student, said hello, and then put down her coffee, opened her notebook, clicked on her pen and sat silent amidst the noisy room.

Her eyes were a bit puffy, and he guessed she must have spent the night crying. How he wished he had known—how he wished she had been able to tell him.

Ross waited as the last to arrive took their seats. It was all very informal, even though it was a difficult subject: 'Recognising Child Abuse in a Ward Environment.'

Ross was a good teacher; he didn't need to work from notes. He turned off the television, told everyone to get a drink quickly if they hadn't already. As he talked, he let his eyes roam around the room and not linger on her. She was probably uncomfortable because it was Ross giving the lecture—not that she ever showed it. She nodded and gave a brief smile at something Cassie said, and she glanced occasionally at him as he spoke, but mainly—rudely, perhaps—she looked at the blank television screen or took the occasional note on the pad in her lap.

'Often,' Ross said, 'by the time a child arrives on the ward there is a diagnosis—perhaps from a GP, or Emergency, or perhaps you have a chronically ill child that has been in many times before. It is your responsibility to look beyond the diagnosis, to always remember to keep an open mind.' He glanced around and saw her writing. 'Babies can't tell you what is wrong, and older children often won't. Perhaps they are loyal to their parents, or perhaps they don't even know that something is wrong…'

'How can they not know?' Cassie asked.

'Because they know no different,' Ross said patiently. 'This is particularly the case with emotional abuse, which is hard to define. Neglect is a hard one too. They are used to being neglected. They have grown up thinking this is normal.'

It was a complicated talk, with lots of questions. None from Annika, of course. She just took her notes and sometimes gazed out of the window or down at her hands. Once she yawned, as if bored by the subject, but this time Ross didn't for a moment consider it rude.

He remembered the way she had sat at the charity ball, ignoring the speaker, oblivious to his words. Now, standing in front of everyone, he started to understand.

'A frozen look?' Cassie asked, when he explained what he looked for in an abused child, and Ross nodded.

'You come to recognise it…' he said, then corrected himself. 'Or you sometimes do.'

There were more questions from the floor, and all of a sudden he didn't feel qualified to answer, although he had to.

'These children sometimes present as precocious. Other times,' Ross said, 'they are withdrawn, or lacking in curiosity. You may go to put in an IV and instead of resistance or fear there is compliance, but often there is no one obvious clue…'

He wanted his lecture over; he wanted a moment to pause and think—and then what?

He felt sick. He thought about wrapping things up, but Cassie was like a dog with a bone, asking about emotional abuse—what did he mean? What were the signs?

'"*Just because I can't see it, I still know you are*

hurting me."' He quoted a little girl who was now hopefully happy, but had summed it up for so many.

And you either understood it or you didn't, but he watched Annika's mouth tighten and he knew that she did.

'How can you get them to trust you?' another student asked.

'How do you approach them?' Cassie asked.

But Ross was looking at Annika.

'Carefully,' he said. 'Sometimes, in an emergency, you have to wade in a bit, but the best you can do is hope they can trust you and bit by bit tell their story.'

'What if they don't know their story?' Annika asked, her blue eyes looking back at him, and only Ross could see the flash of tears there. 'What if they are only just finding out that the people they love have caused them hurt, have perhaps been less than gentle?'

'Then you work through it with them,' Ross said, and he saw her look away. 'Or you support them as they work through it themselves. It's hard for a child to find out that the people they love, that those who love them—'

'They *can't* love them…' Cassie started. 'How can you say they love them?'

'Yes,' Ross said, 'they can—and that is why it's so bloody complicated.'

He had spoken for an hour and barely touched the sides. He didn't want her to be alone now, he wanted to be with her, but it was never that easy.

'Sorry to break up the party.' Lisa's voice came over the intercom. 'They need you in Emergency, Ross. Two-year-old boy, severe asthma. ETA ten minutes…'

And the run to Emergency would take four.

As everyone dispersed Annika sat there, till it was only the two of them left.

'You have to go.'

'I know.'

Her head was splitting.

Don't tell. Don't tell. Don't tell.

Family.

No one else's business.

How much easier it would be to walk away, to shut him out, to never tell rather than to open her heart?

'You know that my brother, Levander, was raised in the orphanages…'

He did, but Ross said nothing.

'We did not know—my parents said they did not know—but now it would seem that they did.' It was still so hard to believe, let alone say. 'I thought my parents were perfect—it would seem I was wrong. I was told my childhood was perfect, that I was lucky and had a charmed life. That was incorrect too.'

'Annika…'

'You want me to be open, to talk, and to give you answers—I don't know them. When I met my brothers' wives, when I saw what "normal" was, I realised how different my world was…' She shook her head at the hopelessness of explaining something she didn't herself understand. 'I was sheltered, my mind was closed, and now it is not as simple as just walking away. Every day it is an effort to break away. I don't like my mother, and I hate what she did, but I love her.'

'You're allowed to.'

'I realise now my parents are far from perfect. I see

how I have been controlled…' She made herself say it. 'How conditional their love actually was. I am starting to see it, but I still want to be able to sustain a relationship with my mother and remember my father with love.'

'I'm sorry.' He had never been sorrier in his life. 'For rushing you, for…'

'It can't be rushed,' Annika said. 'And I am not deliberately not telling you things. Some of it I just don't know, and I don't know how to trust you.'

'You will,' Ross said.

She almost did.

His pager was shrilling, and he had to run to the patient instead of to her. He had to keep his mind on the little boy and, though he was soon sorted, though the two-year-old was soon stable, it was, Ross decided, the hardest patient he had dealt with in his career.

So badly he wanted to speak with her.

CHAPTER NINETEEN

'HI, ANNIKA?'

'Yes.'

'I'm ringing for a favour.' Now that he understood her a little bit, he could smile at her brusqueness. 'A work favour.'

'What is it?'

'I've got this two-year-old with asthma. Emergency is steaming. There's some poor guy in the next bed after an MVA, and the kid's getting upset.'

'Bring him up, then.'

'The bed's not ready. Caroline says you need an hour,' Ross explained. 'Look, can you ring House-keeping and ask them…?'

'Just bring him up,' Annika said. 'I'll get the bed ready. Caroline is on her break. It can be my mistake.'

'You'll get told off.'

'I'm sure I will survive.'

'It will be *my* mistake,' Ross said. 'Just make sure the bed's made—that would be great.' He paused for a moment. 'I need another favour.'

'Yes?'

'This one isn't about work.'

'What is it?'

'I'd like…' He was about to say he'd like to talk, but Ross stopped himself. 'I'd like to spend some time with you.'

The silence was long.

'Tonight,' Ross said.

And still there was silence.

'You don't have to talk,' he elaborated. 'We can listen to music…wave to each other…' He thought he heard a small laugh. 'I just want to spend some time with you.'

'I'm busy on the ward at the moment. I don't have time to make a decision.'

She was like no one he had ever met, and she intrigued him.

She would not be railroaded, would not give one bit of herself that she didn't want to, and he admired her for that. It also brought him strange comfort, because when she had been with him she had therefore wanted to be there—the passionate woman that he had held had been Annika.

He had wanted more than she was prepared to give.

And now he was ready to wait. However long it took for her to trust him.

'He can go up…' Ross said to one of the emergency nurses. 'I've cleared it with the ward.'

The emergency nurse looked dubious, as well she might. The children's ward had made it perfectly clear that it would be an hour at least, but the resuscitation area was busy, with doctors running in to deal with the patient from the car accident, neurologists, anaesthetists… The two-year-old was getting more and more distressed.

He could hear the noise from behind the curtains and gave the babe's mum a reassuring smile, blocking the gap in the curtains just a touch with his body as the toddler and his mother where wheeled out.

'Thanks so much for this.'

'No problem.' He gave her a small grimace. 'They might be a bit put out on the ward when you arrive, but don't take it personally—he's better up there than down here.'

He'd left his stethoscope on the trolley and went over to retrieve it. He considered walking up to the paediatric ward to take the flak, just in case Annika was about to get told off on his account, but then he smiled.

Annika could take it, *would* take it—she had her own priorities, and a blast from Caroline… The smile froze on his face, everything stilled as he heard a colleague's voice from behind the curtain.

'Kolovsky, Aleksi…'

Ross could hear a swooshing sound in his ears as he pictured again the mangled, bloodied body that had been rapidly wheeled past twenty minutes or so ago. His legs felt like cotton wool as he walked back across the resus unit and parted the curtains.

The patient's face had been cleaned up a bit, though Ross wasn't sure he would have recognised him had he not heard his name, but, yes, it was him.

His good friend Iosef's identical twin.

Annika's brother.

'Aleksi…' His voice was a croak and he had to clear it before he continued. 'Aleksi Kolovsky.'

'His sister works here, doesn't she?' A nurse glanced up. 'Annika? One of the students…?'

He stood and watched for a few moments, more stunned than inquisitive. He watched as the powerful, arrogant man he had met just the once extended his arms, indicative of a serious head injury, and grunted with each breath. The anaesthetist had decided to intubate, but just before he did, Ross went over.

'I'm going to get Annika for you,' he said, 'and you're going to be okay, Aleksi.'

CHAPTER TWENTY

THE hospital grapevine worked quickly, and Ross was aware not just that he had to let Annika know, but his good friend Iosef too.

The Kolovskys were famous. It would be breaking news soon—not just on the television and the internet, but the paramedics and emergency personnel would be talking, and both Iosef and his wife Annie worked in another emergency department across the city.

As he walked he scrolled through his phone. He didn't have Annie's number, only Iosef's, but, deciding it would be better for his friend to hear it from his wife, he called their emergency department. He found out that Iosef was just being informed and would be there to see Aleksi for himself shortly.

Ross moved faster, walked along the long corridor at a brisk pace, bracing himself for Annika's reaction and wondering what it would be.

He spoke briefly with Caroline, informed her of the news he would be imparting, and then headed down to room eleven.

'He's settled.' She was checking the asthma baby's oxygen saturation; he was sleeping now, his mother by his side.

'That's good,' Ross said. 'Annika, could I have a word, please?'

'Of course.' She nodded to the mother and stepped outside. 'There was no trouble with Caroline—the cot was prepared…'

'Thanks for that. Would you mind coming into my office?'

Her eyes were suddenly wary.

'It's a private matter.'

'Then it can wait till after work,' Annika said.

'No, it's not about that…' He blew out a breath, wondered if perhaps he should have taken up Caroline's suggestion and let her be the one to tell Annika, but, no, he wanted it to come from him—however little he knew her, still he knew her best. 'Just come into my office, please, Annika.'

She did as told and stood, ignoring the seat he offered, so he stood too.

'There was a patient brought into Emergency,' Ross said. 'After a motor vehicle accident. It's Aleksi, Annika.'

'Is he alive?'

'Yes.' Ross cleared his throat. 'He's unconscious; he has multiple injuries and is still being assessed.' She was pale, but then she was always pale. She was calm, but then she was mostly calm. She betrayed so little emotion, and for Ross it was the hardest part of telling her. She just took it—she didn't reach out, didn't express alarm. It was almost as if she expected pain.

'I'll tell Caroline that I need to…'

'She knows,' Ross said. 'I'll take you down there now.'

Annika only wavered for a second. 'Iosef…'

'He's been informed and is on his way.'

They walked to Emergency. There was no small talk. He briefed her on the little he knew and they walked in relative silence. A nurse took them to a small interview room and they were told to wait there.

'Could I see my brother?' Annika asked.

'Not at this stage,' the nurse said. 'The trauma team are trying to stabilise him. As soon as we know more, a doctor will be in to speak with you.'

'Thank you.'

And then came Iosef and Annie, and Nina, their mother, who was hysterical. Iosef and Annika just sat there, backs straight, and waited as more and more Kolovskys arrived.

And still there was no news.

A doctor briefly popped in to ask the same questions as a nurse had ten minutes previously—was there any previous medical history that was relevant? Had Aleksi been involved in any other accidents or had any illnesses?

'Nothing!' Nina shouted. 'He is fit; he is strong. This is his first time sick—please, I need to see my son.'

And then they went back to waiting.

'Do *we* keep relatives waiting as long as this?' Iosef's patience was finally running out. 'Do they *know* I'm an emergency consultant?'

'I'll ask again,' Annie said.

'I'll come with you.' Ross went with her.

'God!' Annie said, once they were outside, blowing

her dark curls to the sky as she let out a long breath. 'I can't stand it in there—I can't stand seeing Iosef…' She started to cry, and all Ross could do was pull a paper towel out of the dispenser and watch as she blew her nose. 'It was the same when his dad died. You know he's bleeding inside, but he just won't say…'

'He will,' Ross said. 'Maybe later—to you.'

'I know.' Annie nodded and forced a smile. 'I should warn you. They're bloody hard work, that family.'

'But worth it, I bet?' Ross said. Then he crossed a line—and he would only do it once. He looked at Annie, and stared till she looked back at him. 'Annika isn't a lightweight.'

'I know she's not.' Annie blushed.

'That family *is* bloody hard work, and Annika's right in the thick of it…'

He watched her cheeks redden further.

'Imagine if you woke up and found out that the grass was red and not green.'

'I don't get you.'

'Imagine if you'd been told all your life how lucky you were, how spoiled and indulged and precious you were, how grateful you should be.'

Annie just frowned.

'Grateful for what?' Ross demanded, and he wasn't sure if he and Annika would make it, because at any moment she was likely to turn tail and run, so he took the opportunity to tell Annie. 'Go and tell your doctor husband, my good friend, to look up emotional abuse. I can't stand the board at the hospital, but maybe on this they're right—there are charities closer to home. Tell him to wake up and see what's been going on with his own sister.'

He watched her face pale.

'They controlled what she ate, how she spoke, what she thought—have you ever stopped to think how hard it must be to break away from that?'

'We try to help!'

'Not good enough,' Ross said. 'Try harder.'

CHAPTER TWENTY-ONE

THEY could get no information at the nurses' station, so, before Iosef did, Ross pulled rank. He sent Annie back to the relatives' room and walked into resus, past the huddle around the bed, and up to Seb, the emergency consultant, who was also a friend. He was carefully examining X-ray films.

'How's it looking?'

'Not great,' Seb said, 'but there's no brain haemorrhage It's very swollen, though, and it's going to be a while till we know if there's brain damage.'

He was bringing up film after film.

'Fractured sternum, couple of ribs...' Seb was scanning the X-rays and he looked over to Ross, who was scanning them too, looking at the fractures, some old, some new. 'His left leg's a mess, but his pelvis and right leg look clear...' Seb said. The X-rays were just a little harder to read than most. There was an old fracture on Aleksi's right femur, and when he pulled up the chest film Ross looked again and there were a few old fractures there too.

'Any skull fracture?'

'One,' Seb said. 'But, again, it's old.'

'How old?'

'Not sure—there's lots of calcification… The mum says he's never been in hospital. Poor bastard.' Seb cleared his throat. 'Twenty years ago I'd have been calling you.'

'And Social Services,' Ross said, his lips white. 'What happens when it's all these years on?'

'Look, he could have been in an accident they don't know about…' But these fractures were old, and in a child they would have caused huge alarm. 'Let's get him through this first,' Seb said. 'I'll come and talk to the family.'

Nina sobbed through it; the aunts were despairing too. Iosef and Annika just sat there.

Seb was tactful, careful and thorough. He mentioned almost in passing that there were a couple of old injuries, and Nina said he had been in a lot of fights recently, but Seb said no, some looked older. And Iosef remembered a time his brother was ill, the time he came off his bike…

Nina remembered then what had happened.

'Oh, yes…' she said, but her English was suddenly poor, and an aunt had to translate for her.

'Just before the long summer holidays one year he had a nasty tumble. His leg…' she gestured '…his head. But it was nothing too serious.'

Iosef excused himself for some air, and Annika looked at her hands, sometimes at the door, and once or twice at Ross. When he went and sat beside her he gave her hand a little squeeze, and when he started to remove it she held it back. She kept holding it till they moved Aleksi up to ICU.

'Levander's flying over from England,' Iosef said, as he clicked off his phone in yet another waiting room.

'He moved there when he got married,' Annika explained. 'That is when Aleksi took over the company.'

Her face was as white as chalk, Ross noted. When she came out from seeing her brother, he saw her fingers go to her temples.

'Can you take me home?'

'Of course.'

'Will you tell my mother for me?'

'Of course,' Ross said, though he wasn't particularly looking forward to it. He turned to Nina. 'Annika's not feeling great; I'm going to take her home…'

Nina shot up from her seat. 'You need to be here— for your brother.'

'I am here for my brother,' Annika said. 'But the doctor said it is going to be at least forty-eight hours.'

'If he gets worse…'

'I have said everything I need to to him,' Annika said, and suddenly her eyes held a challenge. 'Have you?'

'You should stay.'

'I can't.'

She was so white he thought she might faint, and he put his arm around her.

'Can you give them the phone number?' she said.

He frowned.

'Your phone number at the farm—my phone battery's flat.'

'I've got Ross's number,' Iosef said, and he gave his sister a small hug. 'Look after her,' he said to Ross.

'I will.'

Ah, but Nina hadn't finished, because Nina hadn't yet got her way. 'If you had any respect for my daughter you would not flaunt this in front of her own mother.'

'I have *so* much respect for your daughter.' It was all he could say, the only way he could respond and remain civil, and it was also true. He had so much respect for Annika—and never more so than now.

A few hours in her mother's company was enough for him.

Annika had had a lifetime.

He took her to his car, held her hair when she threw up in the bin, and then stopped at the all-night chemist for headache tablet and a cold drink too. He promised himself as they drove home in silence that he would never question her, never ask for more than he needed to know, and that if she didn't trust him, then that was okay.

He trusted himself. For the first time he trusted himself with a woman. Trusted that he would do the right thing by her, always, and that one day, he was sure, she would see it.

CHAPTER TWENTY-TWO

'WHAT time's your flight?'

A massive backpack was half filled in the living room, and only then did she remember that he was going to Spain tomorrow. She looked up at the clock and amended that to today.

'It just got cancelled,' Ross said. 'Family crisis.'

'You don't have to do that.' She meant it—she would be okay. She was making decisions for herself, seeing things for herself. She didn't need Ross to get her through this.

'I want to,' Ross said, and though she didn't need him, she *wanted* him.

'You need to find your family.'

'I think I just did.' Ross grinned. 'Heaven help me.'

'She *is* difficult.' Annika had had two headache tablets and a bath, had refused a cup of coffee and asked for a glass of wine. 'I don't know if I love her, Ross. I am trying to work it out.'

'You will.'

'Can I ask something?' He nodded. 'What do you think will happen with Aleksi?'

'As a doctor, or as a friend?'

'Can you be both?'

'I can try,' Ross said, and he did try. He stood for a full minute, trying to separate the medical from the personal, then trying to put it back together. 'I don't know,' he admitted. 'As Seb said, we won't know for a couple of days yet…' He hesitated, then made himself continue. 'If he can hang in there for a couple of days, that is. He's been unresponsive since they found him. I spoke to him,' Ross said, 'before I came and got you, and I don't know, I can't prove it, it's more gut than brain, but I think he heard…'

He almost hated the hope that flared in her eyes, but what he had said was true. 'I think he was a little bit aware.'

'I want to go to bed.'

'Okay—you have my room. I'll sleep on the couch.'

'Pardon?'

'I've got some explaining to do,' Ross reminded her. 'I was supposed to be apologising about Imelda, the clothes…'

'I accept.' She gave a tight smile. 'If it's okay with you, I would like you to make love to me.'

'Okay…' he said slowly.

'I don't want to think about today,' Annika explained. 'And I know I can't sleep.' Her very blue eyes met his. 'And I'm not really in the mood to talk.' She gave him a very brief smile. 'And you're very good at it.'

'You're a strange girl.'

'I am.'

'Impossible to work out.'

'Very.'

'But I do love you.'

'Then get me through this.'

His love was more than she could fathom right now, its magnitude too much to ponder, yet it was something she accepted—a beautiful revelation that she would bring out and explore later. Right now, she gratefully accepted the gift.

And Ross took loving her very seriously too.

He had never felt more responsible in his life.

He wanted his kiss to right a thousand wrongs, but no kiss was that good, no kiss could. He wanted to show her how much she meant to him.

She couldn't believe she had asked for sex.

Was it wrong?

Should she be sitting with her mother, being seen to do the right thing?

Did she love her brother less because she was not in a room next door?

She was dreading the days that would follow—the pain, the vigil, the hope, the fear—and she knew she had to prepare, to rest, and to get strong for whatever lay ahead.

His kiss made her tremble. It shocked her that even in misery she could be held, kissed, made to feel a bit better, that she could be herself—whoever that was.

He kissed her so deep, slow and even, and when she stopped kissing him back he kissed her some more. He kissed her face, her neck, and then her breasts, and then he kissed her mouth again.

His bed was a tumble.

There was music, books by the bedside, and a dog scraping on the door down the hall.

But there were coffee beans in the fridge and there would be warm eggs in the morning.

There was a soft welcome any time she wanted it.

And she wanted it now.

He took her away, but he let her come back, and then he took her away again.

She had a fleeting image of being old, of a nurse wheeling her into the shower as she ranted about Ross.

Let me rant.

She coiled her legs around him.

Let me rant about the night when I couldn't survive and I came to his home.

She lost herself in a way she had never envisaged.

She lost herself, and this time she didn't hold back— she dived into oblivion. She swore she could smell the bonfire as she felt the magic and the gypsy in him.

He brought her back to a world that was scary, but there was music still playing, and Ross was beside her, and she knew she'd get through. Then she did something she hadn't been able to do at the hospital, that she so rarely did—she cried, and he held her, and it didn't make things better or worse, it just released her.

'I'm sorry about my family.'

She poured it all out, and it probably didn't make much sense, but she said sorry for the past, and the stuff that was surely to come, because Zakahr Belenki knew the truth and so must others. Between gulps she told him that it was only a matter of time, warned him what he was taking on if he was mad enough to get involved with her.

'You don't have the monopoly on crazy families.' Ross grinned. 'Do you remember meeting mine?'

This made her laugh. Then she stared out of the window and thought about Aleksi. She couldn't be more scared for him if she tried.

'What are you thinking?'

'That you need curtains.'

'He'll be okay.'

'You don't know that.'

But he did.

And so he told her—stuff he had never told anyone.

He told her about intuition, and that some of the stories about gypsies were real, and that, like it or not, she was saddled with someone who was a little bit different too.

CHAPTER TWENTY-THREE

HE WOKE her at six, saw her eyes open with a smile to his, and then the pain cloud them as she remembered.

'No change,' Ross said quickly. 'I just called Iosef.'

'We should go.'

All she had was her uniform, or a suitcase of clothes that belonged to Imelda.

So she settled for his rolled-up black jeans, and a lovely black jumper, and a belt that needed Ross to poke another hole in it—but she did, to her shame, borrow Imelda's boots.

They drove to the hospital. Annika was talking about Annie, how good she had been with her father. It was this that had first made Annika think about nursing. It was a little dot, but it went next to another dot, and then she told him about Elsie. One day he would join up the complicated dots that were Annika.

Or not.

It didn't change how he felt.

'It's going to be difficult these next weeks,' Annika said as they neared the city. 'Mum will want me to move home. I can just see it...'

'You do what you have to.'

'She's so determined that I give up nursing.'

'What do *you* want, Annika?'

'To finish my training.'

'Then you will.'

They were at the hospital car park now.

'She'll want me there, back in the family business, away from nursing.' They were walking up to ICU. 'I'm so much stronger, but I'm worried that once I'm back there…'

'You've got me now,' Ross said. 'Whatever you need, whatever might help, just say.'

And that helped.

It helped an awful lot.

It helped when they got to the hospital and Nina was so tired that she was the one who had to go home, with a few of the aunties too. Annie was ringing around for a hotel nearby.

'Use my flat,' Ross said, and handed them the keys.

It helped when she kissed him goodbye and went and took her position next to Aleksi and held his hand. She told him he'd better get better. It helped to know that Ross was in the building—that he wasn't at all far away.

Every minute of every day was made better knowing that Ross Wyatt loved her.

CHAPTER TWENTY-FOUR

BEING a doctor brought strange privileges.

It brought insight and knowledge gleaned when a person was at their most vulnerable, and it weighed heavily on Ross. He loved Annika, which meant he cared about Aleksi.

And, he didn't want to keep secrets from Annika, but, like it or not, he knew something that she didn't.

He had spoken with his colleague, Seb, who had revealed that Aleksi had refused any attempt to discuss his past. Ross considered, long into the lonely nights while Annika was at her mother's, if perhaps he should take the easy option and just leave it.

Then one day, checking in on a patient in the private wing of the hospital, Ross saw the Kolovsky clan leaving. The door to Aleksi's room was slightly open. A nurse was checking his obs, but apart from that Aleksi was alone.

Ross walked away, and then turned around and walked back again just as the nurse was going out.

'How are you doing?' He wasn't offended by Aleksi's frown as he attempted to place him—after all, they'd met only once, and Aleksi was recovering from a head injury. 'I was in Emergency when you came in.'

'You'll forgive me if I don't remember, then,' Aleksi said

'I'm also a friend of Annika's; I was at the charity function. Ross Wyatt…'

He shook his hand.

'Annika's spoken about you,' Aleksi said, then closed his eyes and lay back on the pillows. Just as Ross thought he was being dismissed, as he realised the impossibility of broaching the subject of Aleksi's old injuries, Aleksi spoke, though his eyes stayed closed. 'How is Annika doing?'

'Okay.'

'She's moved back home?' Aleksi asked.

'Your mum was upset, with the accident and everything. She wanted Annika close.'

'She should be back at her own flat.' Grey eyes opened. 'Try and persuade her…'

'Annika will be fine,' Ross said, because that much he knew. 'You don't need to worry.'

'For her, I do.'

'Let me do the worrying on that score,' Ross said, and Aleksi gave a small grimace of pain as he tried to shift in the bed. Ross saw his opening. 'That's got to hurt. I saw the X-rays…'

'I'm going to bleep for ever going through security at airports,' Aleksi said. 'I'm full of wires and pins.'

'It was a bit of a mess.'

'So, are you an emergency doctor?'

'No.' Ross shook his head. 'I'm a paediatrician. I was

just in Emergency when you came in—and I broke the news to Annika. She asked me to find out more.' He held his breath in his lungs for just a second. 'I was trying to get more information for her. I was speaking to Seb when he was looking over your X-rays.'

'The emergency consultant?' Aleksi checked, and Ross nodded. 'He was up a couple of days ago to see how I was doing.'

And then Aleksi looked at Ross, and Ross looked back, and the conversation carried on for a full two minutes but not a single word was uttered. Finally Aleksi cleared his throat.

'What happens to patient confidentiality if I'm not your patient?'

'You still have it.'

'Even if you're screwing my sister?' Aleksi was savage for a moment, but Ross was expecting it—even if Annika's brother was a generation older than Ross's usual patients, his reaction was not dissimilar.

'I'm a doctor,' Ross said. 'It's my title at home, at work, in bed; it's not a badge I can ever take off. Some conversations with your sister might be more difficult for me—I will have to think hard before I speak, and I will have to remember that I know only what she chooses to tell me—but I'm up to it.'

'Thanks, but no thanks.'

Aleksi closed his eyes and Ross knew he had been dismissed. Inwardly cursing, he turned to go, wondering if he'd made things worse, if he could have handled it better, if he should have just left well alone. And then Aleksi's voice halted him.

'It was only me.'

Ross turned around.

'You don't have to worry that Annika was beaten.' He gave a low mirthless laugh. 'She had it tougher in many ways. My father was the sun, my mother the moon, and they revolved around her. She had the full beam of their twisted love, but they never laid a finger on her. It was just me.'

'I'm sorry,' Ross said, because he was.

'It was my own stupid fault for knowing too much…' He looked up at Ross. 'Every family has their secrets, Ross,' Aleksi said, 'and Levander thinks he knows, and Iosef is sure he knows, but they don't….' He gave a thin smile at Ross's frown.

'Annika told me…' He faltered for a moment. 'Some…'

'About Levander being raised in an orphanage—and my parents conveniently not knowing he was there?'

Ross nodded.

'That isn't the half of it. And I'll save you from future awkward conversations with my sister by not telling you. Suffice to say I know more than any of them. That's why my father beat me to within an inch of my life, and that's why my mother, instead of taking me to hospital, kept me at home.'

'Any time,' Ross said. 'Any time you can talk to me. And I promise I'll keep it confidential.'

He'd had enough. Ross saw the anger and the energy leave him, knew Aleksi had revealed all that he was going to—for now.

It was almost a relief when Annika walked in, for a

quick visit at the end of her shift. She smiled and frowned when she saw Ross with her brother.

'I thought I'd see for myself how he was doing,' Ross said by way of explanation. 'I was just saying to Aleksi that he looks a hell of a lot better than he did last time I saw him.'

'I was wondering why they'd sent a paediatrician to see me.' Aleksi gave a rare smile to his sister. 'I didn't realise at first it was your boyfriend.'

'Boyfriend?' Annika wrinkled her nose. 'He's thirty-two.'

And Ross laughed and left them to it.

He nodded to a colleague in the corridor, chatted to Caroline when he got back to the ward, and then he went into his office and closed the door and sat there.

The cleaner got the fright of her life when she came in to empty the bin and he was still there, in the dark.

'Sorry, Doctor. I didn't realise you were here. Do you want me to turn on the light?'

'No, thanks.'

And he was alone again, in the dark.

With Annika he might always be in the dark.

Might never know the full truth—what she knew, what Aleksi knew… It was like a never-ending dot-to-dot picture he might never be able to join up.

Buena onda. He felt what it meant this time—that vibe, that feeling, that connection. Finally he had it with Annika, and it belonged with Annika.

An ambulance light flashed past and Ross looked around his office. The blue and red lights from the ambulance danced on the walls. He realised he wasn't completely in the dark—there were shades and colour, the glow of the computer, a chink of light under the door, the streetlight outside, the reflective lights of the hospital foyer.

There was light in the dark.

And he didn't have to see it all to know what was there.

He didn't need neat answers, because for Ross there were no longer questions.

There was nothing that could happen, nothing that could be said, nothing that could be revealed that would change how he felt.

More light—his phone glowed as his inbox filled.

And he smiled as he read her meticulous text—no slang for Annika.

My mother just left the building.
I have been told for the last hour how bad you are for me.
When can we be bad? x

He smiled because everything he wanted and needed he already had—everything she was was enough.

Okay, so she had never said she loved him, and she probably didn't yet fully trust him—but slowly she would.

Ross swore there and then that one day she would, and replied to her text.

ASAP x

CHAPTER TWENTY-FIVE

'IS IT possible to request first lunch break?' Annika asked during handover. 'Only, my elder brother is coming from the UK this morning.'

'That shouldn't be a problem,' Caroline said. 'How is Aleksi doing?'

'Better.' Annika nodded. 'A little slower than he would like, but he is improving.'

It had been a tough few weeks.

But full of good times too.

Levander had flown in at the time of the accident and stayed till Aleksi had shown improvement, but had had to return to the UK. Now, though, he was coming with his wife, Millie, and little Sashar for a six-month stay. Levander would take over the running of the Kolovsky empire while Aleksi recuperated. But though it had been wonderful to see Aleksi make such rapid progress, it had been draining too.

Nina had wept and wailed, had made Annika feel so wretched for leaving her alone that she had moved back home. The daily battle just to go to work had begun again.

The control her mother exerted, the secrets of the past, had all sucked her back to a place where she didn't want to be.

The papers had been merciless. It had been proved that neither drugs nor alcohol had been a factor in the accident, but still they had dredged up every photo of Aleksi's wild ways.

And she'd hardly seen Ross.

She'd seen him at work, of course, and they'd managed to go out a couple of evenings, but Nina always managed to produce a drama that summoned her home. Ross had been so patient…

'Oohh, look at you!' Caroline gave a low wolf-whistle as Ross walked past, and Annika gave a rare laugh at his slight awkwardness as nurses, domestics and physios all turned and had a good look!

He *was* particularly spectacular this morning.

Black jeans, black belt, a sheer white cotton shirt and Cuban-heeled boots. His hair was still damp and he had a silver loop in his ear. He looked drop-dead sexy.

'Will your brother be here yet?' Ross asked a while later.

'I would think so.' Annika glanced at her watch. 'Iosef is going to the airport to collect them.'

'So what's your mum got planned for you tonight?'

'Probably a big family reunion dinner, somewhere glitzy where the press can see us all smiling and laughing.'

'I'll give it a miss.' Ross gave her a wink. 'But thanks for the invite.'

'There was no invite.' Annika shot him a short smile back. 'You're a bad influence, remember?'

* * *

It was a busy morning, made busier because it was her last day on the ward and time for her end-of-rotation assessment.

'Well done.' Heather Jameson ticked all the boxes this time. In the last few weeks, though it had been hard at home, Annika had made work her solace, had put her head down, or sometimes up, had smiled when she didn't really feel like it and had been rewarded in a way she had never expected. 'I know you've had a difficult time personally, and that it took you a bit of time to settle, but you have. The staff are all delighted with you.'

'I've liked working on the children's ward,' Annika said. 'I never thought I would, but I truly have.'

'What do you like about it?'

'It's honest,' Annika said. 'The children cry and they laugh and they don't pretend to be happy.' She gave a small smile. 'They forgive you if you are not happy too,' Annika said, 'and so long as you are kind, they don't mind if you are quiet.'

'You've got Maternity next,' Heather said, and blinked when Annika rolled her eyes.

'You might like it—remember you weren't looking forward to Paeds?'

'I think I am too stoic to be sympathetic,' Annika said, 'but of course I will be. Now I know where I'm going.'

It was things like that that set her apart.

There was still an aloofness, a hard edge that bewildered Heather, but, yes, Annika was intriguing.

'Do you think Paediatrics is where you might specialise?' Heather said.

'No,' Annika said. 'I've decided what I want to do.'

'And?'

'Geriatrics or palliative care.' Annika smiled at Heather's slight frown. 'It has everything the children's ward has and a lot of wisdom too. I guess as you near the end of your life the mask slips away and you can be honest again.'

'You did very well in your geriatric rotation.'

'I thought it was because nursing was new,' Annika admitted. 'I thought the gloss had worn off over the last eighteen months or so. But now I realise nothing was ever as good as my time there, because geriatrics is the area of nursing where I belong.'

She thought of Elsie.

Of a white chocolate box filled with mousse and raspberries—and that nothing could taste so perfect, so why bother searching?

Idle chatter had come easily with Elsie and the oldies, and silence had been easy too.

'I want to qualify,' Annika explained. 'I want to get through the next year. I am not looking forward to Maternity, nor to working in Theatre, but I will do my best, and when I get my qualification I have decided that I would like to specialize in aged care.'

Oh, it wasn't as exciting as Emergency, or as impressive sounding as Paediatrics or ICU—but it was, Annika realised, an area of nursing she loved. She had been searching for something and had found it—so quickly, that she hadn't recognised it at first.

It was the care Annie had shown her father that had first drawn her into nursing—the shifts at the nursing home that had sustained her.

She liked old people.

For the most part they accepted her.

It was very hard to explain, but she tried.

'Those extra shifts that I did in the nursing home,' Annika admitted, 'they were busy, and it was hard work, but…' Still she could not explain. 'I like the miserable ones, the angry ones, the funny ones, even those I don't like, I like… They teach me, and I can help them just by stopping to listen, by making sure they have a chance to talk, or making sure they are clean and comfortable. It's a different sort of nursing.'

And Heather looked at a very neat, very well turned out, sometimes matter-of-fact, often awkward but always kind nurse, and realised that Geriatrics would be very lucky to have her. To be old, to have someone practical tend to the practical and then to have the glimpse of her warmth—well, they would be lucky to have her and also she would be lucky to have them.

She needed a few golden oldies bolstering her up, mothering her, gently teasing her, showing her how things could be done, how life could be funny even when it didn't feel it. It might just bring a more regular smile to those guarded lips.

'You'll be wonderful.'

It was the first compliment Annika had truly accepted. 'Thank you.'

'But you have to get through the next year.'

'I will,' Annika said. 'Now I know where I'm heading.'

'Right, you'd better get off for lunch.'

Was it already lunchtime?

Annika dashed into the changing room, opened her locker and ran a brush through her hair and then tied it back into its ponytail. She added some lip-gloss and went to squirt on some perfume—but remembered it was forbidden on the children's ward.

She couldn't wait to see Levander. Last time it had been so stressful, but with Aleksi improving there was much to celebrate, and she was looking forward to seeing Millie too, and little Sashar.

She dashed down the corridor and saw Ross, standing talking to some relatives, and he caught her eye, gave her that smile, and it was as if he was waiting for her, had always been waiting patiently for her.

'Levander.' She hugged her brother when she reached Aleksi's room. It was so good to see him looking well and happy, and Sashar came to her easily. Millie was talking to Annie, who was holding Rebecca.

All the family were together, yet still her mother was not happy, still she could not just relax and enjoy it. She was talking in Russian, even though neither Millie nor Annie understood, telling her children her restaurant of choice for the Kolovsky dinner tonight.

'The hairdresser is at five, Annika.' Nina still spoke in Russian. 'Make sure that you come straight home.

'I'll come too.'

Annika frowned as Annie, for the first time in living memory, volunteered for a non-essential hour at the Kolovsky family home.

'If Iosef takes Rebecca home, I can hang around here and you can give me a lift.'

Annika looked to Iosef, who nodded.

'Hey!' Annika turned to Aleksi and kissed him. His face was pale and it worried her. 'Any better?'

'I'm fine,' Aleksi said, because he said the same each day. He was so tough, so removed from everyone, and so loathing this prolonged invasion of his privacy.

'You'll be home soon.'

'Nope!' A thin smile dusted his pale features. 'I'm sick of bloody family…' He turned to his PA who was there, a large, kind woman, always calm and unruffled, and whispered in her ear. 'Tell them, Kate.'

'Your brother's off to recover at a small island in the West Indies.'

'Very nice.' Annika smiled.

'I'm going into hiding,' Aleksi explained, with just a hint of a wink. That dangerous smile, Annika saw with relief, was starting to return. 'I refuse to be photo-graphed like this—it will ruin my reputation.'

'It's irreparable!' Annika joked, and yet she was worried for him—more worried than he would want her to be, more worried than she could show. She would talk to Kate later—check out as best she could the details of his rehabilitation.

'Come and visit?' Aleksi said, but Annika shook her head.

'I can't. I'm going to Spain for my honeymoon,' Annika said, enjoying her brother's look of confusion.

The door opened, and Nina frowned as a forbidden doctor walked in.

'Family.' Nina said it like a curse. 'Family only.'

'Ross is family,' Annika said. 'Or rather he's about to be.'

She swallowed as the celebrant walked in behind Ross.

'Mrs Kolovsky.' Ross's voice was neither nervous nor wavering as the relatives he had been talking to in the corridor came in—*his* relatives, all happily in on the plan. 'Annika and I want no fuss, but we do want everyone we love present.'

She felt Aleksi's hand squeeze hers, saw Levander smile, and Iosef too. She was scared to see her mother's reaction, so she looked at Ross instead.

It was the teeniest, tiniest of weddings. But she was getting stronger and, with or without Ross, she would make it.

But as he took her hand and slipped on a heavy silver ring she knew that with Ross beside her she would get there sooner.

'By the power vested in me, I pronounce you man and wife.'

He kissed her, a slow, tender kiss that was patient and loving, and then he pulled her back and smiled.

The same smile that had kept her guessing all this time and would keep her guessing for years to come.

'I love you.' It was the first time she had ever said it, Annika realised. He had married her without the confirmation of those three little words.

'I always knew that one day you would,' Ross said. 'What's not to love?'

He made her stomach curl; he made her want to smile. There was excitement from just looking at him, and she wanted to look at him for ever, but for now there was duty.

'We would love to be there tonight,' Annika said to her mother's rigid face. 'Just for a little while.'

For her mother she would face the cameras and allow it to be revealed in the newspapers tomorrow that the Kolovsky heiress was married. She would smile, and she would have her hair done and wear a fabulous dress, but it would be one of her choosing.

'And I would like it if Ross's family could join in the celebration.'

'Of course…' Nina choked.

'Look after her,' Iosef said to Ross.

'I intend to.'

And Iosef could see his wife's tears, and understood all that she had been trying to say to him these past weeks.

His spoiled, lightweight, brat of a little sister was actually a woman of whom he should be proud—and he told her so.

'I am so proud of you.'

She had needed to hear it, and she smiled back at her brother and her sister-in-law, and then to Levander and Millie—and it dawned on her then.

They were all survivors.

Survivors who were busy pulling their own oars, rather than being dragged down—but how much easier it would be now if they pulled together.

There was only one who was still going it alone.

'Aleksi.' She smiled to her brother. 'I was going to speak to the nurse in charge, see if maybe we could come back here after dinner…' And then, much to her mother's annoyance, she changed the plans again. 'Or we could ring the restaurant and eat here.'

Aleksi wouldn't hear of it. 'Go out,' he said, and

then gestured to his infusion. 'I'll be knocked out by seven anyway.'

He was, Annika realised, still rowing all by himself.

'Congratulations,' Aleksi said, and kissed his sister.

'The last single Kolovsky,' Annika teased. 'And still the Kolovsky wedding gown has not been worn.'

'It never will be, then.' He shook his new brother-in-law's hand. 'Take care of her.'

'He already has,' Annika said.

Yes, the tiniest of weddings—and still duty called.

But sometimes duty was a pleasure too.

They walked back down the corridor, laughing and chatting. A nurse and a doctor returning from their lunch break.

The ward was nice and quiet, darkened for the afternoon's quiet time, but Caroline wasn't best pleased. She was talking to Heather Jameson and was stern in her greeting to her student. Good report or not, it was inexcusable to be thirty minutes late back from lunch without good reason.

'Annika, it's forty-five minutes for lunch. I know your brother just arrived, but…'

'I am sorry,' Annika said. 'I was at Security; I had to pick up my new ID.'

Lifting up her lanyard, she offered it to Caroline.

'Well, next time…' Her voice trailed off. 'Annika Wyatt?'

Her neck almost snapped as she turned to Ross, then back to Annika.

'We just got married,' Annika explained, as if that was what people always did in their lunch break.

It seemed the strangest way to spend your wedding day, and no one but the two of them would understand, but there was freedom, real freedom, as she excused herself from the little gathering, smiled to her husband and colleagues, and did what she had fought so hard and for so long to do.

She started to live life her way.

* * * * *

CHILDREN'S DOCTOR, SHY NURSE

BY
MOLLY EVANS

MILLS & BOON®

DID YOU PURCHASE THIS BOOK WITHOUT A COVER?

If you did, you should be aware it is **stolen property** as it was reported *unsold and destroyed* by a retailer. Neither the author nor the publisher has received any payment for this book.

All the characters in this book have no existence outside the imagination of the author, and have no relation whatsoever to anyone bearing the same name or names. They are not even distantly inspired by any individual known or unknown to the author, and all the incidents are pure invention.

All Rights Reserved including the right of reproduction in whole or in part in any form. This edition is published by arrangement with Harlequin Enterprises II BV/S.à.r.l. The text of this publication or any part thereof may not be reproduced or transmitted in any form or by any means, electronic or mechanical, including photocopying, recording, storage in an information retrieval system, or otherwise, without the written permission of the publisher.

This book is sold subject to the condition that it shall not, by way of trade or otherwise, be lent, resold, hired out or otherwise circulated without the prior consent of the publisher in any form of binding or cover other than that in which it is published and without a similar condition including this condition being imposed on the subsequent purchaser.

® and TM are trademarks owned and used by the trademark owner and/or its licensee. Trademarks marked with ® are registered with the United Kingdom Patent Office and/or the Office for Harmonisation in the Internal Market and in other countries.

First published in Great Britain 2010
Harlequin Mills & Boon Limited,
Eton House, 18-24 Paradise Road, Richmond, Surrey TW9 1SR

© Brenda Schetnan 2010

ISBN: 978 0 263 87897 4

Harlequin Mills & Boon policy is to use papers that are natural, renewable and recyclable products and made from wood grown in sustainable forests. The logging and manufacturing process conform to the legal environmental regulations of the country of origin.

Printed and bound in Spain
by Litografia Rosés, S.A., Barcelona

Dear Reader

Thank you so much for reading this book. I hope that you have enjoyed seeing how Mark and Ellie solved the problems between them and found the love they now share.

Regarding the aromatherapy used in this story: while pure essential oils and aromatherapy can certainly be used for a variety of minor ailments, and to promote positive moods, always seek proper medical attention for serious disorders first. You can add complementary aromatherapy later if you wish. There are simple ways to treat simple imbalances such as headaches and skin irritations using natural ingredients. I'm not advocating either/or, but both together to reach wellness. Lavender is my favourite of the aromatherapy oils, and helps to soothe my skin as well as my mind. Try it some time and see what you think.

There is a lot of information about aromatherapy widely available on the internet, as well as some great reference books out there. If you're interested in using the oils make sure that you do your research first, or consult a certified aromatherapist.

Happy reading!

Love

Molly

Molly Evans has worked as a nurse from the age of nineteen. She's worked in small rural hospitals, the Indian Health Service, and large research facilities all over the United States. After spending eight years as a Traveling Nurse, she settled down to write in her favourite place: Albuquerque, New Mexico. In days she met her husband, and has been there ever since. With twenty-two years of nursing experience, she's got a lot of material to use in her writing. She lives in the high desert, with her family, three chameleons, two dogs and a passion for quilting in whatever spare time she has. Visit Molly at: www.mollyevans.com

Recent titles by the same author:

ONE SUMMER IN SANTA FE
THE GREEK DOCTOR'S PROPOSAL
THE EMERGENCY DOCTOR'S CHOSEN WIFE

CHAPTER ONE

Camp Wild Pines
Maine, USA

NURSE Ellie Mackenzie watched a man jog past the camp infirmary as she put away the medical supplies. She didn't mind the task. Frankly, it kept her hands busy and her mind off of the last difficult year of her life, which was what she needed right now. A fresh start. A break from everything that was familiar, habitual, ingrained in her by years of ICU nursing with a side dish of humility for good measure. With a quick glance at the photo of her parents that sat on her desk, she returned to her task. She liked seeing them there.

The jogger was someone she didn't know, so she didn't take much notice as he cruised by the other direction. No business of hers who was running around outside in the sweltering June sunshine in Maine. She was here to work, take a break from hospital nursing for the summer, chase healthy kids around for a few weeks and forget about the recent emotional traumas that had nearly broken her spirit. The man was probably just a counselor enjoying a solitary run before the campers descended tomorrow. After that, there would be no peace and quiet for anyone until the end of summer. At least, that's what her friend, Vicki, had said. Vicki had been a nurse here for several summers, so she should know. Now that Vicki and her husband, Sam, had had a little girl, and Sam had entered a new residency program, they couldn't spend their entire summer here. That's how Ellie had been recruited for the job.

Ten minutes later, the lone jogger ran by in the opposite direction. Catching only a glimpse of long muscular legs, bare torso and a baseball cap turned around backward, she tried to concentrate on the task at hand, but those legs were a definite distraction. She'd likely meet the fellow and the other staff later at the lodge, then she could put a name to the legs, er, face.

Before she finished her task, the squeaky screen door announced a visitor, and she entered the front room to investigate.

"Hello?" Audible wheezes caught her trained ears the second she entered the room.

The jogger had come into the infirmary. Sitting on one of the wooden chairs designated for patients by the front door, the man leaned forward with his hands on his knees, huffing and sweating. "Hi, there." He waved while he caught his breath.

"Hi, yourself. Are you all right?" Moving closer, she gave his thin frame a closer inspection.

He held up a hand, indicating he still needed a minute to catch his breath. "I'm good."

"You don't look good." Wondering if he were experiencing heat exhaustion, she sat on the chair next to him and checked his pulse. It was rapid, but not bounding. The red color of his face indicated he'd been exerting, but he looked as if he were starting to settle down.

Wiping away the sweat on his face with his shirt, he laughed. "Thanks. I'm not used to the humidity *and* heat here."

"Where are you from? Obviously not Maine," she said, more accustomed to it than he was having lived in Dallas, Texas, for several years.

"New Mexico." He wiped his arm across his forehead. "Hot, but not humid."

"Hey, that's cool. I went to nursing school there, but now I live in Dallas where it's hot *and* humid. Are you one of the counselors? I'm Ellie." Now that his color was returning to normal, she relaxed somewhat. Not that she couldn't handle it, but she really didn't want to have to deal with a medical emergency the second she arrived at camp and without the assistance of a backup. Since he was able to carry on a conversation, he wasn't in too much distress, and otherwise he looked healthy.

"Yes, and no. I'm assuming you're the nurse?"

His striking green eyes met hers for the first time. Keen intelligence shone from them. Another time or place she might have been intrigued, but now she looked away. Any interest in men and relationships was on hiatus for the summer. She was too tired to tackle either one. The last relationship had worn her out. Not that she couldn't admire the beauty of the male form; she just didn't want to get close to one just yet.

"Yes."

"I'm the camp's doctor, Mark Collins."

"Oh," she said with a nod and then sat upright as the realization of what he'd just said hit her. *"Oh."* He was *so* not what she'd expected. From what Vicki had told her about her new colleague and his extensive professional experience, she'd thought him to be much older than he obviously was. This put an alarming new perspective on those legs that she would be around a whole lot more than she expected.

He wiped his hand on his shorts, then held it out to her. "Nice to meet you."

Ellie shook the rather sweaty hand, then removed hers from his grip. "Same here. So, do you know Sam or Vicki?"

"Sam. We worked together for a few years at the university hospital in Albuquerque. And you?"

"I'm a friend of Vicki's. We went to nursing school at UNM together. She convinced me that taking a leave of absence and being a camp nurse for the summer would be good for me. Did you get the same line from Sam?" She smiled, suspecting that their mutual friends had begun a small conspiracy.

Mark grinned and put his shirt on. "Nearly identical. Seems they went to great lengths to find substitutes for themselves so they didn't have to come back."

"Right."

Long awkward silences bothered Ellie, so she usually filled them with idle chatter, attempting to keep her patients comfortable. She did the same now, falling back on the best technique she knew. Having a casual conversation with a stranger was something she'd learned to do. Naturally shy, it didn't come easily to her, but she'd learned to hide behind her nurse persona.

"So, are you ready for tomorrow?" she asked. "I hear that it's pure chaos the first day or two, especially with the younger campers who are away from home for the first time." Memories of her own camp experiences as a kid were good, though she hadn't gone to sleepaway camp as young as some of these children.

"Yep. Ready as I'm going to be." He indicated the pile of empty cardboard boxes strewn around the floor. "I see you've been tackling the supplies already. How about a break? Come down to the dock and meet some of the others with me? There's going to be a bonfire just for us tonight, then another one with the kids tomorrow night."

"Sounds great," Ellie said, but hesitated, glancing at the load of trash and boxes scattered about the infirmary. A job left undone was just work to do later, or for someone else to finish, and she hated leaving things incomplete. She simply couldn't do it in good conscience. The nagging voice of her past rolled through her, and she nearly shivered. She hated that voice and thought it had finally left her alone for good.

"Something wrong?" Mark asked, his eyes intense and watching her, unsettling her.

"Didn't a bonfire nearly destroy the camp two summers ago?" she asked, trying to direct his attention away from her.

"That's what I heard, but it all worked out well in the end. Got a new soccer field out of it, too." He pointed to the fire extinguisher by the door. "There are more extinguishers around, but after that experience, it's doubtful there would be a repeat."

Ellie nodded, then stood. "That makes me feel a little better. Well, I'd better get back to it. There are a few more things for me to unpack yet." She hoped that wasn't too straightforward, but if she intended to get this project done before nightfall, she needed to keep moving.

"Want some help? I've finished my run and am happy to give you a hand." He glanced at his watch. "We've got two hours before the bonfire starts."

"No." Again, she hesitated. "I've got it." Stepping back, she moved away from him. He was a very intense man, and she didn't need that right now. She was supposed to be soothing her frazzled nerves, not getting them more so. The energy he had seemed to want to pull her in. She was here to relax, not get embroiled in other people's high energy, no matter how enticing it seemed.

"Can't I at least take some of the empties out to the recycle pile?" he asked and pointed to the stack by the door. "Won't take but a minute."

"Okay. But I've got the rest."

"After that, I'll unpack my stuff, take a shower and head down to the bonfire." He started toward the door and loaded his arms with the empty boxes, then paused. "You really ought to come down, eat some sticky marshmallows and hang out with the rest of us. You'll make everyone feel guilty if they know you're up here working while we're all down there having fun."

She chewed her lower lip, then reached past Mark to open the door for him. "Maybe. We'll see how much of this I get finished first." Though the idea was tempting, she doubted that she'd go. There was so much to do before tomorrow. There was always so much to do, and she never seemed to have enough time in her life to get everything done.

Mark strolled down to the edge of the lake just at sunset and the spectacular rays of orange, yellow and red bounced off of the gentle ripples of water. Breathing deep, he pulled in the fresh, humid air that was so different than he expected it to be. Not that he hadn't been in humid climates before—he had, all over the world, but something was different about this experience. It was fuller, fresher, much more alive than he'd remembered air ever being. Maybe he was being fanciful, but that's what it seemed to him tonight, and he was okay with being a little fanciful now and then. Kept things interesting. Life was too short to be serious all of the time. He'd certainly learned that lesson in spades not long ago.

As twilight deepened, he paused on the dirt path, savoring the moment. Night creatures crawled from their dens to explore their world and created such a symphony of sound that he was compelled to stop and listen for a few moments.

Sam had been right. This remote experience was exactly what he needed after all he'd been through in the previous few years. Tension he hadn't been aware of holding onto began to slowly unwind, and his shoulders relaxed. The persistent gnaw in his gut eased a fraction. Working as a pediatric trauma physician was intense enough, then becoming a patient in his own hospital with a life-threatening illness had brought his world to an abrupt halt. Tension didn't begin to describe the hell he'd been through.

Now that he was past all that—three years past—he was still having difficulty getting back into the swing of having a normal life. He was no longer sure what normal really was. It was definitely not what it had been a short time ago. Nagging doubts, and the agonizing wait of two more years before his body was considered free of cancer, loomed over him every day and influenced him in ways he'd never imagined. Should he rent or have a mortgage? How much life insurance should he buy? Would he die before the tires on his car wore out? Could he engage in a short- or long-term relationship? These were at the top of the list. So many decisions were now based on his questionable longevity.

Chasing after a bunch of healthy kids all summer was going to be a monumental change for him, but one he anticipated being good.

The hoot of a night bird pulled him from his thoughts, and he continued down the hill to the fire blazing at the edge of the water. The smell of charred marshmallows was already heavy in the air, and he hoped that it would entice Ellie into joining the group.

"Hi, Mark. Glad you made it."

"Gil, nice to see you." He shook hands with the camp administrator.

Gil looked up the path. "Where's your nurse?"

"Ellie's finishing up a bit of housekeeping in the infirmary, then she'll be down." At least, he hoped she would be.

"Okay. There's a spot by me *and* the bag of marsh-mallows. You can join me there."

"Just what I wanted to hear." With a laugh, Mark followed the man through the tangle of people who had just plopped down anywhere near the fire. Casting one last glance up the path that had fallen completely dark, he hoped that Ellie would come. She seemed nice, and he needed to make friends with her while they were here for the summer. The community of people he called friends had dwindled during his illness, and he needed to rebuild his support system differently this time. His fiancé, who was supposed to be with him through sickness and health had they married, had bailed during his first treatment. She'd said it was because he wasn't likely to be able to father children, but now he knew better. The shallowness and insecurity he'd never seen had become blindingly clear.

Not wanting to cloud the evening with thoughts of the past, he put her from his mind and followed Gil to the fire.

Though he enjoyed the atmosphere of young adults and experienced counselors who returned year after year, something was missing. Maybe it was just because he was a first-timer here, maybe because he really didn't know the others yet, but something was out of place. Having grown up in a large family that didn't recognize boundaries, loneliness had never been part of his life, but now that was the feeling that came to mind.

Footsteps on the path and a quick, feminine curse alerted them to the arrival of someone else.

"Hello? Is this where the party is?"

Ellie had arrived. A smile covered Mark's face, and

he stood. "Over here," he said and waved, hoping she'd recognize him against the backdrop of the fire.

"There you are," she said and made her way through the tangle of people seated on blankets and camp chairs. She reached for Mark's outstretched hand and grabbed on. Her touch was strong and firm.

"We've got a nice spot here," he said and eased down to the ground with Gil on one side and Ellie on the other, then released her hand. The small groups returned to their conversations now that Ellie was seated. Someone brought out a guitar and began playing softly in the background.

The slap of a hand against bare skin broke the silence, and Ellie jumped. "Ohh. I shouldn't have worn shorts."

"Bugs getting to you?" he asked and swatted away a mosquito buzzing near his ear. "They sound like tiny airplanes, don't they?"

"Yes. These critters are going to have a feast on me. I didn't have time to mix up my own bug spray today and just grabbed the commercial stuff left over from last year." She slapped again. "Obviously, it's not working."

"Maybe you have a sweeter disposition than the rest of us," Gil said and everyone chuckled. Small conversations picked up where they had left off when Ellie arrived.

"I'm an ICU nurse, so *sweet* doesn't really enter into my job description."

"Now, I've worked with plenty of sweet ICU nurses, so I'd have to argue with you on that," Mark said, wondering why she was down on herself.

There was a moment of silence before Ellie answered. "I might have been at one time, but over the years, it seemed to have gotten lost in the job, you know what I mean?" she asked, her voice softer than it had been moments ago, meant for only him and Gil to hear. The others were too far away to hear anyway. "Life gets to be about what you do, not who you are."

"Oh, I doubt that or Vicki wouldn't have recommended you," Gil said and poked a marshmallow onto a long wooden stick. "This is for you. Roast to your preference and enjoy."

"Thanks." She took the stick and focused on putting the fat marshmallow at the edge of the hot coals. "Vicki's a good friend, Gil."

"She said you'd fit right in here, and I believe her." He handed her a chocolate bar and graham crackers to go with the marshmallow.

"I hope she's right." Tucking her head, she focused on making the gooey treat.

Mark's mouth watered. "Gil, can you fix me up with some of that? I haven't had a s'more in years."

"You got it." He reached into the bag and produced a marshmallow that he handed to Mark, then gave him a chocolate bar and a graham cracker.

Mark took the items, watching Ellie as he did. Her focus seemed to move inward as she watched the changing lights in the fire in front of them. The light picked up the reddish hues of her short brown hair. There was a simmering fire in Ellie that he saw, but she probably didn't even know about. Mark hoped for her sake that it wouldn't go out completely.

CHAPTER TWO

HAD she seriously even thought the word *relax* yesterday? Ha! There would be no relaxing at Camp Wild Pines. *Chaos* didn't begin to describe the absolute bedlam that descended on the camp when the four charter buses of kids arrived just after lunch. She'd simply replaced the intensity of the hospital for the madness of camp life. Ellie had never seen so many kids in one place before and certainly none with the level of excitement that sparked off of these campers. Someone must have fed them a bunch of sugar on the bus and let them go.

"Great, stuff, isn't it?" Mark asked her as the campers made their way to the infirmary for exams. He poked bellies, and tickled ribs, as each child made it through, then supplied all with a sweet treat.

"Great?" Ellie gaped at the line of campers, boys and girls, ages seven to fourteen, that trailed its way through the infirmary and out the door, filing all the way across the compound to the lodge, nearly a football field's length away. "Uh, that wasn't quite how I would have described it."

Mark laughed and placed the otoscope into the ear canal of the next camper and leaned forward for a look. "It's great to me."

Ellie gave him a sideways glance and raised her brows. The man obviously lived a crazed life if he thought this was great. "If you say so. Too much chaos and noise kinda makes me nervous. Reminds me too much of work." The thing she'd come here to get away from.

"The noise level with kids is always high. You'll get used to it."

"I doubt it." She'd never get used to it. "There's always too much to do, and never enough time to finish it." Hurrying, she pulled the folders for the next group of kids. "There's only a few minutes before they're supposed to be heading to their cabins, then to the lodge for the welcome reception." She looked at the line of campers and anxiety cramped in her belly. "We're never going to make it." What if they were late, what if she didn't do things the way Dr. Collins liked them, what if—

"Ellie?" Mark touched her on the shoulder, distracting her from her racing thoughts. She hadn't seen him rise and step closer to her.

"What?" She looked up at him. He was so close and tall that she felt small in comparison. Until now she hadn't realized how different they were in height. He just kept going up.

The calm smile on his face didn't detract from the sharp assessing look in his green eyes. "Don't have a panic attack the first day. We'll be fine."

Sweat broke out on her back. Being so nervous about everything wasn't how she wanted to be, but she didn't seem to know how to change. After so many years of being dedicated to helping others and more recently helping her parents through her father's illness and death, something had broken inside of her that she didn't know how to fix. She didn't know if it could be fixed. The last man she had been intimately involved with certainly hadn't thought so. "But the kids will be late, and then—"

"So? It's not like they're going anywhere for the next eight weeks. They can be a little late for the first meeting in the lodge, or we can do the remainder of the assessments tomorrow. Won't hurt anything."

Ellie simply stared at Mark. "Are you serious? Things need to be done on time, not when we feel like doing them or get around to it." How could he be a physician and say that?

"Ellie. We're not slacking. There are simply a few kids I want to take an extra look at right now. There are some campers with chronic illnesses that we need to follow closely over the summer, and if I document well now, it will save me a lot of brain strain later."

Looking away from him, she lowered her eyes. "I see. Sorry, Dr. Collins."

"No sorry about it, and please call me Mark." He squeezed her shoulder once in a gesture that was meant to soothe her frazzled nerves, then turned away. "Let's just get finished with what we can reasonably do, and then we'll go to the lodge with the kids." He called the next camper over. After a quick, assessing glance at Ellie, he carried on with the exams.

Before Mark finished with the next set of eyes, ears and tonsils, the paging system called the campers to the lodge. Without preamble, the kids scattered in a mob of gangly legs and arms and choruses of cheers. "Guess that settles it. Off to the lodge with the bunch of them." He popped off the cover of the otoscope into the trash bin that nearly overflowed beside him. With a look at Ellie, he bundled up the trash and placed a clean liner in the bin.

Stacks of files lay on every conceivable surface; some hung precariously from their perches, and a few had landed on the floor. Ellie hurried around the room picking up trash, putting away files, writing notes on other files. Her frantic pace nearly made him dizzy. He'd had enough of that sort of thing for a while. The change in his life over the past few years had made him much more aware of how he spent his time. He wasn't going to waste his, and he didn't want to see Ellie use up hers on mundane things that could wait. Especially when there was a bonfire waiting. With *s'mores*.

"I guess it's time to head to the lodge," Mark said and motioned for Ellie to join him by the door. Mark paused at the look of panic in her eyes as she surveyed the mess. There was something definitely going on with her and it wasn't files or organization. Getting out of a hospital environment was going to be good for her, too. That was obvious. He knew nothing about her personal life, but the signs of stress she displayed were enough to make him want to reach out to her, want to help her. "Are you ready?" he asked, knowing there could be an explosive answer at the end of that question, but he was ready for it. He hadn't grown up with three sisters without learning a few things about women.

"Uh, no." Ellie shook her head and moved back to the first pile of charts. "I can't go until all of this is taken care of. You go ahead, and I'll join you later." She picked up a stack of files and their contents slid onto the floor. "Probably much later."

He caught a glimpse of tears in her eyes before she hid her face behind the files in her arms. "Ellie, this stuff isn't going anywhere. Let's go meet the kids and let them get to know us a little. We're going to be here all summer, and the charts can wait."

"I just can't leave things undone, you know? I'm not built that way." A sigh flowed out of her. "If I leave things for later, I'll never catch up. You go ahead." She grabbed another stack of charts and began going through them. "It's practically a sin in the nursing world to leave something for the next person to do when you could have done it yourself." She clucked her tongue.

"You're not the only one here. I can help you. I helped create the mess—I can certainly help clean it up." That was logical, wasn't it?

"But that's not a physician's job. This is a mundane task that I should do."

"Ellie, we're not going to be in a hospital setting for eight entire weeks. I won't tell if you don't." Offering her an encouraging smile, he wanted her to respond, but she didn't.

She eyed the piles, but gave another heavy sigh. "I don't know. It's a lot of work. I've always had the philosophy of '*do it now so you don't have to do it later.*'"

"My philosophy is '*don't* waste the now,' and I outrank you. Let's go enjoy ourselves. Before last night I hadn't been to a bonfire for years, and my stomach is growling in anticipation of more campfire food." He paused when she looked as if she were going to resist more. "Please don't make me give you a real doctor's order."

"What?"

Startled brown eyes caught his gaze, and he knew he'd surprised her. Good. "When we come back, we can do it together and get it done in half the time. It's not like it's an urgent matter, and there's no one from Medical Records breathing down our necks."

At that she gave a sideways smile, and her brown eyes lit up for the first time since they'd met. "You're right. I can deal with all this later."

"*We'll* deal with it. Promise. Let's just go enjoy ourselves." This was good. One small step forward.

"Okay. Let me grab a sweatshirt and my special bug spray. They ate me alive last night so I'm not taking any chances tonight."

"Sounds good."

She hurried to her room at the opposite end of the hall from his and returned in minutes. She carried a dark blue sweatshirt with an embroidered loon on it and a white spray bottle in the other hand.

Mark waited by the door, then walked with her to the lodge, wondering what could be special about bug spray. But if it worked, who cared?

The evening was pure delight. Kids ran wild through the camp, and he laughed more than he had in years. Tension began to simply unwind out of him with each passing moment. This was a good change for him, and one he hadn't realized he'd needed. Thank God for good friends who made excellent recommendations. Get out of the hospital for a while. That was the ticket. Oh, what a pleasure it was to be here and simply to be alive.

Tapping his foot to the guitar music, he wasn't watching as one small camper tried to sneak by, but tripped and landed nearly in Mark's lap. The little boy with bright red hair squealed, and Mark helped him to stand.

"I gotta use the bathroom," he said and his blue eyes expressed his urgency.

"Come on, it's this way," Mark said and helped the young boy find the restroom. This was something he knew he might never be able to do otherwise. Not necessarily help a kid to the bathroom, but help *his own child*—get up in the middle of the night with his own children, help them with whatever they needed. For a moment, despair hit Mark; the realization of what he might never have was reflected in the face of each and every camper present. He simply couldn't allow himself to indulge in a relationship when he might not live through the next few years. It wasn't fair to the woman or any children that could come of the relationship. Minutes later, the boy emerged from the bathroom and, for a moment, Mark forgot about his own needs that wouldn't be met so simply.

CHAPTER THREE

ELLIE stirred in her bed the next morning, awakening slowly as the sun crept over the windowsill to invade her room. She hadn't slept so well in such a long time; she'd almost forgotten what it was like. Events of the past few years had disturbed her wakeful time as well as her sleeping time. Maybe fresh air and the quiet Maine woods had helped. A lovely breeze had stirred the pines surrounding the infirmary most of the night, bringing with it the lonesome call of the loons that she loved. The soothing sounds must have lulled her into a state of bliss.

Living in a large city for so long had numbed her senses to what nature had to offer. Cement and skyscrapers and bright lights, and the never-ending roster of critically ill patients, had taken the place of activities she had once enjoyed, and she mourned that loss. Work, and the lengthy illness of her father, had just about worn her out, the breakup with her fiancé only compounding her exhaustion. Mourning had unfortunately become a way of life and one she was determined to shake off during the summer. She knew she would. She just had to figure out how to get started.

The framed photo on the table beside her bed had been taken when her father had been happy and healthy and that's how she wanted to remember him. Memories of his illness had finally begun to fade.

After a quick glance at the clock beside the photo, she bolted upright, panicked. She was late! Tearing off her sleep shirt and quickly dragging on shorts and a T-shirt, she raced out the door, then came to a halt.

Mark sat quietly with about ten kids who waited in a semi-organized line for their morning meds.

"Why didn't you wake me?" she whispered and patted her short, rumpled hair into place, supposing she looked like a porcupine with it sticking out all over.

"No worries. I've got things under control." He gave her a quick assessing glance and his eyes warmed, lingering on her longer than they had yesterday. The flush of heat that rushed through her wasn't entirely from embarrassment. Though she had said she wasn't going to be interested in men during the summer, Mark was intriguing her from the get-go.

"I'm supposed to pull the charts, and the meds, and have things ready before clinic. You didn't need to take clinic this morning. I should have done it." Her heart raced uncomfortably in her chest. This was her job, and the first day here she was already behind.

"Ellie, calm down." Mark handed a camper two pills in a paper medicine cup and a small glass of water. "Down the hatch, buddy." The camper dutifully swallowed the medicine. "Why don't you wake up and get something to eat? It's not a crisis that I take the morning clinic. You can have the one after lunch and the evening one if that will make you feel better. There are a few kids with allergy shots that are due, so you can set them up for the lunch clinic." He gave her a quick glance and adjusted the baseball cap on his head. So far she'd never seen him without it. If he was anything like her brothers, they had to have a favorite team cap on almost before they got out of bed.

"Thank you. I'll do that." Face burning, she headed to the bathroom and closed the door. She splashed cold water on her face, combed her hair and glanced in the mirror over the small ceramic sink. Already, on the first day of camp, she'd succeeded in embarrassing herself in front of the physician and a number of the kids. Determined not to let this setback get the better of her, she pulled herself together. One little problem shouldn't ruin, or set the tone for, the rest of her day. Think positive. Think positive. Wasn't that what she told her patients all the time? Maybe she ought to listen to her own words of advice. If it worked for her patients, it ought to work for her, right? She'd simply make it up to Mark somehow. She'd find a way. Opening the door to the shared bathroom, she re-entered the front, feeling a little better.

"Bear is the man you want to see at the lodge. He said he'd put a few things back for you if you're hungry."

"I can wait. Why don't I take over here?" she said, but as she looked for more campers, she saw that the line had dwindled down to just a few. Mark had handled the task without her help, and no one looked as if they were distressed, so she relaxed a little more. Positive thoughts. Positive energy. If she kept telling herself that, she'd really believe in it one day, wouldn't she?

"Seriously, Ellie. Go ahead and get something to eat. I'm good for a while." He winked at her. "After this I think I might take a run around the camp, get my exercise for the day."

"Yes, Doctor," she said and, with a frown, turned to the door, but paused as she felt a hand on her arm. Turning back, she glanced at him. They were going to be working together for the entire summer, so she should make a better attempt to be friends. Making friends with a handsome man was always a good thing.

"Ellie, my name is Mark, not Doctor. Can you just call me Mark? Please?" he asked and paused, then removed his hand.

"I can do that," she said, then nodded and liked the sound of his name rolling around in her head. "Where I work not too many physicians like being addressed by their first names, so it's just habit."

"A good habit to break, if you ask me. We're all on the same team, right? And if Bear has any of those Boston cream doughnuts left, snag me one for later, will you?" He smiled and the effect made her hold his gaze a second or two longer than she normally would have. Though thin, he was a handsome man. Intense, but handsome.

"Sure." The tension in her flashed away as his vibrant energy seemed to move into her. Energy she seemed to need right now, but didn't know how to find.

"Maybe two if he has them."

That made her laugh and the sensation was warm in

her chest. Laughter had been bountiful in her home as she'd grown up, and she realized now that it was somehow missing in her life. She'd become too serious and that was something she'd never wanted to be. "I'll see what he has. You might have to do an extra lap around the camp to work it off though." The man had a sweet tooth. She'd have to remember that. He was too thin by far, so if she could grab him a doughnut now and then, she'd do it. He'd been nothing but nice to her, so she could do something nice back. Perhaps her payback to him could come in the form of confiscated pastries now and then.

The lodge, a great lumbering building made of rough-hewn timber, was the hub of the compound, and she reached the front porch in minutes. The screen door squeaked as she opened and closed it, and she entered the cool interior to find the place empty. Last night, they had stuffed nearly three hundred people in here, and the din had been overwhelming. Now, every footstep echoed off the log walls. Just as she entered the lodge, a crashing clatter of pans and shattering of glass made her jump. Loud cursing and yelling followed, and she hurried over to the galley.

"Hello? Is everything okay?" She gasped as the biggest, brawniest bearded man she'd ever seen turned to face her, anger blazing in his deep-set brown eyes.

"No, dammit! I'm burned half to death." He held his right hand under the water in the sink and continued to grumble. A thin man covered by a white apron hovered a few feet away, his hands nearly choking the handle of a broom.

"I'm Ellie, the nurse. We haven't met yet."

"I'm Bear, the chief fried cook." He shook his head and continued to mutter under his breath.

"Why don't I look at your injury? Are you hurt anywhere else?"

"No, thanks. I'll be fine."

Now, she remembered something Vicki had said, that Bear took a while to warm up to people. "Vicki Walker said you make a great clam chowder," she said, hoping to distract him a little.

"She did, did she?" Bear cast her another glance. "We'll be missing her around here this year."

"She and Sam and their little girl will be up for a visit or two during the summer, so you'll get to see her."

Nodding at that, Bear turned to face her more fully, though he kept his hand and forearm under the running water. "Think you got anything in the infirmary to help a grease burn as big as this?" he asked.

"Sure. Getting it under the cold water is the first thing, for sure. Let me call Dr....Mark to come over and see you, too. I also have some aromatherapy oils that will take the sting right out of the burn and probably minimize scar tissue."

"I don't care about scars. Got enough of them already, so a few more won't make much difference." He sniffed. "Aroma-what? What's that?" Bear asked, a puzzled expression on his face.

"Plant extracts that have healing properties." She'd studied aromatherapy and used it on her father when he'd been ill, and she was now thinking of becoming a practitioner in addition to her nursing career. Comple-

mentary therapies were helpful to standard tr[...]
and she was a believer in them.

"Like folk medicine?" he asked and his fierce e[...]es-
sion eased a little.

"Something like that." That was probably the sim-
plest way to describe the therapy that didn't sound too
out-there for most people.

"Okay. Phone's on the wall there." Bear nodded to
the wall beside the mess of a desk scattered with magazines and paperwork.

"Thanks." Ellie looked at the numbers scrawled on
a piece of paper beside the phone. Dialing the number,
she waited for Mark to answer. She quickly explained
the situation and hung up. "He'll be here in a minute.
Only one camper left for the morning clinic."

A single nod was the only response from Bear. She
noticed that he had reverted back to his tight-lipped
expression again and suspected the burn hurt a lot
more than he was letting on. "Can I ask you a few
questions, Bear?"

"As long as they're not about my clam chowder
recipe," he said.

"No," Ellie said and hid a grin, knowing that Vicki
had worked long and hard to get that recipe out of him.
"They're medical questions. Are you on any medications or do you have any medication allergies?"

Bear answered her questions and a few minutes later
Mark charged through the door of the lodge, carrying
two medical supply packs. "I wasn't sure what we were
going to need. I brought a few things, then we'll get you
to the infirmary to do a full exam."

"I don't need no full exam. I just need my burn looked at." He held his hand and forearm out to them.

Ellie winced inwardly at the sight of the red, inflamed skin and took a pair of exam gloves from Mark. "Do you think it will blister?"

"Not sure. Might," Mark said and applied exam gloves before touching the wound that ran from Bear's thick fingers all the way to midforearm. "You said he put the injury in cold water right away, correct?"

"Yes. And to my knowledge, the sooner a heat injury is cooled, the better." Burns weren't her specialty, but that much she remembered and the advice made complete sense. Sometimes common sense was the best medicine in the world.

"Should I put ice on it?" Bear asked and winced as Mark touched a particularly tender spot that could have been the initial contact site.

"No. You don't want to apply ice to skin that's already delicate."

"Delicate? There's nothing delicate about Bear," the thin assistant cook said with a snort. "He's as tough as they come."

"You're right about that, Skinny," Mark said. "The injured skin is the only thing delicate here, and we don't want to add anything too cold to it, because skin damaged by heat could then be damaged by cold."

"Makes sense," Bear said and gave a nod.

"If you have no objection, Mark, I'd like to try some aromatherapy oils on the injury, too." She chewed her lip, not sure how he would react to that request. Many doctors didn't understand, or agree with, the benefit of treatments that weren't created in a chemistry lab.

"Aromatherapy?" Mark asked with a quick glance at her, brows raised, silently asking for more information.

Clenching her hands together, she prepared to support her case. "Yes. I know it's considered an alternative treatment, but I like to think of it as complementary. I've used it successfully on a variety of ailments. No adverse reactions, either." Mostly she'd treated her dad and a few friends, but she truly believed in it. Heart racing, she hoped he would agree. She might even be able to document the use of oils on a burn for others to follow.

"Any objections from you, Bear?" Mark asked and turned the man's wrist slightly, looking at the wound that ran all the way around his wrist. "Otherwise, we'll just send you off to the ER in town."

"Nope. She said it's kind of like folk medicine, and I'm okay with that. Anything to take the sting out of it is okay with me, and I don't want to go to the ER. I got stuff to do."

"Aromatherapy is widely used in Europe, and I've used it before on burns, though not one as large as this." In the kitchen she was a klutz and had succeeded in burning herself in myriad ways, so she kept a bottle of lavender essential oil handy to treat herself with.

"Okay, Nurse Ellie. Do your thing."

Mark issued the order, and she was suddenly energized by his open-minded nature. Working with him might not be so bad after all.

"I'll be right back." She raced to her room, grabbed her kit of aromatherapy vials and quickly returned to the lodge. Unzipping the protective neoprene case, she pulled one bottle out and clenched it in her hand. "Keep holding your arm over the sink, will you? In case anything drips off," she said.

"I think you did a good job of cooling the injury right away, Bear," Mark said and stood to observe Ellie's treatment.

"Hurts like hell though," he said, grumbling, but allowed Ellie to minister to him. The first few drops of oil hit his skin and the fragrance permeated the kitchen. "You didn't tell me it was perfume!" Bear cried and tried to pull away from her.

Grabbing him by the apron front, she kept him in position. "It's not perfume. Now live up to your reputation and hold still, will you?"

"Oh, man. The guys will never let me live this one down. My wife, neither." He bowed his head and shook it in disgust, certain his fierce reputation had just been torn to shreds.

Beside them, Skinny snickered, but quieted after a glare from Bear.

"It's better than being in pain, and it's certainly better than a burn that could scar badly and prevent you from cooking for all these campers." Gently, she used her fingers to rub the oil over all areas of the burn. "There are wonderful healing properties in this oil, as I said. Who cares what it smells like, right?"

Bear gave a sniff of lingering disapproval, but relented. "I guess."

"If it will make you feel better, you can tell people I held you down while Ellie poured it on you," Mark said.

Bear gave Mark's thin frame a glance and snorted. "Now, no one's gonna believe that one."

"I'm stronger than I look," Mark said and flexed his left bicep.

Bear barked out a laugh and shook his head. "I make biscuits bigger than that, Mark." Bear relaxed, and Ellie knew that had been Mark's intention.

The tension between the three of them eased. "Did Ellie get her doughnuts?"

"No. I burned myself just as she walked in. They're still in the cooler." He nodded to indicate which one.

Mark rubbed his hands together at that information. "Any others that you want to get rid of, like Boston cream? Breakfast was a long time ago."

"Yeah, help yourself. There's a couple left." Bear held still while Ellie wrapped a light gauze dressing to his injury.

"That ought to do it." She applied one strip of tape to keep the end of the gauze secure.

"I can't cook wearing this thing. I look like a mummy."

"Leave it on through the afternoon. Step back and just supervise for a meal, then come see me before dinner. We'll take it off then and see how it's doing. You might not even blister," Ellie said, pleased that she'd been able to help him right away with her essential oils. The more she used them, the more uses she found for them.

"I'll see you in a couple of hours, then. Get your doughnuts, and I'll clean up this damned mess I made."

Skinny stepped forward with a grin. "I can help you, Bear, since you have a sore paw."

Bear turned quickly with a growl. "Now, don't be

making cracks about me bein' lame…" Bear said and grabbed a towel with his left hand and snapped it at Skinny, but he missed by a long measure. "Put that broom to good use and help me clean this mess up."

The two engaged in what appeared to be a long-standing, good-natured argument. Thus dismissed, Mark and Ellie gathered their medical supplies and returned to the infirmary.

CHAPTER FOUR

THE chaos of the morning settled down and Ellie was able to prepare the allergy shots as well as get the normal lunch meds organized. Accomplishing the task ahead of time made her feel more in control of herself and more comfortable with the job she was supposed to be doing.

While the kids who had received allergy shots waited the requisite fifteen minutes in the infirmary to see if they were going to have a reaction to the injection, Ellie waited with them. A local reaction of warmth and swelling sometimes occurred, although there was always the potential for a serious reaction with each injection. She kept a number of EpiPens handy for true allergic emergencies. Something she dreaded happening to anyone, but especially a child.

Screams and shouts heralded the arrival of someone to the infirmary, and she was on instant alert. A counselor carrying a screaming child in his arms hurried toward the building. Ellie rushed to the door and opened it for them.

"What happened?" The boy screamed as if he'd had a leg cut off, but it was clearly intact.

Mark arrived directly behind them. "I heard the commotion from across the soccer field. That kid's got a good set of lungs. What's going on?" He instantly switched to physician mode, and Ellie was startled to see the visible change in front of her. The intensity and his energy were totally focused on the situation in front of him.

The counselor sat the boy in a chair and dropped into the one beside him. "Bee sting."

Ellie knelt as the boy held out a hand with a bright red welt forming on the back of it. He continued to cry and tremble despite the efforts of the counselor and Ellie to comfort him.

"I don't see a stinger, so that's good." She applied a numbing spray to the site as Mark watched over her shoulder. "This will make it feel better in a jiffy," she said and stroked his arm above the sting, trying to soothe him a little. "What's your name?" With a gentle hand, she wiped his tears away and pressed a cool cloth to his face.

"This is Adam," the counselor said when the boy didn't speak. "And I'm Eddie."

"Nice to meet you both. Is this your first year at camp, Adam?"

The boy nodded and leaned closer into the counselor, who hugged him. Tears continued to flow, but the hysteria had settled down to hiccups and sniffles. Ellie suspected that the numbing spray had begun to do its job. The fear would take a little longer to subside.

Then Adam giggled. And his eyes lit up. And then he pointed over Ellie's shoulder, and she turned. And she clapped her hand over her mouth to stifle the totally unprofessional giggle that threatened to burst out of her.

Mark looked like a rooster. He had taken a large exam glove and placed it over the top of his head. The fingers flopped over to one side, but each time he moved they jiggled like a rooster comb.

"That's more like it," he said and knelt beside them, still wearing the glove on his head. Adam reached out and batted the fingers, trying to make them stand upright. Mark examined the injury closely. "You're right. No stinger, so couldn't have been a honeybee. Looks like there might be two stings though. Must have been a hornet or a wasp. They're a lot nastier." He looked at Eddie. "Where was he when this happened?"

"Over at the edge of the new soccer field."

"Okay. As long as it wasn't in your cabin, although I think the maintenance guys checked all of the buildings for unwanted critters already." He patted Adam on the leg. "Ellie, got any more of that lavender oil handy?" he asked.

"Sure. Want to put some on the sting, too?" She brightened at the thought. Another use for her oil.

"Yes. The numbing spray smells so medicinal, and the oil is a much better fragrance for the kids."

"Got it." She returned in a minute with the oil and put a dab on Adam's hand, smearing it around the entire welt. "This will fix it up quick. I would like him to stay for a few minutes to make sure he's not going to have an allergic reaction." That would be a disaster if Mark weren't close to help.

"Good plan." He rose and removed the glove from his head and put it on Adam's head. "Looks better on you."

For the first time, Ellie was able to look at Mark's hair, which was a dense, thick brown and cropped close to his head. She supposed it was much easier to care for this way for the summer.

"I have some candies, Adam. Want one?" Mark asked and reached for the jar of sweets even before Adam's eyes widened. Opening the lid, he held it over for Adam to reach into and select his own. "You, too, Eddie."

"Thanks."

"Eddie, will you bring him back after dinner so we can check him?" Ellie asked.

"Sure." He unwrapped a candy and popped it into his mouth.

After a few more minutes, when Ellie was sure that Adam wasn't having a more severe reaction to the sting, Eddie picked up the boy and gave him a shoulder ride out the door and back to their afternoon activity. The allergy-shot kids also departed since their waiting time was over as well.

Mark wrote a note in Adam's chart regarding the injury and treatment. Watching him, Ellie knew she had to say something.

"I'm really surprised that you're so open to alternative therapy." She shrugged. "At least to the aromatherapy anyway."

"Why wouldn't I be?" He set the chart aside and focused his attention on her. "It's good practice to be open-minded in all sciences."

"I'm just surprised. So many medical people—nurses and doctors—discount other therapies as being whacked simply because it's not developed in a pharmaceutical lab." Thinking of it still irritated her, but she had to realize that not everything worked for everyone, and people were entitled to their own opinions, even if she didn't agree with them. Alan, her former fiancé, had had nothing good to say about the oils.

"I've heard that said about acupuncture, chiropractic and massage therapies over the years, but they've all proved their worth, haven't they?"

"You're right. I never thought about it that way, but the science of medicine continues to evolve, doesn't it?"

"As it should."

Sitting in the chair beside him, she warmed to her subject and decided to share a little of her personal experiences with him. "My dad was ill not long ago. Seriously ill. One of the best things I did for him was mix up some oils that my mom and I massaged onto his feet and hands." Talking aloud about her father made her miss him right then and a pang shot through her. Being weak and vulnerable in front of Mark wasn't what she wanted to do, but right now she couldn't seem to stop herself. "He said when the pain was coming on, he'd always take his medication, but using the oils in addition helped him relax enough for the meds to work."

"Sounds like a good plan to me. How is he doing now?" Mark blinked and stiffened, his face strangely devoid of emotion that had been so evident moments ago. His green eyes observed her, and she had a hard time holding his gaze. This was apparently becoming a difficult conversation for both of them, based on Mark's reaction.

"He died about six months ago." Tears pricked her eyes, but she didn't want to give in to them. One of the last things her father had asked of her was that she not grieve overly long, that she continue with her life, but she seemed to have become stuck where she was, unable to move forward out of the quagmire of emotions that wanted to tangle her up at odd moments.

"I'm sorry, Ellie. Is it something you want to talk about?"

"No. Not right now, but thanks." She looked down at the bottle of lavender oil in her hand and closed her fingers around it. "Fragrances are very powerful and stimulate memories that we often forget about until we experience the scent again. When I open this particular oil, I always think of what he said."

"He sounds like he was a smart man."

"He was." Rising, Ellie moved away from him and busied herself putting away the items used in the lunch clinic.

Bear arrived around 4:00 p.m. for his checkup. He nearly filled the small front room with his larger-than-life presence. But he didn't intimidate her as she'd expected. She guessed that putting *Teddy* in front of his name would describe Bear on the inside.

After applying gloves, she reached for the scissors and began to cut away the gauze wrapping. The fragrance of lavender filled the air around them and soothed her nerves.

"Careful with them scissors—I still have dinner to contend with," Bear said.

Although his eyes were serious, the words made her smile. There was a sense of humor in there, but it was buried deep beneath the beard and the brawn of the man. "I'll try not to cut your hand off." In seconds she had Bear's arm and hand open to the air again. "How does it feel?"

Flexing his fingers and making a fist, Bear moved his hand in all directions. He gave a grunt. "Hmm. Feels good. The lavender did take the sting out after a while."

"I knew it was going to work!" Excitement bubbled through her. "Let me find Mark so he can have a look."

Eagerly, she turned, but ran right into Mark, and his arms caught her before they both toppled over. "Whoa, Ellie. I'm right here."

"Oh, you have to see this." She grabbed him by the arm and led him to Bear's side. "See? I told you this was going to work."

The contrast in skin tones was obvious, but what had been a fierce red color of the burned skin had mellowed to a dark pink. The center that had been the initial contact site had also faded, though it was still richer in color than the rest.

Mark gave a smile to Ellie, then faced Bear. "My. You're right." He parked his hands on his hips and looked at the burn site. "It's nearly gone." Putting on the gloves that Ellie handed him, he turned Bear's arm toward the light to examine the area around the wrist. "I'm impressed, Ellie. Your lavender oil really worked."

"So am I," Bear said and lowered his arm to his side, then looked up at her, his expression open. "I'm grateful to you for fixing me up so quick."

"You're welcome." She handed him the remainder of her bottle. "Put some more on throughout the day today and tomorrow if it gives you any trouble." Eagerness and joy bubbled within her. Treating people that resulted in such good healing was the epitome of her work. "You have to make sure they are *pure* essential oils, if you ever use any again. And lavender is the only one you can put directly on the skin. The rest have to be diluted with another oil, like grape seed or the like."

"No tellin' how long I woulda sat in the ER." The bottle nearly disappeared in his brawny hand.

A thrill shot through her. "This was the biggest burn I've ever treated, but the oil seems to have done the job."

Bear stood. "Next time you get some, how about ordering me a bottle or two? Someone's always burning or cutting themselves in the kitchen. We'll use this one up in a hurry."

"Absolutely, Bear." She reached forward and gave him a quick hug.

Blustering at the affection, Bear patted her shoulder with his large hand. "I gotta get back to the kitchen. No tellin' what Skinny'll do without me there."

"Okay. Let me know if there's anything else you need, Bear."

"Sure will." He exited the infirmary and returned to the lodge.

Mark turned to Ellie with a grin. "That was good work," he said.

A flush ranged over her face and neck at the compliment. She hadn't been this excited over anything in a long time, and although the sensation was good, it was somewhat unfamiliar at the same time.

"Thanks, Mark." She tossed the fragrant gauze in the trash. The scent of lavender lingered in the air, and she took a deep breath. "Suddenly, the scent no longer has any sadness to it for me." She gave a laugh. "That's kind of a surprise to me."

"A good one, I hope." Mark leaned against the exam table, settling in for a chat.

"Yes."

A frown chased across her face and her eyes were wide and open, but there were secrets hidden in there. "But?" Would prodding her a little help her to open up?

"But what?"

"Sounds like there's a 'but' hiding in that statement somewhere." He had been the champion of hiding his feelings, so he recognized the same trait in Ellie.

"There probably is." Running her fingers along the edge of the table, she looked away from him. "I don't know. It's just that I've not felt like this for so long that I don't quite know how to go about making things different." She blew out a long sigh.

"Change is never easy, it takes time. I know that myself." The life he had known had been changed for him, and he'd had no choice except to go along with it. A memory shuddered through him.

"You don't look as if you've had a serious problem in your life. You're so easygoing. And Vicki told me that you've traveled in many parts of the world, gone on missions for health care and even run in two marathons."

"Well, yes, I have done those things, but the past few years haven't been great." Yes, that was an understatement. He was lucky he'd survived the past few years.

"I'm sorry. I'm prying in your personal life, and I have no business doing that." She picked up the few remaining files from the table and put them in the filing cabinet.

After that, she looked around for something else, but they had finished all of the assessments earlier. He'd made her uncomfortable, and he wanted to remedy that now.

"Ellie, no." He removed his cap and ran his fingers through his hair, then replaced the cap. "I mean, yes, there are things in my private life that are painful, but no, you're not prying." He pulled a chair over and sat backward on it, resting his arms on the back. "We're going to work together for the summer, and we'll get to know each other. For now, I'll just tell you that I was seriously ill a few years ago. It came out of the blue and hit me hard." So hard he'd nearly died from it.

"I'm sorry, Mark." Tentatively, she reached out and touched his arm, offering him a gesture of comfort that he knew she would have offered to anyone. That's just the way she was, giving so much to others. "That's why you're on the thin side, isn't it?"

"Yes. But every day I'm getting healthier and stronger." With a grin he patted his flat abdomen. "If I keep up those Boston cream doughnuts, I won't have to worry about the thin part for much longer."

"I suppose you're right," she said and gave a quick laugh. "If you're not bothered by the illness, then I won't be, either. Serious illness can take over a person's life, so I'm glad you're over yours." She gave a sigh and pulled a chair close to his. "Since you've shared some of your story with me, I'll share some of mine with you. Stress has really been getting to me the past year. My father died of cancer, and working in an ICU setting is no piece of cake. So I'm hoping that some downtime, running after healthy kids for the summer, will lighten me up a bit."

"I'm sure it will. Sounds like we're both where we need to be for a while." He puffed out a quick sigh. It was actually a relief to talk a little about his past, his illness. Not that he wanted to linger on it, but sharing a tiny bit with Ellie was not as difficult as he thought it would be.

"Definitely."

"I think I'll take that extra lap now, if there's nothing else going on."

"Nope. Just dinner at the lodge, then clinic right after." She gave a quick laugh. "No bonfire tonight though, so you'll have to indulge your sweet tooth some other way."

"I'll do that." Turning his hat around the proper way, he left the infirmary and the sudden appeal of Ellie's smile.

Since his illness and recovery he'd been too focused on survival to be attracted to anyone. Now that he was ensconced in a small building with Ellie, trapped for the summer with a beautiful woman in a remote area, he was uncertain that that had been a wise move on his part. Being attracted to her simply because she was available and in front of him didn't seem likely. If another woman had gotten the job, he probably wouldn't have found her as interesting, as intriguing, as Ellie was. She was a woman with depth and caring and didn't hesitate to share herself with others. There was promise in that. He may not be around long enough to cash in on that promise, so he advised himself to steer clear of Ellie and her allure.

After a few leg stretches, he took off at a slow pace around the camp. This time of the afternoon, the temperature was hot and the humidity was high, leaving the skin and hair sticky even after a short exposure. Dark threatening clouds gathered in groups on the horizon, and he supposed they'd have a storm before the night was through. He loved storms and the chaos they created in the skies. External chaos was good. Internal chaos was not so good.

Right now, he needed to put some distance between himself and Ellie, the source of his current chaos in feelings. The vulnerability she gave off appealed to some manly aspect of his personality. He supposed that was why he'd become a physician, because he wanted to help people. He was a doer and a fixer. And he wanted to help Ellie without getting too involved emotionally. That was the downfall of being involved with people. Unfortunately, he wasn't much of a technology man, or he'd consider research in a lab somewhere, limiting his contact with others. But he knew that wasn't going to solve his problems, and he made his way around the soccer field down the path to the lake at an easy pace.

A swim class was in full swing, and he watched the boys and girls splashing around the roped-off lanes of water. With a laugh, he recalled his swim lessons as a kid. He'd sunk like a rock and had almost given up until his gangly body had somehow managed to put everything together, and he'd made it across the pool, sputtering the entire way. From then on, he'd lived in the neighborhood pool every summer. Now, watching the kids learn their lessons, he was once again reminded of something he might never do—take his own child swimming.

As he had moved through college and residency, he'd never thought of being ill himself. He'd always thought of how he could help others, how he could use his skills as a physician. Other people got sick and died, other people contracted chronic illnesses. He'd become one of those *other people*.

Finding a spot on the dock away from the kids, but where he could observe them, he thought back to that time in his life that had nearly killed him.

CHAPTER FIVE

HE'D found a lump in one testicle where there ought not to have been one. Though he'd been in a hot shower at the time, he'd broken out in a cold sweat. He'd experienced all the phases of grief, but had set them aside in order to get a swift diagnosis and treatment. Denial was what got people into serious trouble. Denying a serious illness only gave the illness more time to grow and take over, rather than defeating it quickly in its tracks. He'd had to make a leap over that denial hurdle. Though he knew that his sort of cancer responded very well to treatment, the fear of it never left him.

The cancer diagnosis had laid his family low. His father had been absent most of his life and was no source of comfort or help then. Thankfully, his sisters had come together to help him when he'd needed them the most. Rather than tearing his family apart as many serious illnesses do, his condition had strengthened the bonds between them. Mark wondered if the same thing had happened to Ellie and her family when her father had become ill, if she and her mother were still close. Of course, he'd seen the picture of her parents in the workroom, but she hadn't mentioned her mother at all.

The swim coach blew her whistle, redirecting Mark's thoughts as she called the swimmers from the water. The kids landed in sloppy, wet piles as they sat on the dock and listened to the instructions.

Rising from the wooden dock, Mark knew that everyone would be called to the lodge shortly, then there would be clinic right after. He'd left Ellie rather abruptly, the story of her father's death affecting him in a way he hadn't expected. He wanted to find Ellie and apologize for being rude.

He returned to the infirmary and found it empty.

"Rats," he said.

"Where?" Ellie's voice came from down the hall.

"Where are you?" Good. She was still here.

"In the ward room."

Mark moved around the corner and found Ellie reclining on one of the beds and his stomach clenched at the sight of her there. "What are you doing?"

She held up a book and removed her glasses. "Catching up on my reading. I brought a stack of books a mile high." Closing the book, she avoided looking at him.

"Ellie, I'm—"

"Help! Where is everyone?"

Ellie and Mark bounded out of the ward room and into the front. "What's going on?" Ellie asked.

A counselor and a young male camper were in the front room. The boy was covered in scrapes and scratches. Blood dripped from multiple lacerations on his face, neck, arms and hands.

"What in the world happened to you?" Mark asked, grabbing two pairs of gloves and handing Ellie one.

"A tree happened," the counselor said with a quick glare at the boy.

"What's your name?" Mark asked and motioned for the boy to be seated on the exam table.

"Kevin." Holding onto his left wrist, he climbed onto the table with some assistance from his counselor.

"I'm Scott," the counselor said.

"So how did a tree happen to you, Kevin?" Mark asked and applied a stethoscope to the boy's lungs, looking for more serious injuries than what was already obvious.

"I was climbing and fell out."

"Right into a patch of blackberry bushes," the counselor said and shook his head.

"Ouch. That must have hurt. Why don't I start cleaning up the scrapes?" Ellie suggested. Her heart rate had jumped at first, but it settled down now that the injuries seemed benign. "So what's with the arm? Is it hurting?" she asked. Behind the red cheeks, he had a bit of pallor that made her wonder whether his arm was broken. The way he cradled it was also a classic sign of injury.

"It hurts. Hit it on a branch on the way down and the ground, too."

"Double ouch," Mark said and reached out to touch the injury gently. "Can you make a fist?" he asked and went through the examination with a tender touch.

Kevin winced and tried to pull away. "Ow."

"There's swelling already in his fingers," Ellie said

and began cleaning up the scratches with gauze soaked in normal saline.

"I see that." Mark sighed. "You're probably going to need to go to town for some X-rays, Kevin."

"Oh, man," he said, his voice whining. "My mom is going to kill me."

Ellie laughed at that. "I doubt it. But we will have to call her and let her know what's going on."

"Do you have to? I just got the cast off of my other arm three weeks ago."

"What happened to that arm?" Mark asked with a grin.

A red flush covered Kevin's face and neck, and he dropped his gaze. "I fell out of a tree in the backyard."

"You're going to have to start climbing shorter trees," Ellie said.

Mark laughed and Ellie felt the first stirrings of attraction at the sound. The man had a wonderful laugh. Even though he was engaging with people, she sensed a deep sadness within him. Maybe she was wrong, or maybe it was some nursing instinct firing to life, but that was what she felt.

"Ellie, can you handle things here while I take him in for X-rays?" Mark asked. "I don't think we need an ambulance for this."

"Sure," she said. "Not much else going on right now. Just the clinic after dinner. I'll call his mom and let her know what's going on. Otherwise, if anything serious comes up I can call you on your cell phone."

"Sounds good." He let his eyes linger on her face and mouth a moment before Ellie had to look away. Wow, the man was intense, and something in her was responding to his intensity, his energy, the vibrancy of the man. This was something she hadn't expected of her summer as a camp nurse.

"Come on, kiddo. We're going to town," Mark said. "Scott, want to come along, too?"

"I wish. I hear they have a great pizza joint in town, but I have to round up the rest of the group before they're all in the trees, too."

"Go ahead. We'll take it from here," Mark said, and Scott headed back to his group. "Pizza?" He looked down at Kevin. "You like pizza?"

"Is that a trick question? We have them in school sometimes."

"No. It's not a trick question. I should know every kid likes pizza, don't they? After X-rays we'll stop for some." Mark took a cloth sling from the supplies and fitted it to Kevin's arm, keeping the wrist higher than the elbow.

"Here's a couple of ice packs, too," Ellie and handed Mark a plastic bag filled with ice cubes. She placed another one inside the sling on top of Kevin's wrist.

"Great." They moved toward the door. "Anything you need from town?" he asked.

"Nope. We're good on everything still."

"Okay, see you in a few hours, depending on how many people are ahead of us in the ER."

With a nod, Mark and Kevin left the infirmary, and it suddenly felt too quiet and too empty. Ellie took off her gloves and cleaned up the supplies she had used, then made a quick call to Gil, then a lengthier one to Kevin's mom. Returning to her book on the ward bed, she tried to focus again on the story unfolding between the pages, but she couldn't concentrate on the characters and found herself rereading the same passage several times. Her eyes drifted down, then sprang open again as she fought off the urge to sleep.

Maybe it was too hot in here, she thought and got up to turn on the air conditioner. Maybe she needed some iced tea. A little cool air and cold caffeine should wake her up. After going to the small kitchen and fixing herself some refreshment, she returned to the ward room, but her book no longer held the appeal she'd anticipated.

What she needed was distraction from her thoughts, from thinking about Mark and that last, long, hungry look he'd given her. An involuntary shiver made her tremble, and she pressed the glass of cool tea to her cheek. No man had looked at her like that in a long, long time. Certainly, Alan never had. Maybe it was just her vanity perking up after months adrift at sea.

Something about him appealed to her. But she'd promised herself a rest for the summer, to regroup, to find where she wanted to go beginning in September. Most people thought of spring as a time of renewal, just coming out of long winters, but to her, fall was her time of refreshment and growth. The weather and season changed, kids started back to school and life seemed to have a greater sense of movement for her than in the spring. She always felt stronger and more energized with cool mornings and warm afternoons.

She'd always wanted to see the famous New England autumnal change that she'd read and seen pictures of. It seemed as if the past few years she'd lived her life by reading about places instead of experiencing them.

Perhaps she could stay in Maine or the New England area to experience it firsthand this year. When the fall moved on, then maybe she could as well. Her father had left her a small nest egg that she'd yet to tap into. Until now, there was nothing that she'd really been interested in doing, just going to work. Staying over a week or two in the fall to enjoy the scenery seemed like a good use of her time and would hardly dent the money he'd left.

Returning the novel to her room, she pulled out an aromatherapy encyclopedia instead to read up on some of the new oils she wanted to try soon. Closing the book, she turned it over and looked at the front. Aromatherapy. Hmm. She loved this therapy. Maybe she could realize her dream of becoming a certified aromatherapist. The money her dad had left her would certainly fund such an endeavor. She'd look into that soon, too.

Hours passed with no word from Mark. Restless after the small clinic had wrapped up and no further emergencies had occurred, she tried to walk off her mood outside, but the mosquitoes got to her first, and she made a hasty retreat.

As darkness descended, she lunged onto the screened-in infirmary porch and shook her clothing to rid herself of any unwanted creatures. She was really going to have to remember that bug spray every time she left the building. Then she realized something was different in the infirmary. Something in the air. She sniffed.

Her footsteps hurried as she moved into the front room and her mouth began to salivate at the fragrance filling the air.

Pizza?

"Mark?" she called and looked around. Where was the man? More importantly, where was the food?

"In the kitchen."

Tossing her sweatshirt onto the back of a chair, she followed her nose to the small kitchen and gasped in surprise. "What's all this?" she asked, a bubble of warmth surging in her chest.

"It's called pizza," Mark said and turned with a glass of wine in each hand. "I hope you like red."

"I like anything called wine," she said and reached for the glass. "Oh, this smells fabulous."

"Sit down, and I'll tell you about Kevin. No sense in letting good pizza get cold."

Ellie sat in one chair and Mark in the other, around a small bistro-style table. Beneath the table, their knees rubbed, and they adjusted their positions. Reaching for a slice, Ellie bit into it. Moaning out loud, she chewed.

"I love a woman that isn't afraid to express herself about food." Mark watched her, grinning.

"I'm so sorry," she said and covered her mouth with her hand as she chewed. "I couldn't help it!" She sipped the wine that went perfectly with the pizza. "This is the most incredible pizza I've ever had, or I must be incredibly hungry. And I even had dinner."

"No. It's that good." Mark helped himself to a piece.

"So tell me what happened." Emily watched Mark as he spoke, his face animated, his story engaging.

"It's a break, but not bad. He's casted again." He shook his head. "Kevin reminds me of myself when I was a kid."

"How so?"

"Always getting into trouble in some way or another."

"You?" Ellie looked at him and tried to imagine the young version of him, but failed to see it. "Hard to imagine."

"Not if you talked to my mother. She said she kept her hair color just fine with the three girls, but when I came along, that's when things started to go gray."

Ellie laughed at that. "Was she serious?"

"She says so, but I'm not sure."

They talked a little more about Kevin's case and the plan for keeping him comfortable should the need arise for pain medication. "Should we bring him to the ward room for the night, or do you think he'll be okay in the cabin?"

"I told him that he could make that decision. He has ice packs, and I have a prescription for pain medicine should he need it. Elevation and ice are the best, but if he's anything like me, the cast won't keep him out of trouble, only delay it for a day or two."

"The voice of experience," she said and paused. Maybe it was the wine and the company, but at this moment, with nothing going on around them, she relaxed.

"More?" Mark asked and raised the bottle over her glass.

"Just a little. Red keeps me up at night if I drink too much."

"Then no more after this. Insomnia is no fun."

"Again, the voice of experience?"

"After residency hours, your system doesn't know if it's coming or going sometimes. Took a few years to get it straightened out, then being on call is no picnic, either."

"Is that why you came to camp for the summer? To get away from all that hospital grind?" she asked and watched as his green eyes clouded over. "I'm sorry. I've overstepped my boundaries with that question. I didn't mean to."

Mark reached across the small table and took her hand. "No. It's okay." He took a deep breath and sighed, wondering how much to tell her and decided there was no harm in giving her some information. "Being ill and the recovery took a lot out of me. I was hoping to recharge my batteries here over the summer."

"Have another slice of pizza," she said and slid the last one over to him.

"No can do. I'll explode if I have any more." He patted his stomach.

"Then I'll wrap it up for tomorrow. Maybe you can have it for your midmorning snack or something. That is if you like cold pizza." She reached for the last slice to wrap it up, but stopped when Mark's hand encircled her wrist.

CHAPTER SIX

"You're very sweet, do you know that?" he asked and wondered if she knew that was really true. Many women, especially caregivers, undervalued themselves and didn't even know it. They spent their energies on everyone else except themselves. His mother, his sisters—they were all like that. Not that it was his cause in life, but when he had an opportunity, he wanted to let the people in his life know they were valued.

A shadow crossed her face and puzzled brown eyes met his. This was one of the few times that she met his gaze full on and the effect on him was inspiring and arousing. Two feelings he'd not allowed himself to indulge in for a long time. But now, sitting across from Ellie on a hot summer night, having had a nice evening with her, part of him wanted to reconsider his vow not to be involved with anyone until his five years of being cancer free ended. Provided he was still living.

"What?" she whispered, her gaze locked on to his.

He didn't want to let go of the moment, but he knew he ought to. Taking a deep breath, he released her wrist and tried to return to the comfortable relationship he and Ellie had established. "Oh, nothing. Just wanted to let you know."

He stood and gathered the pizza box, folded it and put it in the trash bin.

"You know, earlier, you left pretty quickly. I hope I didn't say anything to disturb you," she said.

This time she stopped him and her touch on his skin was lightning. Unable to resist the magic in her touch, he paused and looked down at the sincerity in her expression. She cared about people. It was innate in her, something she probably didn't realize she had, and that was very hard to resist.

His vow forgotten for the moment, he didn't try.

Facing her in the small room, he paused. Her natural allure reached out to him almost as tangibly as her hand on his arm. Without taking another second to think about whether it was right or wrong, whether he should or shouldn't, his gaze dropped to her mouth, and he leaned in and kissed her.

Ellie parted her lips beneath his. Instinct made him pull her a little closer to him. The soft feel of a curvy woman leaning into his chest nearly robbed him of all good sense.

Desire vibrated through every cell in his body, but he had to step back. Ellie had been through enough pain recently. He didn't want to add to that. With reluctance, he eased back from her. "I'm sorry, Ellie. I shouldn't have done that."

"Yes, well." She stepped back from him and gave him a nervous glance. "We're both professionals. We won't let this affect our relationship, right?" Turning away, she pulled the box of foil from a drawer and wrapped the last slice of pizza.

"Really, it's my fault, my responsibility, and I apologize for acting inappropriately." Dammit. He should have controlled himself better than that. No matter how attractive Ellie was or how perfect the moment seemed between them, he needed more control that he obviously had.

"You sound like you regret touching me." Hurt flared in her eyes before she turned away from him.

"Quite the contrary." He stepped out of the tiny kitchen that suddenly became stifling. The space was too tight and he was too close to her for his comfort. "I'll say good-night, now."

"Good night, Mark," she whispered and watched as he made his way down the hall. Just what had he meant by that comment—"Quite the contrary"? Had that meant he'd enjoyed the way the electricity had flowed between them for a moment or two? It obviously hadn't been just her that had felt that little sizzle in the air before their lips met. She'd hadn't felt that level of attraction for a man in a long, long time. And now, she wasn't sure she wanted to feel it for the man who was her coworker on a temporary basis.

Perhaps he was right. Though there was definite attraction between them, acting on that attraction might not be the wisest move that either of them could make. She placed the pizza in the nearly empty refrigerator, corked the remainder of the wine and set it in a high cupboard, then washed the glasses.

After her few tasks, she surveyed the front room.

Sighing, she looked around for something else to clean up, but there was nothing. Already prepared for the morning clinic, she had nothing else to keep her occupied.

A few days passed as Ellie and Mark returned to their routine, but without the same level of comfort that there had been between them. Ellie tried to forget the feel of Mark's lips against hers, but at odd moments she'd remember and look up at him. Despite the illness he'd suffered, he was strong and masculine, and made her feel very feminine. No man had interested her much in the past year or more, and now, with Mark under the same roof as her every day, she wondered if it weren't a simple case of coveting thy neighbor, because he was close and handy to her. And she was definitely coveting.

After the lunch clinic ended and the kids found their afternoon activities, she and Mark occupied themselves in the infirmary. She sat at the table and worked on her e-mails. Mark produced some professional journals that he intended to read.

A sudden flurry of activity behind her made her turn. Mark ripped the trash bag from the metal trash can, took one of the clear liners, blew air into it and pulled it over his head.

"What are you doing?" she asked and gaped at him. "Are you out of your mind? Take that off!" Had he gone mad? Lunging toward him, she tried to rip the bag from his head. Goofing around with a glove to entertain the kids was one thing. He was going to suffocate himself with this trick.

"Call 911. Now!" His voice was oddly muffled inside

the bubble of the bag, but she understood. His energy was on high alert, and she stopped struggling with him. This just wasn't right.

"Are you ill? Why am I calling 911?" Confused, Ellie backed up a step, but she still had no idea what was going on.

He tied the ends of the bag beneath his chin. "Because I'm about to get attacked by mad hornets."

"What are you talking about?"

Mark pulled the fire extinguisher from the wall beside the door. "Just do it." Moving toward her, he pressed a quick kiss to her mouth through the bag. "Bring the emergency kit and every anaphylaxis kit you've got."

With that, he raced out the door, looking like a cartoon character dashing across the yard. Horrified, Ellie watched him go, and as her focus changed and narrowed to what he had seen, she exclaimed, "Mark!" and grabbed the phone, terror filling her, and dialed the emergency number. "Oh, God."

During the quick call, Ellie couldn't keep her gaze from the scene unfolding across the compound. Mark raced toward what she hadn't seen at first. The air was dark with it.

A huge swarm of insects. Someone was fighting for their life in the middle of it.

Mark charged right into the fray, at the risk to his own life, spraying the stinging insects with the extinguisher, trying to create some relief from the attack. Shouts and screams filled the air as others noticed the situation, and Ellie's nervous system knotted up. Counselors and campers filled the area, but the adults ushered the children away from the scene, thankfully preventing injury to anyone else.

The emergency pack was in her hand before she was aware of it and, heart wild in her chest, she raced out the door behind Mark, totally uncertain as to what to do, how to respond to this emergency. People died every year from a single sting. How someone could survive such an attack, she didn't know.

Prayers and whispers of safety ran through her mind. This was her worst nightmare come to life. Nothing in her experience had ever prepared her for this. Nearly breathless, she stopped just yards away from them as the white puffs from the fire extinguisher filled the air.

Ellie dropped the equipment and screamed, "Mark!"

As he fell to his knees, he continued to spray the fire extinguisher until it fizzled out empty. By then, the hornets, or whatever they were, seemed to have dispersed to a few confused individuals that posed no further threat.

Mark ripped a hole in the bag and tore it off of his head. He hauled in great gasping breaths, then barked out a few wheezing coughs. She hurried over to him and placed a hand on his back. "Are you okay?"

"Check…him…first," Mark said, panting to catch his breath.

She heard the wheezes as he struggled for breath. But with the injuries to the other person unknown, she had to do as he instructed. Mark was at least breathing. The bees appeared to have dissipated with the majority killed or dying from the effects of the extinguisher.

Skinny, however, lay in a heap on the ground, dead hornets all over his back.

"Skinny?" She called his name and flicked away the dead insects so that she could turn him over. "Skinny, can you hear me?" She struggled to turn the thin man over and found Mark's trembling hands, covered with welts and stings, there to assist her.

"What in the Sam Hill is going on here?" Bear yelled as he charged toward them. "Oh, my Lord!"

"There's been a hornet attack, Bear. Skinny and Mark are hurt." She took a deep breath and choked down the tears that wanted to threaten. She had to help them, and she couldn't be afraid. If Mark collapsed, too, she'd be the only one left to care for both of them. "Let's move him away from here. I'll take his legs—"

"I'll get his shoulders," Bear said and tucked his hands under the injured man's arms. Skinny was unresponsive and his head fell to the side. In seconds they had moved him away from the attack area and placed him on the ground again.

"We need help right now." Despite trembling hands, she tore open the packages of two Epi-kits, and put them together. "Talk to him, Bear. He'll know your voice. Just talk to him."

Bear muttered in a gentle voice, one she'd never heard before, as his brawny hands brushed the hornet carcasses off of Skinny's chest and neck. Eyes, nose and mouth already swollen to an extreme, the man was unrecognizable. He was in *very* serious condition. Ellie pulled back the syringe and plunged it into his thigh, administering the lifesaving medication.

"Give him another one," Mark whispered, his voice strained. "He's gonna need it. Get the oxygen on him, then give me an injection." Though raspy from exertion, Mark's voice was almost normal again.

Without a word, Ellie administered a second syringe into Skinny's other leg. "Bear, can you rub those spots while I get the oxygen?" Nodding, Bear complied. In seconds she had a mask connected to the transport oxygen tank and cranked it up high. She placed the mask on Skinny's face, and Bear held it tight.

Turning to Mark, she winced, but tried to control her reaction.

"That bad, am I?" he asked, but the attempt at humor fell flat.

"Let me give you this, then you have to check Skinny. He's not looking good." She quickly gave Mark the shot in his left thigh and turned back to Skinny.

"Is he breathing?" Mark asked and rubbed the injection site on his thigh.

"Yes, he's got a major stridor though." The swelling of the airway caused the high-pitched crowing sound that was unmistakable in a respiratory emergency. Ellie shook her head, willing the epinephrine to start working, to start counteracting the body's natural reaction to the stings.

"Jake!" Bear called to one of the assistant cooks that stood nearby. "Go show the paramedics over here." With a nod, he ran to the entrance.

Mark crawled on his hands and knees over to Skinny's head and took over holding the oxygen mask from Bear's hands. Mark attached the ambu bag and tried to force extra oxygen through to Skinny's lungs.

"His airway's constricting already. He's really tight." Mark shook his head and clenched his jaw together. "I don't know if this is going to work."

"If he loses his airway completely, we're going to have a problem." Ellie hated to say it, but the man could certainly die right in front of them, no matter what they did. "Can you do an emergency trach if needed?" Sometimes cutting a hole in someone's throat was the only way to save a life.

"Yes, but I'd rather not have to." Mark removed the oxygen mask for a second and opened Skinny's mouth to place an oral airway. It would assist in keeping his throat open despite the swelling. "Dammit. I thought this might have happened." He extracted several dead hornets from Skinny's mouth, then placed the plastic airway and applied the oxygen mask again.

"There was one in his mouth?" Ellie asked with revulsion and shivered.

"Several. I'm certain he has multiple stings inside his mouth and on his tongue. That's why his breathing was affected so quickly."

"Oh, dear."

"Can you use your purple stuff on him?" Bear asked, his eyes filled with worry and concern for his friend, aware of the gravity of this situation. He held out his hand. "Fixed me up right quick on my burn. Can you use it on him?"

"My what?" she asked without looking up from her task, trying to get an IV into Skinny's hand. They needed IV access, and they needed it now. In the next second she had one in and taped it down.

"The folk medicine. The purple stuff you used on my burn."

"Purple stuff?" Then the light bulb in her brain went on. "Oh, the lavender oil!" Ellie glanced up at Mark, and he nodded.

"I'll bag him. Go get your purple stuff."

CHAPTER SEVEN

ELLIE raced the few yards to the infirmary and returned in minutes with her kit of essential oils. Fumbling with the zipper as the paramedics arrived, she sat the kit on the ground and pulled out the lavender oil.

Mark spoke to the rescue crew as Ellie dabbed the oil onto the stings on Skinny's face and throat, not knowing if it would truly help the emergent situation, but it certainly couldn't hurt. The rest of the stings could wait. His condition was too serious to mess around with. If he survived this attack, she could treat the welts later.

"Damned hornets. They keep on stinging. They just don't die like a honeybee," Bear said, anger sparking from his eyes. "He should never have been out here."

"What was he doing?" Mark asked and continued to bag Skinny.

"He was looking for fiddlehead ferns that grow here every summer. Since the fire two years ago, we weren't sure whether they'd come back like usual, and I just mentioned that I had a taste for some. Musta kicked into a ground hornets' nest." Bear shook his head. "They're nasty."

"Let's get him loaded." Bert, the paramedic, said and took over bagging Skinny. They headed off to the local hospital with him.

"Bear, why don't you follow along?" Ellie suggested and gathered the equipment, her heart still not back to normal, the trembling in her hands not finished yet.

"I got dinner to get going," he said, but his gaze followed the ambulance out of the camp.

"Give your instructions to one of your other cooks. I'm sure they'll want to know someone's with Skinny and everyone will feel better if you're there with him."

Bear gave her a look with his dark eyes and nodded. "You're right. They'll do better with something to keep their hands occupied." He placed his on Ellie's shoulder and gave her a squeeze. "Thanks." With that, he picked up Skinny's hat and moved off to the lodge.

Ellie turned to Mark. "Let me see to you now, please?"

"I'm going to be okay. I can feel the jitters from the epinephrine." Stooping, he picked up the fire extinguisher. "Gonna need another one of these for the infirmary."

"Later. Why don't you go shower, and I'll get the rest of this stuff?"

"Here, we can help," Gil said and stepped forward. "We'll get this stuff picked up. Ellie, take him to the infirmary. Then I'm going to call an exterminator to make sure these things are gone for good."

Stiff and sore, Mark walked toward the infirmary building. Ellie approached his side and offered an arm of support around his waist. "Are you sure you're okay? I think you ought to go to the hospital and get checked out, too. I'm concerned about the amount of stings you've gotten, even though they aren't on your face or neck."

"You can take care of me." Unable to find the strength or desire to resist, he put his arm around her shoulders and gave her a little of his weight. Leaning on someone was not something he'd wanted to do and hadn't done in a long time. Not since his illness. But now, leaning on Ellie, having her lithe body giving him some of her strength, was just what he needed. Tremors rattled through him, and it wasn't just the effects of the epinephrine. He was exhausted from the outrageous amount of energy he'd exerted.

Reaching ahead of them, Ellie pulled the squeaky screen door open, and they entered. Guiding them straight to the bathroom, Ellie eased him onto the edge of the tub. With one hand balancing him, she turned on the taps with her other hand. "A cool bath with baking soda will help the stinging some, too. Can you manage while I get the baking soda?"

"I think so," he said. But he really wasn't sure he could get into the tub without disgracing himself or landing on his head. He hadn't needed help to undress or bathe since the end of his treatments. Returning to that state of helplessness was somewhat humiliating, but at this point, he was too tired to care. "Why don't you call the lodge and ask someone to bring it over?"

"You're right. I shouldn't leave you alone right now."

"That's not what I—" he started, but she had charged out the door. ICU nurse with a mission all the way. He smiled. But he supposed that was why she was as successful, and as fatigued, as she was.

God, he hurt. He felt as if someone had taken a hammer and beaten him with it. Each sting site throbbed laser beams through his body. His injuries were nothing like Skinny's though, and he couldn't imagine how much pain the man had been in. Reaching behind his head, he grabbed hold of the neck of his T-shirt and dragged it off over his head. Then he put a foot up on the toilet seat and untied one shoe, then the other.

A soft knock on the door interrupted him. "Mark? Are you in the tub? I have the baking soda. Do you want me to hand it to you or put it in the tub for you?"

"I think you're going to have to help."

Ellie pushed the door open and entered the room.

Sweat broke out on his forehead and chest and a chill soon followed it. Not good.

Ellie pressed her hand to his forehead and gave a small gasp. "You're hot."

"Cold, too." Taking a deep breath, he struggled to maintain his control. "Get me a couple of Benadryl, Tylenol and a shot of whiskey."

"Okay. I get the meds, but what will the whiskey do?"

"Settle my nerves or intoxicate me. I'm not sure which at this point." And right now, he didn't much care.

"I have something better than that. Let's just get you into the tub first, then I'll get the meds."

Mark let out a long sigh. "This wasn't how I had planned to spend the afternoon."

"I know. Me, either. How about you just let someone help you for a change, eh? As medical people, we're really bad about letting others help us, aren't we?" She continued speaking in a soothing voice as she helped him to undress. Grabbing a towel hanging on the rack, she covered his waist. "Let's maintain some privacy and cover your...stuff." Averting her gaze, Ellie blushed prettily, and Mark smiled at that.

"Sure. Like you haven't seen a man's stuff before." He was certain the towel was more for her modesty than his.

"True. Just not *your* stuff. And if we're going to work together the rest of the summer without being uncomfortable around each other, it's better this way."

"Agreed." Easing into the tub was no simple task while keeping the towel intact. "I feel like someone beat me up after pulling an all-nighter."

"You look like it, too." Leaning over him as she helped him ease down into the water, her clean fragrance and the scent of lavender passed over him. Unable to enjoy it due to the next wave of chill that hit him, he regretted that he was not in the tub with her under different circumstances. Any intimacy in his life was a distant memory. He didn't know about Ellie's love life. Unfortunately, the pain of the stings took his mind from going that direction at the moment.

"I can't believe what you just did," Ellie said and knelt beside the tub, shaking her head. "I've never seen anything like it." She dumped the entire box of baking soda into the tub and turned off the taps. With her hand, she swirled the powder so that it dispersed in the water. "Have you ever done anything like that before?"

Mark looked into her eyes as she paused. Something brief and electric passed between them before she dropped her gaze and picked up a wash-cloth. "No. I don't normally go out of my way to commit heroic acts."

"Yet you just grabbed the fire extinguisher and ran."

"I did something else first," he said, wishing he had the courage to try it again. Looking at her so close, maybe he did.

"Well, sure. You had to protect yourself with the bag over your head. It was a brilliant idea." She gave a nervous snort and her amused gaze met and held his. "I wasn't sure what you were doing at first though."

Mark raised his hand from the water, cupped the back of her neck and pulled her closer. "I meant this." And he kissed her. With her off balance in a kneeling position, he had no trouble pulling her the rest of the way to meet his mouth. Entirely too long had passed since he'd really kissed a woman, and he hungered for Ellie now. Her sweetness, her caring—everything about her pulled him in. For a moment, he needed to be just a man, in a tub, with a woman.

Soft and pliant, she opened her mouth to his. She reached across him and braced a hand on the other side of the tub. Imprisoning her face between his wet hands, he breathed in her scent, her warmth, and plundered her mouth with his lips and tongue. She tasted so sweet, felt so tender. Passion as he hadn't experienced since his illness filled him. He was in danger of revealing too much of himself physically and emotionally in the kiss. He eased back from her before he lost all control of the situation, and he was suddenly grateful for the position of the towel. His stuff had come to life.

Startled brown eyes peered at him. "Wow. What was that for?"

Smiling, he pressed his forehead to hers and caught his breath. "Because you're sweet, and I wanted to see if I remembered right."

"Right about what?" Returning to her previous position kneeling by the tub, she created some space between them.

"That your mouth was as soft as I remembered. I couldn't tell through the plastic bag." Was he out of his mind even contemplating getting involved with a woman, even on a temporary basis? A shiver claimed his attention away from making any decisions at the moment.

"You shouldn't be trying to jog your memory right now. Not when you're in this condition." She returned to nurse mode and placed the washcloth in his hand. "Keep washing this over you, and I'll go get those meds."

The phone in the main room rang, and she hurried out to answer it.

Amazingly enough, the baking soda trick seemed to be doing the job. The pain of the stings had begun to ease. He'd have to look more closely at home remedies for the simple things in the future. Minutes later, a gentle knock at the door announced Ellie's return.

"I've got the meds and some water." She handed him the items and sat on the floor beside the tub. "Are you doing any better?"

After downing the pills, he closed his eyes and leaned his head back against the tub. "Yeah. Your remedy is working."

"I'm sure the medications will, too, but when you're out of the tub I'd like to use some oils on you."

"Sounds interesting. The purple oil or what?" He opened his eyes to slits to watch her. At the moment, that's all the exertion he could cope with.

"Yeah, the purple oil." She raised a large amber bottle of whiskey. "If you take this with the Benadryl, you'll probably fall asleep."

"Sounds okay to me." Although he hoped he hadn't made her uncomfortable with the kiss, he didn't regret it, either. Her lips were as soft as they appeared to be, and he liked the feel of them against his. "Why don't I get out, get some clothes on and then you can do the purple oil?"

"It's actually lavender oil."

"I know, but men only recognize primary colors."

"What?" Confusion appeared on her face. "That's not true."

"If you ask a man what color something is, he generally will tell you one of the primary colors. If you ask a woman what color something is, you're likely to get a description of something else, like lavender, or fuchsia, or chartreuse. I don't even know what color chartreuse is."

Ellie laughed, and the sound filled him with joy. This was the first time he'd heard such unadulterated laughter from her, and it was a good sound.

"That's absurd. Men see in more than primary colors—they simply refuse to acknowledge it."

"Not in my world, babe."

"That's so lame." She stood. "Anyway, can you get out and dressed by yourself?"

"Yeah. Just leave me a clean towel, and I'll make it."

Weakness hadn't gotten him through all of the ordeals he'd suffered in the past few years. Leaning on Ellie for a moment had been nice, but he had to find his own inner strength again to finish the job.

"Okay. Just call if you need me." Rising, she moved away from him toward the door, then paused. "By the way, that was the hospital, and they're keeping Skinny in the ICU overnight. He's being intubated as a precaution due to the amount of stings he had on his throat and head, but he's at least responding well to treatment."

"Good to hear."

"Okay. I'll leave you to it."

Ellie left the bathroom and busied herself restocking the emergency kit and tried not to think of what had happened in the bathroom. The kiss.

Mark had *kissed* her. Again!

Why had he kissed her?

Why had *she* kissed him back?

Why was her heart *still* unsteady?

It wasn't as if she hadn't been kissed before. She certainly had. Mark had also given her a tiny kiss after pizza the other night. This kiss had taken her breath away, and she'd felt it to the bottom of her toes.

The door to the bathroom opened, and she heard Mark slowly move down the hall to his room. She'd better get the oils ready. Fumbling with unzipping the pack she kept her oils in, she pulled out her favorite healing ones—rosemary, grapefruit and lavender. The grape-seed oil was in another bottle that nearly slipped from her fingers.

Come on, Ellie. You're a nurse. There's nothing special going on between you and Mark. You're just going to treat his injuries and go on with your life, right? Right. But the second that he entered the treatment room with her, she knew her little pep talk was a complete farce. She swallowed down the lump of desire that wanted to crawl up her throat.

Relying on her professional demeanor had gotten her through many difficult situations in the past, and she clung to it now as the only lifeline in the vicinity. "Moving kinda slow, huh?" She held out a chair and indicated he should sit.

"Being a human pincushion will do that to a man," he said and eased into the chair. "So what are you going to do?"

"I thought I'd start at the top, and work my way down. The first application of oils will be lavender, directly applied to the skin, then I'll do a mixture of a few others with some grape-seed oil." She stood upright, explaining the procedure as if he were a patient. There was no harm in that. Treat him just like everyone else.

"I see. Come a little closer, please." He motioned her forward.

CHAPTER EIGHT

COMPLYING, she picked up her bottle of lavender and moved closer. "Ready to get started?"

Without answering her, he reached out and clasped her behind the neck, pulled her closer and gave her a hard kiss.

Again! "What's with the kissing today?" Not that she didn't like kisses, but something was going on.

"I'm going to do that every time you hide." Green eyes bored into hers, challenged her.

"I'm not hiding," she denied and pulled away from him, gripping the bottle of oil tight in her fist. Seething anger burst through her.

"You are. You've got to be more than your job, or life is going to go flashing right by you. Since we've been here, I've only heard you laugh spontaneously once or twice, and rarely seen you do something just for fun, other than read, and you usually read aromatherapy books." He watched her, his playful mood giving way to a more serious undercurrent. "Why not relax a little, give yourself a break from whatever's bugging you?"

"Nothing's bugging me," she said and tried to find a way to deny the truth in his observations, but couldn't.

"Yeah, right. Ellie, every time something comes up where there's an opportunity to share of yourself or jump into an event with the others, you run the other direction."

She gasped, horrified. "I'm a Mackenzie. I don't *run* from anything."

"I know you value your privacy, but if something's bothering you, I can listen. I can be a sounding board if you need a problem solved."

"I don't have any problems." No, they'd all gone away when her fiancé had left her, and her dad had died. At least, that's what she kept telling herself.

"Ellie, we all have problems."

"Like you know anything about that." Highly irritated without a logical good reason why, she faced him. She opened the bottle and released the lavender fragrance into the room. "I'm sure everything came easily to you, didn't it? Probably went to an Ivy League undergrad school, took European vacations, sailed through medical school, didn't you?" She avoided his gaze and concentrated on dabbing the oil on her fingers, then applying it to the red welts on his shoulders and arms. "Despite the recent illness you mentioned, I'm sure your life has been a piece of cake compared to what I've been through in the past few years. You're too damned happy for it to have been otherwise, so don't tell me about watching life pass you by when you hardly know what it's like, Dr. Perfect." She said it as if it was a character flaw. Why, she didn't know, and didn't want to think about the knot in her gut as the words came out of her mouth. That was so unlike her, so totally uncharitable, but something snapped in her. "You have no idea what it's like to suffer."

He didn't deny or confirm her observations. Mark grabbed her hand and stopped her from her task, holding onto her until she looked at him.

Finally, she met his gaze, nearly trembling with emotion that she had denied lived in her. "What?"

"There's one more thing I am."

"What, football captain? Rugby captain? Debate team captain?" She meant to hurt him. She couldn't stop herself from doing it. The intensity, the look, in his eyes was what stopped her, and she paused in her emotional tirade.

"Cancer survivor."

The shock of his statement nearly drove her to her knees. "What?" she whispered and clutched his hand, despair and humiliation washing through her. Oh, God, she was so stupid.

"I'm a cancer survivor," he said and released her hand. "So I *do* know what it's like to see your life passing you by. Every damned day." His voice was gruff, and he closed his eyes for a moment.

Tears filled her eyes, pain for him shot through her and she closed her eyes to hide her shame. "I'm so sorry, Mark. I didn't know." She knelt beside him and sat back on her heels, her head lowered. "I don't know what's coming out of my mouth sometimes." She covered her face with her hands, unable to look up at him and see the hurt in his face that she had caused. "I'm sorry. It goes against everything that I am to be this way. I just didn't know."

"I know you didn't know. I asked Vicki and Sam not to tell you."

The sound of his soft voice, the forgiveness already there, made her want to weep, and she looked up at him, seeing the strength he'd had to find in himself. Reaching out, he eased her hands away from her face, then drew a line with one finger down her cheek.

"But why? I would never have said those things had I known." Tears leaked from the outer corners of her eyes, and she tried to brush them away on her shoulders.

"So you wouldn't treat me like a patient. Since surviving, I find that when people know of my history ahead of time they treat me differently than people who don't know." He shrugged and brushed away another tear with his thumb. "To them, I'm just a regular guy, and I like it that way."

Biting her lip, she hesitated, then blew out a long breath as she gathered her courage. "I'm sorry, Mark. Can I ask how you are doing now?"

"Yeah. I'm about three years out from the last clean CAT scan." He patted her hand and urged her up from her kneeling position. "Keep going with the oil. It feels good."

"Okay." Now, she would do anything to make him feel better, even if it was only a small physical comfort. She could never make up for the harsh words she'd spoken, but she could sooth his troubled flesh. She stood and continued to dab and apply the oil to the multitude of welts across his back, chest, arms and legs. "Thankfully, you were smart enough to do the bag trick. I don't know what would have happened to you had you been more exposed. Those little beasties are evil."

"No. I'm sure they were just protecting their nest. Some hornets nest in the ground, and Skinny may have simply stepped on one." He sighed and his eyes drooped a little.

"After I dose you up, I'd like to call the hospital and check on him again. Check on Bear, too."

"Sounds good." Mark stifled a huge yawn. "Wow. Looks like the Benadryl is kicking in."

"Didn't even need the whiskey. Why don't you go lie down in the ward room, and I can finish applying the rest of the oils to your legs and back there?"

Nodding, Mark stood and moved to the ward room and crawled facedown onto the nearest bed. "Man, I'm tired."

"It's been quite a day, hasn't it?" she asked.

Chuckling into the pillow, he then turned his head to the side. "Understatement of the year, I think."

"Between the meds and the oils, I think you're going to pass out here in a few minutes."

Another yawn claimed him, and he nodded. "Your powers of observation are astute."

"That's why they pay me the big bucks. One of the best skills a nurse can have is observation." Glad to see that he was truly feeling better and not upset about her comments, a warm glow began in her chest. Her touch and the oils were going to finish the job in just a few moments.

His words—*cancer survivor*—echoed in her mind. He knew what it was to suffer, and he'd survived. There was no greater achievement in her eyes.

Mark allowed sleep to claim him. Undeterred by his lack of consciousness, Ellie continued to minister to his wounds. Actually, now that he was asleep, she felt freer to explore his body with her hands, to satisfy her need to touch him, to soothe him and to bring him a comfort that she wouldn't have been able to do otherwise. After the lavender, she poured her special mix of healing oils into the palm of one hand, then rubbed her hands together to warm the oil. Starting at his feet hanging over the edge of the bunk, she took her time and rubbed the oil into his skin, noting old scars here and there from minor injuries. She saw no surgical scars and concluded that they must be on his abdomen, and she'd simply missed them. Astute observation skills, eh?

His skin quickly absorbed the healing oils, and she moved upward over his calves, thighs, then his back and arms. Each touch, each stroke of her hand, she infused with her own healing energy that she hoped would bring him comfort.

"Ellie, you ought to consider massage therapy," Mark mumbled. "This is incredible."

She bit back the startled gasp that wanted to escape. "I thought you were asleep." She'd hoped he'd been asleep and hadn't heard her words of whispered sympathy.

"I'm kind of in a waking coma right now."

She smiled at that, knowing exactly how that felt after an aromatherapy treatment. Stress was nowhere to be found at that point. "Turn over, and I'll do the welts on the front."

"I'm not sure if I can move." But he turned slowly and collapsed onto his back. With a sigh of contentment, he closed his eyes again. "Go to work, Nurse."

"Yes, Doctor." She poured and warmed more oil and started again at his feet, working her way up. Though underweight a little, he had a beautiful body, and his muscles were toned and well formed. As she reached the top of his chest and neck, she found that her hands trembled as she stroked his skin. He opened his eyes, and she caught her breath at the heat in his gaze. Yet he didn't move. He waited for her.

Her mouth went dry, and she tried to swallow. Unable to look away from the need in his gaze, she froze. She hadn't allowed a man into her life for a long time. She'd been too caught up in helping her parents with her father's illness. Not that she hadn't dated on occasion, but Mark was right. She'd been watching life pass her by, and she hadn't even been aware of it. Did she dare try to stop and savor the moment presented to her right now?

Dropping her gaze to his mouth, some feminine instinct parted her lips. "Mark?" She didn't know what she was asking him. The question wasn't clear in her mind, and she didn't know how to translate that to him.

"Yes." He swallowed and raised his hands to cup her neck, drawing her slightly toward him. "Whatever it is, the answer is yes."

Unable to resist the draw of him, the pull of her heart toward him, she let herself go, and lowered her mouth to his. Though he'd kissed her earlier, this contact was completely different. This was need like she'd never known and it drew on her own suppressed needs.

He devoured her. Parting her unresisting lips, he drew her tongue into his mouth. Unable to suppress the heat of desire that gripped her, the glide of his tongue against hers tightened the knot in her stomach. Lord, the man knew how to kiss. Tremors that started somewhere in her middle spread through her body. Turning her head to the side, she parted her lips more and gave herself to Mark's heat.

Struggling to control the reaction of his body, Mark dragged Ellie against his chest and groaned. The feel of her weight against him, the taste of her sweetness and the fragrances mingling between them drew on every sense he had. For the moment, time ceased to move.

Ellie relaxed against him, and he savored every movement she made. She was lovely and caring, and he wanted to know her more than he'd suspected when they'd met. After thoroughly exploring her mouth, he released her and eased her upright.

She took in deep breaths, as did he. With one hand, he brushed her bangs back from her face. He liked her face and the animation she allowed to show now and then. There were mysteries and secrets hidden inside Ellie, and he wanted to discover what they were.

"Wow." She sat on the edge of the bunk beside him, and he was pleased that she didn't move away. One of her hands rested on his chest, and he liked the contact.

"Wow is right," he said. There was spark and chemistry between them, but he knew it took more than that to have a relationship that meant something. "Another surprise in a day full of them."

"Yes. Well." She glanced away, the movements of her hands busy and nervous now. "I have evening clinic in a little while. Dinner's in a few minutes, but I'm sure you'd rather stay here and rest." Reaching behind him, she straightened his pillow, and avoided his gaze. Back to nurse mode again. "I'll see if Bear can make a tray for you."

"Just a sandwich or two will work. Don't go to much trouble. I'll probably just sleep an hour or two."

Nodding, she rose, but he took her hand before she could get too far away. The medications and the events of the day were taking their toll on him, and he struggled to stay awake. "Will you stay with me tonight? In the ward room, I mean?"

"Yes. I'll stay." She brushed her hand over his face. "Go to sleep for a while now though. I'll be back in a bit." She moved to the foot of the bed and pulled a sheet up over him, then untucked it at the bottom. Leaning over, she kissed his forehead, then left the room.

A few hours later, after dinner and the clinic, Ellie reentered the ward room. Mark had adjusted his position and lay more on his right side, facing the doorway. His breathing came slow and deep, and she hoped the sleep was restorative for him.

Easing a bed closer to his, she tried to make as little noise as possible, but the feet of the bunk screeched across the wooden floor. "Darn it," she whispered.

Mark shifted and opened his eyes a crack. "Hi."

"Hi. I'm sorry I woke you." She leaned over and touched the back of her hand to his neck, then his forehead. He felt okay. "How are you doing? Did the sleep help?"

"Yeah. Yeah." He stretched and then took her hand. "What time is it?"

"About ten."

"I've slept for six hours?" he asked, his voice husky with sleep.

"Yeah."

"And you let me, didn't you?"

"Yeah, I did. You needed it. I'm still having waking nightmares about hornets, and I'm frankly not sure I'll be able to sleep tonight." She shivered.

"Don't worry. It's over, and everyone's okay." Mark rose and scrubbed his face with his hands. "I'll be back in a few." He allowed his fingers to trail down her arm as he left the room. Returning in a few minutes, he had foraged in the kitchen and found the sandwiches that Bear had sent, and a two-liter bottle of soda.

Ellie settled down on her bunk with one of her books and watched as Mark plowed through the food and downed the entire bottle of soda.

"That was fast. Are you going to need an antacid now?" she asked and parked her reading glasses on her nose, then turned on her book light.

"Nope. There are times when my appetite goes from zero to ravenous in a nanosecond, and this was one of those times. My metabolism kicks into overdrive." He patted his stomach and lay back on the bed; a contented sigh rolled out of him.

Though he had kissed her a couple of times, and she had offered him the comfort of her touch and healing oils, she didn't quite know what was really going on between them. Though they lived and worked together, she really couldn't say they were dating, and he'd not yet asked her out. This was a strange situation. Focusing on her book, she tried to see the print in front of her, but she'd read the same passage three times already and sighed, trying to remember what oil went with what.

"What are you thinking so hard about over there?" Mark asked.

Ellie looked up. Mark hadn't changed positions and remained with his eyes closed. "What makes you think I'm thinking hard about something?" she asked.

"I know the sounds of a female with something on her mind," he said and opened his eyes to peer at her in the near dark. "I grew up with three sisters. I know how the female mind operates."

"Ha," she said and snapped her book closed. "Did your sisters ever tell you that?" Secretly she smiled, but kept her face neutral.

"Hardly. They're too sneaky for that." Turning onto his side, he faced her and she put her book down. "Is there something you want to talk about?"

"Aside from hornets?"

"Aside from hornets." The bunks were just inches apart and he reached out to take her hand.

Looking down at the way their fingers intertwined, she wondered if that was how people's lives intersected. So far she'd been too preoccupied with school, work and helping her parents that she hadn't been entwined with anyone since Alan. Had she gone too far to be able to find her way back? To be able to truly reach out for another and risk getting hurt? "I'm sorry, Mark. I should go back to my room. I don't want to keep you up."

"No, you shouldn't. I'd like you to stay with me here tonight. Will you?" He squeezed her hand, and his eyes drifted down again. The effects of the medications and the stings still remained in his system. She thought of offering him another aromatherapy treatment, but decided that sleep would probably be the best thing for him.

"I will."

He brought her hand to his mouth and kissed her knuckles. What a sweet gesture. She closed her eyes and listened to him breathing. The sound comforted her in a way she didn't know was possible. She extracted her hand from his grasp without waking him and covered him with a sheet.

In the darkness, she listened to the sounds of the night and wondered if she were already falling for a man she barely knew.

CHAPTER NINE

Ellie woke the next morning to find Mark already up, showered and ready for the clinic. The horrors of the previous day had been slow to leave her brain. Every noise in the ward room had startled her subconscious until the wee hours of the morning, preventing her from having a good sleep. A yawn, a stretch; she rose and staggered to the coffeepot in the kitchen. Filling a ceramic mug, she took it with her into the shower and let the water pound her brain awake.

Mark stood in the doorway of the kitchen as she left the bathroom. The way he looked at her made her breath pause. He was so vibrant and alive in that moment. The welts had faded to pink overnight, and she almost didn't notice them. Then he smiled, and her heart fluttered erratically in her chest. She knew that a man like Mark couldn't go for a woman like her. Not long-term. She was too shy, too focused on her work, too ordinary to really attract him. At least, that's what Alan had told her over and over. Sure, while she was right under Mark's nose he was interested, but the second their ways parted, she'd be just an addendum to his summer in Maine. And she didn't want that. Couldn't handle it. What she wanted, and what she needed, was what her parents had had together. She glanced at the photo of them on the worktable. She'd settle for nothing less than that.

"I called and checked on Skinny."

"Oh, how is he?" she asked and stepped forward, then paused as a small herd of about fifteen children roared into the infirmary.

"I'll tell you right after clinic," he said and looked at the group of kids. "Now who's first?"

All of them shouted, "Me!"

Despite waking up on the tired side, Ellie had to laugh. The sight of Mark surrounded by the squealing children all vying for his attention was something to see. His laughter overrode the noise of the kids. When he looked over their heads and his gaze locked on hers, something in her heart cramped. "I gotta go." Before she could give herself a chance to fall into the trap of his green, green eyes, she turned and fled to her room.

Frowning, Mark watched Ellie rush down the hall. "What was that about?" he mumbled aloud.

"Dr. Mark, I need my inhaler," one child said with an audible wheeze that captured his attention. "I'm Tommy Brooks."

"You sure do." Each child had a medication file of their own. Mark reached in to Tommy's file and extracted the requested rescue inhaler and shook it. "One puff, wait a few seconds, then the other, okay?"

"I know. I'm not a kid," Tommy said with a roll of his eyes.

"You're right. Go for it." Mark tried not to laugh at the expression on the boy's face.

Tommy raised the device to his mouth and administered the medication as instructed.

Mark finished the short morning clinic, then knocked on Ellie's door. "Are you okay?" he asked.

With a smile that looked artificial, she opened the door. The glance she darted at him didn't meet his gaze. "Sure. I'm fine. Just didn't sleep well last night."

"Did I snore or something?" he asked, hoping he hadn't talked in his sleep. Who knew what secrets a man could reveal under the influence of Benadryl and aromatherapy? Now he was glad he hadn't added the whiskey on top of that.

"No. It's okay." She left the room with her pack of aromatherapy bottles in her hand. "I think I'm going to do a treatment on myself. I'm still a little freaked out by yesterday." She looked up at him and her face brightened. "Oh, you said you had a report on Skinny."

"Yeah," Mark said and followed her to the common room. "He's off the ventilator, breathing well on his own and out of ICU. Should be out of the hospital in a day or two."

"That's great news. Does Bear know?"

"He's the one who told me. He must have been over at the hospital at dawn." Mark wanted to reach out and ease the vulnerability and skittishness that he saw in her today, but thought better of it. Maybe it was just having spent an ill night that made her so jumpy. He hoped so. He hoped that the intimacy of helping him yesterday hadn't interfered in their professional relationship or the friendship he was beginning to enjoy with her. Though he knew he couldn't truly reach out to her the way he would have wanted to had circumstances been different, something about her continued to attract him. Clenching his fists, he resisted the urge that tried to draw him closer to her.

"I'm glad he's doing better." For a second she held his gaze, then dropped it to refocus on the pack in her hand. "I'm going to use the ward room to do an inhalation treatment on myself."

"I'll clear out, then, and give you a bit of privacy." This was the best way. They could work together, but not get too close. He could take the hint that she was obviously uncomfortable in saying it out loud, but her body language spoke the same message if he'd only open his eyes and put his libido on ice.

"It's nothing special, just a few oils that stimulate energy and pull the cobwebs out of my brain."

"I wish I had had that in medical school," he said.

She stepped back without comment and entered the ward room, then closed the door. Somehow the room had turned into their private living area when there were no patients in it. With a sigh he decided to have his run now before the heat of the day peaked. Summer was full upon Camp Wild Pines, and his time there was nearly half over. With a quick glance at the ward room door, he sighed, grabbed his ball cap and a bottle of water and headed out.

Refreshed after her aromatherapy session, Ellie sailed through lunch and the afternoon clinic, energy in every movement. With afternoon as the quiet time coming up, she was going to take the opportunity to catch up on her e-mails that she missed yesterday and drop a line to her mother. Several days had passed since she'd e-mailed her, and Ellie knew that her mother worried. Though her brothers were both in the same general area as their mother, they were married with kids and had busy lives that revolved around sports and summer activities for their kids. With a sigh, Ellie took her aromatherapy supplies back to her room.

When she returned, she stopped short and put her hands on her hips and looked down at the floor at an object that hadn't been there just moments ago. "Where did you come from?"

The little baby girl sitting on the floor looked up at her. "Ga?"

"Yeah, you." Ellie knelt down beside the baby when the screen door squeaked. She looked up, then screamed, "Vicki!" Ellie leaped to her feet to embrace her friend. "I can't believe you're here. Why didn't you call?"

The baby still on the floor gave a happy squeal and flailed her arms at the excitement in the room.

"Takes that surprise factor right out of it," Vicki said and pulled back from Ellie as Sam entered the infirmary. With another squeal the baby raised her arms to her daddy, who picked her up.

Vicki introduced Ellie to the little girl. "This is Myra. I know you've seen pictures, but this is the real thing."

Sam moved closer to Vicki, then leaned over and kissed Ellie's cheek. "Nice to see you again, Ellie." The baby wiggled to get down, and Sam returned her to the floor with a stuffed animal that she grabbed by the nose.

"Same here." Warmth filled her heart as she watched the family together. Joy mingled with a touch of envy in her heart. She was so happy that Vicki and Sam had worked things out between them, proving once again that good relationships could be had.

"Where's Mark?" Sam asked and eased his arm around Vicki's shoulders. Vicki looked up at him and the affection between them nearly filled the infirmary.

Ellie had to take half a step back, the energy nearly overwhelming her. "I'm not sure. Let me page him." She used the phone to access the camp intercom and asked Mark to return to the infirmary. "He's never far, so he should be here in a few minutes."

They chatted, and Ellie knelt to eye level with the blonde, curly haired girl. "She's just darling," Ellie said.

"Who's darling?" Mark asked as he entered the building from the side door.

Ellie looked up as Mark's long strides carried him closer to her. Seeing him so full of life and energy, vibrant and masculine, an overwhelming flood of attraction hit her. "What?"

"I said, 'Who's darling?'" He squatted down beside them. "This little one? Where'd she come from?"

"Right here," Sam said.

Surprise covered Mark's face and, for an instant, she saw the boy beneath the man. "Sam. Vicki." He charged forward and encased his friend in an exuberant hug. "Why didn't you call? We'd have made it a party."

"We can still make it a party," Vicki said and held her arms up for Mark's hug.

He kissed her cheek and gave her a squeeze. "Motherhood agrees with you. You look marvelous."

A quick flush colored Vicki's face, and she glanced at Sam. "I think you're right."

The group left the infirmary for a tour of the grounds, viewing the changes that continued to evolve since the fire two years ago. As they neared the wooded area beside the soccer field, Ellie noticed a patch of wild onions growing. She pointed to them. "Would you look at that?"

"Maybe that's why Bear's soups are so good. He's got his own private stash of wild herbs," Vicki said.

"Yeah, he mentioned something about you trying to weasel a recipe out of him." Myra wiggled in Ellie's arms and held her hands out to her mother.

"It took years, but I finally got it," Vicki said with a grin and took Myra back.

"What happened to you?" Sam asked and pointed to Mark's arms and legs and the fading welts. "Looks like someone mistook you for a pincushion."

"Hornets happened. Hospitalized Skinny yesterday."

"It was horrifying," Ellie said and told them how Mark had charged into the fray to save Skinny.

Vicki took one of Mark's arms and looked more closely at the marks. "What did you use on them?"

"Ellie fixed me up with some aromatherapy oils."

"In addition to some meds," Ellie added, not wanting to take credit for his entire healing process.

"I slept for twelve hours, and when I woke up they were like this, nearly gone."

"That's amazing," Vicki said. "I'm just glad you weren't hurt too badly." Vicki gave a full-body shudder.

"I did a lot of that yesterday," Ellie said. "I'm still a bit freaked out over it."

After the tour, they settled down at the lodge for a visit and to renew their friendships.

"I should go to the infirmary and put a note on the door, letting people know we're over here in case something comes up," Ellie said and stood.

"Good idea," Mark said.

"I'll be right back."

She left the lodge and placed the note, returning moments later to find Mark huddled in what appeared to be a serious conversation with Sam and Vicki. "You need to tell her," Vicki said in an urgent whisper. "There shouldn't be any secrets."

"I know. I know. It's not a topic that comes up in casual conversation though." Mark removed his cap and ran a hand through his hair, seeming more distressed than she'd ever seen him. If this was a private conversation, she didn't want to intrude. The three of them obviously had things to talk about that didn't include her, so she backed out of the lodge without letting the screen door make a sound and stayed on the porch a few more minutes.

Bear strode up the stairs to the lodge with a basket of wild greens and a pair of kitchen shears in his hands. Now Ellie knew there were definitely some secrets in Bear's recipes.

"Hi, Bear, what do you have there?" she asked and tried to see into the basket.

"Oh, this and that. Some wild greens. Those fiddlehead ferns Skinny was looking for. Nothing special," he said and scooted around her, opened the door and entered. Ellie followed him inside and the trio broke up their conversation. Bear didn't slow down until he was safely tucked away in the galley.

"So what's the word?" Ellie asked, trying not to reveal that she'd heard part of the conversation. "Any plans while you're here?"

"I think we're going to let the men go have some catching-up time, and we'll do the same," Vicki said and held her hand out to Myra. "Let's go, girl."

"Mama, mama," she said and toddled her way through the lodge to the door.

After returning to the infirmary, Vicki settled Myra for a nap in the ward room, and they sat at the table in the kitchen.

"Last year we had part of the ward room turned into a nursery. She was just three months old, then."

"I'm glad things have worked out with you and Sam."

"So am I," Vicki said. "Though not without struggle, we finally found the place in our relationship where we could both be happy."

"Do you miss the ICU nursing?" Ellie asked and poured a glass of iced tea for each of them. If she didn't have her work, she didn't know what she would do. So much of her identity was wrapped up in her career, being a nurse, caring for others. If that was not in her life, it would be hard for her to imagine her life otherwise.

"No. Not a bit right now. My hands are full enough." Vicki raised her glass to her cheek and pressed it to her skin with a sigh. "This is lovely."

"I see." Ellie looked away.

"Are you missing the ICU already?" Vicki asked. "You can tell me."

"No. Not really." She looked around the small infirmary that had turned into her summer home. Moving from the ICU into a small building that had become the center of her life had been a drastic change.

"You sound surprised." Vicki sipped her drink, waiting for Ellie to reply.

"I guess I am. The chaos of the ICU is something I kind of got used to and didn't know until I left it how bad it really was for me, how overwhelming." Now that she said it aloud, she realized what a revelation that was. Her entire nursing life had been geared toward the high-tech side of saving patients. With that went high-level stress. And that wasn't what she wanted. She spent too much energy trying to de-stress, that she wondered if it was worth it. "Maybe I'm just not cut out for ICU work after all."

"It's amazing what taking a step back from things will do for you. I know the beginning of my nursing career was all about everyone else, and I nearly didn't have enough time or energy left for me." Compassion and understanding seemed to flow out of Vicki. She'd been where Ellie was now. She knew the difficult miles that Ellie had walked, and had walked many of her own.

Tears of unexpected grief burned Ellie's eyes. The pain in her chest came out of nowhere, and she leaned forward over the table. Vicki sat with her, not saying anything, but scooted closer and patted her back. The soothing gesture only made Ellie cry more.

Long minutes passed and so did the storm of tears.

"I'm sorry, Vicki. I don't know what got into me." Wiping her eyes, she pulled herself together and took a few cleansing breaths.

"I don't, either, but it certainly wanted out." She patted Ellie again. "Do you feel better?"

"Marginally. I usually end up with a big fat headache after crying, so I really try not to do it." Crying just wasn't for her. She knew that some people derived great comfort from a good cry, but it had never worked for her.

"Then you need some other sort of emotional release."

"Definitely. Like what? At this point, I'm open to just about anything." Really. "As long as it doesn't involve sports."

Vicki thought a second, then her entire face brightened and her eyes twinkled. "I don't think it's really considered a sport, per se, but it might work for you."

"What? Tell me. I'll do it." Anything.

"How about sex?"

CHAPTER TEN

ELLIE burst out laughing. She'd never heard such a funny thing coming out of Vicki's mouth. But maybe that had been her intent. "Sex? *Sex*. What are you talking about? I haven't been in a relationship since Alan and, frankly, the thought of returning to him almost frightens me. Who am I supposed to have sex with, my imaginary lover?" She shook her head, totally dismissing the idea. That just wasn't going to work.

"How about Mark? He's available and right under your nose." Vicki watched her closely.

Narrowing her eyes at Vicki, Ellie sat back in the chair and crossed her arms. "Now I see what you're up to. This is a total matchmaking weekend for you, isn't it?" she asked and took a sip from her glass, eyeing Vicki over the rim. "Won't work."

"I really don't know what you're talking about, so what do you mean by that? Don't you find Mark interesting and attractive?" Vicki asked the question and somehow maintained a completely innocent look on her face. Oh, she was sneaky.

"Well, yes, of course," Ellie said and felt the burn of a blush begin in her chest and move up her neck. "He's very attractive. If you like that tall, lean, athletic stuff." She cleared her throat. "He's nice, too." She was going to get herself in trouble if she kept talking, so she clamped her mouth shut and looked at her friend.

"If you're looking uncomfortable and blushing, then something must be going on. Did he say he was attracted to you?"

"No. Not really." Ellie shrugged. "Though he did kiss me. A couple of times."

Vicki leaned forward across the table. "Aha. You don't call a kiss 'something'? What's it take to get your attention, woman?"

"I'm not sure anymore." Again, she shrugged, not certain of the point of this discussion since she and Mark would head their separate directions at the end of the summer, despite what could be called a mutual attraction going on. "After the first time, he apologized." That apology stung more than anything.

"But? There's more, I know it. I've known Mark for a long time, and he doesn't go around laying his lips on just anyone."

"Well, I said he sounded like he regretted touching me, but he said something I haven't quite figured out yet." She frowned as the memory of that tugged at her.

"What?"

"'Quite the contrary.'" Puzzled, she looked at Vicki. "What do you suppose he meant by that?"

"You *have* been out of it too long. It means he has

the hots for you, but respects you, too, and wouldn't jump your bones simply because you were convenient."

"Why do you think that is?"

The humor fled from Vicki's face. "He's been seriously ill."

"Yes, he told me a little about it."

"Did he tell you his fiancé left him in the early stages of his illness? In fact, during his first treatment?"

Ellie gasped, horrified that someone would abandon their fiancé when they were needed the most. She would never do that. "No, and I'm not sure that you should be telling me, either. If he'd wanted me to know any more he would have told me." Though it felt like a violation of his privacy, she was glad to know a little more about him.

"I know. I know. He's a very private, very proud man. But he's also overprotective, way overprotective, of those he cares for."

"I'm not sure what you mean, but it's his life to live, isn't it?"

"Yes. Sam and I just want to see him happy and healthy, and part of that is having a good support system of loved ones around him." She sighed. "There's no more healing power in the universe than the power of love. But I'm not certain Mark can take that leap of faith and reach out for it after what he's been through."

"Now you're confusing me even more. Why wouldn't he be able to reach out to someone? He seems perfectly healthy now." He'd more than proved that yesterday.

"I don't mean to confuse you. The rest is for Mark to tell you if he chooses. Just don't shy away from him if there's attraction between the two of you. It would be good for both of you." Looking around the infirmary, a dreamy smile came over her face. "There's something magical about this building, I swear. This was really where Sam and I worked out the problems between us, and where we fell in love all over again. Doing that a second time made us stronger together than we had ever been." This time tears made Vicki's eyes shine, and she waved them away. "Making me sentimental just being here."

"I think Bear is going to want to see you. He said he was going to miss not having you around here this year," Ellie said.

"He did? What a fooler he is. You just never know about that man." She shook her head. "As tough as he is, he's just a big old softy on the inside."

Ellie filled Vicki in about the grease burn and her use of aromatherapy oil on it. "You would have thought I dumped a bucket of perfume on him, the way he carried on about it."

Vicki laughed. "I can just see him now."

"He was really shook up about Skinny."

"They've been friends for a long time," Vicki told her, her eyes filled with concern.

"You should have seen Mark with that fire extinguisher. It was a brilliant idea, and I never would have thought of it. It was like watching something out of a horror movie." Ellie shivered as the memory of seeing both men covered in stinging insects hit her. "Still gives me the creeps."

"You were telling me Bear was pretty upset about the attack."

"Yeah. He went to the hospital this morning before

Mark or I were even out of bed. Skinny's due back tomorrow, but he had a close call of it. Why don't you go over to the lodge and say hi? I'll watch Myra. She's sleeping, and I can handle her for a while."

"Good idea. I'll be back in just a bit." She rose and returned to the lodge to visit her old friend, Bear.

"Ellie?" Mark called as he entered through the side door into the infirmary. "Where are you?"

"In the ward room."

Again. It was definitely more comfortable than being in her cramped bedroom all of the time. He made his way down the hall and turned into the room, then felt as if someone had punched him in the gut. He stopped, because he couldn't move farther, and his breath froze in his lungs.

Eyes closed, humming softly, Ellie sat in a chair and rocked Myra, who was fast asleep on her shoulder. The sight almost made his knees go weak. Together, they were simply stunning. And something he wanted with every fiber in his soul. He didn't dare to try to make the dream a reality. Disappointment like that would destroy him.

Gathering his strength, he moved into the room and sat on the bunk nearest to them. Reaching out, he touched the small, perfectly shaped little foot with his finger. He was an uncle and had been around babies a lot, but the sight of such miniature perfection made him appreciative of the process of Mother Nature all over again.

Ellie opened her eyes and met his. The softness, the beauty in her face, made him want more than he knew he should. Wanting her, wanting a family of his own, was a dangerous undertaking when his illness could return at any time. That thought never left him.

"Is she asleep?" Ellie asked.

"Yes," he whispered and swallowed down the desperate needs trying to surface inside of him.

Ellie moved Myra and placed her back on the bunk, covering her with her light blanket. "Isn't she just beautiful?" Ellie asked, looking at the baby, then she looked up.

Holding her gaze, Mark had to agree. "Yes. She certainly is beautiful."

"You're not even looking at her." Ellie swallowed, and her gaze flashed to his mouth.

The tension between them was suddenly palpable, and he wanted to reach out to her more than he ever had. "That's okay. I see a beautiful babe right in front of me."

Ellie walked out of the ward room, and Mark followed her to the front. She turned to face him and opened her mouth to speak, but didn't have a chance to say a thing.

Mark was right behind her and stepped in close, cupped her face and kissed her. Hot and hungry for her, he gave her no options except to answer him with the same heat. Parting her lips, he delved his tongue and found her eager response. Oh, she was so sweet and pliant to his touch.

In an instant, his body hardened, ready to take this little embrace to its final fruition. Though his bodily functions had returned to normal since his illness, he hadn't tested himself yet with a woman, not wanting to fail her or himself. The humiliation and disappointment of being impotent after surviving his life-threatening ordeal was something he hadn't wanted to discover one way or another, but now, while folding Ellie into his arms, he was more motivated than ever to test himself. With her approval, of course.

Her approval came in the form of a throaty moan and melting softly against him. Not wanting to resist the sweet temptation of her, he knew he had to. So many conflicting emotions swirled inside of him, he couldn't make sense of any of them. And for the moment he didn't try. He simply enjoyed the sweet feel, the sweet taste, the sweet fragrance, of Ellie in his arms.

Finally, he lifted his head and pressed his forehead to hers as they caught their breath from the embrace that had taken them both by surprise. With his hands still cupped around her face, he held her softly. She was what he wanted, but his future was so unknown, so uncertain, that he knew he didn't have the right to want her so badly. She was backed up against the worktable, and he wanted to lie her down on it and strip her bare. The needs raging inside him nearly made him tremble.

Reaching up, she clasped her hands around his wrists and squeezed, though she didn't move away. "Wow. What was that for?" she asked.

"I don't know. I just needed it." And that was the base truth. He needed to be touched, to feel again, to express the emotions churning inside of him. Curving her hair back behind her ears he lifted his head, and she looked at him, cautious desire filling the depths of her eyes and her face. "Not that this is your problem, but I haven't made love since my illness." He smiled at the surprise on her face. "And to be brutally honest, Ellie, you're the first woman I've wanted to make love to since then."

"Oh." Her brows shot up. "Oh! Well, then." She dropped her gaze and started to move back from him.

"I've made you uncomfortable now, haven't I?" Damn. Sometimes he didn't know when to keep his mouth shut.

"No. Well, maybe a little." She fidgeted with the hem of her shirt and gave a nervous laugh.

"I'm sorry, Ellie. I just wanted to kiss you." Turning away, he ran a hand through his hair. "There's something going on between us. An attraction I hadn't looked for or expected to find. Especially not here at camp."

"Me, either. It's certainly surprising, but not unwelcome."

Dammit. He knew he should tell her the entire story, but somehow, in the speaking of it aloud, he almost gave life to the fears he didn't want to acknowledge. Vicki had said he should tell Ellie everything, but he didn't know if he should, wasn't sure he had the right words. What purpose would it serve if they were going to go their separate ways in a few more weeks?

"Mark?"

The sound of her soft voice made him turn back to her.

"There's more to your story than you've told me, isn't there?" She patted the worktable beside her and hopped onto it. Joining her there, he gave a deep sigh and decided to tell her the story that had been eating him alive inside.

"There's way more. So much more I'm afraid to say it out loud." His voice was rough with the emotions he'd tried to hide from her and from himself, but it obviously hadn't worked.

She took his hand and held it. "Why don't you just start talking, then stop when you're done?"

Compassion flowed from her into him, and he knew this was why she was such a good nurse, a good person, and needed this break from ICU nursing. She gave a lot of herself to others, but he didn't see that she was able to take much back from others who wanted to give a little to her.

"When I was diagnosed with testicular cancer just over three years ago, I thought for sure my life was over."

At her shocked gasp, he cringed inside. Maybe that wasn't the best way to say it, but he just had to tell his story. It was nearly alive inside him, clawing to get out.

"I'm sorry. Keep going." She squeezed his hand and urged him on.

"After diagnosis and surgery, I spent months in treatment hell. I developed a new appreciation for what our patients go through. There's no way to describe the experience, other than to say I survived it."

"Vicki did tell me that your fiancé bailed on you when you were sick."

"Yeah. She bailed all right. In the first week of treatment." He snorted and shook his head in disgust. "She couldn't bear being around 'all those sick people,' which included me."

"How selfish." Ellie clapped her hand over her mouth a second, then touched his arm. "I'm sorry. You must have loved her once."

"Not really. Amazingly enough, what I thought was

love was somehow not. She was beautiful, but so shallow you could see right through her. For some reason I was looking for a woman who would make a good 'doctor's wife,' rather than looking for a friend and a life mate." He took a deep breath. "Having her take off really made me realize what was important in life and what was simply icing."

"Surely your family was with you through your treatment and recovery."

"Yes, they were. You mentioned your father died from cancer, so you know it's tough on a family, but it pulled us together, and we're closer than we ever were."

"Mom and I are much closer, too. So at least that's one good outcome from Dad's illness." She turned to face him. "So you told me that you've been clear of the disease for three years?

"That's right. Three years and counting."

"And you haven't found anyone of interest in that time?" The surprise in her eyes warmed him. "Seriously?"

"No." It was that simple. "Seriously." Until now at least.

"I find that hard to believe, Mark. You work with a lot of women in the hospital."

"Yep, I do. My sisters have even tried to fix me up with their friends, but there's just not been the right chemistry with anyone."

Silence hung between them. "You said you haven't made love, but have you…test-driven…yourself?" She clapped her hands over her face and turned a glorious shade of red. "I can't believe I just asked you that. I'm so sorry, don't answer that."

Mark chuckled, then a laugh, the likes of which

he'd not felt in years, burst out of him. And he laughed until tears dribbled from his eyes. Off the table, he couldn't hold himself upright and he doubled over, laughing and laughing.

Ellie joined him. Reaching out, he hugged her to him, until the laughs subsided to small tremors that still shook him, and he had to sit down. "Yes, I have, so the parts work. However, taking my engine for a *test-drive*, as you say, and putting it through an *endurance race*, are two entirely different things."

"I suppose they are." She wiped away a tear from her face.

"The big issue, too, is that I don't know whether the sperm I make is viable." That was something he hadn't wanted to tackle yet, either. Somehow not knowing the answer to that was better than knowing he was infertile.

"You haven't done testing since the treatment?"

"No." He shrugged, the humor of the moment beginning to fade. "I haven't wanted to find out. If I'm not in a serious relationship, what's the point?" And since he wasn't going to be in a serious relationship until he made it to his fifth cancer-free year, there was no point. Having the information wouldn't solve anything if he was still going to die.

"The knowing might bring you some peace of mind, don't you think? I don't know a lot about testicular cancer, but I've read that storing sperm before treatment can give you some hope for children later."

"If you survive the treatment and the first five years, you mean?" He squelched the bitterness that wanted to leap out of him. Sometimes the emotions of it all just got to him, though he tried not to let it take over his life.

"Well, yes."

"I did save sperm, but I always preferred doing things the old-fashioned way, especially when it comes to children. I'd rather not create my children in a lab if I don't have to." He shook his head and took in a breath, willing the pain of that thought to go away.

"That would probably be everyone's first choice. For some people, that's the only way they can have children."

"I know. I know. And it's a wonderful option, but at this point, for me, it's just moot, since there isn't a line of women beating down my door to marry me and bear my children, is there?" The last one had left him when he'd needed her the most, and he'd not wanted anyone in his life since then.

"Mark," she said, and he heard the reproof in her tone. "That's a nasty thing to say about yourself. There's a lot more to you than being a sperm donor and making babies. You could have a wonderful relationship with someone, even if you never had children."

"I know. I know. I didn't mean to unload my problems on to you, Ellie, I'm sorry." He ran a hand down her arm. "You've started to become a good friend, and I didn't need to do that to you." Irritated with himself, he started for the door, but her hand on his arm stopped him.

"You weren't unloading problems, Mark. And you *are* starting to be a good friend. Until that last crack, we were good."

Anger in her face and eyes surprised him. He hadn't expected that. "But?"

"Friends share things, and you don't need to police what you say to me."

The compassion, the interest, in her eyes nearly made him want to reach out to her in a way he hadn't allowed himself to reach out for years. But something stopped him. "There are just some things that you don't need to hear. That's all." Some things he could hardly stand to hear himself.

"Mark! Just stop it, will you? Have you listened to yourself? You sound like you're ninety-five years old and ready to give up."

"I can't help it, Ellie! Until you go through this experience yourself, face your own death, you can't know how deeply you're going to be affected." He was surprised at how emotional he'd gotten. Tremors of rage he thought he'd suppressed pulsed through him. Clenching his jaw tight for a moment, he refused to give in to the emotion of the moment.

"I understand that. I'm not saying that I know what you're going through, or what you've been through, but I have suffered in ways that you don't know." Her voice cracked, and she cleared her throat. "I just want you to know that I can be here for you, that I can listen when you need to talk." Pausing, she knelt beside him and took his hands in hers, but she didn't look at him, keeping her gaze on their entwined hands. She pointed to her left ring finger. "There used to be an engagement ring on this finger." Her voice dropped to an emotional whisper.

"What happened?" Sick with anticipation, he gripped her hands in his, almost knowing what she was going to say. Now he knew he didn't have the right, shouldn't have the want, to desire her. She'd been through too much emotionally already, and he'd only give her more.

"The man I was to marry, to build a life with, wouldn't share me with my family. We had been together for years and had every intention of fulfilling the all-American dream."

Unable to resist, he reached out to stroke her hair. "And the dream faded?"

"More like it was shattered by a narcissistic idiot who thought the world revolved around him." Now, she looked up at him, the passion of righteous anger blazing from her eyes, and he almost pulled away from the intensity of her. "When I paid more attention to my father during his illness than Alan, he couldn't take it. He got pissy, then angry, then he sulked. Do you know that when a man sulks, it's a massive turnoff?"

Suppressing a grin, he said, "I'll try to remember that."

"Anyway, he never said it in so many words, but he wanted me to choose between him and my dying father. Do you believe that one?" She stood and paced in front of him.

"Obviously, you chose your father."

She snorted. "Obviously. I figured if we were truly meant to be together he'd still be there after things settled down with Dad, but it didn't, and he wasn't."

"I'm sorry, Ellie," he said, and meant it. A bad heartbreak could scar a person for life.

"He made a promise to me, and he broke it. It's that simple." She turned to face him, giving him a stare that all nurses seemed to possess. "There are no guarantees in life, Mark. You know this. People say one thing and do another. They change, they change their minds, they simply just go away. You'd do well to reach out and embrace whatever you can in life, because you don't know how long it's going to be there. If you're waiting for some miracle woman to show up at the right moment in your life, you may be waiting a long time." She huffed out a sigh and seemed to withdraw into her own mind for a second. "I loved a man and lost him. Yes, it hurt, but I've moved on. I don't want to get hurt again, but we don't know what's around the next corner, or the next one, or the one after that. All we can do is reach out to what's right in front of us and hold on."

Cries from the ward room halted their conversation. Saved by the baby. "Guess this conversation is over." How could he tell her that he simply couldn't reach out the way she suggested? She'd been through enough pain in her life and though she said reaching out was the way to go, he didn't want to knowingly cause her pain.

Ellie moved toward Myra, then paused. "For now. But it's not over, Mark. We still have more than half the summer left."

Nodding, Mark left the confines of the infirmary, and wished he could leave his dark mood behind as easily.

CHAPTER ELEVEN

VICKI and Sam returned to the infirmary, collected the baby and headed to their hotel for the night. There simply wasn't enough room in the infirmary for all of them to stay comfortably. That was okay with Ellie. She liked her space as well as her friends.

The summer heat loaded with humidity had descended, and she couldn't sleep anyway. Pressure in the air seemed to force her muscles to work harder than usual to accomplish the same tasks. The air-conditioner unit in her room blasted away, but it was heated dreams and raw desires that kept her from falling into a deep sleep. Humidity was just an excuse.

Mark's touch, the scent of him, the taste of him and the feel of his body against hers, drove her to a state of restlessness that she hadn't anticipated. Desire was something she'd put on hold through her father's illness and now that she'd found some freedom outside of the hospital and the controlling relationship she'd had with Alan, it appeared that her body had also found the freedom it needed to respond as fully as it wanted to.

Dreams were hot and sweaty, with familiar bodies straining together, and she woke with a desperate need in her, a need that had been awakened and refused to go away. Mark was down the hall. He was the source of her current situation. He was also the solution.

Could she take that tiny step, that giant leap, toward him, to what he could offer her, even if it was only temporary? Didn't all relationships start out as temporary anyway? Who needed commitments or promises that were unwisely given in the heat of a moment, when the heat could change to ice in a millisecond?

She'd rather not have broken promises, only shared moments, between them.

Desperate to cool off and hose down the desire rumbling inside of her, she left her room and sought out a glass of ice water in the kitchen. That only succeeded in quenching her thirst; the heat of her inner turmoil persisted.

"Stop it!"

Ellie jumped and flashed around. "Mark?" She knew she'd heard his voice, but he wasn't behind her as she'd expected.

A muffled voice came from his room, and she hurried barefoot to him. "Mark?" She pushed the unlatched door wide and saw him fighting with his sheets. He had to be asleep, struggling with his dreams as she had been doing. Getting close to a thrashing person in the throes of a nightmare could be dangerous, as she'd experienced in her hospital work. So she called his name from the doorway.

"Mark? Wake up. Mark. Wake up."

At the sound of his name he stilled, his chest heaving.

Though his eyes opened, she doubted that he was fully awake yet. "Mark, it's Ellie. You're having a dream."

"Oh, my God." He sat up on the edge of the bunk, rested his elbows on his legs and held his head in his hands. His breath wheezed in an out of his lungs as if he had just been running through the camp.

Sitting beside him, she placed a hand on his back. "Are you okay? Want a drink of water?" She handed him her glass and he drained the frigid water in seconds.

"Wow. Thanks." He tried to peer through the darkness at her, though with only the hallway light, she couldn't tell how much of her he saw. "What are you doing up? Did I wake you?"

"No. My own dreams woke me. I got up for water, then heard you."

"Sorry."

"Not your fault. The heat kept me from sleeping." At least that was a partial truth. "Want to talk about it?"

"I'll tell you my dream if you tell me yours." He pressed the glass still filled with ice against his cheek, trying to cool off.

"Uh, I'm not sure that's a wise idea." Really unwise if she intended to keep her secrets to herself.

"Why not? Didn't you just flay me on that point earlier tonight? It's just us, we're friends, it's the middle of the night and we're sitting here in the almost dark." He placed the glass on the floor. "There's no one except us, Ellie. Tell me about your dream. I want to hear about it to distract me from mine."

Oh, she knew she was going to regret this. "Okay." She huffed out a sigh. "I was dreaming about you. And me.

About our conversation earlier tonight." The dark lent some sort of secrecy, some anonymity, though she knew exactly where she was and to whom she was talking.

"What about it? I really didn't mean to burden you with my problems."

Ha. "It was no burden at all. It was quite the opposite." She licked her lips, which had suddenly become dry. Hmm. Her throat was dry, too, though she'd just had some water. "It was exhilarating actually."

"I don't follow."

The darkness seemed to expand and fill her mind as she remembered. Images from her dream flashed through her mind; electricity zinged through her as desire began to once again unfold. "We were together in my dream."

"Together?"

She nodded, even though he couldn't see her. "And…naked."

"Aha. Now I see what kept you awake. You were taking me for that test-drive, weren't you?"

There was humor in his voice, and she responded to that. Laughter bubbled in Ellie, though she tried to hold it back. "Uh, yes. I was taking you for a test-drive."

"How was the engine performance?" he asked. Though she couldn't see him clearly, she felt him shift position to face her, but more than that, she sensed a shift in the air between them. She wasn't the only one who was affected by her dream. In telling Mark, he responded as she had in the dream.

"It was going well until I doused it with ice water."

"Ouch. That brought things to a halt, didn't it?"

She licked her lips, trying to find some of that moisture she'd recently downed. "Temporarily." She paused. "Until I came in here."

He huffed out a sigh and placed his hand on her arm, stroked it down to her hand. "You know I want to make love with you, Ellie. I'm not just saying that because you're here with me now, you know that, don't you?"

"Yes. I feel the same way. And it's not because of the dream, but it's because of who you are, and what you are, and everything, that I… God, this just isn't coming out right."

"What?"

"Will you hold me, Mark? Just for tonight, will you hold me?" Could it be as simple as that? Just two people holding each other in the dark and allowing the rest of the world to go away for a time.

"Ellie. Don't pity me because of what I told you. I couldn't handle that." His grip on her hand tightened.

She snorted. "Believe me, it's not pity that's pounding through me, Mark. It's pure, unadulterated lust."

"Oh, Ellie. You make it hard for a man to say no." His hand clenched hers and the tremors in him shot through her.

Reaching out into the dark she found his face and turned it to her. "Then don't say it." Moving closer, she pressed her cheek against him, rubbing, feeling the scrape of his overnight beard against her skin. "Please hold me, Mark. I need you to hold me." The world needed to go away just for a little while.

"I don't think holding you will be enough," he breathed and cupped her face in his hands. "At the moment, I can't muster the strength to resist you, resist what's going on between us." He turned his face toward her.

This was just where she wanted to be. "I'm not sure if I remember how to make love anymore, Mark. It's been so long." Desperate desire overwhelmed any self-doubt. She needed him.

"Try," he whispered against her lips.

Already charged up by the erotic dream she'd had, Mark's touch was magic, and ignited her in ways she'd never imagined. Each kiss, each stroke of his tongue against hers, each gentle press of his hands on her skin, stoked the fire higher. She wrapped her arms under his and cupped his back with her hands.

They lay back on the bed, and Mark shifted his position until their legs tangled together, his hips pressed against hers. Yes, his engine was definitely ready for high performance now. The heat of his arousal pressed hot and hard against her belly. With only a thin nightshirt that rode up high, she felt every inch of him through his boxers, and she suppressed the groan in her throat. Desire that had blossomed now surged in electrical pulses through her.

He kissed her cheek, her neck, and made his way down to tug at a nipple through the fabric, and she arched at the wet heat of his mouth. Reaching for the hem of the nightshirt, he tugged and pulled at it until it was up over her head, trapping her arms at her sides. "I want to touch you," she whispered. "My arms are stuck."

Without replying, he opened his mouth over her nipple and pulled it inside, and she forgot what it was that she was protesting. Surges of electricity shot through her, and her mind no longer functioned properly. This was definitely what they both needed.

Each stroke of his tongue on her tender flesh was an agony of the senses. Low in her belly, her flesh came alive. Surges of heat and moisture shot through her, quivers of desire made her gasp as he took her deeper than she'd ever been. The past had no place here.

Mark lifted his head and ringed his tongue around her other nipple while his hands got busy and tugged at the scrap of panty she wore and dragged it off of her.

Following his hands downward, he kissed the slight curve of her belly, the flare of her hips that his hands had itched to touch for days and days. Her skin was so soft, and she smelled of lavender and honey, and some essential feminine fragrance he knew he'd inspired in her.

"Mark, wait—" She breathed quickly, seeming to sense his destination.

"Shh. Shh. Easy, love." Urging her knees farther apart, he kissed her thigh and rested his face against her lean leg and sighed, totally content in this position and the moment between them. "You are so beautiful, Ellie. So beautiful."

Restless, her hips moved, and his mouth watered to taste her. Unable to deny himself any longer, he turned his face to her center and opened his mouth over her.

At the first touch of his mouth on her feminine flesh, Ellie cried out and stiffened, clutching the sheets in her fists. Then, her knees drifted slowly apart. Allowing himself to explore her soft body as he wished, he teased and tugged and stroked until her breathing hitched. Easing a finger inside of her heat, he took her over the edge. Her choked cries filled his ears; the spasms of her body let him know that he had satisfied her. Easing upward, he pressed a long hot kiss to her mouth, and she held tight to his face. Then he drew away.

Pulling himself upright, he fumbled around in his nightstand. "Where are those things?" he mumbled aloud, then he found what he was looking for.

"What?"

"I confiscated some condoms from a few of the older boys who were using them to make water balloons," he said and tore the box open, spilling them all over the place. Grabbing one, he opened it and brushed the rest to the floor.

"This is a much better use for them."

She reached for him and, with her hands assisting his, eased the condom over his erection. Her touch was magic, and he was rapidly losing any control he might have once claimed.

"Are you sure about this, Ellie?" he asked, hoping that he wouldn't fail her with the rest. Stopping now might render him incapable for life.

"Come here," she said and pulled him to her. With a groan, she found his mouth, and he lost himself to her eager touch. Kisses deep and hungry, her touch setting him on fire, he knew that this was what he wanted, what they both needed, and he raised himself above her, then paused.

The feel of her nails digging into his hips, urging him forward, gave him the last little bit of courage he needed, and he eased inside her moist sheath.

"Oh, Ellie." She was so soft, so hot, so incredibly firm around him, that he thought he might explode right there. But as his body seemed to remember what to do, he released the control of his mind to simply feel and enjoy Ellie's body as sensations took over. He knew that no matter what happened between them, he would never forget this night.

"Mark," Ellie cried as she clutched him closer, her breathing faster.

She tipped her hips up, and he surged into her. Sweat broke out on his skin as he pulled back, then moved forward, easing into her again. She wanted to please him as much as he seemed to want to please her.

Sighs and moans, and the sounds of flesh against flesh, filled the air between them. Sensing that Mark was close to a release, she wrapped her legs around his hips and pulled him hard into her, her fingers digging into his hips. Tension mounted as her body surprisingly prepared again for surrender, and she pressed her face against his moist neck. Holding him tight with her legs, and squeezing him with her arms, her body took over and tremors shook her.

An instant after the orgasm took hold of her, Mark trembled in her arms, and he cried out with the ferocity of his own release. Rocking back and forth with her, he drew out the pleasure for the both of them as long as possible, then he collapsed on top of her. His breath wheezed in and out of his lungs as heavily as it had the first day she'd met him.

Then he laughed and it was pure joy that came out of him. "Ellie. I think you remembered just fine." He pressed quick kisses all over her face that made her smile. Then he dove in for a long, hot kiss that ended with a gentle touch of his lips on hers. "You are so wonderful. Thank you, Ellie. You have no idea how much I needed this, how much I needed *you*." The trembling of his body told her how much.

Without moving, she held onto him. Now that she'd reached out to him, she didn't know if she wanted to let him go.

CHAPTER TWELVE

THE next morning there was absolutely no time to reflect on whether it was right or wrong that Ellie and Mark had made love, or if great sex was really one of life's ultimate stress busters.

Starting at the time her alarm went off, the infirmary was in crisis. Highly contagious stomach flu had hit the camp and left no cabin unaffected. At least three campers from every cabin went down at once. When those kids recovered, three more replaced them in the infirmary. Ellie dispensed all of the stomach medication that she had available and sent Gil to town for more.

"Here it is," he said as he charged through the door with several sacks of medication in his hands. He placed the bags filled with pink liquid medication on the worktable. "I went to the pharmacy and the store and bought every bottle they had. They'll have more tomorrow."

"Thanks, Gil." Exhausted, Ellie opened the bags, took out three bottles and handed them to Gil with a bottle of hand sanitizer. "Mark's out making rounds in the cabins, and I've got a ward room full, so I can't leave. Can you find him and give these to him?"

"Sure." He took the items from her.

"After that, wash your hands and lock yourself in your office if you can."

"Got it." He left and the phone rang.

"Infirmary from hell, Ellie speaking." It was Vicki. "We've got a massive case of stomach flu here, so you three ought to stay away for a few days." She sighed with regret. "That will probably be the end of your visit here, but I don't want you to get sick, too. This is awful." She'd lost track of how many kids came and went, how many brows she'd mopped and how many doses of medication she'd administered. Everything was beginning to take on the same pink hue.

"I'm so sorry. We wanted to spend some time with you and Mark, but we leave in two days."

"I'm not certain we'll be over the worst of this by then and it's not worth the risk, especially for Myra." From the looks of the ward room, the bug wasn't going to be over until it had infected every person in the camp.

"Is there anything you need me to bring? I can do a shopping trip for you and drop it off at the back door of the infirmary without risking exposure."

"Oh, Vicki. If you could get me a couple of things, I'd totally appreciate it." She gave Vicki a short list of necessary items. "You're such a good friend. You have no idea how much I need that right now." Tears nearly sprang to her eyes, but she resisted them. Fatigue was what was getting her down, and her emotions were just raw right now.

"I do know. I was having trouble myself a few years ago, remember? You helped me a lot by just listening, so now it's my turn to help you out. Just let me do this for you, will you?"

With a tired laugh, Ellie said, "Okay. I'll let you." She hung up and returned to the ward room to the sounds of renewed retching from one of the children.

"Oh, you poor little ones," Ellie said and emptied yet another emesis basin, then dosed the child with the pink stuff. She sat by his bedside stroking his hair until he drifted off to sleep. Washing her hands in between each bed, she moved on and on until she could hardly stand upright. The skin on her hands was raw and cracked from so many washings and applications of hand sanitizer. She'd definitely need some heavy-duty oils after the crisis was over.

A phone call from Vicki alerted her to the delivery of her supplies. Vicki had set three bags of items at the side door without Ellie even noticing that she had come and gone. She put away the perishables, then let the rest sit on the counter until she had time to deal with them. At this rate, camp might be over by the time that happened.

During the three days of exhausting, repetitious tasks, Ellie and Mark caught naps and showers and food when they could, spelling each other at intervals. Any discussion of what had occurred between them had had to wait.

The tidal wave of campers flowing in and out of the infirmary slowed down to a trickle, and Ellie collapsed facedown on a clean bed in the ward room. She'd scrubbed with soap and water, then applied anti-infective spray for good measure to each surface of every bunk, every door handle and all possible sources of contaminant. Fomites were not going to reinfect anyone if she had anything to say about it. She'd washed all of the sheets and put them back onto the clean bunks. Exhaustion nearly claimed her. There were now four potentially un-disturbed hours between now and the next clinic, and she intended to sleep through every minute of them.

Groaning, she let out a long sigh and settled down for a nap. The scent of lavender oil soothed her fraught nerves and she breathed deeply, then frowned. Lavender oil? Where had that come from? Had she left a bottle open somewhere? She opened her eyes and saw Mark standing beside the bunk, her bottle of mixed aroma-therapy oil in his hand. "What are you doing?" she asked and heard the fatigue in her own voice. If she could hear it, then obviously Mark could, too. Although he didn't look it, he couldn't be in much better shape than she was at the moment. She pushed her arms against the mattress and eased into a sitting position.

"You're exhausted, so I thought I'd give you some of your own medicine." He poured a dollop of oil into his hand. "Go back to the way you were, and I'll give you a purple treatment."

"Aren't you tired, too? You've been at this as long as I have." Although he looked a little rough around the edges, he didn't look nearly as bad as she felt.

"Yeah, but I had half a pot of coffee and a shower, and I'm good for a while. Residency was good training for these past few days." He grinned and the light in his eyes darkened. "No worries. It's time you had a little re-laxation time of your own instead of taking care of everyone else."

"Mark, no. It's really okay. You don't have to spend

time on me when you should be resting, too." He wasn't going to do this. "It's an unnecessary use of your time when you don't have any more than I do."

"Ellie."

The drop in his voice made her pause and look up at him. "What?"

"Be quiet and lie down. Doctor's orders."

Resistance boiled strong inside of her. "But—"

"You're not being a very good nurse by disobeying doctor's orders. Why are you resisting me?"

"It's not you," she said and dropped her gaze, wondering when the pulse of anxiety within her was going to go away. They'd made love. It wasn't as if he hadn't ever touched her. He knew her intimately. "It's just not necessary. I don't need it."

"I most heartily disagree. You need this as much as the kids needed your touch, your calming influence that you don't even know you have. How are you supposed to fill up your soul if you don't stop every now and then to try? Giving of yourself so much has put you right where you are."

"Where, Maine?" The attempt at humor fell flat.

"No. The edge of exhaustion. And besides, I want to touch you the way you touched me. The way you helped me." He knelt beside her and placed his oily hands on her thighs. "Just breathe, Ellie. Just breathe."

The gentleness in his voice was nearly her undoing. She couldn't be weak, especially not in front of him. Tears spilled from her eyes. Where had those come from? She brushed them away. She didn't cry. Ever. Tears were an indulgence she couldn't afford. Unable to refute his claim, she remained silent. Unfortunately, he was right. "I just don't know how to allow myself to enjoy things like that anymore. Not since…well, not in a long time."

"Sure you do. Things you don't think are important for you really are. But I have to tell you from experience that the human touch, connecting with another person, is one of the things that got me through my illness."

"Which was so much more serious than my silly problems. What's a case of fatigue compared to a near-death experience?" It was nothing. She knew that. But the memory of his touch made her want to do exactly as he suggested and surrender to him, to give up the need to be strong all of the time. Honestly, she was simply too tired to fight anymore. A sigh rolled out of her, and the burning in her eyes made her close them for a second.

"Ellie, quit talking and lie down."

Unable to resist him or herself any longer, she gave in. Exhaustion made her weak and tears continued to dribble down her nose and wet the pillow under her head. "I'm sorry."

"That's it," he said in a soothing voice and touched her with his oil-soaked hands. "That's my girl. Quiet, slow breathing. Empty your mind. Close your eyes and just enjoy."

Strong and sure, his hands began the journey at her bare feet, applying the oil and massaging her tired muscles. She ached everywhere and a groan of pure bliss came out of her throat as he pressed his thumb firmly into the arch of one foot. "Oh, God, Mark. If I had *any* government secrets, I would give them away right now."

He chuckled. "Feel good, eh?"

"Beyond description," she said and allowed a long sigh to unfold from somewhere deep inside of her. "I feel so weak admitting that to you."

Moving up to her calves, he poured more oil into his hands and began to massage the stressed muscles there. "Why is it weak to admit you enjoy something? The human touch is very important in well-being. You've had a tough year. Being an ICU nurse is no easy thing, then to have your dad's illness piled on top of the fiancé rejection. That is beyond the ability of most people to sanely handle without needing some sort of break."

"Until the other night, with you, I haven't had the human touch, that intimacy, for a long, long time. Alan wasn't very demonstrative unless he wanted something. For him, intimacy was a means to an end, rather than something you do when you care about someone." Tears that she thought she'd finishing shedding began to fall again. Sniffing, she tried to hide her reaction from Mark and turned her face away. "I don't want to think about that part of my life anymore."

"I think you need the connection with others more than you realize or that you've allowed yourself to have." He soothed her with his touch and with his voice. "Don't be afraid to be vulnerable with me, Ellie. Don't be afraid to feel your emotions."

"I've had to be strong for so long, that I don't quite know how to do that."

"Just let go for a little while. Give yourself a break and lean on me for a little while. It'll be okay," he said and pressed a kiss to the back of her head. He straightened her arms by her sides, applied the oil, then stroked her back. No one had offered her such comfort since she'd been a child. After another breath filled with the healing fragrance of lavender, she finally gave in to the exhaustion that overwhelmed her.

Mark watched as she fell asleep, amazed at the personal strength and sheer stubbornness that had seen her through some troubled times. Though impressed by the things she'd accomplished, there was something else about Ellie that reached into his spirit and made him want to stay by her side for more than the rest of the summer.

She was lovely, and courageous, and strong, and before the end of the summer he was going to convince her of it. If he left her with nothing else, he would do that for her.

Voices alerted him to the arrival of a camper. He left the ward room to catch them before they woke Ellie.

CHAPTER THIRTEEN

NIGHT fell before Ellie woke. Unable to tell the time from the light, she entered the main room to find it empty and the clock reading well after clinic hours had ended. She'd missed it, and Mark apparently had handled it without her. The thought of that didn't disturb her as much as it had just a few weeks ago. Maybe she was learning to be more of a team member instead of being the entire team. That was just getting to be too much work.

The rustle of papers drew her to the screened porch. She stepped out, and Mark looked up. He wore reading glasses perched on his nose, a glass of water sat beside him on a small table and he was reading from a professional journal. The smile that lit up his face stopped her. He was simply the most wonderful man she'd ever known. He was kind, generous, sexy to a fault, had a sense of humor that she enjoyed and he didn't let her take herself too seriously. Had she fallen in love with him without even knowing it?

"Hi, there. Have a good rest?" He removed his glasses and tucked them into the collar of his shirt.

"The best in a long, long time." Admitting that wasn't as scary as it might have been a few weeks ago. Maybe she was finally healing from the rigors of her job and the lingering grief of the past year. Life moved on, and she had to move along with it.

"Must have been the aromatherapy oils. Good combination you made." He patted the seat beside him.

"Yes," she said and moved to the swing and sat with him. What would it be like to enjoy the same sort of relationship that Sam and Vicki did? They'd been through their tough times, and she knew every relationship had them. Finding the right person was something that happened to people, but so far hadn't happened to her. She'd begun to think that the relationship fairy had skipped over her. Perhaps that fairy had returned now with an unexpected gift. After Alan, she had some making up to do.

"Where are you?" he asked and closed the journal.

"What?" She blinked several times and peered at him. What had he said?

"I asked where you were," he said and tapped her temple with one finger. "You were miles away there for a minute."

"I think I was." There was no harm in admitting that, was there?

"There's something I want to ask you," he said and turned more closely to face her.

Without verbally answering, she raised her brows.

"The kids will be heading out for a long day trip in a few days."

"Yes, I know. It's going to be a project getting everything ready." She was just glad the medical team didn't have to go along. One whole day to themselves was going to be pure bliss.

"I was wondering if you'd consider going somewhere with me." He uncrossed, then recrossed, his legs and shuffled the magazines in his lap.

"Sure, where?"

"How about a date?" He hadn't really intended to ask her like that, but the second she appeared, warm and sleepy, on the threshold of the porch, he knew he'd had to ask. He wanted time with her, away from the camp, away from everything that represented any sort of illness or work. Just for one day, he wanted to forget his own limitations, his own potential life limits, and just be a man out on a date with a woman.

"What did you have in mind?" she asked and gave him a crooked smile.

"I didn't really have much in mind other than to spend the day together." Yes, he was Mr. Spontaneity.

"Sounds good to me. By the way, what's the word on Skinny?"

"Bear took him home, but he stayed out of camp because of the bug. Three days in the hospital was about to do him in. Not a man that takes life lying down."

"I'm just glad he did so well," she said. Settling against the back of the swing, she allowed the motion of it soothe her, though right now she didn't seem to need much in the way of soothing. Problems and stress were remarkably absent. All seemed to be right in the world. For now. "Thank you for the treatment. I thoroughly enjoyed it."

"Any excuse to touch a beautiful woman works for me," he said.

"You're a beast, you know that?" she said, but grinned. He was taking all the starch right out of her, and she hadn't even been aware of it. Giving a small kick against the floor, she set the swing into higher motion and tucked her feet beneath her.

"I do," he said and laughed, then pulled her closer. "It's a status I thoroughly enjoy."

The campers left on their day-long trip, and the grounds of the camp were thoroughly, eerily, silent. Mark approached Ellie with a medium-size box in his hands. "Come on, time's a-wasting."

"What are we doing?" she asked.

"It's a surprise, but you'll need your bug spray, a hat and a bottle of water. Swimsuit's optional."

"Optional, eh?" She narrowed her eyes at him, but his playful attitude drew out the lighter side of her. This was going to be fun, whatever it was. "I'll be right back." She returned in minutes with a beach bag slung over one shoulder and sunglasses perched on her nose.

"Let's go." He put on his backpack, then led the way down to the lake. "I thought we could take one of the canoes and have lunch across the lake."

"Oh, that sounds fun."

After securing their items in the bottom of the canoe, they paddled quietly out onto the stillness of the water. Ellie sat in front, Mark in the back. They moved around the lake for a while, watching birds and other wildlife at the edge of the water. The fragrance of her custom bug spray drifted back to him and the mosquitoes were remarkably absent.

They eased into a quiet cove away from the busy activity farther down the lake and pulled the canoe out onto the rocky shore. Mark opened a bottle of wine he'd brought along, poured a plastic cup full for each of them and handed Ellie one. She sipped and savored the sharp taste on her tongue. Then, without preamble, Mark leaned toward her and kissed her. It began as a quiet exploration, but soon turned hot and demanding. His arms moved around her, and she didn't resist. She'd somehow lost the will to resist him and her own natural needs that blossomed around him. The day seemed to be a time somehow out of time. They had no responsibilities for the moment, no place to be, nothing urgent required their attention. They needed the break, and they were wildly attracted to each other. Who could argue with long, slow kisses on a day like this?

"Ellie, you drive me crazy," Mark said and ran his tongue from the lobe of her ear down to her neck and nibbled his way across the sensitive skin exposed there. She'd removed her shirt to reveal the pink bikini beneath, and he cupped her breast, thumb stroking the peak of her nipple through the clingy fabric.

"Then I know exactly what we need to do," she said and eased back from him.

"What's that?"

Standing, she removed her sandals and eased her shorts down, then kicked them aside. "Have a cold swim! I'll beat you to the water," she said. Picking her way over the few feet to the water's edge, she stumbled into the frigid lake with a squeal.

The chase was on, and Mark dashed after her. She

was a few strokes ahead of him, but he swiftly caught her. His daily swims in the lake had begun to pay off.

Catching up to her as she struggled to swim while giggling was easy. In seconds he grabbed her ankle and held on. It was like holding onto a slippery mermaid. Reeling her in, he caught her under the knees, then hauled her closer and clasped her hips to his.

The second their bodies touched, all play ended. Looking down into her dark brown eyes that changed from playful and startled to heavy with desire, Mark knew he was lost to her. He loved this woman with every breath he had in him. Life just wasn't fair. He'd found the woman he would have chosen for himself had he met her under any other circumstances. She was strong and proud, but compassionate and kind as well. She didn't deserve to have a death sentence hanging over her head the way he did. Dammit. The joy of the day fogged over as surely as the afternoon clouds ranging in from overhead.

He pulled away from her and released her legs. She floated away onto her back, uncertainty on her face. Though he wanted her, had wanted to make love to her again, he didn't dare. One chance at intimacy was all they had, and he'd do well to leave her alone now. She didn't deserve the heartache he could bring to her, especially after her previous fiancé had hurt her.

"I'm sorry, Ellie." Releasing her, he swam away, leaving her staring after him as she treaded water.

"Mark? What's wrong?"

The sound of her voice echoed off of the rocks and through his heart. He owed her an explanation, but couldn't form the words in his mind, let alone speak them aloud. This wasn't what he wanted, but he had no choice. He'd never put her or any woman through his illness again. Until his five years were up, he had no choice, and he'd never ask her to put her life on hold for that long. She deserved any chance at happiness that came her way, whether he was in it or not. She'd suffered in the romance department already.

"I think I'm ready to go," he said and hauled himself out of the water onto a rock to dry. The picnic box remained untouched. What a waste. "Maybe this wasn't such a good idea after all."

"What?" She swam over and climbed onto the rock beside him. "What's wrong? One second we're having a good time, then the next second you're acting as if I've developed leprosy. What's up?" She pushed her wet hair up and away from her face.

What could he do, lie to her? She'd felt his touch; she knew the depth of the passion between them when they'd made love. Ellie was not someone he could easily turn his back on, even though he knew he had to. She was smart and vibrant and that's what had attracted him to her in the first place. He wanted to kick himself for allowing himself to touch her, even once. But he would cherish that memory forever.

"I'm simply ready to go back to camp. The water's colder than I thought." The chill in him wasn't due to the temperature of the lake water, but the cold that had lived inside of him for too long.

"Well, we're out of the water and up on a nice warm rock sitting in the sunshine." She crossed her arms and stared at him. "I'm not leaving until you spill whatever it is that's bugging you."

"Me, spill?" he asked. "I have nothing to spill."

"Mark. Just because we've been intimate once doesn't give me the right to tell you what to do, but maybe you could share a little more of yourself with me. It might do you good to talk about it."

"It?" Was he so damned shallow?

"Yeah. Whatever it is that's bothering you." Reaching out, she put the lunch box onto her lap and opened it. "Oh, this looks good. My mouth's watering already."

Unable to resist the aroma, his mouth began to water and his stomach actually growled. His appetite knew no shame. He glanced at her from the side. She was smarter than he thought. Sneaky, too. "You knew I would respond to that food, didn't you?"

"Pavlov ring a bell?" She grinned and held out a cold chicken leg to him and waved it back and forth. "If you want it, you have to answer one question."

"Does that go for you, too? Fair's fair."

For a second she looked as if she would reconsider participating in this game. "I guess. But I go first."

As long as he got that piece of chicken, he'd answer just about anything. He was too easy. "Go ahead."

"What changed your mind back there?" she asked and held the chicken out in front of him.

Sighing, he didn't know if this was a good idea. Then his stomach growled again, and he knew he had to answer her or he was going to starve to death right here and now. "You did."

At her gasp, he grabbed the leg from her, then tore

off a bite. Oh, this was good. Bear was a magician, not a cook.

"Me? What did I do?" Stunned surprise remained on her face and her hand lingered in the air with no chicken in it.

"You didn't do anything."

"Then how can you blame your change in behavior on me?" Reaching into the box, she retrieved another chicken leg, but held it without taking a bite. "You're a very confusing man."

He chewed a minute as he thought about how to answer that. "It's because I care about you, Ellie. That's why I stopped." He finished the chicken before she spoke again, and it turned to a cold lump in his gut instead of the nourishment he'd anticipated.

"I don't understand." Tears formed in her eyes and his insides cramped at the sight. "I truly hadn't expected to find a friend here, let alone someone to…care for, but I have. Are you telling me you don't want to take our relationship any further than it already has gone?"

"I'm telling you, Ellie, that I *can't*." His voice had grown gruff with emotion, and he heard it himself, so he knew that she heard it, too. Damn. He hadn't expected this out of today. Selfishly, he'd just wanted to spend some time with her, and now he saw what a big, fat, bad idea that had been. "I didn't mean to mislead you—"

"Then why the hell did you even ask me out if you didn't want to get to know me? What was the point in this? Just something to do so you wouldn't be bored?"

"No. It was nothing like that." Running a hand

over his head, he closed his eyes. "It was an impulse, nothing more."

"An impulse?"

Anger snapped in her eyes, and he knew he deserved all of it.

"I'm not buying that. There were days between when you asked me out and now. Why not just cancel the date?" She leaned forward and narrowed her eyes at him. "I know there's something else going on, Mark. Now, tell me."

"We're simply not right for each other." That sounded so lame. "I'm sorry, Ellie."

"Yeah, right. Let me remind you, Doctor, of your own medicine. Just a few days ago you lectured me about opening up and sharing of myself emotionally. Do you recall that conversation?"

"Yes." And he recalled touching every inch of her body while he was at it.

"Then take some of your own medicine. You expect me to open up and unload my problems on you, but you aren't willing to open up and share a little bit of yourself with me? How fair is that?"

"It isn't, and I know it, and I'm sorry." So very sorry that he couldn't put words to how badly he felt. So very sorry that he would never again know her touch.

"And what about all the crap you fed me about taking advantage of everything life had to offer? Was that just for everyone else, not you?"

"No, of course not—"

"Then, what?" Her breathing came fast, and she twisted the napkin in her hand.

Unable to speak what was really in his heart, he remained silent. It was for her sake, not just his, that he couldn't reach out to her any longer.

"Well, okay, then. I guess we're done here." She stood. "Mark, you're a hypocrite. Let's go back to camp." She closed the picnic box and didn't look at him again as they gathered their gear.

He knew he'd hurt her, but he didn't have the words to make it right. He didn't have the time he needed in order to make it right.

The canoe trip back to camp was long and silent and painful for both of them.

CHAPTER FOURTEEN

ELLIE stayed in the lodge after they returned from the lake and sipped a cup of coffee in silence. Rain had begun to drizzle by the time they reached the camp's shore, so she grabbed her stuff and ran. The rain was a good enough excuse to get out of there. She simply couldn't return to the infirmary right now. Not with Mark so close at hand, but so far away emotionally. She hadn't pegged him for an emotionally distant man, not with the way he related to the kids and shared of himself with them. The way he'd risked himself to save Skinny had taken so much more courage than she could ever think of having. She'd been silly to even consider that there had been a chance for them together. The relationship fairy was cruel indeed.

Heavy footsteps approached, but she didn't look up, hoping whoever it was would simply keep moving. A coffee carafe appeared in front of her, and her vision expanded to include Bear. Without a word he placed an empty cup on the wooden table, filled it, then refilled her own.

"Looked like you could use some more." He sat down across table from her and picked up his mug.

She looked down at the steaming black liquid. "I think it's going to take more than a cup of coffee to help me out, Bear."

"I got a bottle of good Irish whiskey in the back for emergencies if you need it. Purely medicinal, you know."

Warmth at the gesture heated her chest. "Thanks, Bear. I'll let you know."

"Good enough." Companionable silence filled the air between them for a few minutes. Ellie listened to the song of the wind through the trees, and mourning doves cooed outside the lodge as the rain continued to drizzle. Though the sounds should induce peace and well-being, she couldn't find it in her. Not now. Not after Mark's announcement. Not after the way her heart had reacted.

"Might not hurt to talk to him," Bear said. He sipped from his cup and sat across the table from her, a great hulk of a man with compassion pouring out of him. Something else totally unexpected from the man.

"What do you mean?" Could he seriously mean Mark?

"Dr. Mark. You need to talk to him."

"Why should I?" Anger now replaced any warmth in her chest. Men always stuck together, didn't they?

"He needs you. He needs to talk to you."

"Believe me, he doesn't need anyone." He'd made that more than clear today.

Bear nodded. "I can see how you might think that, but you're wrong."

"Bear. I tried to talk to him, just today. We were having a good time, then he shut down on me. You can't have a conversation with someone who won't talk."

"Yep. That's the truth of it. Sometimes you just have to talk without saying any words." He scratched his beard and frowned. "Maybe *communicate* is a better word than *talk*."

"You lost me." Were all men so complicated?

"I'm not one much for giving advice. You and Dr. Mark have been good to me, so I hate to see you both hurting."

"Bear—"

He held up his hand for her to stop. "You might not know about this, being a woman and all, but men have fears. When we think we can't do right by our woman or our children, now that's the worst fear of all."

"I don't know what you mean by 'do right by.'" This was confusing her more than ever. A dull pain was beginning at the base of her skull.

"Men take care of things. We get things done. We're not much on feelings unless they're so powerful we can't help it. But give us a job to do, and we can get it done. That's how we show our true feelings."

"I got that. My dad was a fixer. Any problem you took to him, he could fix it or figure out how to get it straightened out."

"See? Your dad was a real man and a real dad."

"He was." Now, thinking of him wasn't as painful as it had been at the beginning of the summer. Time did have a way of healing things, though it was the world's biggest cliché to think of it that way. It was true. The ache that had lived in her heart for him no longer had the influence it once had. At least that was something.

"Now what did he do if he had a problem he couldn't solve?" Bear asked and took another sip.

"Oh, that was bad." She chuckled at a memory. "He wouldn't give up until he figured it out. Not a good time to be around him, either."

"Did he ever have a problem he couldn't fix or solve on his own?"

"Sure. When he was sick. He went to the doctor, but the doctor couldn't fix him, either." Enlightenment struck Ellie, and she stared at Bear. Reaching out, she clasped his wrist and squeezed. "He's trying to protect me, isn't he?" she whispered.

Bear simply smiled, and his eyes curled up at the outer edges. "Might be. A real man takes care of what's his. Sometimes the way we go about things might not be the most intelligent way, but we protect what's ours."

"I'm such an idiot," she said and closed her eyes. She should have seen it. Her father had done the same thing. When he became ill and knew that he wasn't going to be getting better, he went through every insurance policy, every bank account, and ensured that her mother would have everything paid for, everything in order, and there would be no reason for her to worry financially the rest of her life. It was the last thing he could do for her, aside from love her until he no longer could. It was what had made him such a good father and husband. And one of the reasons they missed him terribly. He'd taken care of things until the very last.

"When my mother figured out what he was doing she was furious. Then she cried, then he cried." She shrugged. "It wasn't what she wanted."

"But it was something he needed to do, right?"

"Yes."

"And somehow they met in the middle, didn't they?" Bear asked.

"Yeah. They were like that. They had their own way of working things out together." She shook her head. "I know I'll never have that."

"Of course you won't."

A pang of disappointment and longing shot through her. "Bear, this would be a good time to reassure me and tell me that I'll find it, right?" That faint hope that had blossomed in her chest faded to dust at his words. She was going to choke that fairy.

"Nope. This would be a good time to tell you to quit moping around in the lodge. I gotta wax the floors before the kids get back. If you want to work things out with Mark, you go after him and do it. If you do, you'll have your own version of what your parents had, just not exactly what they had."

"I see. Thanks, Bear. That was one of the more interesting pep talks I've ever had," she said. Standing, she moved around the other side of the table before he could get up. She leaned over and hugged him, then kissed his cheek. "It was just what I needed to hear."

"Good. Now get outta here. I saw Mark getting ready for a run, so you'd better hurry."

"Thanks!" With a wave she dashed out of the lodge and sprinted for the infirmary. She nearly ripped the hinges off of the squeaky screen door and leaped through the entrance. "Mark! Where are you?"

Only silence greeted her, and she stopped. Damn.

She'd missed him, and she had no idea where he'd gone running. "Fooey." Shoulders drooping, she caught her breath. What in the world had she been thinking? No matter what Bear said, Mark didn't want her. He'd made that abundantly clear out on the lake. He had a life elsewhere. Just because they'd made love one time didn't mean that he was going to want to have a relationship with her. How could they have a relationship when they lived so far apart anyway? Long-distance relationships sucked. And hadn't she told herself that she was simply going to take care of herself over the summer and not even think about relationships until the fall?

Well, she hadn't thought, she'd just jumped right in to one. She huffed out a sigh and turned.

Mark stood right behind her, and she shrieked. Grabbing her arms, he hauled her against him. "I don't care if it's wrong. I don't care if I get hurt, Ellie. I don't want you to get hurt. I don't want to hurt you." The fierce look in his eyes would have frightened her once, but now she knew it was fear and not anger behind them.

"Let go of me," she whispered and shook her hands to free them of his grip.

"I shouldn't handle you that way, sorry." He released her.

Reaching out, she grabbed him around the shoulders and pulled him close to her. Automatically, his hands reached for her hips. "No, you shouldn't. I want to put my hands on you and I can't when you're holding them."

On fire, she hooked her hands around the back of his

head and dragged his mouth down to hers. She didn't kiss him so much as she devoured him. Parting her mouth she slid her tongue inside his, teasing and tasting him, daring him not to respond to her. With a groan, he pressed her back against the wall and leaned into her. Hands ranged over each other, teasing skin and tugging at clothing.

"Oh, God, Ellie. I want you." His breath was harsh in his throat. Unable to prevent himself, he clasped the straps of her swimsuit and drew them down over her shoulders. When she figured out where he was headed, she gasped and kept her eyes on his. She didn't stop him and didn't look away. The desire in her eyes was a beautiful thing to see.

He'd stopped earlier, but now he didn't know if he could. He certainly didn't want to.

She reached for his hand and pulled it up to her breast. She closed her eyes as he held the soft flesh, brushed his thumb over the hardened peak. She was luscious in her desire and watching her enjoy the passion between them sealed his fate. He loved her.

Somehow his mouth found her breast, and he breathed deep. Aching for her, he pressed his hips against hers, and she rubbed hard against him. She touched his ear with her mouth, and her breath was hot and harsh. "Take me to bed, Mark. Take me to bed, now."

Unable to resist her plea, he moved with her down the hall to his room and opened the door. Without letting go of her, he found the bed, and they collapsed onto it. Clothing and swimsuits flew across the room until there was only skin between them.

* * *

Two o'clock in the morning had always been his bewitching hour. For whatever reason, when 2:00 a.m. came, he woke. If he had pain, or dreams, or something on his mind, no matter if he slept deeply at first, when 2:00 or thereabouts arrived, he opened his eyes.

The same thing happened tonight. He and Ellie had made love again and it was as magnificent as the first time. His body had remembered what to do and had less of a problem figuring things out than his mind did. It had always been his mind that caused him trouble.

Rising from the bunk, he moved to the kitchen for something to eat. Though he and Ellie had been together earlier in the evening, the ability for two people to successfully *sleep* together in one of the bunks was impossible, so she'd moved back to her bed after a long, lingering kiss by the doorway.

He opened a bottle of soda and sat at the bistro table, put his elbows on it and dropped his face onto his hands. How was he going to survive the remainder of the summer without hurting Ellie any more than he already had? What was going on between them was magical and totally wrong. There were years left until he could reach out to a woman and not let go. He had to let go of Ellie. For her sake, he had to.

A sound drifted into his consciousness, and he looked up, expecting to see a camper in the doorway. Ellie hovered there instead.

"Are you okay?" she asked.

"Yeah." He turned to face her and smiled. She was all sleepy eyes and rumpled nightshirt, bare legs and feet. What he wouldn't give to be able to crawl into bed with her and sleep away the rest of the night. "I'm okay. Did I wake you?"

"Mm-hmm. It's okay though." Taking a step forward, she placed her hand on his bare back, then sat in the seat beside him. "Sleep's overrated, right?"

"Not in my book."

"Do you want to talk?"

She was giving him an opportunity that he could no longer avoid. He had to talk, had to tell her everything, or he couldn't live with himself any longer.

"I want my life back, Ellie," Mark said and turned away from her. He shoved both hands into his hair and clutched the sides of his head. Agitated didn't begin to describe what he was feeling. "I can't take it anymore. I can't take it."

"Why can't you have a life? I don't understand." She'd gone perfectly still, intently focused on him.

"Because I…I have cancer."

"No, you don't. You told me you were treated and free of disease. You have been for three years. " The agitation in her voice made it raise an octave.

"I was. I am." He groaned loud, hating to hear the words come out of his mouth, but they had to be said. "But my life is on terminal hold for another two years."

"Why? What's two years got to do with anything?"

"Until I'm free of cancer for five years I can't have a life or a relationship with anyone, no matter how much I want it. Not even you." There. He'd said it out loud and to the one person in the world he never wanted to hurt. If he wanted to spare her in the long run, he had to do it now.

"Mark, that's ridiculous." She leaned back in the chair, a stunned look on her face.

"Ridiculous? Is that what your mother thought when your father died?"

"Of course not. She didn't want him to suffer any more than he already had. She was grateful, as was I, for the time we had with him."

"Didn't it break your heart to love him and lose him?"

"Yes, it did. But we didn't love him any less because he was only going to be with us a short time. We probably loved him more."

"You were an adult when you lost your father. What would happen if I fathered a child and then died? How fair would it be to that child and the mother? Not at all." He just couldn't do it.

He had to break out of this cage that trapped him, and he left the kitchen and strode to the main room. No matter what Ellie said, no matter how she tried to rationalize things, it wouldn't work. Couldn't work. He wouldn't do that to her or a child. Not the way it had been done to him.

"Mark!" She reached out and stopped his movements. "Stop it. Will you listen to yourself? You have a right to have a life. You have a right to live it." She took a deep breath. "You have the right to love, and be loved, well for as long as possible. We all do."

Trembling from the bound-up rage inside him, he clenched his teeth against the emotional pain that was tearing a hole in him. "I can't, Ellie. I can't. I won't knowingly do that to someone I love." And he knew he loved her or the pain wouldn't be this bad.

"But you have friends, you have family, that love you. You're worthy of being loved, Mark. I don't know where you've been living, but there are no guarantees in this life anyway. I could go back to Dallas and get hit by a bus. Should I have waited until I was certain it was safe to live my life?" Anger snapped in her eyes. "Weren't you the one who lectured me about reaching out to grab life with both hands? And here you are afraid to do it yourself."

He clasped her shoulders. "Ellie, I can't take the chance I'll develop cancer again within the first five years. It's my worst fear, and I simply can't do that to another person. To you."

"What if someone cares for you already and wants you to love them back, no matter what, no matter how much time you have?"

The tears she'd been struggling to hold back brimmed in her eyes. Mark knew what she was saying, knew that part of him wanted to reach out to her, to take what she offered and to hell with the rest of it. Cancer was the bus that was going to run him down.

"I would tell this person that I can't be what they need right now and to find someone who can be."

She jerked away from him and hugged her arms around her middle. "You're being so unfair to yourself. You must know the cure rate by now? Why not simply monitor your blood levels every six months or so? Keep track of it, stay on top of it. Can't it be that simple?"

"I do that already. I just don't know if it will be enough." The fight seemed to run out of him. "I know what it was like to grow up without a father, so I won't willingly or knowingly inflict that loss on a child. He could have made a difference in the lives of me and my sisters, but he chose not to. I won't create a life that I won't be around to raise."

"Do you hear yourself? You sound like the ultimate martyr, sacrificing yourself so that those around you won't have to suffer if you get sick again."

"Say it, Ellie. It's not just sick—it's *dying* from a recurrence of cancer."

"So you think you're the only one who's faced this issue? How many cancer survivors are down on their knees every day, grateful to have just one more day with their families and loved ones?"

Furious, she stormed from the infirmary and ran outside into a rain that neither of them had noticed. Her tears mixed with the rain and dribbled down her face. He was so much more valuable than he knew. Not just in what he could offer someone in support, but in his humor, in his friendship.

"Ellie, I'm sorry," he said.

Surprised he'd followed her, she turned. They were both soaked in minutes. "Don't be sorry, Mark. Go back to your calendar and start ticking off the next two years, and then you can come out of your cocoon."

"Do you think I like this? That I'm enjoying putting any sort of life I might want, any future I want, on hold for two more years?" He grabbed her roughly by the shoulders. "Do you think I want cancer more than I want you?"

"Apparently, you do. You get something out of this or you'd already have taken your life back. You wouldn't let the cancer win. You're a coward, Mark Collins.

Somehow, along the way to recovery, you left your courage behind." If he couldn't see it, then there was nothing for them.

"I died, Ellie! Everything in me died when I found out that I had cancer. Then it took whatever I had left to find the strength to survive the treatments. I lost my fiancé. I had to quit my job because I could no longer function."

"I know, Mark. I know. And now, faced with an opportunity to rebuild your life, to make it better than it was before, you don't reach out, you won't take the chance—you simply turn away. When there's someone who loves you standing right in front of you, you walk away because it's easier."

"Easier! Do you honestly want to love someone, start a family even, with someone who might leave you?"

"Who said anything about starting a family, or marriage for that matter? Is that all you want? Right now, all I want is a chance to be with you to see where we might get to, and you won't even take it. There are no guarantees in life, Mark. I could marry someone and have children with him, and he could die in a car accident, or leave me for someone better than me." That had happened to so many of her friends that she didn't even want to think about it.

"There's no one better than you," he said, his voice husky with emotion.

"Then prove it. Take a chance with me, Mark. We have something to build on that I've never experienced in a relationship before. I wasn't expecting to find someone I could love here, and I certainly didn't expect it to happen so quickly. I care deeply for you." Her voice cracked. "But I can't have a relationship on my own. You have to be willing to take a chance on us, take a leap of faith with your future, and reach out for it, no matter the consequences."

Stunned into silence, Mark simply stared at her. The rain appeared unaffected by their storm of emotion and continued to pour down on top of them. "I don't know what to say."

"You've already said it. You've won the battle to save your body, but you've lost the war and let it eat your heart and your soul. If you can't take your life back, no one can do it for you." Calmer now, she wrapped her arms around herself. He'd made his decision, and she'd have to accept it. "I'll write up a schedule for us to divide the clinics. That way we can avoid each other for the rest of the summer."

"I don't want to do that, Ellie."

"Then you'd better figure out what you do want. We've got another few weeks of camp to get through yet, and I won't be able to do my job if we keep on this way."

"I know. Me, either. I didn't expect to find a situation like this."

"What do you mean, 'a situation like this'?" She narrowed her eyes at him.

"Finding someone I could have loved had the circumstances been different."

"Had your attitude been different, the circumstances wouldn't matter." With that, she walked back into the infirmary, and Mark let her go.

CHAPTER FIFTEEN

DAYS passed with Ellie and Mark in a stalemate. They worked together and slept in the same building, but that was about the extent of their interactions.

Carnival weekend arrived and so did Sam and Vicki for their second scheduled trip to camp. This event was planned for the next to the last weekend before camp ended, that way the kids could have a few days to recover from all the fun before heading home.

"Well, I've never seen two more miserable-looking people in my life," Sam said. He and Mark had taken a canoe out onto the lake and left the women to the infirmary with Myra.

"Ellie and I had a bit of a philosophical disagreement." That was a polite way to put it, wasn't it?

"A bit?" Sam barked out a laugh that echoed off the water.

"Okay, a major philosophical disagreement."

"Anything you want to discuss?"

"Not really."

The only sound was of their oars dipping into the

water and the birds chattering in the trees at the edge of the water. A red-eyed common loon lazed about in the middle of the lake, but flipped under the water and swam away at their approach.

"Vicki and I had some trouble over the years, but we worked it out."

"I know, everyone has trouble now and then. But you didn't start out that way. Beginning a relationship with problems only leads to a quick end and pain for everyone."

"But you're crazy about Ellie, I can tell. Being wild about Vicki made me want to work that much harder to keep her with me and happy." He paddled and paused. "To be able to change."

"Yeah. You two were suited to each other from the get-go." Not everyone had the stability that Sam and Vicki had.

"That's possible for you to have, Mark. You've got a lot to offer a woman like Ellie."

"Sure, illness, caretaking when I'm infirm again, holding the bucket for me when I have to take chemo again." Not going there.

"You keep saying *again* like it's a sure thing the cancer's going to come back. Statistics are with you, man. That hasn't hit you yet?" He paused, then returned to paddling. "You haven't had any signs have you?"

"No."

"Then what's your worry?"

"It's like walking around with a guillotine around my neck, just waiting for it to drop. I can't relax or make plans until I know for sure that my life is my own again."

"It's already your own, you're just too afraid to see it."

"Dammit, it's not mine to share. Ellie deserves someone who can give her what she wants, what she needs, someone to love her the way she should be loved. Not someone with one foot in the grave."

"No one would love her the way you do."

Mark let the pause between them hang. "That's why I have to let her go at the end of the summer."

"Sounds like you've already let her go."

"I guess I have. It's better this way." Didn't mean it wasn't tearing him apart on the inside to do it.

"I respectfully disagree with you, Mark. When we were here a month ago, you were both excited and happy. You were on the verge of discovering what was between you. There was magic in the air around you. Vicki and I both felt it."

"I was deluding myself at the time." Severely.

"About what? Being happy?"

"Yeah. That's what Ellie said, too." The heaviness in his chest grew more dense. This wasn't the way things were supposed to have worked out in his life, but this was what he had gotten. He was just lucky to be alive, and although he immensely appreciated that fact, he wasn't free.

"Think we might be right?"

"No. It's not that I don't have the right. It's just that what happens if we work it out, if we make a good thing between us, then I get cancer again?" He sighed. "I couldn't live with myself if that happened and I died, leaving her to fend without me. If I start something, I intend to finish it."

"Statistics are with you, my friend. I thought you did some research on this."

"I did. I did." Over and over and over.

"You don't believe the research?"

"It's not that I don't believe it—I'm afraid to believe it. What if I'm the odd statistic that doesn't stand up to the research? It does happen and people do die from this, no matter what the statistics read like."

"Then you face life the way the rest of us do, man— no guarantees. You take your chances and grab life with both hands, and you don't let go." Sam half turned in the canoe to face Mark.

"Sometimes having a friend who's a psychiatrist is a royal pain in the ass." Mark jerked his oar forward and splashed Sam a good one.

Sam laughed and shook his head like a wet dog. "I'd have to agree with you on that one."

Mark left the conversation at that point and focused on paddling the canoe, one stroke at a time.

"Guess we ought to head back. They'll be ready for the carnival to start soon and something unexpected always happens," Sam said.

Mark followed his lead, and they turned the canoe back to the camp.

Before the carnival got into full swing, Ellie and Vicki set up a first-aid clinic on the porch of the lodge in readiness for the flurry of bumps and bruises and minor injuries they were sure would occur.

The mail arrived while they were waiting for little customers, and Ellie accepted the giant mail sack from the postman, as well as a small package addressed to her.

"Oh, this is for Bear," Ellie said after opening the box containing an order of her new essential oils. "He wanted some lavender oil for the kitchen to put on burns right away."

"How is his?" Vicki said.

"It's nearly invisible. At first I was really surprised that it worked so well, but I really shouldn't be. Lavender is such a great oil."

"You did a good job with that. He could have had a serious scar."

"Thanks. I was just surprised that Mark went for a complementary therapy. Most docs I know wouldn't have. Too alternative, not scientific enough." She'd heard that argument for years, but it hadn't stopped her from trying the oils on herself and her friends who were open to new ideas.

"Mark's full of surprises." Vicki grabbed a bottle of water from the ice-filled cooler beside them. Though they were in the shade, the humidity made the air feel hotter.

"Yeah, I know." He'd surprised her in so many ways in the past few weeks, she couldn't keep track. The last surprise she could have lived without.

"Let's sit for a while. The relay races are about to start, so that's pretty benign unless someone wipes out at the finish line."

"Okay." Ellie huffed out a sigh and reached for a bottle of water.

"So, how are you and Mark doing?" Vicki asked the open-ended question.

"We aren't." It was as simple as that. Though they

had connected for a while, that connection was now broken in a way that couldn't be mended.

"This is just an observation, but you both look pretty unhappy."

"I can't speak for him, but I'll be glad when camp is over, and we can go our separate ways, get back to what I'm familiar with." Away from the heartache. Although coming to Maine had seemed like a good idea at the time, it had obviously been a mistake.

"What happened? Things were okay when we were here last."

How much should she tell Vicki? Not that she wouldn't guess anyway, so she might as well spill it. "We made love."

"What? *What!*" Vicki leaned forward, intent on hearing everything. "Was it that bad?"

Tears pricked Ellie's eyes, and she gave a sad smile. "No, silly. It was wonderful. That's what makes the situation so bad. We had a wonderful few days, maybe a week, as lovers, then Mark decided that he was more into protecting me than being with me."

"Oh, Ellie, I'm so sorry. Did you tell him he's an idiot?" Vicki placed a comforting hand on Ellie's shoulder.

Tearful, Ellie gave a watery laugh. "Basically. But he doesn't want me to get too attached to him, then have something horrid happen, like his cancer return." She took a gasping breath, still unable to see the logic in his thinking. "He can't see the benefit of being together even if something bad happens in the future. He doesn't see that I could help him, that I would support him, that I would love him no matter what."

"Part of his resistance may be because of his former fiancé."

"Another thing we have in common. He told me about her, and I told him about Alan. I think he's over the hurt of that breakup, but not the fear, and that's something only he can conquer."

A camper with a splinter interrupted their conversation and, from then on, their time was filled with little bits of this and that.

When Vicki dispensed the first aid, Ellie gave a kiss to the cheek of the injured camper. When Ellie treated, Vicki gave a kiss, and they applied a red, red lipstick for each one. Soon there were campers all over the place with lipstick imprints on their faces. Some kids began to fake injuries in order to get another dose of loving from the nurses.

"This is turning into a kissing booth," Vicki said and kissed another cheek.

"We should start charging." Ellie laughed and started to give kisses to anyone that came by.

"Charging for what?" Sam asked as he and Mark approached the first-aid station.

"Kisses," Vicki said and gave Sam a smooch on the cheek.

"Sounds good to me," he said and smooched her back.

They were so good together. They were more comfortable and happy than Ellie had seen them in years. Their lifestyle adjustments had paid off for them in happiness, and she was thrilled that their marriage and friendship had survived the rocky times. As Ellie watched, envy twisted in her, and she glanced at Mark, who also watched their friends. The expression on his face mirrored what was going on inside of her. If she could only convince him to take a chance…

Sudden screams rent the air and the hairs on Ellie's arms stood straight up. She rose and looked around for the problem. Mark's energy reflected that his system was on high alert, too.

Together they stepped off the porch, and Mark reached for her hand. Somehow Ellie had an emergency pack in her hand before she became consciously aware of it.

"Help! We need help over here." A counselor raced over to the lodge and waved for them to follow.

"What's wrong?" Mark asked as he and Ellie ran behind him.

"Ricky's choking."

Oh, no, Ellie thought. One of her worst patient scenarios. If they didn't clear the airway in a few minutes, a child could choke to death right in front of them.

They arrived at the scene to find a crowd of campers gathered around a boy of about ten years of age. Immediately, they could see that this situation was serious. The boy had already lost consciousness, his face a ghastly blue.

"What was he eating?" Mark asked as he shot into action and dropped to the ground beside Ricky.

"Hot dogs." The counselor shoved his hands into his hair and paced back and forth. "We were having a contest."

"Bad idea. Ellie, send someone for the oxygen tank."

"I'll go." The counselor raced away.

Mark didn't waste any time. She'd never seen such focused intensity in him. She assisted Mark to turn the boy onto his back and began a series of chest thrusts to try to dislodge the object occluding the trachea.

She looked into the boy's mouth for anything, but nothing had loosened. "Again," she said, trying to control the anxiety surfacing in her. The boy was turning a dreadful shade of bluish gray now.

Mark again thrust on the boy's chest. "Come on, kid. Come on!"

"Turn him," she said and again checked his mouth. "Nothing."

"Dammit," Mark ground out. "We might have to do a tracheotomy right here."

"Can Sam help you?"

"Yeah, but I'm better at the quick-and-dirty stuff." He cursed nonstop under his breath.

Sam arrived with the oxygen tank, the anxious counselor trailing behind him. "Vicki's calling 911 right now."

"We don't have time to wait," Mark said. Sweat poured out of him from his efforts.

"I'll go get the trach kit," Sam said and ran to the infirmary just a few short yards away.

"Come on, Mark. You can do it. Just one more time," Ellie said, urgency, anxiety and somehow hope pouring out of her. "You can do it. I *know* you can."

The glance between them took a split second, but in that time, Ellie gave every confidence, every desire, every spark of powerful energy, she had to Mark. He clenched his jaws together and performed another series of five chest thrusts.

Hands shaking, knowing this was the deciding moment, Ellie looked in the boy's mouth. "Turn him more, there's something there, but I can't get it," she cried. Mark turned the boy to his side, and Ellie scraped out the remnants of a half-chewed piece of food with her fingers. "Oh, you did it, Mark!"

They eased him back and place the oxygen mask over Ricky's face. Ellie's joy turned to fear. "He's not breathing."

"Bag him."

Quickly she switched oxygen devices and pushed oxygen into the boy's lungs with the ambu bag. "You can do it, Ricky, you can do it," she whispered with each squeeze of the oxygen bag. "Come on, buddy, breathe."

Sam returned with the kit that was now unnecessary. "Wow. Good work. You got it."

"Yeah, but he's not breathing on his own," Mark said and reached for Ricky's arm. "Pulse is really fast, but at least he has one." Sweat dripped off of Mark onto the ground.

"Where's that ambulance?" Ellie asked, not looking up from her task, and she took up Mark's cursing under her breath.

"Easy, Ellie. You're doing great. His color's improving, too," Mark said and applied the oxygen monitor to Ricky's finger. "Slow down, take your time and give him good breaths."

"My hands are getting tired." Her arms were shaking from the effort.

"I'll take it for a while." Crawling close to her, Mark placed his hands over hers, and she took his place to monitor the vital signs. The tension between them had evaporated and now they were the team they had been not so long ago. Ellie looked up and met his gaze. They looked at each other for a moment, and she could see the longing in him. A blink of his eyes, and the connection between them broke.

Sirens cut the air and Ellie breathed a sigh of relief. "Oh, thank heaven, they're here."

"Vicki will show them where to come," Sam said.

After they turned Ricky over to the ambulance crew, who took him to the ER for further evaluation and monitoring, a gloom settled over the camp. Even the skies seemed to sense the discord of what should have been a happy day and a light drizzle chased everyone into the lodge. The carnival was over.

Ellie grabbed the equipment and headed to the infirmary with Mark right behind her.

"You did great back there," he said and wiped his hand over his face.

"So did you." She shivered as her wet clothing began to chill her. "I don't think I've ever been so scared. I thought we were going to lose him."

"Takes a real pro to not lose your cool like you did."

"I was just glad it wasn't more hornets," she said and another shiver crossed her flesh. "Ew."

Mark laughed, and Ellie joined him. They needed the break after sharing such an intense case.

"Me, too," he said and took a step closer to her.

She caught her breath, afraid to move, afraid to hope. Her gaze latched on to his and wouldn't let go. "I hate hornets."

He stepped closer still, all playfulness gone in an instant, his green eyes intense and focused on her. "Me, too." With that, he pulled her into his arms and hugged her. "Ellie."

Tremors vibrated through him and into her as she clasped her arms around his back. This was what she needed—to be touched and loved by Mark. And he needed to be touched and loved by her. There was no one else for her, and she knew in her heart that she was what he wanted, too. Somehow she had to convince him of it.

They stood for long moments simply holding each other and coming down from the high anxiety of the shared case. Mark's soothing strokes on her back soon gave her the strength to pull away from him to tell him what he needed to hear and what she needed to say.

"Mark Collins, I love you." Reaching for his face, she pulled him down and laid a gentle kiss on his mouth.

"Ellie."

She stopped him before he could deny her. She had to speak the words in her heart that were bursting to be free. "Whether you love me or not, you must know that I love you. Vows that are spoken in sickness and in health I give to you now, between just the two of us." Tears formed in her eyes, and she dragged in a ragged breath as the beating of her heart nearly closed off her throat. "With all my heart, with all my soul, I will be with you whether you're healthy or not. I love you and want time with you. What matters is not the amount of days we have together, but the joy and the love within those days that counts."

"Ellie." His voice was a hoarse whisper, and he swallowed quickly.

Desperation was in every movement he made as he reached out and yanked her back into his embrace. He trembled and so did she. The power of the feelings between them nearly scorched the air in the room. If he didn't speak soon, she was going to die of embarrassment right here in his arms. He pulled back and cupped her face with his hands.

"I've never known anyone like you." Energy and passion and love nearly glowed in his eyes. "You mean more to me than I ever thought possible. I don't know what my future is, but without you in it, it's going to be awfully sad and boring."

Tears that formed in her eyes now overflowed down her cheeks, and hope began to ease the ache in her chest. Mark dropped to his knees in front of her and took her hands.

"Let me give back the vows you've just given to me, because they are the most beautiful words I've ever heard." He took a breath and squeezed her hands. "I, Mark Collins, vow to adore you for as long as we have together. We are a beautiful team that no one, not even me, can tear apart. You are the life that breathes within me and keeps my heart beating. Each step of every day I will take part of you with me." He kissed the knuckles of her left hand. "I love you, Ellie Mackenzie. Will you honor me, and marry me, possibly bear my children some day, and love me until the day I die? Whenever that is?"

She drew him up to stand in front of her. Happiness that she'd never experienced in her life filled every cell of her body. "I *do* love you, and I *will* marry you, and we *will* have children and a long, long life together. I just know it."

He pressed a hard kiss to her mouth, then held her against him.

The squeak of the screen door let them know that they weren't alone any longer. "Man, there's just no privacy around here," Mark said and they turned, holding onto each other.

Sam and Vicki came through the door with a sleeping Myra on Sam's shoulder. "What's going on?" Vicki asked, concern etched in her face as she moved toward Ellie. "Did something happen?"

"Yeah." Ellie nodded and looked up at Mark. "We just got married."

"Wh-what!" Vicki yelled and gaped at them.

"Well, not really, but Mark proposed, and I said yes," she replied and squeezed Mark's waist. She wasn't going to let go of him any time soon.

Vicki clasped her hands to her cheeks and turned to Sam, her eyes wide.

"Wow. You work fast," Sam said with a grin and held a hand out to Mark. "Congratulations." He leaned over and gave Ellie a one-armed hug. "To both of you."

"Okay, okay, okay," Vicki said and waved her hands as if trying to make sense of things. "You two sit down right now, and tell us what happened. Last thing we knew you were coming up here to decompress from the emergency."

"I guess we did that, too." Ellie laughed and it was free and happy. "We'll tell you everything, but first I have to call my mom." She reached into her pocket, pulled out her cell phone with a hand that still trembled and dialed. In two rings her mother picked up. "Mom? It's Ellie. I'm getting married!"

"What!" her mother yelled into the phone, and Ellie jerked it away from her ear.

"Why does everyone shriek when I tell them?" she asked Mark.

"Because you are a wonderful person who deserves happiness more than anyone I know," her mother tearfully replied into the phone.

"I'll call you again, later." Ellie finished the conversation in a minute, then hung up.

"We need to celebrate," Vicki said and headed to the kitchen. "Hey! This bag of stuff I brought you weeks ago is still sitting on the counter." She turned narrowed eyes on Ellie.

"What? What bag?"

Vicki pointed to a grocery bag that lay rumpled on the counter, forgotten since it had been left there. "This. It's part of the stuff I brought you when we were here last time and the stomach flu was running rampant."

"Oh, yeah. I kinda forgot about that bag since everything I needed was in the other one." Confused now, she headed into the kitchen. What could she have overlooked?

"Not *everything*. You're going to have to open it now." Vicki brought the bag out just as Sam returned from putting Myra on a bunk in the ward room. "Sam, they didn't even open my present."

"How rude," he said and grinned. "What present?"

"Present? I didn't know it was a present or I definitely would have opened it. I thought it was just more stomach medicine." She took the bag from her friend.

"Open it." Vicki crossed her arms and tapped a toe, waiting.

Reaching into the bag, Ellie pulled out a bottle of

wine and handed it to Mark. "Oh, lovely. We can share it and toast our engagement." She smiled at Mark.

"The rest we're not sharing together. I don't care how much we love you," Vicki said and snickered.

Reaching again into the bag, Ellie pulled out a small box, then shoved it back into the bag with a giggle. "Vicki!"

"Hey, those were meant for you and Mark. If you'd opened the bag at the right time you wouldn't be turning three shades of red now."

"Just why *is* she turning three shades of red?" Mark asked and reached for the bag that Ellie shoved behind her back.

"No reason."

Before Ellie could think, Mark grabbed her around the waist and took the bag from her, opened it and laughed.

"Am I the last one to know?" Sam asked.

Mark hugged Ellie to him while he continued to chuckle and handed the bag to Sam.

"Hey! We could use some of these, too." He looked at Vicki. "Just because we're married, and they're not, doesn't mean they get all the fun."

She reached up and gave him a quick kiss. "True. Very true."

Mark looked at Ellie, and the future no longer held fear for him. With Ellie by his side, he knew that he could conquer whatever challenges life and his health threw at him. "How do you feel about moving to New Mexico? Or I could move to Dallas?"

"My home is where you are. New Mexico has fond memories for me."

"With you there, I think we'll make some more."

"Absolutely."

He kissed her, seeming to find doing so in front of his friends, who witnessed the love between them, a vow, sealing his love for the woman who would soon be his bride.

"You know, Sam and I renewed our vows here at camp. Gil even gave us the use of the main house and grounds for a week before they closed things up for the winter. He might be willing to extend the same offer to you."

"My mom and brothers will kill me if I get married without them." Although enticing, the idea might not work for everyone.

"Then invite everyone here for the ceremony. Have a collective family reunion or something," Sam said. "I think we can swing a long weekend, then. How about over Labor Day? Most people are off an extra day for that anyway."

"What do you think?" Ellie asked Mark. The light in her eyes nearly brought him to his knees. He would do anything for this woman who loved him.

"I'm up for it. All we can do is ask Gil and ask the family to come." He brought her hand to his mouth and kissed her knuckles. "I want to marry you, Ellie. I don't care where or when, but I will be there."

Vicki whispered in Sam's ear, then he nodded. She looked at them and cleared her throat. "You know, Sam and I have reservations at a lovely bed-and-breakfast in town. Since Myra's already asleep, why don't you two take our reservation for the night? We can handle anything that comes into the infirmary for one night."

"Vicki, Sam? Are you sure?" Ellie asked. The generosity of their friends was overwhelming.

Reaching out, Mark grabbed the key that Vicki dangled in front of her. "They're sure, now go pack a bag." He nudged Ellie toward her room. "All you're going to need is your toothbrush and that bag of stuff Vicki bought you."

"Mark!" She giggled as she walked down the hall. "I think I need a little more than that."

"Okay. A bottle of aromatherapy oil, but no more than that," he said and turned toward their friends. "Thank you. We'll owe you one."

"Just be happy. That's all the thanks we need." Vicki embraced him and then Sam did as well, with a hearty clap on the back.

"We'll do that," Mark said and knew that it was going to be true.

EPILOGUE

Just a few weeks later

SAM stood with Mark, who fidgeted, on the dock by the lake. "Are you okay, man?" he asked.

"Yeah," was Mark's tight-lipped response. "I'm good."

"You'd better hold onto me, because when you see her, you're going to want to faint. I don't want you to fall in and drown on your wedding day."

Mark laughed and some of the tension in him lifted, the positive energy of the day now filling him again. "I won't, I promise."

Vicki and Myra walked down the path to the lake dressed in matching summer dresses. "Now I think *I'm* going to faint. They're so beautiful," Sam said.

"Be strong."

"You're next," Sam said and gave a small wave to his daughter, who waved back.

"I sure hope so." Mark's dreams of a family of his own were uncertain, as was his future, but at least he was beginning by marrying Ellie. She was his family and his future. The rest would fall into place as long as they loved each other.

When Ellie appeared, Mark's heart, which had been doing fine, began to race in his chest. Each pulse he heard in his ears until it drowned out any other sound. He was hers; there was no doubt about it.

Soft and dreamy in a beige summer dress and sandals, she looked like a dark-haired fairy come from the forest to tempt him. Giving in to the temptation, he held out his hand to her and brought her by his side, where she would remain the rest of their lives together.

"Friends and family of Ellie Mackenzie and Mark Collins, you have been invited here to this grove to witness the love shining between these two people who have promised themselves to each other." The words rang out and were forever etched into the hearts of Mark and Ellie.

At the end of the reception in the lodge, Skinny turned to Bear. "Think I could work in the infirmary next year?"

Bear frowned at the man. Had he gone daft? "No. You're not a doctor or a nurse. Whatcha want to do that for?"

"There's so much romance going on in there, I was hoping some of it might rub off on me."

Bear laughed and clamped his arm around Skinny's shoulders. "Sorry, son. You're stuck with me and the boys in the lodge. We're as romantic as you're gonna get."

* * * * *

★

⊙™ MILLS & BOON®

are proud to present our...

Book of the Month

Their Newborn Gift
by Nikki Logan
from Mills & Boon®
Romance

When Lea became accidentally pregnant she
decided that she would go it alone. Rodeo star
Reilly wasn't the sort of man who'd want to
be tied down. But five years later she needs
to tell him her secret...

Mills & Boon® Romance
Available 4th June

Something to say about our
Book of the Month?
Tell us what you think!
millsandboon.co.uk/community

0610/03a

MEDICAL™ 2-in-1

Coming next month

DARE SHE DATE THE DREAMY DOC?
by Sarah Morgan

Nurse Jenna Richards did *not* come all the way to Glenmore
to fall head-over-heels for the first sexy doctor she saw.
But what's a single mum to do when devastatingly
dreamy Dr Ryan McKinley has his eye on you?

DR DROP-DEAD GORGEOUS
by Emily Forbes

Plastic surgeon Ben McMahon has stepped out of Melbourne's
society pages and into nurse Maggie Petersen's life. He
sweeps Maggie well and truly off her feet— then the city's most
eligible bachelor discovers he's about to become a daddy!

HER BROODING ITALIAN SURGEON
by Fiona Lowe

Whilst Dr Abbie McFarlane appreciates eminent surgeon and
temporary colleague Leo Costa's skills, his famous Italian
charm she can do without! Abbie doesn't do flings – if she's
going to open her heart to Leo, she wants it to be for ever…

A FATHER FOR BABY ROSE
by Margaret Barker

Romance isn't something gorgeous, but guarded, surgeon
Yannis Karavolis cares about. Until he meets vulnerable
Cathy Meredith and her lovable infant daughter Rose,
Yannis begins to wonder whether fatherhood, marriage
and happiness could be his once more…

On sale 2nd July 2010

Available at WHSmith, Tesco, ASDA, Eason and all good bookshops.
For full Mills & Boon range including eBooks visit
www.millsandboon.co.uk

0610/03b

MEDICAL™

Single titles coming next month

NEUROSURGEON...AND MUM!
by Kate Hardy

When Amy Rivers' dreams of a family were shattered, she
dedicated herself to neurosurgery, where she's kept her
head – and her heart – ever since. Then she meets new
village doctor, Tom Ashby, and his motherless little daughter
Perdy... Life has been tough for all of them, but together
can they make each other whole?

WEDDING IN DARLING DOWNS
by Leah Martyn

Dr Declan O'Malley has just sauntered into Emma Armitage's
medical practice and revealed himself as her surgery's new
partner! Country GP is not what high-flying ex-surgeon
Declan imagined as his ideal job, but there is one plus-side
to Darling Downs: working with beautiful, and feisty,
Emma is a *very* enticing challenge!

On sale 2nd July 2010

Available at WHSmith, Tesco, ASDA, Eason and all good bookshops.
For full Mills & Boon range including eBooks visit
www.millsandboon.co.uk

0710/26/MB293

FROM PLAIN JANE HOUSEKEEPER TO WEALTHY MAN'S WIFE?

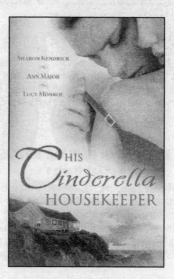

Italian Boss, Housekeeper Bride
by Sharon Kendrick

Shameless
by Ann Major

What the Rancher Wants…
by Lucy Monroe

Available 2nd July 2010

www.millsandboon.co.uk

M&B

0710/009/MB294

A RUGGED RANCHER...
A TEMPTING TYCOON...
A COMMANDING COP...

MARGARET WAY
BRONWYN JAMESON
MELANIE MILBURNE

MASTERS
OF THE
Outback

These powerful Australian men are
ready to claim their brides!

Available 18th June 2010

www.millsandboon.co.uk

M&B

0710/25/MB296

Three gorgeous and sexy Mediterranean men

– but are they marriage material?

The Italian's Forgotten Baby
by Raye Morgan

The Sicilian's Bride by Carol Grace

Hired: The Italian's Bride by Donna Alward

Available 2nd July 2010

www.millsandboon.co.uk

M&B

WEB/M&B/RTL2

Discover Pure Reading Pleasure with

**Visit the Mills & Boon website for all
the latest in romance**

- **Buy** all the latest releases, backlist and eBooks

- **Find out** more about our authors and their books

- **Join** our community and chat to authors and other readers

- **Free** online reads from your favourite authors

- **Win** with our fantastic online competitions

- **Sign** up for our free monthly eNewsletter

- **Tell us** what you think by signing up to our reader panel

- **Rate** and review books with our star system

www.millsandboon.co.uk

Follow us at twitter.com/millsandboonuk

Become a fan at facebook.com/romancehq

2 FREE BOOKS
AND A SURPRISE GIFT

We would like to take this opportunity to thank you for reading this Mills & Boon® book by offering you the chance to take TWO more specially selected books from the Medical™ series absolutely FREE! We're also making this offer to introduce you to the benefits of the Mills & Boon® Book Club™—

- **FREE home delivery**
- **FREE gifts and competitions**
- **FREE monthly Newsletter**
- **Exclusive Mills & Boon Book Club offers**
- **Books available before they're in the shops**

Accepting these FREE books and gift places you under no obligation to buy, you may cancel at any time, even after receiving your free books. Simply complete your details below and return the entire page to the address below. You don't even need a stamp!

YES Please send me 2 free Medical books and a surprise gift. I understand that unless you hear from me, I will receive 5 superb new stories every month including two 2-in-1 books priced at £4.99 each and a single book priced at £3.19, postage and packing free. I am under no obligation to purchase any books and may cancel my subscription at any time. The free books and gift will be mine to keep in any case.

Ms/Mrs/Miss/Mr _____ Initials _____

Surname _____

Address _____

_____

_____ Postcode _____

E-mail _____

Send this whole page to: Mills & Boon Book Club, Free Book Offer, FREEPOST NAT 10298, Richmond, TW9 1BR

Offer valid in UK only and is not available to current Mills & Boon Book Club subscribers to this series. Overseas and Eire please write for details.. We reserve the right to refuse an application and applicants must be aged 18 years or over. Only one application per household. Terms and prices subject to change without notice. Offer expires 31st August 2010. As a result of this application, you may receive offers from Harlequin Mills & Boon and other carefully selected companies. If you would prefer not to share in this opportunity please write to The Data Manager, PO Box 676, Richmond, TW9 1WU.

Mills & Boon® is a registered trademark owned by Harlequin Mills & Boon Limited.
Medical™ is being used as a trademark. The Mills & Boon® Book Club™ is being used as a trademark.